The Conjurer and the Corpse

by

C.E.Colemane

Cover Design by: @ehsan221b https://www.fiverr.com/ehsan221b

This book is dedicated, with love, to the Cool Kids. You know what you did.

Also, I bet £10 that Will won't find this.

"And he that strives to touch the stars oft stumbles at a straw."

— Edmund Spenser, The Shepherd's Calendar: Twelve Aeglogues Proportionable to The Twelve Months

CONTENTS

CHAPTER 1

Before Her Time

"Temporal Displacement: theoretical phenomenon whereby an individual or object moves from one point in time to another. Such movement may occur spontaneously or by a magician's direction. However, though anecdotally attested, there exists no conclusive proof either that the phenomenon is genuine or that it may be induced artificially."

Keening's Magical Glossary, Volume 7, (21st ed.) p 116. Trewcester University Press (2012)

Redwald de Cordonnay was bleeding again, and Alice Hawtree was sort of dead. The latter bothered Redwald immensely. He had not yet noticed the former.

Outside the carriage window, Kingsmarch Station rustled and heaved like forest undergrowth swarming with insects. Hurried travellers weaved around Giant porters burdened with luggage trolleys, while black-furred and yellow-eyed Hob technicians scurried across elevated walkways, tending to orcite charging contacts.

Redwald, however, sat alone, sealed in a second-class compartment. Academic gown gathered up and away from the dusty floor, briefcase stood neatly behind his legs and umbrella to one side, he was peering through his glasses and down his long nose at the letter in his hand. A frown creased his high forehead as he read it again and again, his eyes flicking back and forth like the carriage of a typewriter. He grumbled to himself.

Somewhere on the platform a conductor blew her whistle, and the glistening green engine at the head of the train roared and screeched as it pulled away from the station. Steam billowed into

1

the wrought iron recesses overhead, incense into the vaulted ceiling of an industrial cathedral. Redwald ignored it all. His thoughts were swarming the letter like bees on an invading hornet. The hornet, however, was winning. And still his bleeding went unnoticed.

He turned the facts over and over in his head, reading, re-reading, checking and compiling, sorting and filtering them to try and force them into some kind of order. Giles Hawtree, the letter's author, had this own theory of course, but that idea was . . . difficult for a magician to stomach.

Suddenly the glass door rattled open and his focus broke.

"May we join you?" The speaker was a thin woman in middle age, out of breath and with a twist of bitterness in her lips.

"I'd be delighted," Redwald lied, but she had not waited for his response. Her heavy suitcase thudded on to the floor before he could offer to help her with it, barely missing his feet, and she lowered herself rigidly onto the seat in the far corner, patting sweat away with her handkerchief.

"Do hurry up Elisa!" The woman tutted at someone down the corridor. Redwald nudged her case away from his gown with the tip of his shoe as Elisa appeared in the doorway.

"I'm sorry Mama," she wheezed, manoeuvring her own case through the doorway with a clatter. "They adjourned later than I expected." Shorter and broader than her mother, Elisa's cheeks had reddened with exertion to match her hair. She sought a place for her bag, but only the overhead racks were free. Foreseeing further clattering, and stirred as much by a desire to restore quiet to his compartment as by a sense of chivalry, Redwald stood and helped her with the bag.

"Be careful, it's heavy," she said, but Redwald swept it from the floor and up onto the rack with only a slight grimace. She blushed.

"Thank you. So sorry to be an inconvenience". Redwald realised with a jolt that he had been scowling at the letter and his expression softened.

"It's really no bother at all," he said kindly, "apologies if I . . ." he gestured vaguely at his face. "I'm a bit distracted with work."

"Oh no, I understand," Elisa said as Redwald shuffled past the older woman's bag and back into his seat, "We've just come from the Court of Feudatories. My sister is a clerk there and . . . Sir, you're bleeding!" She was looking at his hand. Redwald glanced idly down. He was not yet thirty, but his hands looked much older, cracked, dry skin stretched painfully over thick bones. One of his knuckles had split deep and now a trickle of blood was running down to the heel of his hand.

"So I am," he said, taking a blood-spattered handkerchief from his top pocket and dabbing the crimson away. "Thank you." He smiled at her, before returning to Mr Hawtree's letter and his obsession once more. He needed to get this right. Time could be running out.

Elisa took the seat opposite him and fidgeted for a moment, looking out the window as the copper dome of the Merringham Theatre flashed past. She turned to her mother, who was by now deep into a pocket novel, before looking back at Redwald.

"I'm so sorry, I should have introduced myself, I'm Elisa. And this is my mother, Agnes."

"Mrs Bewley," Agnes snipped.

"I'm Redwald," the magician replied, smiling briefly up at her, "pleasure to meet you both." Elisa paused.

"Are . . . are you travelling for work?" She asked tentatively. "You're a magician, aren't you?"

"Yes, I am." Redwald smiled and lifted the letter a little higher.

"Oh that's amazing! And which . . . what are they called?"

"Inns of Sorcery," Agnes interjected, "and he's with Vanehurst's, just like the Lord Conjurer." She turned superciliously back to her book. Redwald glanced down at the case she had flung so glibly into his orbit.

"Actually, I'm with Furneaux's," he said, folding the letter, "as is the Lord *High* Conjurer. It's not often that one of ours gets the job." Elisa's mother sniffed; she must have mistaken the deep purple of Redwald's gown for the crimson of Vanehurst.

"But you're only a Journeyman, yes?" She added, as Elisa looked away embarrassed. "Shouldn't you be with a Master?" She may have got the colour wrong, but she had clearly recognised the lack of gold embroidery on Redwald's bell sleeves.

"I am," Redwald conceded, "but *senior* Journeymen do take on cases alone." Albeit not cases like this; another reason he couldn't afford a mistake.

"And may I ask, where are you going?" Elisa said before her mother could escalate. "Are you going to Stenmoor too? To the Air Docks? My uncle is a captain in the Aerial Fleet, we're going to visit him. Apparently, their hangars are bigger on the inside that the outside. Is that the sort of magic you do?" Redwald digested this conversational deluge, still grasping Mr Hawtree's letter in the vague hope that he might continue reading it.

"No, not anymore," he said, wearily. "Although I did work on the Air Docks as an Apprentice."

"Oh that's amazing!" Elisa said, "But you're not going back to Stenmoor, then?" Redwald hesitated, but as his stop was before theirs, he could hardly disguise it from them.

"No, I'm going to Martingale-on-Trew. It's a small village in the Hundreds, I suspect you may not have heard of it."

"I haven't, but I bet it's beautiful!" Elisa said, "I'm told the Hundreds usually are. It's a shame you're not coming to Stenmoor, though, you could have stayed with us!" Mrs Bewley tutted. There was a pause then and Redwald watched as Elisa's eyes settled on the letter. The paper vanished into his inside pocket before her question could fully form.

"You said you were at the Court of Feudatories?" Redwald said, consoling himself that, by now, he must know the contents of the letter by heart. "Was that the Duke of Hasselton's trial?" If Elisa was determined to talk, it was best to talk about something besides Redwald's work. Mr Hawtree had requested a mere Journeyman precisely so that publicity could be avoided; a more prominent magician would attract attention. Happily, Elisa took the bait.

"Oh yes, it was quite exciting!" She beamed. "I've never been to a court before, but Audrey, that's my sister, said it was being held in the Gryphon Chamber, which is the biggest, most spectacular courtroom they have and that it would be a rare one to watch, so we sat in the public gallery. She drafted the order, you know. Big job, difficult too apparently - do you remember the Earl of Barrowmill's trial?" Redwald nodded. "Well - can you believe - it was sixteen years ago, and they've not confiscated a fief since then!" Redwald raised an eyebrow.

"Hasselton has lost a fief?"

"Oh yes," she nodded gleefully, "Just the one though, the Barony of Rightingham. But then, he didn't kill anyone I suppose, not like Barrowmill." She paused, turning to her mother. "I remember the scandal of all of it, but what did he actually do again?"

"Killed his Seneschal," Redwald said, looking out the window as the suburbs of Athonstone faded away into low green hills, "to cover up his own corruption and abuse of feudal privilege. I think the Seneschal was a vicar called Leofric, they found the poor man with a crushed skull under his own altar cloth and a bloodied candelabra nearby. Unfortunately for the Earl, the mirror in the vestry was facing the altar at the time, so they called in a magician. One spell later and they had all the evidence they needed to convict." Redwald had just been a boy, but he could still picture the towers of newspapers on street corners, all bearing photos of the murderous Earl and his family. His rat-like features swam before Redwald's eyes.

"You have a good memory." Elisa murmured. Then her face lit up. "Is that the kind of magic you do? Do you investigate *murders*?!" Redwald laughed.

"Not necessarily," he said. "I do a variety of things; my expertise is quite . . . esoteric." Mrs Bewley snorted from behind her book.

"And what *exactly* does that mean?" Redwald looked across the compartment, grinning. His frustration with the letter subsided briefly in favour of cautious excitement.

"It means that my work covers the areas that fall outside everyone else's, the very old bits, the very new bits, the undiscovered or obscure bits, the magic we've forgotten and don't fully understand anymore, or the spells we've yet to learn. I answer the questions that no other magician really wants to touch."

"What sort of questions?" Elisa whispered, awestruck.

How do you solve a murder that hasn't been committed yet?

This was the question posed by the letter, which gnawed at Redwald from the inside, and which he alone must answer. Before it was too late. And even as the countryside flashed past the window and Redwald diverted Elisa onto cases past and other questions answered, the picture painted by Mr Hawtree's letter lingered, burnt into his brain.

Alice Hawtree lay dead behind her husband's desk, her head wrapped tightly in bedsheets, blood seeping through from the gunshot wound to her eye, livid red scars on her wrists and ankles. And there were screams. The bloodcurdling, desperate, terrified screams of the woman who found Alice Hawtree's body in the first place; Alice Hawtree herself.

CHAPTER 2

The Vicar and the Double Standard

"Transformation, augmentation or mutation of sentients

29. It shall be an offence, subject to the provisions of Schedule 7 (National Security Exemptions) and Schedule 8 (Medical Exemptions) from time to time in force, for any person to employ any spell, by any means whatsoever, to effect in respect of any person, including, but not limited to, the spell caster themselves:

a) the augmentation, reduction or removal of any body part, mental faculty or other physical or psychological trait;
b) the transformation from their natural state into any object, animal, race, vegetable, mineral, phenomenon or other concept not heretofore expressed;
c) their disappearance, invisibility, immateriality, trans-temporal or spatial relocation; or
d) the concealment of any physical or other features for the purposes of effecting an unlawful act."

Section 29 Abuse of Magic Act 1876 (Published Courtesy of His Majesty's Grand Chancellery)

The Reverend Charteris blinked absently in the fading twilight as he stood waiting on the platform at Martingale-on-Trew, orcite lantern in hand. He was alone. It was a small station; little more than an elevated scaffold with a smartly painted sign indicating the name of the village. On the vicar's right-hand side and just beyond the circle of yellow lamplight, a small dirt road swerved across the rails, past the end of the platform and away into the woods. He turned to squint up the tracks, pushing his thick-rimmed glasses back up his broad nose, and looked for any hint of steam that might signal the end of his wait.

Shortly past the hour the 14:15 from Athonstone, capital of the Kingdom of the Tempest, rounded the corner and thundered towards the station with all the weighty presence of a warship. Dragging a trail of steam behind it, which smothered the platform as the engine passed, the great green train ground to a halt, the carriages shunting into place. Charteris looked expectantly down the platform, one knobbly old hand clasped authoritatively in the small of his back.

Although steam still obscured much of his view, Charteris reckoned he heard a wooden thud and a metallic click as a carriage door was opened and then shut again. Then, only as the train began to pull away, did the outline of a broad, straight-backed figure and his briefcase begin to materialise. Finally, Redwald emerged from obscurity.

"Mr de Cordonnay, I presume?" Charteris asked, a broad smile stretching from jowl to jowl. His voice was rich and unctuous, with an accent that denoted an easy birth and extensive education. Redwald could picture him sat in a well-worn groove in a well-worn chair, back in one of the gentlemen's clubs of Athonstone, brandy in hand. Charteris offered said hand to Redwald, who paused for a moment. His eyes flickered from the vicar's straggly grey comb-over to his dusty old shoes.

"I'm one of them," he confirmed, "Redwald." He took Charteris' hand, uncertain as to why Mr Hawtree had sent a vicar to meet him. "Forgive me, I was expecting to meet Mr Hawtree tomorrow . . ."

"Ah, not to worry, I'm not from the Hawtree Estate, I'm Charteris, uh, Charles Charteris, the rector at St Alia's, shall we . . . ?" He gestured down the dirt road that, Redwald assumed, led towards the village.

"Uh, of course, after you," Redwald said, non-plussed. With that, Charteris turned on his heel and shuffled away down the platform, head bowed in a permanent stoop.

"I thought I might show you to the Double Standard," Charteris said, before Redwald could ask why he was there, "If you'd like that, of course. I gather you're staying there for the duration." The two men descended the creaking steps at the end of the platform and turned right along the dirt road.

"Yes, I think so, but . . ."

"I suppose you'll be looking forward to a bite to eat and a rest, you must be tired from your journey." Indeed, Redwald was tired. He found small-talk difficult, for all that he had rather liked Elisa. Nor, having expected a solitary walk into the village, did he relish the prospect of further chatter, even if it came with a lantern. His fingers twitched compulsively in the direction of his hipflask, but he restrained himself.

"Yes, I'll be glad of a pint, too."

"Ha! You and me both."

"Listen, I . . . . I don't want to seem ungrateful, it's very kind of you to come and meet me. . . ."

"Not at all, my boy. I just thought you might like to be shown the way. That is what the clergy is for, after all." He chuckled at his own joke.

"But, not wishing to be blunt, why are you here? You say you're not from the Hawtree Estate?"

"Oh no, my dear fellow, my apologies, I ought to have said. I've come on Lord Martingale's behalf, just to make sure you found your way alright, and to welcome you, of course."

"Lord Martingale? Is he . . ."

"The Lord of the Manor, that's right," Charteris said, beaming. Redwald started at that. He had never been greeted at the station by a Lord's representative before.

"Oh, that's . . . very kind of him. I hadn't expected . . ."

"Oh no bother at all, old boy. It's a small fief and his Lordship is very active in its affairs; he cares deeply about all his tenants. Sadly, our Seneschal – Dr Asplund – is not around today, so I volunteered to come and meet you."

"I see," Redwald said, somewhat bemused.

"In any case," Charteris continued, as they strolled between the trees, "the Hawtrees are parishioners of mine too. And given what's happened to poor little Alice . . . given that, it only seems right to help them out where I can." Redwald furrowed his brow.

"Oh . . . do you . . . do you know what's happened, then?" Charteris nodded. "It's just, I was under the impression that Mr Hawtree wanted to keep this as quiet as possible."

"You're right about that old chap," Charteris said with a bitter note of distaste that caught Redwald by surprise. "It seems Giles is so concerned about negative publicity that he's even refusing to bump this up to the liege-lord's constabulary. Not that Lord Martingale minds, of course. He and the Earl of Ellswych . . . don't necessarily get on. Means the whole case is being dealt with by Norris, though; he's our local constable."

"Yes, I have a meeting with him tomorrow. How many people . . ."

"It's a small village," Charteris said, pre-empting him, "most of us know the details, but," he added, upon seeing Redwald's shock, "Lord Martingale has asked us, and we have agreed, not to discuss it with anyone from outside the fief, except your good self, of course."

"Will that work?"

"His Lordship is very well-respected," Charteris said, as evening songbirds chirruped in the canopy, "probably because he *is* so involved in the running of his fief. Even if he weren't though, I'm sure the whole village would do it just for Alice. Anything for Alice, that's what I always say."

"You know Mrs Hawtree?"

"Of course, she grew up here, a tremendously sweet little girl she was. Quite shy, as you'd expect with a father like hers, but so very lovely. We're . . . we're all rather fond of her. Anything for Alice. Not that I wouldn't do the same for my other parishioners, mind you."

"And Mr Hawtree, what's he like?" Redwald asked, by way of conversation. Charteris paused and frowned, his features shifting in the swinging lamplight.

"He . . . he's quite . . . I would say that . . . that he's an interesting character," Charteris finished, nodding his head as if that concluded the matter. Redwald allowed himself a smile, the small talk was proving more engaging than he had anticipated.

"You don't like him."

"Oh no no no, that's not it!" Charteris exclaimed, raising his hands almost defensively and shaking his head. "No, that's not it at all." He paused. His spare hand returned to the semi-permanent groove at the base of his back. "Anyway, I'm glad you're here to support Alice, support them both. No one deserves what she's had to endure, to see your own death like that. What happened, do you suppose?" Charteris said, attempting to herd the conversation to greener pastures. Redwald hesitated for a moment before remembering that, since the entire village already knew what had happened anyway, he was hardly likely to breach confidentiality.

"Well, when Mr Hawtree wrote to my firm, he said he thought it was a murder, combined with a deliberate temporal displacement. He said that his wife had been murdered; a gunshot wound through the eye, but that she was, concurrently, alive and well." Redwald paused for a moment, this was the bit he struggled with. His fingers twitched for the hipflask once more. "He thinks she was killed and then sent back in time to intimidate the family."

"Yes, that's what I heard. But surely that . . . temporary . . . temperature . . . terminal . . ."

"Temporal displacement, it's just a fancy term for time travel."

"Thank you, surely that . . . that isn't possible?"

"I don't know. Few magicians have ever given the question serious thought and those that have are short on answers. It can apparently happen spontaneously, but I don't know how you'd even begin to do it on purpose."

"Spontaneously?"

"Well, there's the obvious example . . ."

"The Ærestian Advent," Charteris intoned, recalling the tale. "That's just a legend, though, surely?"

"True," Redwald agreed, "but there are other, slightly more convincing cases. Are you familiar with story of the Storburgh Gangs? Usually known as the Ladies of Wellinghouse Wood?"

"Wellinghouse Wood rings a bell," Charteris said, frowning, "but that's a children's story, no? C.F. Twistle?"

13

"A fictionalised account of an *apparently* real event," Redwald said. "Gangs were not deemed child-friendly, I suppose, so Twistle turned them into a pair of women on a walk." Charteris grinned.

"Do tell, old boy."

"Well, the story goes that two gangs met in Wellinghouse Wood near Storbugh, in the small hours of a summer's day in 2160. They were meeting to settle a feud. I don't know what exactly, but before they could kick each other's heads in they heard a distant rumbling. It grew louder and closer, until finally they realised that they were hearing hoof-beats. Then an 18th Century knight crested the ridge between the trees and charged towards them on horseback, followed by another and another, appearing out of nowhere."

"Surely it's nonsense old boy?" Charteris retorted, shaking his head. "Could have been anything; a mirage perhaps, shared hallucination, even a re-enactment! They might even have been . . . *dishonest* gangsters?" He beamed wickedly.

"All very plausible," Redwald agreed with a smile, "although difficult to reconcile with the facts. Having been tipped off as to the impending fight, the Guard arrived at the woods once the knights had vanished and arrested the would-be brawlers. Interviewing them all separately, the Guard found the majority of the thugs to be in shock, but in agreement on the details of what they had seen, right down to the designs on the knight's shields."

"Good actors, perhaps, who had taken the time to rehearse?" Redwald grinned.

"Quite, with rave reviews in contemporary chronicles." Charteris frowned up at him. "You see, one Guardsman recognised the description of the heraldry from her time at school. After a bit of digging, she discovered that the gangs' description of the coats of arms matched precisely those of the knights in the employ of Baron Blackspur in 1769, when the Battle of Wellinghouse Wood

14

was fought. After a bit more digging, she discovered that Eadric of Gharford, in his account of the battle, mentions the sudden appearance and disappearance of some oddly-dressed peasants in the middle of the woods. Which appearance, by the way, he says caused the Earl of Storburgh to lose control of his horse and consequently, his head." Charteris raised his eyebrows, surprised.

"So . . . it might actually be possible, this . . . time-travel thing . . ."

"It *might* be," Redwald conceded, "I certainly can't rule it out. I just can't see how someone could write a spell to induce the phenomenon, though. That would require an understanding of the nature of time, you see."

"Oooof, I don't know, old boy. All sounds a bit beyond me," said Charteris, shaking his head.

"To be honest," Redwald conceded, "I'm not sure it isn't beyond me, too." He caved at that last thought. With his free hand, he pulled his hipflask from within the folds of his gown and took a swig. The vicar's nose twitched.

"Ah, a man after my own heart. Askander?"

"Single malt. Distilled near Hepburnham," Redwald confirmed.

"Good taste, old boy, very good. Smells peaty," the vicar observed. "I don't suppose I could trouble you for a snifter, could I?" Redwald handed him the hipflask.

"I mean, there are other ways of making people or things appear to be somebody's duplicate," Redwald continued, thinking out loud, "but if I can rule those out, then. . . then I somehow have to . . ." He paused and sighed, re-gathering his thoughts. "The thing is, knowing how it happened is just half the battle. I need to . . . to try and stop it, her murder, before it even happens." Charteris took a draught of the hipflask and handed it back to Redwald, who surreptitiously wiped the mouthpiece, took another swig and continued. "Which really does beg a bigger question, doesn't it? Can one change the future, if one knows what is coming? Or is time linear and our fates immutable?" Charteris whistled through his teeth.

"Well," he began, in an attempt to lighten the mood, "at the very least, it sounds like you've got an interesting time ahead, old chap." Redwald perked up momentarily at that.

"Oh no, I can't deny it's a fascinating case," he said, his storm-cloud eyes flashing for a moment, "but I just wish there weren't so much riding on it, so much uncertainty. You see, if the future really is set in stone," he said darkly, "then I may have failed before I even begin." Charteris looked up at him, concerned.

"Now listen here, young fellow, you mustn't think like that. Just remember," he said, looking skywards, "Oryn, the Vaeltava, and the stars have a plan for all of us."

Redwald did not reply to that. He, like many magicians, could not deny the power of the stars. Yet he had never seen evidence of a plan, much less a benevolent one. Instead, his dealings with stars had taught him that they were staggeringly powerful and wild in the extreme; not so much celestial guardians as forces of nature. "Ah," Charteris said as the road began to flatten and widen, "here we are."

Ahead, the dusty road sloped down between the trees and out onto a village green. The two men, now chatting warmly, strolled out of the woods and into the silver moonlight cast by Bethin, hanging low in the sky.

Martingale-on-Trew, it seemed, was a village characteristic of the Hundreds, the hilly, green region in which it sat. To the left of them rose a tall, rocky hill that sank in craggy steps down to the village itself, nestled at its base. Ahead and to the right, a wide river

16

valley stretched to a ridge in the distance that sloped and fell to the flat flood plain beyond that. The major buildings were stretched around the village green; a broad, grassy common, with a single weeping willow that stooped wearily and draped its long tendrils over the river. The river Trew was, at this stage, slow and shallow, little more than a large stream, forded by a multitude of small stone footbridges and flowing in parallel with the long central street that passed through the village.

To their immediate left sat the village pub, the Double Standard, and to their right, beyond the Trew and perched on a slight rise, was a little church that Redwald took to be St Alia's. The buildings were all built of the same Hundred Stone, a honey-coloured rock, and were ancient. Redwald imagined, as he stopped to place his briefcase at his feet, that the village had probably looked this way for at least the last 600 years.

"Right, this is where I leave you, I'm afraid," Charteris said, taking Redwald's hand and shaking it vigorously before the magician could offer it. "There's the pub – I'm sure the Landlord will have your rooms ready by now. If you need any help or simply fancy a chat, I live just beyond the church. We really do appreciate what you're doing for Alice and if I can help in any way, you must let me know. I . . . I just hope you can save her."

"So do I," Redwald said grimly. "Thank you for showing me the way, too."

"No problem, my boy, thank you for the whisky! Tell you what, if you're inclined to decent tipple, you should pop along to try my mead one day; made with honey from my own bees!"

"That sounds lovely, perhaps you can show me around the church at the same time?" Redwald said.

"Absolutely, I'll have the mead waiting!" Charteris chuckled as he turned to amble off across the river. Feeling a damn sight more relaxed than when he pulled into the station, Redwald stooped for his case and made his way towards the Inn. The thatched building seemed bent double with the weight of ages, the white and black timber of the upper floors spilling over the stony walls of the ground floor like a beer belly over a belt. Outside, there were a number of stone benches and the odd table, arranged haphazardly at the side of the road and occupied by a few wind-burned locals, who regarded his approach with undisguised curiosity. Redwald passed beneath the painted sign, swinging with a metallic creak from the bracket over the door, and entered the pub.

A wave of heat met him as he entered. To his right there sat a great stone fireplace, surrounded by dry logs, and to his left, a flight of narrow, crooked stairs staggered up to the lodging rooms above. In front, the pewter-topped bar curved around the room, set at intervals with smoothly polished beer pumps, hung with tankards and guarding shelves glinting with half-empty spirit bottles and stacked glasses. The remaining floorspace was occupied by a sparse and motley collection of ragged, well-worn furniture and equally ragged and well-worn people, all standing on a tapestry of old rugs that covered the stone flag floor.

The air hummed with quiet conversation as Redwald made his way to the bar, leant his umbrella against it and introduced himself to the Landlord, a large man, whose brow glistened with sweat above a sandy moustache. He leaned over the bar and looked Redwald up and down.

"You must be the magician."

"I am."

"Welcome to Martingale-on-Trew, sir." He said, a tad dutifully. "Come to see to the 'awtree case?" he asked.

"That's right," Redwald said, raising an eyebrow.

"Ah. Nasty business. 'Course no one talks much 'bout it. His Lordship asked us to respec' Mr 'awtree's wish for privacy. So we 'ave."

"I'm sure Mr Hawtree appreciates that." The Landlord growled in response.

"Ain't doin' it fer 'im. We does what our Lord asks of us, all there is to it. Anyway, what can I get you?" he said, slapping his hand on the bar.

"I might pop down for a drink later, actually," Redwald replied, "but first I'd like to put this in my room." He lifted the briefcase into the Landlord's view.

"Ah right, follow me." He turned and walked to the end of the bar nearest the stairs. There he stopped to rummage in a cabinet for a moment, before extracting a key. "'Ere, give us that, I'll carry it up fer yer."

"Ok," Redwald said, warily. He passed the case to the Landlord who almost dropped it.

"My werd," the Landlord said, "'eavier than it looks."

"It's larger on the inside," Redwald explained, as the pair climbed the creaking, winding staircase up to the first floor. "Helps me carry more books." It was a source of some comfort to Redwald that, in the unlikely event someone tried to run off with his briefcase, they would be hard-pressed to actually lift it.

"Ooooh, by Oryn, ain't that clever," the Landlord said, failing in his attempt to sound interested. The staircase opened out into a long, crooked corridor, with the lodging rooms branching off at odd intervals. The landlord leaned into the one at the very top of the stairs, turned the key and pushed it open.

"This is you," he said as he made his way in, dropping the briefcase at the foot of his bed. "Loo is through tha' door, lock-up is at 'alf past midnight. Think that's 'bout it, unless you got anythin' you need?" Redwald replied that he didn't. "Well if you do think of somethin' just let me know! Always 'ere to 'elp." He said, before closing the door with a snap.

Redwald sighed, paced around the bed and opened the window. A breath of fresh air gusted through, reviving the otherwise stale room. Tomorrow he would meet his client; tomorrow he would start work. He sat down heavily on the bed and clasped his head in his hands. The Reverend Charteris' encouragement notwithstanding, this case remained a tricky one.

This part always made him anxious. It was the stage before he could gather the information, before he could do the research, the point at which things were least inclined to fit into a pattern. Agitated, he stood and went to wash his hands in the adjoining bathroom. They weren't dirty, but the action soothed him all the same.

As he returned to the bed, the breeze swept in again and ruffled his dark hair, the lonely greys glinting in the pale light. It was then that the temptation hit him.

He hadn't done it for a while. There was always a risk of being caught, especially in Athonstone, but occasionally he would do it anyway. Even as he reasoned heartily against it, he could feel that he was losing the argument with himself. The urge was too strong and, after all, had he not earned it? It might even be useful to get a proper lay of the land. Yes, not only was it a pleasure, but necessary for work too. That settled it.

He walked over to his briefcase and began to rummage within. Crouching low, his arm inside the briefcase up to his shoulder, he eventually pulled out a pair of soft, well-worn, leather gloves. As he felt the material between his fingers, he felt too the echoes of the wind, the sensation of rising far, far above his worries. Washing his hands, drinking, these might soothe him temporarily, but nothing helped quite as much as this.

He locked the door to the room and sat on the edge of the bed, looking at the sky beyond. They had been a gift from his grandfather, the gloves. An unexpected, but welcome gift, and completely illegal. He began to pull one glove on to a dry, cracked hand and drew a long, expectant breath, his stomach knotting with the child-like excitement that only this instilled in him. Standing up in readiness, he made to pull on the other glove. He closed his eyes. But, before he could finish, there was a rapping at the door.

"Mr de Cordonnay, sir!" it was the Landlord. Redwald growled, pulled the gloves off and dropped them on the bed. He jerked the door open, more angrily than he had intended.

"Sorry to disturb you sir . . ."

"No problem, what is it?" Redwald asked, curtly.

"Your umbrella, sir," the Landlord said, presenting it to him. "You left it on the bar."

"Ah," Redwald said, underwhelmed, "thank you. It's not the first time I've done that."

"My pleasure, sir. Will ye join us fer a drink this evening?" Redwald turned to look at the open window and sighed.

"That would be lovely," he said, "give me a second, I'll be down in a moment."

"Course, I'll 'ave one ready fer yer." The Landlord turned and headed back down the stairs. Now committed to an evening in, Redwald carefully folded the gloves and put them in one of the two external pockets of his briefcase. Placing that flush to the foot of the bed, he then made to shut the window. As he fiddled with the

21

mechanism, he felt a cold breeze on the back of his neck and heard what he took to be a long, ragged gasp. He spun on his heels, heart pounding, expecting to see . . . *him*. But there was no one there, and no noise besides the creaking of the hinge which, he realised, he had taken for a gasp. The bedroom door, improperly closed, had swung open. Redwald shivered at the thought and cursed his own stupidity, but as he locked the door, checked it and headed down to the bar, he could not help but dwell on it. He was due, after all.

CHAPTER 3

Client Relations

"Once upon a time there was a little village, far out in the south, where it was always cold. In that village there lived a very large family; a father, a mother and 11 children. The father worked the grey fields and the mother fed the children who, once they were grown, also worked the grey fields. This work was hard for them as the crimson flower Alynore would grow in dry furrows where their crops would fail and it pained them to remove it. Sadly, their lord was greedy and vain. He taxed them heavily and made them work his lands, so they could not afford to eat very much. Twice a week they bought a loaf of bread and cut it up as small as it would go; 13 pieces exactly. Each member of the family kept their piece to themselves and carefully saved it up until the next loaf was bought.

They lived this way for many years, but then, a terrible thing happened. The mother realised that she was with child. Sure enough, sometime after, a little girl was born. She was so tiny that she could fit in the palm of her father's hand. But despite her size, she was another mouth to feed and the family could not keep her. So when the father took his meagre crops to market for sale, he also took his youngest daughter. . ."

The Tale of Alynore – Traditional Tales for Growing Children, collated by Dr C.F. Twistle (Allpress) 1992

Redwald awoke to an overcast morning. Pale grey clouds hung low over the valley, too weak to threaten rain, but thick enough that the village seemed to have had the colour washed from every surface. He rose quickly and, eschewing breakfast, set out for Hawtree Manor. Upon being asked where it was, the Landlord had scoffed and advised Redwald to "'ead to the other end of the 'igh Street, turn lef' and look for the 'eap behind the trees."

The village was mostly quiet, but the few people who were pottering around the green turned to look as he passed. The large, stern magician carrying his heavy black briefcase, with his gown flapping as he strode, cut a figure wholly out of place. Redwald, noting their ill-disguised stares, suppressed a smile.

At the end of the high street the buildings ended abruptly and opened out on to the dirt road again. A little way beyond the end of the village the road forked. If one followed the road to the right, Redwald knew, you would follow the Trew downstream. You would pass Oswillow, Manninghurst, Treddaby and Fealton before eventually reaching Trewcester as the valleys flattened and the river broadened and deepened. Instead, he turned left and walked up the slight incline that led to the base of the craggy hill which, as the Landlord had explained, was called the Rise. On the other side, clinging to the gentle green slope and below the exposed rock, was Martingale Castle, the seat of the fiefdom, where Lord Martingale himself lived, while the Hawtrees and their manor occupied this side.

Although the case continued to weigh on his mind, Redwald was pleased to find a slight spring in his step as he climbed the hill that morning. He was not unused to such tension, his very career was predicated upon it. You see, Redwald could not bear disorder, imbalance, or dirtiness. He could walk into a room and spot in seconds every picture frame that wasn't even, every book out of alphabetical order and every spot of dirt, and be compelled, by something deep within him, to correct each one. His cases were the same; puzzles with ill-fitting pieces, tormenting him like an itch for as long as they remained unsolved. Yet, for all that such puzzles might itch, there was an excitement in the scratching of them, in anticipating the catharsis of solution, that now drove him inexorably closer to the scene of an impossible murder.

The incline was just beginning to become steeper and more bothersome when the trees opened and a great brick and stone arch, stretching across the road and marking the entrance to the estate, loomed over him. It was ornate, a little showy and quite new, supporting a carved swan at the apex, wings open in welcome, and surrounded by false crenellations and mock canopies.

Beyond the arch, the trees opened out onto the steep, chequered lawns of Hawtree Manor, neatly cut lines of grass rolling down the hill. Above, the house itself sat at the top of the drive which sloped around the lawns on the left, clinging to the treeline. Built in brick within a stone framework, the manor resembled the old houses built by the lords of minor fiefs; those who could not afford a castle or were not licensed to build one.

Tall and long, its glittering windows looked out over the valley, the criss-crossing mosaic of lead and diamond glass shimmering like a multitude of glassy compound eyes. The ornate crenellations, artistic imitations of those found on real castles, crowned leering gargoyles shaped like lions, gryphons, dragons, and other heraldic beasts. The upper floor jettied out over the lower and from the overbite hung carved stone bosses, with the Hawtree swan and the monogram JH etched in florid, intertwined lettering.

Indeed, it seemed to be a fine example of the old manor houses of the 15th-16th centuries, storied and august. That, of course, was the point. Yet, for all that it was technically well-executed, for all that this monument must have been raised by the most skilful - and expensive - hands, it was still an imitation and, to Redwald, obviously so. It simply didn't fit. The colour of the bricks was too livid, as red as bloodied clay, and the stone was too clean and too new. The entire assembly lacked the patina of age and, rather than forming part of the landscape, gracefully and slowly taking root over the course of centuries, it had been forced awkwardly into place. With time it might mature, like a fine wine or a cheese, but for now it was red, raw and new, like a painful spot in the middle of a forehead. You could fake so many things, Redwald thought, but faking time was difficult. He unconsciously wrinkled his nose as he approached. Next to a village so old and beautiful in its simplicity, the mansion was a crass parody.

Redwald ignored the wrought-iron bell-pull hanging by the door and rapped forcefully instead. It swung open almost immediately. Redwald's gaze quickly slipped downwards and he saw that an elderly Hob in butler's garb had opened the door, a long, spindly claw wrapped around the handle.

"Welcome to Hawtree Manor, sir," the Hob said. Though short by Human standards, he was actually quite tall for a Hob and possessed of a certain worn gravitas, like an old cabinet or a tattered manuscript. He wore a look of tired disdain on his jowly face, which seemed to slope to either side between his bat-like ears, themselves wilting like neglected flowers. This physical malaise, Redwald suspected, was partly due to old age. Although Hobs were generally long-lived, this one looked to be nearing 210, which was venerable. His once-black fur greyed towards the back of his head and was sparse across his face, framing his small, tired, but fiercely orange, eyes. He had the look of one who had spent far too long polishing forks. Doubtless an easier task for him than for most, Redwald thought, since Hobs generally had two pairs of arms. "What is your business sir, may I ask?"

"I'm here about the murder." The Hob cast an uninterested eye over Redwald.

"You are the Magician?"

"Redwald de Cordonnay," he extended a hand to the Hob, who seemed momentarily shaken from his stupor. He took Redwald's hand slowly in his long-fingered claws and they shook. "Morrimer," he replied. "I will inform Mr Hawtree of your arrival."

"Thank you," Redwald said curtly, but the expression caused the Hob's large ears to quiver slightly, as though the words were someone's name he had long since forgotten. Morrimer ushered

26

Redwald through the entrance hall - a grand affair with wooden vaulting and ersatz coats of arms - and into the drawing room to the right, which looked out over the valley and down the sloping lawn.

"Please have a seat sir, Mr Hawtree will be with you presently. Can I get you anything to drink?"

"That's kind, but no thank you."

"Very well, sir." He shuffled off, both pairs of hands clasped behind his back. Redwald heard his claws clacking as he made his way across the wooden floor of the entrance hall and up the staircase. Redwald did not sit down, but instead walked over to the window and gazed out over the woods and valley. There was very little that could improve that view, he thought, before reaching surreptitiously into the folds of his gown to take a swig from his hipflask. He stowed it with practiced speed upon the approach of footsteps.

"Mr Courtney!" a voice called. Redwald turned to meet his host.

Giles Hawtree burst through the doorway and threw his arms open in welcome, beaming. He was shorter than the magician, and much thinner, his lean features drawing to a point at the tip of his neat triangular nose. Although into his fourth decade, and older than Redwald, his hair was devoid of greys. Instead, it was thick and mousy, oiled into a messy quiff over his square forehead and cropped short upon his face. Redwald felt a startling flicker of recognition as he proffered his hand, which Hawtree grasped and shook furiously with both of his own, a perfectly enamelled grin tensing his hollow cheeks.

"Mr Courtney, it *really* is a *pleasure* to meet you," he said, placing unctuous emphasis on his chosen words in a clear, crisp and controlled tenor. Redwald inferred almost instantly that he was a practiced public speaker.

27

"Likewise, I'm sure," Redwald said, "though are you sure we've not met already? You seem familiar."

"Ah yes, people often say that. But no, I don't believe we have. After all Mr Courtney, I'm sure I would remember meeting a Vanehurst man," he concluded, name-dropping the Inn and continuing to shake Redwald's hand.

"Ah, I see. My mistake," Redwald said, gently retrieving his hand. "Although I should note, and sorry to correct you," he continued, in a voice utterly devoid of contrition, "that my name is *de* Cordonnay and I actually trained at Furneaux's. Will Mrs Hawtree be joining us?"

"Alice? No, not for the moment, I'm afraid, she's a little ill."

"Oh, I'm sorry to hear that, I imagine the shock . . ."

"Ah don't worry, it's nothing serious. She's always been a delicate little thing, you know, often sickly," Hawtree said, gesturing indiscriminately to the furniture, "please, do have a seat. How did you find the Double Standard? Sleep well?"

"Uh . . . yes I did thank you, well enough," Redwald said as he lowered himself heavily into an armchair, placing his briefcase to one side, "it's quite a nice pub actually." Although he was doing his best with the small talk, his thoughts lingered upon Mrs Hawtree.

"I wouldn't know, I'm afraid," Hawtree said as he poured himself languidly onto the adjacent sofa. "Not my sort of place, really. It's fine for the locals of course, but it's not quite up to . . . well it's not for me, that's all. I prefer a place with a slightly . . . higher level of service, you know," he said, nodding encouragingly.

"I see," Redwald said distractedly as he produced a pen and notebook from an inner breast pocket, "Mr Hawtree . . ."

"Giles, please," Hawtree said, grinning. Redwald swallowed.

"Giles . . . I hope you don't mind my being so forward, but given your hypothesis . . ."

"Time travel?"

"Precisely, temporal displacement. Given that, and assuming it's at all possible to prevent this . . . event from occurring, the sooner I begin investigating the better. However, I think it's only fair that, before I begin, I explain what I intend to do."

"I'm all ears," Hawtree said, his grin now starting to verge on the unsettling.

"Excellent," Redwald said, adjusting his glasses, "I have of course read your letter, that was very thorough, but I would still like to ask both yourself and, if possible, Mrs Hawtree, a number of questions relating to the event, just in case that throws up any further details that may be useful. I would also like to inspect the room in which you say the body was found and, indeed, the body itself. Does that sound reasonable to you?" Redwald asked.

"Of course, anything for my dear Alice," Hawtree said, though Redwald was surprised to see his grin suddenly vanish. "Oh I'm sorry, you don't have a drink! The damn butler should have . . . ."

"That's fine," Redwald cut him off, "I'm not thirsty, thank you. Mr Hawtree . . . Giles, I think that, to start with, it would be useful for me to establish how the body was discovered."

"I think I said, in my letter . . ."

"That Mrs Hawtree found the body, yes I know. Sorry, I should have been clearer, please set out for me *exactly* what happened that day, and don't worry about repeating your letter. Just tell me what happened in full. How did your wife come to be in that room in order to find the body? Who else was here, what was going on?

29

Leave nothing out; even details that seem irrelevant might be of use."

"Well of course," Hawtree began, but he quickly paused. "It's just . . . I'm not sure where to begin." He looked across the room to the fireplace, almost for reassurance. There, hanging over the mantelpiece, was a portrait of a severe, distinguished-looking man with disproportionately large hands. Bullishly broad-shouldered, with a furrowed brow and sharply hooked nose, he seemed to scan the room with ice-blue eyes, like a hawk waiting for a mouse to make a fatal error.

"Does it begin with him?" Redwald asked. Hawtree jerked to.

"Oh no, my apologies. I just . . . it's hard, there isn't much to tell really, but I'll try my best. We're hosting the annual Hawtree Fund Gala, tomorrow actually, and so some of the guests, especially those from abroad, came earlier in the week. We have a few staying with us until the event."

"Gala?" Redwald asked.

"Oh, have you not heard of it?" Hawtree said.

"No, I have," Redwald explained, frowning. He doubted there was anyone who hadn't heard of the Hawtrees or their Gala. Sir Julius, the late Hawtree patriarch, whose portrait scanned the room from above the fireplace, had been one of the wealthiest men in the Realm and its most prominent industrialist. The Hawtree Foundry had managed to patent the magical process of creating skyron, the light-as-air metal that coated the flotation hulls of His Majesty's airships. The resulting lead in airship manufacture had put both the Hawtrees and the Aerial Fleet on the map, making Sir Julius obscenely wealthy. Although, Redwald noted to himself wryly, he could not remember the name of the magician who had discovered the skyron process. In truth, what surprised Redwald was the fact that the Gala hadn't been cancelled. He nevertheless kept his reservations to himself.

"Oh, right." Hawtree paused again. "Well anyway, Alice agreed with me that we should have a shoot on the Dransday morning, so we all rose early and headed out . . ."

"That's Dransday just gone, is it? The 35th?" Redwald cut in.

"Yep," Hawtree said. "We own most of the land in the valley, so we have our pick of the fowl. We were out from about dawn, and then we were going to head back about midday in time for lunch. I naturally set off early to ensure that everything was ready. Alice followed later with the guests."

"May I ask who these guests were?"

"Oh, we only have a few staying over this year, but now I come to think of it, most have arrived *since* Dransday. We did have one at the time, though; Countess Laetizja of Oštrouman. . . ."

"Czerganzan?"

"Yes, exactly. She lives in Eupleion now, fled the Revolution I think. Can you imagine something so awful, the natural order turned so completely on its head? So traumatic for her." Redwald made a non-committal noise and kept his memories to himself. "She was the only guest present at the time."

"I see, I would like to speak with her," Redwald said, making a note.

"She's taking in the countryside for the moment, but she's staying until Borsday the . . . the 1st, isn't it? Yes, so you've got a few days. She'd be delighted to assist you at some point, I'm sure."

"I'm grateful," Redwald said, still scribbling, "now where were we?"

31

"Ah yes. Well I headed back early, as I say, and was talking to the butler. He's a bit on the elderly side now, so he needs a strong hand in these things. To tell the truth," he said lowering his voice, "I don't think he's all there, but I keep him on for Alice's sake. She is terribly fond of him and you know, they can be so sentimental. Anyway, as he and I were talking, I heard Alice and the Countess arrive back. I told the butler to serve lunch and made to join the girls, but before I could get there, I heard . . . I heard Alice scream. I've never heard her make a noise like that." He looked away from Redwald then, staring into space as he recalled the sound. "I ran to the study and the butler followed. By the time we'd arrived, Alice was slumped against the doorpost, crying. That's when we found the . . . the body."

"Where was the Countess at this point?"

"Waiting for Alice in the Dining Room, I believe. She arrived shortly after me when she heard . . . heard the screams."

"And what did you make of the scene? Did anything stand out to you as odd?" Hawtree looked up at Redwald incredulously, but the magician quickly corrected himself, "beyond the fact of finding her at all, was there anything about her or the room, for example, that seemed out of place?"

Hawtree looked up again at the portrait of Sir Julius, though Redwald could not tell why. Perhaps the image of the thuggish-looking man, with his hands thrust forward assertively on the pommel of a gilded ceremonial sword, was somehow comforting to Giles.

"I suppose . . . the state of it was the first thing. The body, that is." Hawtree looked down from the portrait. "It was bloody and bruised. The wrists and ankles were sore and cut and the face was . . . wrapped up . . ."

32

"Wrapped up?" Redwald asked, his pen skittering across the surface of the notebook with every word Hawtree spoke.

"Uh, yes. Wrapped in bed linens, tightly. It was so tight you could see, see the . . . the features pressed against the cloth. You could even see the mouth was open like it was screaming and . . . and the blood seeping through . . . from the eye," he paused, looking at the empty space between his feet and grappling with the memory.

"So the cloth was generally clean, apart from the blood from her eye?"

"Yes, but . . ." he paused again, as he grasped around his memory for more information. Bit by bit, the facts tumbled from him in disarray. "But the body . . . the body was covered in it, blood, I mean. It had run down from the face and dried on the neck and chest. But the room, the room was . . . clean. Completely clean. There was no blood anywhere else. I mean, you'd think there'd be spray or something, given the . . . given the wound, but there wasn't, not a speck anywhere but on the body. And the room was tidy. No sign of a struggle or anything."

"I see," Redwald said, quietly. "Given that her face was covered when you found her, how did you know that the body was Mrs Hawtree?"

"We didn't at the time. I . . . I unwrapped the head. That's when we saw the face. There was a . . . a hole in the left eye socket and burn marks. I tried to move Alice out before she noticed but she . . . she saw . . . . herself. Passed out with the shock."

"And what did you do after that?"

"Well, I reassured the Countess and had the butler call Dr Asplund, the family doctor. He suggested that we move the body to the icehouse out the back." Hawtree was regaining his composure a little and the grin was threatening to resurface like a persistent, unwelcome smell. Redwald, however, was frowning at the sound of Asplund's name.

"Asplund, as in Lord Martingale's Seneschal?"

"He wears many hats," Hawtree said, airily waving the objection away, "he came down immediately and saw to Alice. I then had the butler call the Guard too, who came to inspect the body."

"And what were their conclusions?"

"He said she was killed by a shot to the eye. At . . . at close range. Norris, Guardsman Norris, has prepared a report, for all the good that will do you," Hawtree said, rolling his eyes. "Anyway, he's got all the details on the injury; I'm afraid I don't know any more about it myself. You're seeing him today though, aren't you?"

"This afternoon, yes."

"Excellent. He also has Parnell's report by the way," Hawtree prompted, gesturing to Redwald's notebook.

"Ah yes, I meant to ask you about Dr Parnell. You said in your letter that she was a . . . generalist?"

"Yes that's right, first magician we could get to attend, really. Obviously, given the magical aspects, I knew Norris couldn't deal with this sort of thing himself – it's a bit *beyond* him – so once he was done I contacted a firm in Trewcester saying it was urgent and they sent Parnell out. She was good, but obviously not quite up to your standards."

"You said in your letter that she had performed some tests? Can you remember what they were?" Redwald asked, ignoring both the compliment to him and the slight to Dr Parnell.

"Can't you just read the report this afternoon? It's all in there."

"That will be helpful for the detail, certainly, but if you can remember what she did, I would appreciate it. It stops me repeating her work when I inspect the . . . the body." Though Hawtree's glistening smile was still nailed to his face, he seemed mildly ruffled. Perhaps he was unused to contradiction.

"Well, if you insist. Let's see . . . I think she said she was doing . . . the Morney-Crosling Process?"

"Murray-Crossan?"

"That's it," Hawtree replied, watching as Redwald's face lit up, "what is . . ."

"Was the outcome positive or negative?" Redwald said, interrupting as he continued to write.

"Uh . . . negative, I think."

"Really?" Redwald said, failing to disguise his interest. "Lovely."

"So, what does that mean?" Hawtree asked.

"The Murray-Crossan Process is a series of tests designed to determine whether or not an object, animal, or person, is, or has been, subject to an aesthetic or transformative enchantment," Redwald replied, reeling off the definition by heart. "In this case, a negative outcome indicates that the body has not been enchanted in that way."

"I don't understand, why else would you enchant the body, if not to send it back in time?" Hawtree asked, confused. Redwald raised his eyes from his notes. He would need to be delicate.

"Although your theory is that the body was sent back in time, that may not necessarily be the case. Before we pursue that line of investigation, we need to rule out the other possibilities. We need to establish, in short, that this body is, in fact, your wife's . . ."

35

"I don't understand, of course it's her; it looks like her," Hawtree said, in a tone that veered dangerously close to patronising.

"It's quite possible to make animate or even inanimate objects look like other things," Redwald explained, "I myself am aware of a spell to animate piles of fruit to make them appear to be living, breathing, talking people. Though I've yet to find a use for that one, I admit," he said, as much to himself as to Giles, "I guess the process would be even easier if movement weren't required. For example, if you were imitating a corpse. . . I mean a deceased person."

"Right, I see," Giles conceded reluctantly, "I suppose . . . I suppose that's why Parnell did the blood test, is it?"

"Blood test?"

"Yes, Parnell tested samples of blood from the . . . body and from Alice. I hadn't realised why before now."

"Do you know the result?"

"She said the samples matched. The same blood flows . . ." Giles fidgeted uncomfortably, "*flowed* in those veins as in my wife; there can be no doubt it's the same person."

"I see," Redwald said quietly, though the gravity of that conclusion was not lost on him. "One final thing Mr . . . Giles, since it appears that we really are dealing with a temporal displacement event, did Dr Parnell establish age at time of death?"

"No, I don't think so."

"Ok, that's one for me then," Redwald said, making a note. There was a brief moment of quiet as the magician continued to scribble. Hawtree looked at him expectantly and ended that moment.

"So . . . can you stop it, this time travel thing? What can you do to save my wife?" He asked, his green eyes glistening faintly. Redwald sat back in the armchair and removed his glasses.

"First of all, although temporal displacement events are very rare indeed, I think you are probably correct to say that we are dealing with one here; the facts fit the pattern. Given that, please understand that this is unprecedented territory. My suggestion is that we gather more information. Given that we have forewarning of the mode of death, it strikes me that our best hope is to close off possibilities and reduce the chances of a murder occurring, using what we know now to direct our efforts."

"What more do you need?" Hawtree asked, in a tone which suggested that the magician surely had enough to solve it there and then.

"Perhaps now would be a good time to inspect the study?" Not waiting for a response, Redwald rose in one smooth motion, and stooped to pick up his briefcase. "After you," he said, inclining his head slightly. Giles rose, looked the magician over and made for the second door out of the drawing room, the one closest to the fireplace. As Redwald followed, he quickly became aware of how imperious he had sounded. "So . . . how long have you been married?" he asked, seeking to mollify his client. People did like to talk about themselves.

"A little over a year now, but we've known each other for much longer," Hawtree replied as he led Redwald out into the corridor. The dark wood panelling gave the place a solid and comfortingly enclosed feeling, like the tunnel of a badger's sett.

"Oh lovely, and how did you meet?" Redwald asked.

"I worked for her father," Hawtree replied, turning to meet Redwald's eye as he answered. "I now run the Hawtree Estate, what with Sir Julius' passing, but when we married I was still in

37

management at the Foundry." Something clicked in Redwald's head.

"Oh, you're not Sir Julius' son?"

"Only in law."

"I was going to say, you don't much look like the portrait."

"Alas, no blood relation, but I thought I'd take Alice's name when we married," Giles replied. "After all, who wouldn't want to be a Hawtree?! Right," he said, unlocking and opening the door on their left, "this is the study. Norris has inspected everything, so don't worry about moving things around. I'm not sure what you'll get from looking in here, though."

Redwald stepped in and began to scan the room. Bookshelves clad every wall, stacked with volumes that were clean, new, and largely untouched, their green and red bindings embossed with unblemished gold. A desk and tall chair occupied the centre of the room, overlooked by another oversized portrait of Sir Julius Hawtree, garbed in hunting dress astride a large black horse, his right hand looking like a bound pork joint as it grasped the reins. The portrait itself hung over an empty fireplace and beside a long, decorative deed, recognising the sale of the Rise to the Hawtree family. Behind the desk, windowed doors opened out on to a broad flat patio area behind the house.

Exactly as Giles had said, there was no sign of any mess at all apart from the lightly blood-stained carpet behind the desk and near the window. Redwald walked over to it and looked out through the doors. There was an area for entertaining, seating, and a large, ornate fire-pit. Giles followed him into the room.

"We roast hogs there in the summer," he piped up.

"Hmmm," Redwald murmured, largely ignoring him. Just as Giles had said, the walls, windows and bookshelves were completely devoid of blood; inconsistent with a shot to the head in that vicinity. The only visible blood was that which stained the carpet more or less at Redwald's feet. He knelt to examine it. It was a very small stain, no more than a half-empty wine glass, and located closer to the window-door than to the desk. Again, it appeared that Giles was right. If the body had been as bloody as he said it was, this tiny stain was not nearly enough for the killing to have happened in this room.

With a groan, Redwald rose to his feet. He began to tread slowly around the study, peering intensely at the spine of every book, every nick in the leather desktop, every crease in the wallpaper. If there were any other clues here, he could not afford to miss them. Yet the room remained silent as the grave and would speak to him no more, its last word on the matter being the modest little stain by the window. "You said there was a gunshot wound to her eye. Given the displacement, I assume you didn't find the actual murder weapon with the body, did you?"

"No, the body's all we have." Redwald scowled.

"All the same, did Guardsman Norris say anything about a likely murder weapon, perhaps based on the wound itself?" His frustration was beginning to colour his voice more than he would have liked.

"Yes, but I didn't fully understand what he said to be honest, I'm not an expert myself. Sir Julius would have known; he was a collector of weapons, albeit mostly antiques. It will be in the report, though. I made sure Norris put it in for you."

"I see." Redwald paused, rubbing his fingers into his temples. "Although I'm afraid to say it, I think I have got all I can from this room, for now. Having said that, I would set a guard here. It's likely that in order to travel back in time to this location from the future, Mrs Hawtree will have to start here too. Can we do that?"

"Absolutely," Hawtree said enthusiastically. "I'll get the butler on it. Do you need anything else?" Redwald nodded.

"If possible and provided it won't disturb her at all, I'd like to speak to Mrs Hawtree next. I don't intend to quiz her on specifics, but her input could be useful here."

"Of course."

"Only if it won't disturb . . ."

"Nonsense! She won't mind. Follow me." Giles turned on his heel before Redwald could object. The magician swept from the room and walked behind his host as they headed down the corridor towards the entrance hall. Morrimer crossed their path as Hawtree turned right and up the stairs to the first floor. Giles paused.

"Where have you been?" Giles snapped.

"I have . . ."

"You *should* have been getting Mr de Cordonnay a drink. Terrible that a guest has been left unattended to . . ."

"Actually," Redwald cut in, "he did offer, I declined." Giles had the good grace to look a little abashed. He turned back to Morrimer. "Well, we're going to see Alice. Bring up some tea will you and be sure to use the good set this time." Morrimer nodded and headed back the way he had come. "See?" Giles confided in Redwald, "a little on the slow side, but then, even Hobs get old someday." With that, he grasped the carved wooden swan at the bottom of the banister and swung himself up. Redwald, taking two steps at a time, followed him up onto the balcony that ran around the upper walls of the entrance hall. Here the plaster bosses hung just a few feet over their heads and the sun spilled through the tall arched window over the front door. Hawtree turned left and headed to a room at the very end of the balcony.

"We put her in here; she didn't seem well enough to stay in the master bed," he explained, pushing the door open and walking into the room. Redwald hesitated on the threshold. "Don't worry, she's awake." Redwald gingerly made his way into the room and discovered that Mrs Hawtree was indeed awake, though he surmised this was a nascent state of affairs. She sat herself up in the grand four-poster in which she had been sleeping and shivered nervously, one hand grasping at her hair, the other holding her upright as she shook like a new-born foal. Giles pulled back the curtains, washing away the uterine red light that had comfortably ensconced the room in semi-darkness and replacing it with dazzling sun. Mrs Hawtree blinked and squinted, making no sound.

Redwald watched as Giles moved around to plump her pillows, before easing her back to lean against the headboard.

"Alice, dear, this is Mr de Cordonnay, the magician. He's come to see us all the way from Athonstone." He turned to Redwald, "You'll have to forgive my wife, she's not feeling too well. The shock has affected her quite badly."

A pale woman with livid red lips, she was on the verge of being unhealthily thin; had he been so minded, Redwald might have touched his thumb to his middle finger around her upper arm. Her dull brown hair, which rose and fell in waves, seemed thin and brittle and although it might have been a trick of the light, Redwald thought he could see her scalp in places. Indeed, when she pulled her hand away from her head to support herself, strands of loose hair fell limply from her crown, entangled in her fingers. Redwald was also struck by how young she looked for one so frail. If told she were a day over twenty he would not have believed it.

"Good . . ." Alice began, looking towards the window.

41

"Morning, dear." Giles cut in, patting her on the back as he smiled at Redwald.

"Yes, I thought so," she said wearily. "Good morning Mr de Cordonnay. Thank you so much for coming." She smiled weakly up at him, a thing as miraculous in itself as the appearance of her corpse in the study. She wore her smile like flowers in her hair; natural, unaffected and quite beautifully. Giles' own smile, by contrast, was an overt, practiced grin, as showy as the Manor's ersatz heraldry and only half as pleasant to behold. "I'm sorry I'm a little out of sorts at the moment . . . I should have . . ." she motioned as if to get up.

"No, the fault is mine," Redwald said, almost brusquely, as he placed his briefcase at the foot of a tall mirror. "I *am* sorry for disturbing you." Besides his guilt at disrupting her sleep, Redwald was discomfited by another, new, feeling. It was strange, he was at *most* ten years her senior, but as he watched Alice prepare to answer his questions, he felt oddly paternal towards her. It didn't seem *right* that she should have to deal with this. It was an ill-fitting pattern.

"No that's fine Redwald, please go ahead," Giles said. "You have questions for her?" Morrimer entered with a pot of tea on a silver tray and several cups. Redwald politely refused, but the Hawtrees each took a drink.

"Thank you Morrimer," Alice said as he placed the tea tray on the bed side table and shuffled from the room. "Please do ask, Mr de Cordonnay," she continued, turning back to the magician, "it's in my best interests to help you, after all." Her weak chuckle turned quickly to a cough and she placed her tea on the nightstand to avoid spilling it. It was then that Redwald's eye settled on the photograph.

Alice had placed her tea directly in front of a small pewter picture frame. Inside, there was a photo of Alice with her father, who looked every bit as stern as he had in his portraits, but not,

Redwald noticed, as big. In fact, the more Redwald examined it, the more peculiar the picture began to look. Sir Julius, ever serious, was dressed in drab business attire and sat in a wicker chair as he gazed icily into the camera lens. By contrast, Alice, then only a girl, was sat on his knee, wearing a much jauntier flowered dress and looking up at him lovingly.

Most peculiar of all, however, were his hands. Although it appeared to be summer and they were sat outside, he was wearing gloves, with his left hand grasping the head of a cane and his right on Alice's shoulder. But then, Redwald noticed, it wasn't actually on her shoulder. Instead, it seemed to hover just over the printed flowers, rather than clutching her affectionately to his side. At the very least, he had put a hand on her back, as if winding a baby, but left his fingers taut and straightened. Redwald narrowed his eyes.

"Mr de Cordonnay?" Alice said, delicately prompting him.

"Oh I'm sorry," Redwald said, snapping back to the present, "Yes, I just have a few questions for you, if I may." He hurriedly reorganised his thoughts, but even as he continued, he had the uneasy feeling that Sir Julius was watching him from the photo.

"Of course. Take a seat if you like." She gestured to the foot of the bed.

"Oh no, don't worry. I prefer to stand. Mr Hawtree has helpfully walked me through the day's events, but would you mind giving me your version of what transpired?" Redwald asked, as he extracted his notebook once more. She did; clearly, precisely, and in order as Redwald listened intently. Despite the physical effort it took, she omitted no relevant point and her story aligned with Giles' exactly. It took Redwald some effort to stop the latter interrupting, but the stories matched.

"And can you think of anyone who would wish to do you harm?"

"In the village?"

"Anywhere," he replied. Alice paused, ran her fingers back through her fraying hair and sighed.

"It's possible," she said. "I don't know who it could be, though. I've lived here my entire life; I was born here. I've always felt like I'm a local and, well, they do look after each other. Lord Martingale in particular has always been very protective of the village and kind to me . . ."

"To both of us," Giles said, taking his wife's hand in his own.

"You can't single anyone out, even tentatively?" Redwald said, directing the question to Alice.

"Honestly, no. You may think I've lived a sheltered life, Mr de Cordonnay, but it's all been spent here. Whoever is responsible for . . . this . . . they're not from around here." Redwald saw then, perhaps for the first time, the emotional weight she bore. He knew logically that she did, of course, but with no outward sign from her, he had consigned the fact to the back of his mind. Now, her voice quavered very slightly and she struggled to swallow.

"May I ask, Mrs Hawtree. . . "

"Alice, please." He overrode his preference for formality.

"Alice, may I ask how old you are?"

"Well, uh . . ." she seemed a little taken aback.

"I'm not asking to be vulgar, but for the sake of the investigation." He smiled as warmly as he could.

"She's 19, Mr de Cordonnay," Giles interjected.

"Thank you," Redwald said, irritation seeping into his voice, "and your birthday?" He continued, addressing the question to Alice. Giles, he noted, suddenly took an interest in the wallpaper.

"34th of Sussureme," she replied. Redwald noted it.

"2306?" he said, after a long pause, the strain of the arithmetic showing on his face.

"Yes." Redwald sighed heavily. She had been born after the turn of the century; that always made him feel old. Old*er,* anyway; he always felt old. Perhaps the memories of his former lives bled through more than they ought.

"I see. Thank you Mrs Hawtree."

"I told you, Alice." She smiled. "I'm sorry I couldn't be of more help, but . . . . I really don't know who could want this." A sense of frustration tinged her voice as tension gripped her frame, but she held it under control.

"Any information is useful . . . Alice," he replied. "Now I feel I should leave you to your rest. Thank you for your help and . . . I hope you recover soon."

"So do I," she said. A chink in her armour bared itself then, as tears began to pool in her eyes. "But . . . please . . . please give me a reason to recover. If I'm to die that way . . . I may as well end it now." Far beneath his taut features, Redwald felt his chest lurch.

"I will do everything I can." He paused. "I swear it." The oath was made.

"Thank you," she said, wiping the tears away with embarrassment. She collected herself, turned painfully around and lowered her head into the narrow groove in her pillow, her ragged breathing barely audible as Giles rose from the bed, pulled the curtains, put his cup of tea by Alice's and led Redwald out into the corridor. Retrieving his briefcase from the foot of the mirror, the magician quickly followed, and shut the door behind him.

"That should be enough to be going on with, I think?" Giles said, leaning forward expectantly.

"Almost." Redwald flicked his watch out of his pocket and looked down his nose at the time. "There's just one more thing I need to do here and the sooner I do it, the better. Should have time before my meeting with Guardsman Norris," he rumbled, largely to himself. He turned and made his way down the staircase, Giles in tow. "I would like to see the body, please," he said as he descended the staircase, free hand in his pocket.

"I can arrange that."

"Excellent. To confirm; Guardsman Norris has made his investigations?"

"Yes."

"Then I have leave to examine it in any way I feel fit?" Giles looked uncomfortable.

"Within reason."

"Funny you should say that," Redwald said, turning to look up at Giles on the higher step, "because they say that reason has no place in matters of the heart, and it's hers I will be needing."

CHAPTER 4

The Humming Heart

"My Dearest Lauranna,

I thank you for your last letter, it cheered me greatly to hear that you are well and that Georgina is excelling in her studies. She will be a fine Baroness one day, I've no doubt. You are both constantly on my mind and I miss you terribly, every sunrise and glittering swell reminds me of you, though neither can surpass you in beauty and I know how excited Georgina would be to see Carus. I have therefore bought her a Carussian sabre, which I shall use to instruct her in swordsmanship on my return, provided she is grown enough, of course. Although my homecoming is now on the horizon, my heart aches to see you both again.

Fortunately my longing is, if only a little, tempered by the action we have seen in the face of the enemy. Excitement of this kind does distract one so well. You need not fear though, we have not been in the thick of any real danger, just a few mild skirmishes off the coast and one more sizeable engagement chasing the EHS Ranitavia away from a convoy of orcite ships. Enough to excite a fellow, but not get him killed! My man Commander Asplund (I feel I may have mentioned him to you before, he's a medical sort) lost an eye to an Empyreal Marine at close quarters for example; engaging stuff. I think it's some consolation to him that he managed to blow a hole through the blighter's head in exchange and, as I said to him, the eyepatch is only an improvement. If you'll forgive the rough talk, my darling, I'm sure he'll be glad of his scars when he hits port. The lads will be trampling each other for his attention.

On that note, I'm thinking of offering him a position as my Seneschal, should he be so inclined. The village is short a doctor too, so we'll kill two birds with one stone. I know you like the Reverend as Seneschal and I agree he has done well, but if Asplund accepts, I think a military man would make just as good a job of it, if not better.

In any event, I must go now my darling, the night is short and there is much to do tomorrow. Know that my love goes with this letter and will be with you always.

Archie"

Letter from Lord to Lady Martingale, sent from HMS Hartspur, 2nd Durrember 2305

It had taken no small amount of time to convince Giles of the necessity, but it was done. Having been led out towards the woods behind the Manor and into the icehouse set into the slope of the hill, Redwald now stood over the body of the 'future' Mrs Hawtree, his breath billowing into mist in the freezing air around him. The low-ceilinged room they occupied was empty; the ice, meat and other sundries having been moved from their shelves into adjacent chambers, away from the corpse. Alice herself lay on a marble slab in the centre of the room, her pallid features lit by the soft glow of dimmed orcite lamps.

The corpse in the icehouse however, looked subtly different to the woman Redwald had seen earlier. The dead Mrs Hawtree was even paler, her lips almost white and much less of her mouse-brown hair remained to her. There were livid red rope marks at her wrists and ankles and, though not malnourished, she was even thinner and more wiry than her former self. She must have suffered before her death, Redwald thought, as bruises had blossomed on her skin like mould spots on linen. Giles was stood in the corner, shivering. Perhaps due to the cold, but it was more likely the gaping red wound in his wife's eye socket.

On the opposite side of the slab stood Dr Asplund. He was a quiet man in his late fifties, unusually short and broad with greying unkempt whiskers, yet sporting a full head of black curly hair. This he had slicked forcefully, but unsuccessfully, back across his head. From the tangled mass at his hairline, a fleshy scar traced its way down to his cheek, passing beneath the black patch that covered his left eye.

The family doctor, Mr Hawtree had demanded, should assist if this experiment was to be done, and so the loyal servant and physician to the Hawtree family had been summoned from his practice in the village and brought up here to remove, for Redwald's sake, the lady's heart from behind her ribs.

"I'm not a mortician," Asplund said.

"I'd trust no one else with this," Giles replied.

The Doctor, arms gloved up to the elbow, was leaning over the body. He had sawn through the breastbone (as respectfully as possible), clamped open her chest cavity, and was about to remove the heart itself.

"We shouldn't be doing this," Asplund said, looking at Giles. "Why . . .," he grunted as he pushed past her lungs, "why didn't Parnell do this? She seemed perfectly competent. I don't see what this city magician has to do that's so important. If it needed doing it would have been done already."

"You worked for Sir Julius for how long?" Redwald asked, ignoring his objections.

"Since he moved here." He continued to huff as he struggled with her organs.

"How long precisely?"

"Twenty years or so, I don't know."

"And you're fond of Alice?"

"You ought to call her Mrs Hawtree," the Doctor snarled, severing her arteries deftly.

"You're fond of her though?"

"Of course," he grumbled, as he held her heart carefully in his hand and manoeuvred it to make her aorta more accessible. "I helped deliver her; I was there when she was born. Every scrape, every illness, I've been up here looking after her; keeping her safe."

"Then I'm sure you want to keep her alive, don't you?" Redwald said. "We are in a unique situation of having forewarning of a murder; we may very well prevent it occurring at all if we're clever. This will help."

"Still," Asplund said, appealing to Giles, "I don't like this. Doesn't seem right."

"Father would understand, I'm sure," Giles said of his father-in-law.

"In any event," Redwald continued, "I only need her heart temporarily. When the time is right, she will be properly cremated. I only hope she's the only Mrs Hawtree we have to burn." The Doctor cut through the final blood vessel attaching the heart to the body. Lifting it clear of her chest he proffered the organ to Redwald.

"Not for me, thank you; just hold on to it for a moment." Redwald leaned down and pulled a black chalkboard and a battered book from his briefcase. The book was an old and ugly thing. Stamped in silver on the placenta-coloured front were the words *Medical Magic Series Vol VII – The Heart and Circulatory Systems – Prof. Sir Thibald Otway*. The board, on the other hand, was well cared for and well-used, the brass frame that supported it glinting pleasingly in the light. Redwald placed it on the table a comfortable distance below Mrs Hawtree's feet.

He flicked through the pages of the book and lay it open beside the board at his chosen page. By reference to both the book and his pocket watch, he then proceeded to draw a series of patterns on the surface of the chalkboard. He started with an off-centre, web-like pattern in white chalk, upon which he plotted a set of seemingly random circles in red, before linking the latter circles with precise blue lines, all drawn immaculately with the aid of a pair of compasses and a ruler. The brass-sprung frame of the chalkboard clicked as he lifted the compasses from the board each time and placed them down again, swinging the polished arms around once, twice, maybe ten times or more and drawing as many circles. Once these were done, he took a separate golden chalk and began to write along the blue lines. Try as they might, however, the magician's scrawl was next to illegible and neither Giles nor Asplund could make out any words.

Once done, Redwald stood back for a moment and examined his work, scrutinising both the chalkboard and his watch in detail. Giles had always wanted to see a magician's watch. They were famously complex contraptions, fiendishly difficult to make and equally hard to use. They always had two faces; the first was a functional timepiece as anyone might carry, but it was the second face, the thaumograph, that made them so useful to the magician. Sidereal magic harnessed the forces of the universe by making offerings to and calling upon stars in combination with one another. This relied on the magician's ability to locate the relevant stars, with the attributes desired, and map them out in their locations at the time of casting to form the spell. So went the First Law of Magic - *As above, so below.*

Redwald twisted the dials around the edge of the thaumograph, re-positioning the star map as necessary. Although each star was labelled with a unique symbol, these were as numerous as they were undescriptive, so most magicians would have a sidereal reference book as well. Redwald, however, appeared to be doing his checks from memory. After some considerable thought, he made a single correction: highlighting one of the red circles in yellow.

51

Finally satisfied, Redwald reached into his briefcase and retrieved a large articulated frame. It looked a little like a laboratory stand and consisted of a sturdy brass pole, hinged into sections, and a weighted base. He unfolded it to a full height of about 3 feet and stood it on the marble surface behind the chalkboard. Diving into the briefcase again, he quickly re-surfaced with a round mesh cage. Split into two halves, it resembled a pair of sieves connected by a hinge, albeit that each sieve had another smaller hole at the top and the bottom of the cage. Redwald clamped the device to the stand and opened the sphere, before directing Asplund to place the heart inside. The doctor did so with steady, blood-soaked hands. Upon closing and fastening the cage, Redwald gave the mesh a light touch, whereupon it gently contracted to match the organ's contours.

"What does that do?" Giles asked.

"This," Redwald explained, gesturing at the frame, "supports the heart, protects it from interference and keeps it upright. It also holds this . . ." he stooped and rummaged in his briefcase once more, producing a large glass water bottle, with a rubber pipe protruding from the top and a cork stopper at the base. He clamped the bottle to the stand upside down and directly over the cage, the rubber tube trailing down towards the heart. He then asked Dr Asplund to insert the tube into the aorta via the cage's uppermost opening, while making a small incision in the heart's base at the bottom-most. As the Doctor carefully complied, Redwald pulled an empty flask from his briefcase. He studied it for a moment.

"Mrs Hawtree turned 19 last Sussureme, yes?"

"That's right."

"20 in a few weeks, then," Redwald muttered to himself, "I'll need another one." Rummaging a little more to the sound of clinking, he pulled out a second flask, which he deftly slid into the space between the base of the stand and the incision in the heart. Marked in numerals up the length of the spindly tube were minutely painted lines of differing colours and lengths, denoting years, months, and days.

"Almost there," Redwald assured the waiting Hawtree, whose shivering had become gradually more acute. Redwald then returned to the varied contents of his briefcase, picking out tiny jars, terracotta pots and vials. One by one he would read the label, uncork the container, sprinkle a small quantity onto an empty circle on the blackboard, replace the container, and repeat. Slowly the empty spaces began to fill with dried lavender, fish eyes, powdered garlic, fingernails, even a small crystal of iron pyrite, amongst other things, and some substances that neither Asplund nor Giles had ever seen before. Finally, only one empty space remained. Redwald turned to Asplund.

"Would you oblige me Doctor?" Redwald said, gesturing to the last empty circle; the one highlighted in yellow.

"How?"

"I see you have some spare blood there," Redwald remarked of Asplund's livid red gloves, "please wipe some of it into that yellow circle." Asplund hesitated for a moment, but at a nod from Hawtree, he complied.

"Right. I think we're ready," Redwald said, removing the cork from the top of the water bottle. "Gentlemen, I would ask you to please remain silent for a few moments. I need to time this perfectly or the whole thing will be thrown off". Very carefully, he reached up to the tap at the base of the water bottle, a tap which, when turned, would allow water to flow through the rubber tube and into the heart. He then performed one final check, his grey eyes examining every inch of the apparatus with absolute and exacting precision. The smallest mote of dust would not have escaped his attention.

While he paused for a moment, Asplund and Giles each stepped back, unsure as to what to expect. Redwald closed his eyes and drew three deep breaths, just as he had practiced. Mustering all his focus, he reduced the raging tempest of his mind to a pitch-black, glassy ocean, mirroring a starless sky. The spell was written, the tribute offered; this was casting. Having stilled his thoughts, he allowed the concept of the spell to float up from the depths. It was one thing to write a spell down, but to give it effect, one had to lift it beyond the mere written word, one had to *feel it, to understand it, to believe it.* As smoothly as it had risen, the concept evaporated from the surface of his mind as he conveyed his message to the stars. He waited; hand poised on the tap. Then he felt it, that inimitable sensation, familiar yet foreign, as power surged through his veins and crackled through his nerves. He turned the tap.

Three things happened in an instant; the water began to flow down into the heart, the objects on the board sagged a little, greyed, and turned to weyste, and the heart started to beat furiously, pumping at a rate far faster than was natural. It hummed. A tiny, almost imperceptible trickle of red liquid began to drip from it into the flask below, while the blood in the yellow circle, the only tribute not to have turned to weyste, glinted in the lamplight.

Giles and the Doctor stared aghast, but Redwald, apparently satisfied, opened his eyes and stepped away.

"What's that?" Giles asked, as Redwald cleaned the weyste off the chalkboard. It was the colour of grey riverbank clay and had the consistency of wet sand, though it was neither wet nor dry to the touch.

"That is weyste," Redwald said, as he wiped the blood off with a clean cloth, folded that carefully, and returned it and the chalkboard to his cavernous briefcase, "the by-product of magic. When the tribute is offered to the stars they accept the essence of those things, the smell, the colour, even the taste of a flower, for example, or the sliminess of the eyes and leave the material behind. This is, to put it unhelpfully, the nothing that everything is made of."

"And what's that doing?" Asplund asked gruffly, gesturing at the heart.

"It's a spell to determine age. Or rather, age at death. The subject usually has to be dead for this to work."

"Usually?" Asplund asked. Redwald ignored him and turned to Giles.

"Your wife is both dead and yet has still to die. By seeing how old the dead Mrs Hawtree was when she died, I can tell just how far in the future she was murdered, by reference to how old your wife is now. I do that by having the heart re-live every beat it ever made, from the first beat after birth to her very last. I specify in the spell that it's after birth, otherwise it's hard to tell how many days we're dealing with." He looked at the apparatus, now humming, with a dark look in his eyes. "It's an elegant, if unsettling spell; seeing a life pass at speed. It will still take time though, and when it's done it will only be a rough guide, no more accurate than a day. However," he continued, as if arguing with himself, "it's still better than nothing and I'm hoping we won't be working on margins that narrow." He paused for a moment, his eyes resting on the raw flesh at her wrists and ankles.

"Restraints." Asplund said, noting the gaze. Redwald hummed agreement.

"Which might make her time of death academic, to some degree, if she's kidnapped well in advance."

"Do you think they sent her back deliberately?" Hawtree interjected, "to remind us to pay a ransom perhaps, to intimidate us?"

"Hard to say, but I doubt it. Sending her back would require magical knowledge currently unheard of. Besides," he said, looking at her dull bruises and glistening cuts, "this seems personal. This can't just be a ransom demand, this is . . . vindictive. Or not; I'm not a detective. Please leave that," he said, changing the subject abruptly and gesturing to the apparatus, "alone, for the time being. I imagine it will take about four days to give a result. It must not be tampered with, is that understood?"

"I will have the butler check it hourly and place two guards on the door," Giles said.

"Excellent," Redwald replied, "I'd also suggest you place guards on Mrs Hawtree's door and keep her under close protection. If we can prevent her kidnapping, that may be one way to head off the murder." He flicked open his watch.

"Right, well thank you for your help gentlemen," he said, looking at Dr Asplund who simply replied with a grunt, "but I had better be off, I have an appointment with the Guard."

"When?" Asplund asked.

"Oh, Guardsman Norris wouldn't settle on a time, he just said this afternoon."

"Yes that sounds like Norris," Asplund snorted, "but you're out of luck; the Guard Station closes at four, they'll be shut now."

"Four?!" Redwald blurted, incredulous.

"It's a quiet village."

"So it seems," Redwald said with an arched eyebrow, looking at the Doctor over Mrs Hawtree's body on the table. "In that case, I shall have to speak to the Guard tomorrow. Mr Hawtree, would you mind sending a message on my behalf to Guardsman Norris to arrange a meeting tomorrow morning? He can find me at the Double Standard if he wants to discuss."

"Of course, my pleasure," Giles said, "I'll set the butler on it right away. Is there anything else you need here?"

"No," Redwald sighed, "I've done all I can for the moment. Thank you both for your help, I do appreciate it."

"Our pleasure," Hawtree said, grinning, "please, allow me to show you the way out."

"I'll clean myself up in here," Asplund said, peeling the bloody gloves off of his hands. Redwald cast one last look at his apparatus, the humming heart, and the woman on the table with the open chest before picking up his briefcase and heading out of the icehouse. It was a cool spring afternoon and the wind rustled his dark hair, the speckled greys catching in the sinking sun. Giles was talking animatedly, but Redwald himself was silent, as the two men gently meandered out along the gravel walkway towards the turnaround in front of the house. As they turned the corner and arrived in front of the Manor, Giles was engaged in describing the construction of the house and Sir Julius' difficulties therein, but Redwald's attention was caught by something else; a distant tower, silhouetted against the ochre sky.

"What is that?" he asked, looking out across the wide valley below and towards the opposite hill. Wooded, green and low, like the mossy hull of a capsized ship, it sloped down to the banks of the Trew, guiding the river's course as it snaked downstream.

"What, the hill?" Hawtree said, somewhat irritably. "It's just a hill; the locals call it *Martingale's Work*, or something like that."

"No, sorry, I meant the tower," Redwald pressed. It was the look of the thing that had struck him. Built of patterned red brick, much like Hawtree Manor, it was fancifully crenelated and exaggerated to look more like a castle than a real castle would have. Whoever designed it had even tacked a secondary tower, replete with tall slate spire and fluttering banner, onto the primary one, like a limpet clinging to a pillar. Even from this distance, the initials JH were clearly visible, patterned into the brickwork. In keeping with the overall aesthetic of the Manor, Redwald thought, it looked sorely out of place. Giles stopped and turned to look.

"Oh, *I* built that!" He said, gleefully.

"Yes," Redwald said, slowly, "and what is it?"

"It's a monument to Sir Julius. Before he acquired the land here, he was going to build his home on that side of the valley, he even laid the foundations. When he died, I decided to build on those foundations and dedicate a memorial to him, so that Alice could see it from her window."

"Oh, that was thoughtful," Redwald said, taking exceptional care to maintain a neutral tone.

"I thought so," Giles replied. "The locals call it Hawtree's Folly and make the *brilliant* jest that Hawtree's Folly is built on Martingales' Work, but they can say what they like. Lord Martingale has so very kindly asked that they desist, but I'm sure they haven't. As long as he and I get along, I don't see that it matters."

"Yes, I suppose you're right," Redwald said, attempting a smile. Before he had a chance to say anything further, however, the sound of carriage wheels rattled up from the woods below them.

Through the arch at the base of the drive emerged a tradesman's van. The large, painted wagon was drawn by four black horses, driven from the coach box by two attendants in black and gold livery, and bore the legend; *Acewood & Thurlow: Wine Merchants.* Redwald watched as the horses trotted up the steep incline and

58

brought the wagon parallel to the front door. Giles called for Morrimer before turning to Redwald.

"A terrible business really," Giles shook his head. Redwald mused that, so long as he lived, no wine merchant was likely to struggle in business, but he kept that thought to himself.

"How do you mean?"

"Oh, this is all for the Hawtree Fund Gala tomorrow. I hardly feel up to it, but we do have a name to maintain."

"I confess, I'm surprised it's still going ahead." Redwald's disapproval was as well disguised as blood on snow. Hawtree's grin faltered for a moment, but he quickly regained his composure.

"Oh, you mustn't think that way. I've sealed off the wing where Alice is sleeping; she will not be disturbed if she chooses to miss the event. Besides, Norris confirmed that he has all the evidence he needs and my own men will be on duty for safety. The Annual Gala is a crucial event in the Society calendar. It would shame Alice and her father if I were to fail as a host." Redwald said nothing. "Besides, we have been organising it for months, even before the . . . well the . . . you know."

"The murder, yes."

"May I extend you an invitation?" Giles said.

"Me?" Redwald asked, genuinely surprised.

"Certainly, as an advance form of thanks. The *Hawtree Estate*," he said with more unction than the phrase deserved, "would truly like to show you how much your efforts in this case are appreciated. I don't know what I would do if I lost Alice. It's just that, with the Gala, a man of my status has a lot of obligations you see. It really is a bore, but you understand my position. Would you do me the honour of attending?" Redwald looked off down the lawn,

59

uncertain as to how to respond. "It would be an opportunity to represent your firm to some very exclusive clientele," Giles urged.

Redwald sighed inwardly. *Networking.* Having said that, his superiors might be less than forgiving if he turned down the chance to schmooze the great and questionably good. . .

"I've ordered fifty cases of the Reichort Arrovênnes . . ."

"I'd be delighted," Redwald relented, his face betraying the lie. "Time?"

"Tomorrow, 7:30." Giles beamed. "We are so looking forward to having you!" Redwald thanked him curtly, before turning and heading back into the village.

The magician trudged slowly down the hill, the springy steps that bore him up it having faded with the passing of the day. It *was* a start, he consoled himself, but not much of one. Of the event itself he had learnt very little and knew even less about how to stop it. Of the Hawtrees, however, he had learnt rather more. He turned around to look up at the Manor. Somewhere in that house, that gaudy testament to a dead man's over-inflated ego, lay a young woman who needed his help; help that might not materialise in time. He swore and headed for the nearest pint.

CHAPTER 5

Dulled Senses and Sharp Tongues

"... At the market, the crops would not sell as they had gone bad. The little girl's father was very sad and, after drinking himself witless, went out to sell his daughter. It was raining and he held the little girl up in his hand calling for someone to buy her. Then a man in a smart coat rode up and told him to take better care of her. Seeing that this man was rich, her father explained that his family was poor and could not feed the girl and that, if the rich man did not buy her there and then, he would leave the baby in the mud and the rain. The man on the horse gave the father eleven gold sovereigns, one for each remaining child, and asked the baby's name. Her father replied that she had none and told the rich man he must provide one. The rich man thought about it and took the baby away ... "

The Tale of Alynore – Traditional Tales for Growing Children, collated by Dr C.F. Twistle (Allpress) 1992

"Knock!" roared Djereff Altoon, Bowmaster-General of the XII Tenyran Guard, his jet-black horns slick with fallen snow. Either side, ranked Giant archers knocked arrows on bows half again the height of a man, their Human and Hob slaves hurrying between them, bearing sheaf after sheaf of new arrows. "Draw!" Below them on the plain, the massed cavalry of Supreme Magistrix Parothia VIII of Jenever charged with insane abandon towards the massed Tenyran ranks, the Supreme Magistrix herself watching from the walls of the city. The archers lifted their bows. "LOOSE!" The black arrows rose like a murder of startled crows. Arcing through the frigid air in their thousands and flying in the face of the soft white snowflakes, they began to fall, skewering the cavalry and spattering the freshly fallen snow with Avenar blood.

"Evening!" Charteris said merrily as, red faced and beaming, he dropped backwards into the opposite chair. Redwald slowly closed his book and returned to the present, leaving the Third Siege of Jenever far behind him. "I see you've made a decent start!" Charteris pointed out. In his book-free hand, Redwald held a glass of ruby ale, while the prior four glasses were stacked neatly on the table in front of him.

"Yes I have," Redwald admitted, a warm smile spreading slowly across his face like burning incense. He lifted his glass in Charteris' direction, slopping a bit of beer over the rim. "Cheers!" The Reverend groaned as he leaned forward in his chair to clink glasses.

"Cheers!" he said, before taking a deep draught from his own pewter mug. It was warm and pleasantly snug in the bar of the Double Standard. Redwald had managed to burrow into an alcove by the stairs and had spent the past few hours leaning back into the pocked leather of an ancient armchair, drowning the stresses and concerns of the day in wholesome, warming ale. Outside of Redwald's little corner, the bar was humming like a finely tuned engine and the walls of the pub seemed to lean inward to coddle the occupants. Behind the bar the Landlord rushed to and fro with surprising agility for a man of his girth, while his daughter pulled pints with a healthy vigour. Meanwhile, the people of Martingale-on-Trew were chatting, laughing, and drinking, whether stood at the bar, nestled into the ragged furniture, or gathered around the crackling fire.

"So," Charteris said, easing himself back into his seat and glancing at Redwald's tower of empty glasses, "I see you met Giles." Redwald barked a laugh.

"Don't be unkind, Reverend," he said, permitting himself a beery grin.

"I wasn't!" Charteris replied in mock outrage. "I am simply acknowledging that he's a bit of an acquired taste."

"An *interesting character?*"

"Your words, not mine," Charteris winked.

"No Reverend, I'm afraid those are your words." Charteris rolled his eyes back as he recalled their prior conversation.

"Bugger, so they are, but you see what I mean . . ."

"He was nothing but polite to me," Redwald replied, "however, it did feel a bit like talking to an actor *playing* Giles Hawtree, rather than to the man himself." Redwald wondered briefly if that's why he recognised Giles. Did he resemble an actor? Charteris jerked forward and clicked his fingers.

"Exactly! That's exactly how I'd put it," he said, before allowing himself to sink slowly back into the chair like a deflating balloon. He sighed then, an expression of guilt creeping into his wrinkled features. "It's a bit unfair though, really. I know we laugh, but I do feel for the poor fellow."

"Why on Awn would you do that?" Redwald asked, grinning to himself as he took a draught.

"Oh well, you know, I think . . . I think he feels he has to play a role . . . for his career, you see?"

"How so?"

"Well, he was promoted ever so quickly at the Foundry. I wonder if he doesn't feel a bit out of place, deep down. He was a jobbing servant when he arrived here, after all. Honest work, to be sure, but very different from what he does now. It's a terribly quick change of scene."

"He was a servant?"

"Oh yes. Don't suppose he told you that? I think Sir Julius transferred him to work here from his Athonstone properties in about 2310, 2311." Clearly Redwald didn't recognise Giles from Athonstone, he himself had only moved to the City a few years after. "Yes, must have been," Charteris said, clearing his throat, "I remember my bees suffered quite badly that year; lost a lot to the cold. A few years later, he suddenly got a job at the Foundry. Probably why Giles is the way he is, come to think of it; having Sir Julius as a mentor."

"Oh?" Redwald prompted, before finishing his pint.

"Well, with all due respect for the departed," Charteris said, raising his hand and performing the sign of the Cycle, "the blighter was terribly aloof."

"Perhaps he was shy?" Redwald sympathised a little. He had often been accused, not without justification, of being aloof.

"No, it wasn't quite that. Never had much to do with the village, never really *involved* himself personally, you see. Never once shook my hand either. Perhaps I'm being old-fashioned, but I consider that a common courtesy. Having said that," Charteris sighed, "I can't say he didn't contribute *financially*, even if he didn't deign to contribute personally. Gave bits of money to the village from time to time, new church bells, bridge repair, that sort of thing. Mostly raised from that Gala, you know."

"Hmmm," Redwald murmured, "I'm going to that tomorrow, actually. Would be grateful if you could introduce me to a few people, if you don't mind."

"I'd be delighted old boy, but I'm not invited." Charteris smiled, kindly.

"Oh," said Redwald, abashed, "I'm sorry. I didn't mean to . . ."

"No, quite alright, he only ever invites Lord Martingale and Dr Asplund from round here."

"Friends of the family?"

"No, the Lord of the Manor and his Seneschal. Thank Oryn I lost that job to Asplund, I don't know if I'd fit in very well up there." He said, swigging his pint.

"Well," Redwald said diplomatically, "I only got an invite when I saw the wine coming up the drive. I suppose he felt he couldn't avoid it."

"He avoids it with us!" Charteris chuckled. "Maybe you qualify because you're a city-type, I suppose." Redwald baulked a little at that; he never thought of himself as a city-type. Woodlow, the village of his childhood, was near Athonstone to be sure and within the Royal Demesne, but as leafy green as Martingale-on-Trew itself. "Anyway, another celebratory pint for you? First day on the job?" Charteris said, gesturing again to Redwald's empty glasses. Redwald felt his stomach drop; he had, until now, successfully forgotten about the case.

"Oh, yes please. Only if you don't mind, though," Redwald said, distracted.

"Of course, I'll get you a pint of my favourite," Charteris said, staggering away to the bar. Redwald placed his book on the table and leant forward in his seat, fingers on his temples. The tension swept over him like a dust storm as he remembered what he had deliberately forgotten; having been in the village a full day, he still had no real leads. Although to the rest of the pub he looked perfectly calm, he was flailing internally. Hurriedly trying to review the facts he could remember, he found himself unable to make sense of them. *That*, he thought to himself, *is probably because of those.* He looked across at the glasses and felt a pang of guilt. The vision of Alice Hawtree's corpse floated before his inner eye.

"Here!" Charteris said, setting a pint of pale ale on the table in front of Redwald, "Hobson's Choice!"

"Thank you, that's very kind." Redwald said, smiling weakly.

"To the case!" Charteris said, proposing a toast and inadvertently mashing salt into Redwald's wound. "Good luck, old boy!"

"Thank you," the magician said, clinking glasses once more, "I'll need it." He took a draught large enough to momentarily still his mind, but the relief was short-lived.

"That bad eh?" Charteris asked, sympathetically.

"I just . . ." Redwald said, on the cusp of a rant. "No, never mind," he said, restraining himself, "it's my problem, not yours."

"Anything I can do to help?" Charteris asked, hopefully.

"No one can help, I'm afraid. It's just . . . it's just that . . . there's so little to work with here. Aside from the event itself, the magical aspects of this are extremely limited." He took another draught.

"How so, old chap?"

"Well, how the hell . . ." he stopped himself abruptly, "Apologies Reverend, I didn't mean . . ."

"Nonsense, old boy. You should have heard *me* when one of the bees got past my veil. Not much to work with?" It was perhaps the first indication that Redwald had given of being drunk. His diction, while a tad slower than his usual brisk patter, was as crisp and formal as it always had been, if not more so.

"Well, having established that it *was* a temporal displacement, I'm now left to try and *solve* the murder before it happens, you see? And because of the time travel aspect, I have to do it with only half the evidence; there's no murder weapon, no fingerprints, just the body."

"That sounds difficult."

"Really bloody difficult," Redwald confirmed, arching an eyebrow. He briefly fixed Charteris with a penetrating stare, but his gaze slipped away into the middle distance as his mind continued to race. "Need to talk to Guardsman Norris. His conclusions may be crucial. Really hacked off I missed him today, actually. If I'd been able to talk to him, I might have been able to move this case forward a bit quicker."

"There's always tomorrow," Charteris said, kindly. Redwald shook his head.

"No . . . I can't afford to waste time. She might . . . she's . . . I can't leave it too late." Charteris watched with concern as an agitated darkness crept into Redwald's eyes.

"Listen, old boy, you must try and relax. You'll be no good to Alice if you're fraying at the edges, no good to anyone for that matter." Redwald grumbled quietly to himself, unconvinced. "But if you're really that worried about it, I'm sure Osbert wouldn't mind a *quick* chat now. He's just over there, by the fire." Redwald's head flicked around as though he were a raptor about to kill something.

"Where?"

"The young fellow with the blonde hair. He's sat next to Asplund; the chap with the eye-patch. I don't expect he'll be able to help you much tonight, but . . ." Redwald muttered a distracted thanks and promise of imminent return to Charteris, before seizing his pint and swooping across the pub to where Norris sat. He swayed a little as he walked, but quickly righted himself.

"Guardsman Norris?" Redwald asked. Raising his voice above the hum of conversation, he rather abruptly barked at the young man, who turned to look at the magician hurriedly and with some measure of shock.

"Yeah?!" he blurted.

"I'm Redwald de Cordonnay, pleased to meet you," Redwald said, leaning over the seated Guardsman. He offered his pint-free hand. Osbert Norris, whose round face, guileless expression and untidy blonde hair indicated that he was Redwald's junior, regarded the latter with a mixture of interest and wariness, like a shy toddler being introduced to an adult acquaintance. He took the magician's hand. "Doctor," Redwald said, shaking Asplund's hand too.

"Come to join us, de Cordonnay?" Asplund growled through his beard.

"I was hoping for a quick chat with Guardsman Norris actually, about the case," Redwald said, his dark eyes flicking across to meet Norris' head on.

"Have a seat . . ." Asplund said, gesturing to the larger of the two chairs on the opposite side of the fire.

"But that's . . ." Norris began, before Asplund silenced him with a look.

"Thank you," Redwald said, enthroning himself in the gigantic armchair, possibly the oldest and scraggiest seat in the pub, and placing his pint on the table to the left of it. He did not notice the looks directed surreptitiously at him from around the room. "I'm sorry I wasn't able to make our meeting earlier today, Guardsman, but I hadn't realised the station would close at *4*."

"That's alrigh'" Norris said, breezily and completely innocent of the quiet condemnation that laced Redwald's apology, "a fella of Lord Hawtree's popped down earlier, we can meet tomorrow?"

"*Lord* Hawtree?" Redwald asked, confused.

"Just a little nickname we have for Giles," Asplund said, "he doesn't mind."

"I see," Redwald replied, eyebrow raised, "anyway, tomorrow would be fine, Guardsman, thank you for making the time, but really . . ."

"Oh yeah sounds good," Norris said, interrupting, "we can talk about the reports." He smiled, clearly trying to appear cooperative. It did little more than rankle Redwald, who sank some more beer to smother the rising sense of frustration.

"Thanks," Redwald said, "but really I was hoping to ask you a few questions this evening if I may? In particular," he said, without waiting for Norris' response, "I would value your opinion on the type of gun used. I appreciate the weapon itself isn't available due to the displacement, but do we have any other evidence that might identify it? Is this a standard-issue revolver, say, or are we working with a narrower field?" Norris looked somewhat bewildered.

"Um, it's an old gun, but it's all in the reports and I'm off-duty. Maybe tomorrow . . ."

"Yes, I appreciate that you're off-duty," Redwald said, irritably, "but time is short, and I'm already behind schedule, so if you could just give me a *few* details, then I can at least start to think . . ."

"Sorry, just can't remember the specs off-hand," Norris said, shrugging.

"All your other time-travelling murder cases cluttering your memory, are they?" Redwald snapped. Sweat glistened on Norris' forehead.

"Everything alright Osbert?" The voice came from over Redwald's shoulder. Its owner, a man in his late 50s or early 60s, was robust, tall and accompanied by a pair of muddy Wedron Bloodhounds. He was dressed in mud-caked boots and well-worn tweeds, offset by a row of medals at his chest. Although their reliefs were worn and the ribbons sun-bleached and frayed, the medals were clearly treasured, arranged in immaculate order and polished to a mirror-sheen. This was in stark contrast to the man's hair, which was wild about his head and face like a lion's mane and as white as he was black. Redwald shifted uncomfortably in his seat, his eyes fixed on the panting, filthy dogs.

"Yessir," Norris replied, "Mr Cord-neigh was asking about the Hawtree case."

"Oh I see, so *you're* Hawtree's magician are you?" The robust man said scornfully, looking down at Redwald.

"Yes . . ." Redwald replied, reluctantly diverting his attention from the dogs, "I was just asking . . ."

"Well could you *just ask* somewhere else? You're in my chair."

"I'm sorry, what?" The suppressed frustration began to bubble anew.

"You're in my chair. Move." Redwald looked across at Norris and Asplund, but neither said a word.

"*Your* chair?"

"I hope Hawtree isn't paying too much for you; waste of money if he is," the robust man said. The dogs whined at his feet, itching to be released. "That's the problem with these city-boys," he continued as he stooped to let the dogs off the leash, "rich in qualifications, poor in brains" Redwald felt a rush of hot, irrational anger consume his insides then, but not due to the remark. As soon as they were free, the dogs had padded up to Redwald and begun to sniff at him with their wet noses and filthy muzzles, pawing at his legs. He tried to gently prod them away with his shoe, but they simply ducked and continued to sniff. Redwald could see the loose hair and mud accumulating on his trousers with each passing second, dirtying them, tainting them, disordering them. It was an imposition; in Redwald's eyes, the man may as well have spat in his face. It enraged him in a way that few other things could.

"Would you get your bloody dogs away from my legs?!" Redwald snapped compulsively, his chest tight with an overwhelming mix of panic and fury. The robust man merely smirked as the dogs continued to inspect Redwald, trying to place their paws in his lap and leap up on to the chair with him.

"Sorry, can't help you. I think they're confused; seeing a stranger sitting there. After all, *it's my chair.*"

"Oryn's sake!" Redwald barked, oblivious to the increasing number of onlookers. Gathering his gown close to him, he frantically pushed past the dogs and stumbled away from the chair.

"Good boy," the robust man said, smiling down at Redwald as he took his place opposite Dr Asplund, the dogs settling at their master's feet. Redwald was now immensely uncomfortable. Though not visibly soiled, he *felt* the imperceptible dirt hanging heavy on his trouser legs, contaminating them and everything they touched. He jerked briefly towards the door as if to leave, his body betraying his gut instinct; to leave, to be clean, to rid himself of the discomfort that only he could feel. But he couldn't, not yet. Suppressing his compulsions as best he could, Redwald grabbed his pint from the side table and made for the remaining empty chair, directly opposite the Guardsman. His eyes never left the dogs.

71

"Oh no you don't, that's my wife's chair," the man said, grinning. Redwald swept around to meet his gaze.

"Excuse me?!"

"My wife's chair."

"And is she currently using it?!" In response, the robust man simply spoke the name of one of the dogs and patted the empty seat beside him. It promptly hopped up onto the cushion and rested its head on the chair's arm. "Fine," Redwald spat, "but I still have questions for Guardsman Norris." Norris, who had been cautiously watching this exchange, suddenly found himself sweating again.

"I'm sorry, I *do* know it's an old gun, but I don' remember all the details. Talk tomorrow?" He suggested desperately.

"Don't let him bully you, Osbert," the robust man cut in, "Hawtree doesn't run this place yet." His hand shaking, Redwald took a slow, deliberate drink before continuing.

"Fine, the weapon can wait. However, you may still be able to help me with motive. *Who*," Redwald said, silencing Norris' objection before he could even form it, "could kill Alice? Who would want to? You're from around here, is there anybody you can think of who might want to do the Hawtrees harm?" The robust man jerked in his seat to face Redwald.

"You can't suspect someone from the village?"

"Guardsman Norris?" Redwald said, suppressing the urge to rail at the robust man with every insult he knew.

"No!" The man rose from his seat and stepped towards Redwald, the smirk he had hitherto been wearing burned off by an expression of fury beneath. Redwald stood his ground, despite the fact that the man was much, much taller than him. "How *dare* you

72

even imply that anyone from my village had anything to do with this?! Promise me that none of us, *absolutely none of us*, is a suspect."

"I can't promise that!"

"*I* COMMAND IT!"

"AND WHO ARE YOU?" Redwald bellowed. It was as if every conversation in the room had been a burning candle, and Redwald's reply a wintry gust through an open door. The robust man's smirk returned as he recognised that he had an audience.

"*I* am Lord Martingale, these are *my* people, and I *will* not be denied by some . . . MAGICIAN!"

It was at this point that the Reverend Charteris, having amused himself until now with his pint of Hobson's Choice and Redwald's book, arrived at the magician's side.

"See here now Archie, what's all this racket?" he beamed, as if he were completely unaware of the furious row that had just taken place across the room from him. The Baron looked a little ashamed of himself but stood his ground.

"Listen Charles, I'm not having Hawtree send some city magician down here to make accusations about my people!"

"I don't believe, my Lord, that Redwald has done any such thing, have you Redwald?" Charteris said, turning to the magician.

"Not in so many words," Redwald conceded.

"Well good," Charteris said, looking around the group. He appeared to be assessing the mood. "Redwald," he said, turning to the magician, "would you like some mead? I think we should have some of my home-brew. Yes," he decided, before Redwald could object, "let's have a snifter of that, I'll show you the church at the same time, come on." Charteris stumbled off towards the door. Redwald paused for a moment, before looking back at Martingale.

"If you accuse *any* of my people . . ." the Baron began, but Redwald cut him off.

"If they're innocent, I won't have to," Redwald replied, finishing his pint. "See you tomorrow officer," he said, directing a look at Norris, who nodded hurriedly in reply.

Placing his empty glass on the bar, Redwald marched between the glaring villagers and out into the cold night air, where Charteris stood waiting for him. Redwald could still feel the dirt upon his legs, the lingering sense of contamination. Irrational anger flashed through him again, but not enough to smother the tumescent worry that was slowly replacing it. Would he come to regret that outburst?

"Come on old fellow," Charteris said, turning towards the bridge, "let's have a stroll, you and I." Redwald braced himself for a sermon, but none came. The night was quiet. Aside from their footsteps, the only noises on the green were the muffled chatter emanating from the pub and the pleasing rush of the Trew as it coursed towards the sea. Bethin's light settled like silver frost upon the shimmering surface of the river and the tendrils of the willow, lighting their path as they crossed the bridge and ambled up the hillock towards St Alia's.

Finally, Charteris said, "He's a good sort really. You mustn't judge him for . . . for *that*." Redwald remained silent. "It's a tricky time of year for him anyway, but this . . . this case has hit him especially hard. He's very upset about it all."

"Why is that?" Redwald asked, coolly.

"Not all fief-holders are this way, I know. Some are more distant, some leave the running of their fiefs to Seneschals, but the Baron .

74

. . he takes it personally. He cares about his tenants; he's their friend."

"I can't rule out any suspects."

"And you shouldn't, but see it from his point of view. If it *is* one of his tenants, he's responsible for the consequences they must face. Which means . . ."

"He's not just sending a tenant down, but one of his friends too," Redwald admitted, reluctantly.

"Precisely," Charteris replied, as the pair came up to the churchyard, "Hard enough to believe one's friends could be responsible, let alone to mete out punishment if they are." Standing beneath the lychgate, he gestured Redwald through the open door. The magician paused, doubt stirring inside him. It had been months since his last episode. Would an attempt to visit consecrated ground bring *him* back?

Charteris noted the hesitation. "Don't worry, you won't burst into flames," he joked. Redwald wondered briefly if Charteris knew more than he was letting on, but quickly dismissed the thought. He smiled, steeled himself and followed Charteris across the threshold, closing the door behind him. As they walked between the headstones, worn to varying degrees by rain and the passage of time, Charteris failed to notice that Redwald was tense, on edge. The vicar couldn't know, but Redwald was listening intently for the familiar ragged gasp, waiting for the rush of a cold wind.

Upon reaching the church, Charteris heaved open an iron-studded door and ushered Redwald through into the dark expanse. The only interior light came from the Flame Eternal which, flickering in the centre of the floor, picked out the constellations painted in gold leaf on the octagonal dome above. Redwald stood by the door, but Charteris quickly bustled off into the shadows, muttering to himself as he went. Redwald peered after him and found him again only when the Reverend struck a match to light a long wax taper. Taper in hand, he moved slowly around the church, lighting the candles one by one, each a pinprick of light, stuttering into being in the vaulted darkness. Redwald felt the tension drain from him as, candle by candle, the ancient church blossomed into view.

The walls were lined with funerary busts and memorials to the dead, each adorned with painted coats of arms over the engraved names and dates. To his right, on the wall just inside the door, a list of incumbent vicars stretching back eight centuries had been painted directly on to the stone, the colour of the paint brighter with each new vicar. Columns, arranged around the Flame Eternal, swirled up and around and were adorned at their capitals with carvings of green men, coal men, stars, beasts, and demons. One of these in particular caught Redwald's eye, hanging high above the door. Its demonic face was grotesque, bald and scarred, with fangs filed to points and a screaming raven crushed between its teeth. Its eyes seemed to bore into Redwald's own, as if in reminder. He *was* due.

"Drink?" Charteris called from the far end of the church. Snapping to, Redwald headed down the nearest aisle, past the Flame Eternal and through the rood screen, to an area set aside for Charteris to prepare himself for services. There, among the spare chairs, hassocks, and vestments, Charteris was leaning on a chiselled marble monument. A small mahogany cabinet was open in the corner, key in the lock, and two cut-glass goblets rested at the feet of the two enthroned statues which towered over the vicar. Seeing Redwald, he inclined his head in query and sloshed a decanter full of liquid gold in his direction.

"Yes please," Redwald said, before hesitating, "I should apologise, though. First of all." Charteris lifted the stopper from the decanter with a clink.

"What for old boy?"

"For earlier . . ."

"Oh don't worry about it."

"No," Redwald said, firmly, "I do worry about it. I'm very sorry for . . . for my behaviour. It's not how I like to go about things and I'd hate to think that I had caused *you* any embarrassment, especially." Charteris smiled, filled one of the glasses and thrust it into Redwald's hand.

"Do you think that's the first time I've stepped in to calm Archie down? As I said, he cares about this place. He can be overprotective."

"It wasn't just him. I . . . I was short-tempered. I was rude."

"You're under a lot of pressure."

"That's no excuse. Usually I . . . I don't . . . I can't lose control. If I can't control myself what chance do I have of solving this case?" Charteris ignored the rhetorical question and instead took a sip from his glass, his lips pursing with pleasure as he tasted the mead.

"That is a particularly good one actually, if I say so myself," he looked across at Redwald. "What do you think?" Redwald hesitated before lifting the glass to his lips and trying the subtly sweet, warming drink.

"It's wonderful," he said, his frown slipping away like the night before sunrise. He drew a long, cleansing breath. "Thank you for this."

"It's my pleasure old boy. Besides, since you're here to help Alice, I wanted to show my support."

"Thank you. I'll do the best I can for her," Redwald promised.

"I don't doubt it." Charteris raised his glass. "To Alice." Redwald echoed the toast and the two friends drank the honeyed gold together. "So, would you like me to show you around?" Redwald, gripped by a childish flush of excitement, beamed.

"I'd love that, if you don't mind, of course," Redwald said.

"I'd be delighted. Where to start, though?" Having prioritised the pouring of more mead, Charteris decided that the best place to start would, in fact, be with the seated statues directly in front of them. He enthusiastically explained that the couple were Sir Effray and Lady Marian Martingale, the Founders. She had identified the Rise as the ideal spot for a castle and he had laid the foundation stone. The village, he explained, was named for them, not vice versa, and the statues and the base on which they sat contained their ashes and those of their successors.

"Until . . ." Charteris continued, leading Redwald back out through the rood screen and towards the opulent funerary bust of a dour-looking knight, "Errol, 1st Baron of Martingale." He, Charteris explained, had been ennobled for services to Emphoras II and therefore decided that he deserved his own resting place, thank you very much. The tour continued in this vein for some time. Charteris, who knew every inch of his church inside out, revelled in having someone receptive to its story and Redwald, pleasantly warmed by mead, indulged his interest for the historic, the peculiar, and the arcane.

Charteris showed Redwald the 6th Baroness' urn crowning a monument to her sons, all lost at sea in the High King's service. He told the story behind the tattered heraldic banner of Sir Wentworth Cooper; a peasant foot soldier of the 4th Baron, whose seizure of two enemy standards in a single battle led both to his being knighted and to his gallantry being commemorated in the name of the local pub. He even sang the praises of the 7th Baron, who rebuilt the Double Standard after the fire of 1624 and, as he led

Redwald through centuries of history, the latter drank it up as eagerly as the mead. Redwald noted, as the two men walked, that the grandeur of the Martingale monuments receded with each generation, until they finally reached that of the 20th Baron and his wife.

"Interestingly," Charteris said, coming to a halt at a brass panel in the floor decorated with escutcheons, "Lady Emily was herself the only child of the last Vysearl of Maidensworth. You've already met her son, Archie, which brings you to the present day," Charteris said, evidently pleased with his presentation.

Redwald looked up and around the church. "It's quite a place."

"It is, isn't it?" Charteris replied, as he sighed and lowered himself onto a pew. "Perhaps . . ." he continued carefully, "perhaps you can see why Archie is a bit overprotective at times."

"I suppose I can," Redwald conceded, "but I must continue my investigation as planned. I can't rule anything out."

"I don't think that you should. I'm not asking you to do exactly as he says, just to be sensitive to him. He's a good man, but he just . . . I suppose it's fair to say he's a man of action. Unlike us, he doesn't always *think* before he *does*. I was able to moderate that tendency a little when *I* was Seneschal, but then he gave the treasury keys to Asplund and . . . well . . . Asplund is a man of action too, Navy men both; they served together. We're not like that; we're thinkers." He looked away towards the Flame Eternal then, in quiet contemplation. Redwald peered at the old vicar, curious.

"Why are you telling me this?" Redwald asked, quietly.

"After tonight, I'm worried that the two of you won't understand each other." Redwald was taken aback.

"That's very kind of you to be concerned but . . ."

79

"And because you both have the capacity to harm the other, if you're not careful. This is his fief; he has the power to interfere in your investigation, which means that Alice . . ."

"I understand," Redwald said, taking a seat across the aisle from him. "I will . . . try and apologise, when I see him next." He felt again the searing rage as he remembered the dirt upon his trousers and the humiliation inflicted, but he suppressed it. Charteris was right. It would do him no favours to make an even greater enemy of Lord Martingale.

"I appreciate that. He was rude to you, I know, but please remember that this investigation pains him too. He fears for Alice, he fears that one of his friends might be responsible and then . . . then there's the anniversary on Borsday as well. It's just a bad time all around for him."

"Anniversary?" Charteris' face darkened at the memory and he drained his glass.

"The Great Storm of 2306. It was . . . horrendous, one of those awful ones off the sea that doesn't get caught in the mountains. Even the Rise seemed to shake. It did so much damage; pulled down the church spire, lightning struck the rectory, houses lost their roofs, their walls, or were split by falling trees. It even tore down Errol's Tower up at the castle and . . ." he paused then, as if he were restraining himself.

"And?" Redwald pressed.

"And . . . and Lord Martingale had to pay to fix it all," Charteris said, stifling what he had been about to say, "he owed a feudal obligation to do so of course, but he would have helped anyway. His pride demanded it. He took the village and lifted it from its knees at his own expense, everything was put back exactly as it was. It cost him a great deal that storm, and not just financially. As you can see," he said, gesturing to the shrinking monuments, "the

80

Martingales' fortune has been lost over the years, so the expenditure put him into debt. He had to sell something, but what did he have, apart from the village itself? He couldn't sell that, abandon his home and his tenants to some stranger, to use as they liked, not when his very name was attached to the place."

"What *did* he do?"

"He sold his other lands and a good portion of his heirlooms to the highest bidder."

"The Hawtrees?"

"Precisely. He sold them the Rise, that's how they were able to build Hawtree Manor, on land that Archie's ancestors have guarded for centuries past. He sees himself as a King who sold his crown if you like. The only parts left to him are the Castle and the village itself." Redwald was quiet for a moment.

"He did repair everything, though. Surely he can take comfort in that?"

"Not everything," Charteris said, looking up.

"Ah," Redwald sighed, as the realisation clicked into place, "Errol's Tower is still a ruin?"

"I wish that were all . . . ." Charteris said, finishing his mead.

CHAPTER 6

A Short Sharp Shooter

"And lo Angacetiphon, servant of Bethin, did descend unto Oryn and spake thus:

'Fear not the trials through which you struggle, nor the yoke that chafes you, for these are but the birthing throes of a mighty empire, which shall be boundless. Glory shall be your garb and Holy Right and Just Dominion shall be your sword and shield'[228]

And lo did Oryn ask:

'Shall my dominion extend unto the seas of Hsenia?'

'It shall' spake Angacetiphon.

'Even unto the Hatuvae Mountains and the people who dwell there?'

'It shall,' spake Angacetiphon.

'And what of the lush forests and treasures of the Racythian Isles; shall these also be in my realm?'

'Yes, Your Empyreal Holiness.[229] Your realm will cover all the world in Glory. There shall be no people, race or tribe untouched by your magnanimity and enlightened rule.[230] All those that now live, and have yet to live, kneel at your deathless throne. Your empire shall thrive for a thousand, thousand cycles and more, and its furthest outposts shall be set within the bosom of Heaven itself.'[231]"

The Sakratu Orynaea, Dürrendaal Authorised Version (translated), Recollections 228-231

Redwald awoke the next morning to a throbbing headache and a mouth like old carpet. Rising from the bed with a groan, he pondered whether his prowess with alcohol was fading with age, but hurriedly concluded that that couldn't possibly be the case. No, he thought, it must have been the *mixing* that did it, rather than anything terminal. Somewhat comforted, if not cured, he stumbled across to the window and drew the curtains. Blinking in the dreary grey light, he looked out across the green and smiled. Sheets of rain swept over the village like murmurating starlings, falling so thick that Redwald could hear each gust as it pattered across the windowpanes.

He had always loved the rain. In his darker moments, when an uncaring world felt contaminated and close, he would conjure water from the sky to wash it clean and steady his nerves. The rain occupied a special place in his affections for another reason, however. That conjuration spell was the first he had ever cast, just to please *her*. He smiled at the memory; the blazing Czerganzan heat, the wilting of her favourite flowers in the woods, and the joy in her dark eyes when she saw what he had done. He sighed as he pulled himself away from the window.

Bleary-eyed, he washed, brushed his teeth and dressed himself at a leisurely pace, ensuring that his watch-chain was even and his cravat tied *just so*. Sweeping his gown over his shoulders, he squeezed down the ancient, crooked stairs of the pub, his briefcase held out in front of him and his umbrella tucked under his arm. He crossed the bar, elbowed past the pub door, and snapped open the umbrella against the wind and rain.

Redwald found it a pleasant walk to the Guard Station, though many others might not have thought it so. Clouds covered the village in semi-darkness, painting the usually yellow stone a slick grey colour as he strode past the rows of terraced cottages. They were picturesque things, their windows set at odd angles and their doors so low that even a Hob might be forced to stoop beneath the thatch. The plants in the kitchen gardens glistened wet and clean in the rain and the earth smelled rich and damp.

At the end of the row of houses a newer, sturdier, less crooked building jutted out into the road. Built of the same sandstone as the rest, it looked a little like a schoolhouse, with a low roof and steps leading up to an elevated door. Swinging over the entrance, an austere black sign bore the legend CONSTABULARY GUARD, MARTINGALE STATION in white typeface. Rendered beneath the lettering itself were the royal cypher of Emphoras IX, split in the middle by a depiction of the Oromanth, its twisted branches hung with writhing pennants, and an animal that Redwald took to be Lord Martingale's badge, a bull. Redwald smirked.

Stepping onto the portico under the sign, he shook the rain from his umbrella and pushed past the front door. The interior of the station was plain. To Redwald's left, a row of decrepit-looking chairs, with varying levels of discolouration, were arranged before a railing fastened to the floor. Windows barred by distinctly flimsy-looking iron grilles framed the white-washed walls and spilled drab light onto the single desk which sat opposite the entrance. Guardsman Norris, who was poring over some papers spread across his lonely desk, started as Redwald entered.

Redwald paused. He suddenly remembered having brow-beaten the young Guardsman the night before and felt his face burn with the shame of it. He attempted a smile and shut the door behind him.

"Morning," Redwald stated, "how are you doing?"

"Not . . . not bad . . . thanks," Norris said, somewhat uncomfortably.

"Look, I'd . . . I'd like to apologise for my behaviour yesterday," Redwald said, walking slowly towards him, as if going any faster would cause the Guardsman to bolt. "It's absolutely no excuse for the way I spoke to you and behaved . . . generally, but I'm just anxious . . . *very* anxious, to make progress on this case as quickly as possible. May I?" he said, gesturing to the chair in front of the desk.

"Oh sure," Norris said hurriedly, compulsively shuffling his papers into a bundle. Redwald sat down, carefully ensuring that his eyes were on the same level as the Guardsman's.

"Thank you. Anyway, given the importance of this case, I was very keen to ask your views on what happened, but I appreciate that I . . . that I picked a bad time to do that; I'm sorry."

"You want . . . *my* views?" Norris asked. Redwald paused.

"Yes . . . of course. I need your expertise here; I'm not a Guardsman. Your input could be crucial to my investigation; to saving Alice."

"Oh, I thought you just wanted . . . the reports an' that. You . . . you really think I could be . . . crucial?" Norris said, the tone of suspicion giving way to subdued eagerness.

"Yes, I do. *Hence* my hurry to speak to you last night. So, while I'm sorry for my behaviour, please understand that it's just because I got . . . *overexcited* and . . ."

"Do . . . do you wanna talk about it *now*?" Norris asked.

"Erm . . . yes please. . ." Redwald began, but Norris was already spreading his papers back out across the desk as if they were playing cards. This time, however, he twisted them all so that they faced the magician.

"Sorry, *these* are the reports, thought I'd better brush up after last night." There was no malice in the comment, but Redwald's ears burned all the same. "So, we got Parnell's report, the medical report, *my* ballistics report . . ."

"Oh that's all brilliant," Redwald said gently, "but for the moment, I'd really just like to ask you a few questions. Then maybe we can dive into the file? Would that be alright?"

"Oh yeah . . . ok," Norris said, mildly deflated, "so . . . what do you wanna know? Uh, Mr Cord-neigh, sir."

"*De* Cordonnay," Redwald said, smiling as he retrieved his notepad and pen and placed them on the desk in readiness.

"Sorry sir."

"No worries; everyone does it. So, perhaps you could tell me what happened from your perspective first of all. How did you find out about the incident? What did you do immediately thereafter? What did you make of the scene?" He held the pen poised in readiness.

"Well," Norris began, launching gleefully into his account, "first I heard of it was when Morrimer, uh, the Hawtree Butler, sent a boy down on Dransday morning, saying that Alice had been killed, but not proper killed, like. They found her body, but it was her what found it, see?"

"Yes, I see," Redwald assured him, surmising that he needn't start scribbling just yet.

"I went up there immediately, 'course. Wasn't much past 11:45 when I got there. Can't be sure, though, watch is a bit slow, see. Anyway, I went in and saw the body, and then I . . ."

"Where was the body?"

"The study, sir."

"And what did you make of the room?" Norris paused for a moment in thought.

"It looked right clean, I'd say," he replied, nodding to himself, "given the wound in her head an' all."

"Any blood on the walls?" Redwald hinted, "I assume you inspected it fully."

"I did sir, no blood anywhere but under her head. Had to have appeared there suddenly."

"Is it possible that any bloodstains could have been cleared away prior to your arrival?"

"No way. It takes me 10 minutes to get up there from the station. If you was cleaning up blood in that room, you'd never be able to get it off all the walls and books an' that in only 10 minutes, would you?"

"What if the scene had been cleaned *before* you were called? Could someone clean that room up in the time between her death and your arrival?" Norris raised his eyebrows. He clearly hadn't considered the possibility.

"Nope," he said after a moment of thought, "you'd still not have much time; an hour, two at most. An' that wouldn't be enough to find all the spray."

"1-2 hours? Is that how long she'd been dead when you arrived?" Redwald asked, scribbling.

"At most. Depends, but mostly bodies don't start going stiff until they've been dead for 3 hours. She were still . . . floppy. Gerritt took her temperature too . . ."

"Gerritt?"

"Dr Asplund, sorry. He said she couldn't have been dead much more than an hour."

"I see", Redwald said, "so you inspected the room, what did you do then?"

"Then we moved her into the icehouse, and called for that, er, that other magician from Trewcester. The one who did them tests?"

"Dr Parnell?"

"That's her, all right."

"I see, excellent. Which of these is her report?" Redwald asked, looking down at the papers. Norris reached forward and prodded a few ribbon-bound pages across the desk towards him. Redwald flicked through them but saw nothing Giles had not already told him. The report confirmed that the body had not been aesthetically enchanted and that blood tests showed her to be the same woman as the living Mrs Hawtree, before concluding with a recommendation to seek specialist assistance.

"Any remarks on the wound?" Redwald asked, closing Parnell's report.

"Ah yes, that's the interestin' bit," Norris replied, this time indicating a report by Dr Asplund. Redwald tried to skim-read that as well but had to admit fairly quickly that it was beyond him. "It's not hard to see how she got a wound like that," Norris continued, "there's burn marks on her cheeks and brow, so the shooter was close by; face-to-face, like. Can even tell the angle she was shot from."

"Let me guess, she was kneeling?" Redwald's stomach turned a little. The image of Alice, clumps of hair missing, hands bound and knelt before her killer, begging for her life, flashed across his mind.

"No sir." Redwald's ears pricked.

"No?"

"No sir. The shot went in her eye and left her skull a few inches above her left . . . chef . . . chef-droy shooter."

"Chevroid Suture?" Redwald said, having found the term in Asplund's report.

"Yeah, sorry, that's what Gerritt said."

"So it exited at a level above her eyes? Her attacker was shooting up at her?" Well, that was a feat in itself. Although it was hard to tell when seeing her in bed, Alice appeared to have been a fairly short woman. Her attacker would likely be short too, especially if he were shooting from directly in front of her, rather than from a level some distance below.

"Yeah exactly," Norris said, "but better than that, you know you was asking about the type of gun last night? You can tell that from the wound too; it's an *antique*." He beamed.

"Yes, you mentioned it was old," Redwald said. "How do you figure that out from the wound, though? Bullet fragments in the skull?"

"Nope. Never were any bullets, won't be neither. See, in the olden days, they couldn't purify orcite as well as they can now, and they couldn't really purpose it at all. If you can't purpose orcite, all you can do is charge the crystal and release energy when you compress it, right? Like in an explosion. None of these slow-release crystals like in today's lamps. If you can't purify it, or can't purify it very well, there's a risk of cracking when you compress the crystal and the energy is released. *But,* you can sort of get over that by having bigger crystals, less likely to crack. You following?"

"I think so," Redwald said, knowing just enough about the processes of purifying and purposing orcite to keep up.

"So, what they used to do in older guns was stick a big multi-use crystal into the gun itself, instead of single-use charges into bullets like we do now. You'd just pull the trigger, the hammer'd come down on the crystal and energy'd shoot out the barrel, right? No bullets. So when they built these things, they had to fit the barrel size to the crystal size."

"Meaning old guns tend to have wide barrels?"

"Right. Better than that, though, as they got better at purifying, they could afford to put smaller and smaller crystals in the guns, so . . ."

" . . . So the width of the barrel relates directly to the age of the gun?"

"Mostly, yeah. Course there are always exceptions, but that's the general rule. So, because it was such a close shot and the energy blast didn't have time to dissipate, we can roughly tell the size of the barrel from the size of the wound."

"And therefore it's age," Redwald said, looking into the middle distance as he chewed over the revelation like a fillet steak. "How old . . ."

"About 200, 250 years old, I'd say. I'm no expert, though. All the same," Norris said, tapping another report marked 'Ballistics', "I wrote the likely specs down, see, based on the wound. Couldn't remember them at the pub, I'm afraid, but if you found an expert, they could tell you roughly what the gun'd look like and even how old it were."

"I see," Redwald said, thinking. It was more information than he had started with, certainly, and a picture of the potential killer was slowly forming in his mind. The nameless silhouette grew, piece by piece like accumulating driftwood, yet the picture that presented itself was an odd one. "So, what you're saying is," Redwald continued, "we need to be on the look-out for a particularly short suspect with an antique weapons collection?"

"Might be easier than you thought, eh?" Norris said, grinning, but Redwald merely frowned, deep in thought. He pulled the reports to his side of the desk and pored over them one by one, as Norris sat and watched the process patiently. After a pause, Redwald looked directly up at the Guardsman, fixing him with his dark-rimmed eyes.

"What do you think?"

"Me, sir?"

"You're the local Guardsman. You must know everyone pretty well, must be party to some of the . . . less seemly things that go on here. As I said last night, who do you think it could be? Who might want to kill Mrs Hawtree?" Norris shook his head hurriedly. "Anything you say will remain between us, I promise," Redwald said, "Lord Martingale need never find out."

"No sir, that's just it. I really can't think of anyone. Everyone likes Alice 'round here." Redwald paused, assessing the Guardsman. He did not appear to be lying.

"But don't you think this murder seems . . . *vindictive?*" Redwald continued. "Alice wasn't just murdered, she was held captive first; we know that from the wounds. If the killing's *that* premeditated, surely you need a strong motive? A feud, a grudge, perhaps?"

"I s'pose so, sir. Still don't see who it could be, though. Like I says, everyone's fond of Alice." Redwald paused for a moment in thought.

"And how do they feel about Mr Hawtree? Seems to me he's not half so popular as his wife." Norris looked away then, clearly reluctant to meet the magician's stony gaze.

"No sir," he said, finally, "he ain't popular, nor were Sir Julius, but you wouldn't kill Alice if you hated them would you?"

"Would you not?"

"I don't . . . I don't follow sir, sorry."

"Well," Redwald said, leaning forward, "it strikes me that killing Alice is the best way to get back at both of them isn't it? She's the lynch-pin; the heir to the Hawtree legacy and its fortune. Sir Julius would have wanted his name to live on and Giles depends on Alice for his wealth precisely *because* she's the heir."

"I don't know sir," Norris replied, shaking his head again.

"How so?"

"Well, Giles don't depend on her for his wealth, see. He's heir to the fortune too."

"Oh really?" Redwald said, raising his eyebrows.

"Yeah, so I understand it, sir. Part of the arrangement Giles had with Sir Julius. He changed his name an' all."

"Yes, he told me that," Redwald said, as much to himself as in reply. "And how do you know this, may I ask?"

"Oh . . . uh Gerritt told me." Redwald turned to look out of the window and frowned. He spoke to the rain that brushed against the glass then, as he voiced an unpleasant truth.

"So . . . what you're saying is that you can't think of anyone in the village who might want to kill Alice, because she was so well-liked?"

"That's right sir . . ."

"But also that her husband has a financial incentive to do it? In that he would gain full control of the Hawtree fortune?"

"Well," Norris said hurriedly, "I don't know that *he* would kill her, but . . . yeah, yeah I suppose he would make money. Don't explain why he would send the body back though."

"Unless he didn't," Redwald said, musing.

92

"Maybe it's a short antiques dealer?" the Guardsman said, forcing a nervous laugh.

"Possibly." Redwald smiled a little, humouring the guardsman as he rested a hand on the scattered reports. He paused, thinking. "Are these all we have, or is there anything else . . ."

"Oh no, we've got interviews with witnesses, their statements, like, and these too, sir," Norris said, reaching into his desk draw and retrieving another folder. He upended it over the desk so that a mass of paper flumped onto the wood like fallen snow cleared from a roof. He then separated the witness statements from two further documents, which he handed to Redwald.

The first document was a small booklet, through which Redwald flicked before casting it quickly to one side. It was probably standard procedure, he imagined, but fingerprinting people *before* the crime had actually happened struck him as unutterably stupid, as did fingerprinting *both* the dead and the living Mrs Hawtree. The next document was rather more interesting. It was Alice's birth certificate.

"That's odd," Redwald said, showing the sealed certificate to Norris. "Does the Guard usually ask for records like this when investigating a murder?"

"No sir, Mr Hawtree provided it voluntarily."

"Did he say why?"

"Don't remember I'm afraid." Redwald paused for a moment. Then it clicked.

"Oh no, I see," he muttered, frowning at the dates, "It's probably for the experiment, Dr Parnell will have told him I'd need it. I'd like to read the witness statements later, if I may. Do you mind if I keep these?" He asked, gesturing to the documents spread out across the desk.

"Don't mean nothin' to me." The Guardsman said.

"Excellent," Redwald replied, as he gathered the papers up, tapped them into order on the desktop and secreted them in the folder that Norris handed to him. He paused for a moment and looked across at Norris. "Did you have anything else you wanted to tell me? Anything at all?"

"No sir, that's all we got." Norris said, nodding at the folder tucked under Redwald's arm.

"I see," Redwald said, looking into the middle distance. "In that case, I think I will leave you to it. I need to . . . to mull things over." He slotted the folder into his briefcase before standing abruptly and offering his hand to Norris. "Thank you for your time, you've been really very helpful and . . . sorry again about last night."

"No worries," Norris said, smiling. Redwald made for the door but stopped and turned with his fingers on the handle.

"One more thing, if anything, *anything*, reaches your ears that might be pertinent to this investigation, please do let me know as soon as possible."

"Understood, sir. Enjoy the Gala!" Redwald attempted a smile, but instead simply nodded a grimace in the guardsman's direction, before sweeping across the threshold.

Outside, Redwald paused. He looked up at the wet, grey sky from under the portico, before closing his eyes and pressing his fingers to his temples. His headache lingered, exacerbated by the onrush of new information. His mind, rarely at rest, was now crackling and exploding in a hundred different directions like an arsenal ablaze.

In response, he stepped out into the rain and stood quietly, allowing the water to run down his face.

Forcing calm upon his unquiet mind, he began to mull over the case like the words of a spell, dousing the flames and allowing the facts to float upon the resulting waters. He considered the shape of the wound, the proximity of the attacker, and the lack of blood in the study. He pictured the scarred wrists, the thin hair, the bandaged head and the burn marks around the eye socket. His thoughts even alighted on the heart that hummed away beside the corpse, even as it beat simultaneously in Alice's chest, before finally coming to rest conclusively upon *the weapon*. He opened his eyes, snapped his umbrella into place and descended the steps. That weapon, shapeless, nameless, but very, very real was out there already, waiting to fire the deadly shot. Find the weapon and he could prevent the murder. Find the weapon and he might even find the would-be killer. This, he thought, was progress.

Considering that he now deserved a break, he took his lunch in the Double Standard. When the Landlord's daughter arrived with his steaming steak and kidney pie and crispy roast potatoes, she waited patiently as he first moved his umbrella out of her way and then swept the table clear of the witness statements he had been reading.

"'Ere you are, ale . . ." she said, placing the glass brimming with ruby beer on the table.

"Thank you," Redwald said, fixated on the glass.

" . . . and pie. Anythin' else you'll be needin'?" She looked at Redwald's umbrella, which he had temporarily positioned on his lap. "I can 'ang that up, if you'd like?"

"Oh no, that's fine, thank you," he said.

"Sure?"

"Yeah, I'll just stick it in here." He opened his briefcase, which stood upright on the floor beside him, and lazily dropped the umbrella into its magically expanded interior. He snapped the clasps shut and made an eager start on his pie, smiling to himself as he cut the crust and smelt the meaty, rich filling that awaited him. He quickly noticed, however, that the Landlord's daughter was still stood beside his chair, her eyes wide. "Oh, I'm so sorry, I should have said. I'm in Room 4; would you mind putting this on the tab?"

"Yer wha'? . . . Oh, oh sure, yeah," she said, her eyes meeting his as she tore them away from the briefcase. "I'll . . . I'll do that fer you now."

"Thank you so much," Redwald said, smiling. He speared a soft bit of beef with his fork and growled with pleasure as it melted in his mouth. As he ate and drank, he retrieved the documents and made a start on reading the witness statements.

Norris had taken statements from Giles, Alice, the visiting Countess Laetizja of Oštrouman, Morrimer, Asplund, a few of the Hawtree guards and a couple of servants, including Mrs Ofcross, the housekeeper. These Redwald read patiently and carefully, his grey eyes flicking from page to page as the ale sank down his glass and his pie and potatoes disappeared piece by piece.

The statements, irritatingly, all seemed to align, both with each other and with what Giles had told him the day prior. He would have preferred some disjoint, some outcrop from the smooth surface onto which he could cling and pull himself higher, but there were none. The reports, however, which he re-read after finishing the witness statements, provided surer footing and none more so than Norris' ballistics report.

Redwald sat back in his chair, thinking, Norris' report open in front of him. *Find the weapon, prevent the murder.* Redwald looked down at the weapon specs. The Guardsman had been right; Redwald would need the advice of an expert to interpret these, but once he had it . . . Would it be feasible to lock away or hide any suspect weapons, now they were more identifiable? Even if it were, would that actually stop the murderer getting their weapon? Would *that* stop the murder? *Worth a try. But then,* Redwald mused, *where would you even get hold of . . .?* The thought petered out before he could finish it, replaced by another. *Sir Julius collected antique weapons.* Redwald smiled. *Vindictive.* And if the suspect guns were already in the village . . . *Find the weapon, find the would-be killer.* For the first time since his arrival, he had a lead.

Downing his final sliver of ale in a small gesture of triumph, Redwald rose from his table and walked over to the bar. The Landlord's daughter, who was scrubbing the pewter counter-top, looked up and smiled as he approached.

"Anythin' else I can get fer yer, love?"

"Possibly," Redwald said, leaning on the bar, "but it's a slightly odd one. Might you have a map of the village and local area anywhere around? I just want to copy it. Oh, and do you have any twine or string or something, anything that can be tied."

"Can probably find summit'. What d'you need 'em fer?"

"Magic." Her eyes widened.

As the Landlord's daughter bustled excitedly around, Redwald returned to his table, put his plate and glass to one side and began to prepare the spell. He pulled the casting board from his briefcase, set it on the table and began to draw the off-centre white web, blue lines, and red circles by reference to his watch-mounted thaumograph.

"'Ere you go," the Landlord's daughter said, returning with a roll of crimson ribbon, scissors, and a framed map of Martingale-on-

Trew. "Map's off the wall, so let us know when yer done and I'll put it back."

"That's perfect, thank you," Redwald said, drawing two yellow circles outside the web itself and connecting each to a red circle by means of a blue line. "Do you mind if I hang on to the scissors for a while? Just for tonight, I expect."

"A'right . . ." She said slowly, looking down at his work. "Can I watch, though?" He gestured to the chair across from him and she eagerly took a seat. He began to write in gold along each line, extracting the relevant tribute from his briefcase and putting it in the appropriate circle as he went.

"What're them circles?" the Landlord's daughter asked.

"This," Redwald said, pointing to the white web, "is Bethin's net. We use it to map out the stars, which are the red circles, so we can ask them a question or make a request. Because each star represents a particular concept, I can ask the question by selecting the relevant stars in red and then linking them to one another, in the right order, with the blue lines. However, they won't do anything for free, so I also offer a tribute to them; these things I'm putting in the red circles. I can also link them to the yellow circles on the outside, so that I can enchant particular objects, which aren't accepted as tribute. That's, basically, how you write a spell." She exhaled through her teeth.

"Where'd you learn all that?" He smiled.

"Trewcester, then Athonstone, but it was my wife that taught me this spell, actually. Or one like it anyway."

"She a magician too?" He grimaced.

"No, she . . . she does something else. Anyway, we're about ready." While they had been speaking, Redwald had placed the ribbon on one of the yellow circles and roughly copied the village map across two pages of his notebook. "Just one more thing," he said, reaching into his briefcase. He pulled out a small bottle of red ink and pushed it into the final yellow circle, before rubbing some of the circle's chalk onto his hand-drawn map.

"What's gonna 'appen?" She asked, as Redwald closed his eyes.

"We'll see." Clearing his mind as usual, he allowed the spell to bubble up to the surface of his consciousness and evaporate, before feeling the sidereal power surge through him once more. The spell was cast. He heard the Landlord's daughter gasp as the tributes sagged into weyste and he opened his eyes to see her staring at him.

"What'd you do?" He leaned over to the roll of ribbon and the inkpot, the only two items not to become weyste, and placed them to one side before clearing the board away. He opened his notebook to the hand-drawn map, unscrewed the inkpot, and allowed a drop of livid red ink to fall onto the top right-hand corner of the double page spread. It settled there for a moment, glistening wet, before it ran down the paper, over the little pencil Hawtree Manor and across the green to the Double Standard itself, leaving no trace as it went. The Landlord's daughter seemed confused. "I don't geddit." Redwald held up the ribbon, rose from his seat and crossed to the far side of the pub with it. "Ooooooh."

Once he had helped the Landlord's daughter tidy up his plate and glass, Redwald looked down at his watch. By now it was late in the afternoon and the Gala just a few hours away. There would be little point asking Giles about the weapons or their expert until then. In the meantime, Redwald decided, he would take advantage of the restored spring in his step by taking a walk up the Rise. Now that he had this map, it would do him good to get a lay of the land from above and, alas, the rain was still too heavy for him to use the gloves with ease.

Depositing his case in his room and pocketing the ribbon, he left the pub and headed out of the village towards the station. He held his umbrella aloft as the rain pattered gently around him, lighter now than it had been and muffled by the trees which sheltered the path. As he walked, he flicked open his notebook to the map. The little red ink spot was now inching away from the Double Standard. *Excellent.*

Arriving at a fork, he turned right, away from the station and towards the peak of the Rise, which towered above him through the canopy; a craggy, grey-capped outcrop, shorn of foliage by the wind and rain. As he walked, the route turned gradually from road to path and the trees began edging in on him like a gang of muggers. Shortly, even the path dwindled and Redwald found himself picking his way over fallen trunks or pushing aside cool, wet branches. Eventually, however, the greenery began to thin and the woods faded like night before the dawn. Redwald emerged from among the last of the trees and looked up the grass-covered slope.

There, built upon a rocky outcrop that rose like an island from a steep green sea, stood Martingale Castle. Made of the same Hundred sandstone as the village, the castle was built into the very Rise itself and crouched close beneath the crag that dominated the valley. The central keep stood tall over its encircling curtain wall and towers, while around it all snaked a dry moat, dug from the soil around the castle's rock. Once, it would have been a mighty fortress. Redwald could almost see it through the rain, sunlight shining on clean, new stone, the Martingale banner flying from the battlements and two stone bulls set into nooks either side of the gatehouse.

Now, however, it was a ruin. The wall was breached in numerous places, the crenellations of those towers that still stood were worn and broken like an old man's teeth, and the interior of the keep was open to the elements where the roof and part of the east wall had

100

collapsed. One tower adjacent to the keep was no more than rubble, spilling down the side of the rock into the moat and tearing part of the wall down with it. Through the breach, Redwald could see that an old, crooked manor house had been built up against the foremost wall of the keep, clinging like a chimeric limpet to its older, grander predecessor.

Yet, somehow, that felt *right* to Redwald. The whole place seemed to fit, to be whole. Everything here, he felt, was in its proper place. The rain fell upon the Rise, the rain ran down the Rise to the river and the river flowed away to the sea, only for that water to one day return, borne along with the storms that gave the Kingdom of Tempest its name. In the same way, Redwald mused, the castle, having been lifted from the Rise itself, was now sinking back into the rock whence it came. Redwald closed his eyes and drew a deep breath of clean, wet air.

"What are you doing here, boy?" Lord Martingale snapped. Redwald started and turned to see the Baron emerge from the woods astride a gigantic, slate-grey horse. He sat lazily back in the saddle, a brace of rabbits strapped to the harness behind him, and he went without any protection from the rain; his long messy hair slick down the back of his neck and his white beard peppered with droplets. The dogs padded along beside him, their breath steaming in the air and their lips wet with drool.

"I was going for a walk . . ."

"Here? You've got a bloody cheek rocking up on my doorstep after last night," he said, riding past Redwald and reining his horse in so that he and the dogs occupied the high ground between the magician and the castle.

"About that," Redwald began as he warily eyed the dogs, "I should like to apologise, I . . ."

"Stuck your big nose where it didn't belong?"

"*Overreacted*," Redwald replied. "I had had a bit to drink, I was stressed and I shouldn't have spoken to you that way."

"No, you shouldn't have." The dogs growled.

"I appreciate that we got off to a bad start, but . . ."

"No, we didn't *get off to a bad start*. I just don't trust you," Martingale said, his jaw set. Redwald raised an eyebrow in spite of himself.

"May I ask why?"

"Because you're just like *him*." The Baron inclined his head in the general direction of Hawtree Manor. "Because you're a city type with no concern for anyone besides yourself and no respect for the ideals that *my* people subscribe to."

"Such as?"

"Loyalty, for one. I can see your distaste for that, clear as day," he said, looking down at his dogs. "You'll never understand what it is to give and to receive loyalty. You're loyal to whoever pays you."

"Loyalty, like anything, is good in moderation." The Baron leaned forward in his saddle, and smirked.

"Spoken like the filthiest back-alley whore." The Baron spat on the ground between them. "Get off my land." He whistled at the dogs and made to ride home, but Redwald wasn't done.

"And what of Alice?" Redwald asked. Martingale paused mid-turn. "You may not like Giles or me, but Alice speaks very highly of you. I'm here to save her, all I ask is that you let me." The Baron's fingers tightened on the reins.

"I said . . ."

"And what if it were *your* wife; *your* daughter?!" Redwald barked, stepping closer, his pretence of civility washing away with the rain.

"Would you not do anything to protect her?!" Martingale stared in silence at the ruined castle.

"Of *course* I would have," he whispered after a time, "but some . . . some things are inevitable. You see, unlike you, de Cordonnay, storms cannot be bought." Redwald's eyes flicked again to the ruined tower; *Errol's* Tower. *I wish that were all.* Charteris' words glimmered anew. "I don't want the girl to die, but mark this, Giles *will* lose his family to a storm the same as I did. Only difference is, it will be of *his* making. Now, for the last time, get off my land. I have rabbits to skin." Before Redwald could say anything further, Lord Martingale violently spurred his horse and galloped away towards the castle, yapping dogs in tow.

Redwald turned back to the woods. A knot of nerves began to twist and tighten in his navel. He contemplated lingering for a while as he watched the horse and her rider thunder up the slope, but he didn't. Instead, he turned and headed back down the Rise. It was getting darker. Dark enough that the trees were twisting into monsters with leering fingers and gaping mouths. One such figure made him start, a small creature hiding between the trunks, hooded and squat, but barely perceptible in the shadows. Redwald blinked through the strands of falling water, but when he looked again, the figure was gone. Perhaps his drinking really had gone too far, he thought, reaching for his hipflask and fastening his grasp on his umbrella.

CHAPTER 7

Knowledge and Nobility

"Many wise men and magi were called to Sussurin VII's Holy Presence, blessed be his name, and commanded there to halt the Withering on pain of death and damnation. Yet none amongst them could offer any succour, for the Withering was a reckoning from the Vaeltava and not to be undone by mortal hands. As the pestilence spread, Ærestius alone saw what was to pass and so removed his family and twelve companions to his ship, bearing with them the Oromanth. Yet it was not before time. Even as they fled, Giant hordes brought low the walls of the Citadel, despoiling earth that cradled the feet of Oryn Once-Man, and rendering the Oromanth alone."

The Stenmoor Chronicle, author unknown c.1580

"De Cordonnay." Redwald said, smiling. The Hawtree footman looked at the paper and ran a finger down the list of notables to be admitted to the Gala, checking for his name. As she examined the list, Redwald turned to look up at the night sky. He had been tempted not to come. After all, the air had become so clear and calm with the passing of the storm, that it had seemed a perfect night to use the gloves. Yet, once again, he had resisted. For even as Alice Hawtree's heart hummed away in the icehouse, so too ticked away the final days, possibly hours, of her life. He needed to discuss *the weapon* with Giles; he needed to see Sir Julius' collection.

Donning his white tie and tails, he had trudged through the village to find a line of carriages leading from the base of the Rise all the way up to the Manor's gravel turnaround. Here, another footman had directed him away from the front door and towards the *Sir Julius* entrance which, Redwald discovered, was every bit as imposing as its namesake. Following a curving pathway around the slope-ward wall of the Manor, Redwald had found a brightly lit courtyard with an enormous pair of doors set into the rear wall. These doors, surmounted by a carved swan, opened onto a strip of purple carpet that snaked between two merrily burbling fountains and out onto a sizeable cast-iron pier, jutting out into thin air where the lawn sloped to the valley below. Taking a coupe of Arrovênnes from an obliging footman, Redwald had bypassed those guests milling around the courtyard and joined the queue to be admitted to the Gala.

"Not here I'm afraid sir."

"Pardon?"

"I'm afraid I can't find your name, sir." There was a muttering in the line behind him, but Redwald ignored it.

"Are you looking under 'D' or 'C'?"

"Oh sorry, sir. I'll check 'C' as well."

"Thank you," Redwald smiled. For want of something to do, he looked up at a man three behind him in the queue and instantly recognised the face of the Duke of Hasselton, a good head taller than he and several times as heavy. Notwithstanding the recent loss of his barony, the man's enormous frame was hung with so many medals and decorations that he tinkled like a windchime. Redwald absentmindedly began to worry the buttonhole of his own lapel.

"Sorry sir, I'm afraid you're not under 'C' either."

"Look, I think there's been a mistake, Mr Hawtree invited me yesterday, you see."

"If you're not on the list sir . . ."

"No I understand that, but honestly, it was only yesterday. Perhaps he forgot to add me?" More than likely, Redwald thought bitterly, as the muttering behind him intensified.

"Sir, if you're not a guest . . ." It was at that moment that the double doors behind the footman swung open. The rush of noise and warmth broke on Redwald like a wave on the beach. Through the archway he could see the glittering lights of the entrance hall, the coloured dresses, furs and sashes of the attendees, and hear the strains of a string quartet. The smell of the food, however, excited him most.

Two servants, who had just pulled the great doors apart, stepped to either side of the entrance and inclined their heads. Giles Hawtree, accompanied by a man in uniform who seemed to be his head of security, appeared in the doorway and looked out over the valley.

"I can't see her," Hawtree said.

"They said she was expected imminently," the security guard replied.

"Excuse me Mr Hawtree . . . Giles?" Redwald said, seizing the opportunity.

"Hmmm, what?" Hawtree said, not taking his eyes off the sky.

"I'm glad I caught you, I've got something I'd like to discuss . . ."

"Uh-huh, yep."

". . . and there appears to be some confusion about. . ."

"Oh, there she is!!" Hawtree crowed, bustling past Redwald and the other guests without a backwards glance. Redwald, eyebrow raised, watched as Giles marched across the courtyard to the start of the pier, where he adopted a broad stance and looked out into the darkness. It was at that moment that Redwald became aware of a humming, almost imperceptibly quiet, like the buzzing of a distant fly. Following Giles' gaze, he looked out into the sky and found the source both of the noise and of the excitement.

Far away above the valley a speck of light was flying towards them. Redwald followed the speck as it moved downriver, increasing in size as the noise grew louder and closer. Giles anxiously teased his quiff into place before clicking his fingers at the attendant footmen and snapping an order at his head of security. The footmen scattered. Some bustled the queuing guests away from the purple carpet, others stood with their silver drinks trays on either side of the doorway, and two more hurried back inside, returning in tabards of the Hawtree arms and each carrying a heraldic banner. Meanwhile, Giles' head of security had ordered his men out on to the pier, where they stood as an honour guard on either side of the purple carpet.

By this time, the humming had grown to a roar and the skyron-hulled airship, HMS Eilmer, had emerged from the darkness. Great, angular flotation hulls, crouching low over the decks and clinging to either side of the aft cabins, looked like sturdy black sails beneath the royal banner, which cracked from the very top of the mast. In the Dragon's Nest between the fore and aft flotation hulls, orcite engineers tended to the compressed crystals, glowing white-hot inside each hull, while on deck, officers of the King's Own Aviator Corps prepared to anchor the ship.

She descended over the drive and gradually came to a standstill at the end of the pier. At a shout from Hawtree, a few of his guards made to assist in securing the vessel, but they proved surplus to requirements. Instead, six Aviators flew chains across the gulf, the insectoid wings of their cuirasses shredding the air, and secured the Eilmer to the mooring posts. Having lowered the gangplank with a crash, they stood to attention, wings erect and raised their sabres to their chins.

Those in the courtyard watched, transfixed, as two Guards of the Blood, both Giants, crossed the gangplank and joined the Aviators. The tallest must have been over 9 feet tall and they each grasped a wicked halberd in their rust-coloured hands, four black horns protruding through slits in their ceremonial helms. They were quickly followed by a tall young woman in a high-collared military tunic, who passed between the Giants and advanced up the pier towards Giles.

"Welcome to my home, Your Exalted Highness!" Hawtree said, his pink cheeks burning as he sank to one knee and inclined his head. Redwald and the rest of the courtyard followed suit, though Redwald did not bow quite so deeply, fearing he might break his nose on the floor if he matched Giles' stoop.

"It's just *Your Highness*, Mr Hawtree, but I thank you for the welcome. Please do stand up," the woman said, surveying the tabard-wearing footmen and the impromptu honour guard.

"May I offer my most sincere thanks for coming, Your Highness," Giles said as he got to his feet, "the Hawtree Estate is so very grateful for the favour you bestow on us."

"My pleasure," she replied crisply, before continuing as if from a script, "His Majesty the High King wishes to convey his sincere thanks to your family and to the Hawtree Foundry for their work on the Aerial Fleet."

"On the contrary, it is *we* who should thank *you*, Your Highness. Service to the Crown is a pleasure in and of itself. Now, if I may, please do follow me," he said, turning to lead her into the party as the other guests got to their feet.

Redwald watched as the woman and her guard followed Giles down the carpet, a gloved hand resting on the pommel of her sabre. She seemed *precise*. Her black hair was pulled back from her forehead and tied neatly in a plait, revealing a prominent widow's peak that was echoed in the tilt of her angular, mahogany eyes. Her uniform was unornamented, apart from golden epaulettes and an aiguillette, and she walked with the sort of quiet command that was born of hard-won, well-earned competence.

It was by her sole untamed, *im*precise feature, however, that Redwald identified her. Running from beneath her collar, up her throat and onto her left cheek was a livid port-wine stain, flush to her skin, as though someone had spilled a glass of wine on to a tablecloth. Princess Alesancyn, great-granddaughter of High King Emphoras IX, was clearly Giles Hawtree's guest of honour. As Giles, the Princess and her guard arrived at the door, she lifted a coupe from one of the silver trays and thanked the footman.

"After you, Your Highness," Hawtree said, stepping to one side, "the toastmaster is ready to announce you." The Princess, having just finished a sip of her wine, shot Hawtree a look of confusion.

"Is there not a queue?" she asked, gesturing to the waiting guests and meeting Redwald's eye as she did so.

"Not for *you*, Your Highness, of course," Hawtree chuckled. "Please follow me." Redwald returned the Princess' look and merely shrugged at her. Alesancyn gripped the hilt of her sabre and followed Giles inside, her guard in tow. Redwald could not be sure, but he thought he saw the faintest stirrings of a stifled laugh beneath her taut features.

As the chatter resumed in the queue behind him, the footman coughed pointedly and Redwald was quickly reminded of his predicament. He was saved almost immediately, however, by the timely appearance of Morrimer, who had come to ensure that the guests were being speedily admitted.

"My apologies for the inconvenience, Mr de Cordonnay," Morrimer said as he ushered the magician past the embarrassed doorman and into the entrance hall, "I thought I had added your name to the list, but I was clearly mistaken."

"No inconvenience at all."

"That's kind of you, sir. May I ask, have you anything to leave in the cloakroom?"

"No, it's just me," Redwald said, before gently leading the Hob to one side, away from the party proper. "However, I would appreciate your help with something else."

"Yes sir?"

"I had hoped to speak to Mr Hawtree about the case this evening, but I understand he's with another guest for now. Do you happen to know if he'd be free later tonight?" The butler smiled wanly.

"Mr Hawtree has not kept me fully informed of his plans tonight, I'm afraid."

"Ah, I see."

"*However*, I would note that he does make a point to speak to every one of his guests who are important to him." Redwald smiled.

"In that case I shall stand next to someone important." At that moment, a panicked young footman rushed over and stooped to whisper something to Morrimer. The Hob's great veined ear twitched as he listened, before nodding and sending the boy away. "I gather we're having a fish-related emergency, sir. May I excuse myself to attend to my duties?"

"Oh yes of course, just one further question; Mr Hawtree mentioned Sir Julius was a collector of antique weapons, is that right?"

"That's correct sir."

"Are they kept here, or . . .?"

"The collection is stored in the Gun Room, sir," Morrimer said, gesturing across the entrance hall to a door up on the first-floor

110

gallery. "You are most welcome to view it, should you wish. Will that be all, sir?"

"Yes, of course," Redwald said, before adding, "thanks ever so much for your help."

"My pleasure, sir." The Hob, both pairs of arms clasped behind his back, moved like a wraith through the party, looking entirely unfazed at the prospect of an emergency, fish-related or otherwise.

Redwald gratefully accepted a top-up of Arrovênnes from an attentive servant, before turning and scowling at the assembled masses. He did not like society parties as a rule, much like train stations and for similar reasons, the sole advantage of a train station being that it remained a socially unacceptable venue to press-gang someone into a dance. As such, he decided, it would be unwise to linger. Heading for the Gun Room door above him, he skirted around the mass of chattering people that barred his way and made to cross the room.

As rooms went, it was enormous and about as subtly turned out as the rest of the Manor. Each of the four chandeliers that hung precariously over the assembled guests was the size of a carriage and composed of thousands upon thousands of putative glass water droplets, hung from the flared wings of four crystal swans joined at the tail. Across the hall, two marble staircases swept up and around a gigantic golden statue of Sir Julius Hawtree, who was thrusting a miniature airship into the aether with his enormous right hand. From the mezzanine, two doors opened onto a mass of music, colour, and movement that Redwald surmised was the ballroom, while a gallery fanned out around the upper walls, the balustrade supported by a perverse selection of carved beasts.

Redwald began to suppose, as he followed the wall opposite the stairs, that this wing of the Manor was especially designed for entertaining and therefore inaccessible from the residential side. This latter suspicion was quickly disproven when the wall opened

111

without warning and a doorman flew out with a newly stocked tray of drinks, narrowly missing Redwald. As in many other grand houses, the door had been magically concealed so that it blended into the wall, maintaining the illusion that servants didn't exist beyond the limits of their utility.

Turning right beneath the overhanging balustrade, he made for the grand staircase that would take him up to the gallery. As he walked, however, the smell of food reached him once more and a heaped buffet table emerged from the crowd like an island paradise from a tropical mist. Floral salads from Jenever surrounded crispy suckling pigs, while fruits from the jungles at the edge of the Desert Impassable were piled in sweet, fleshy towers beside great vats of cheesy potatoes. Whole schools of fish swirled around the edge of a silver platter, as though caught in a metal maelstrom, and slices of lean, bloody venison were served in a rich chocolate sauce. This bounty was largely neglected by the other guests, who seemed far more interested in one another. Redwald intended to pass the table by but found himself gradually coming to a halt. He stopped, pausing for the briefest of moments, before helping himself to as much as he could carry on one plate. *May as well enjoy myself.* At the end of the table and having balanced a truffle on the last bit of free space, he swapped his empty coupe for a glass of Carussian red and thanked the bewildered-looking servers for their assistance.

Full glass and loaded plate in hand, Redwald continued on towards Sir Julius' collection, climbing one of the grand staircases and following the banister around to the left as it snaked along the gallery. Upon reaching the furthest door as Morrimer had indicated, Redwald turned right and entered the Gun Room. He stopped dead in his tracks. *Shit.* Sir Julius' 'collection' ought rightly to have been called an arsenal. Tall glass gun cases lined most of the sizeable room's walls and were stacked with enough weapons to arm a small garrison. Albeit that some of the guns were not antiques and some of the antiques were not guns, the vast majority of the collection could, to Redwald's inexpert eye, be counted as suspect weapons. He reached into his pocket and felt the roll of ribbon. Did he have enough? Without expert advice, there was no way of knowing and much as he would have liked to, he could not do this alone.

His enthusiasm somewhat blunted, he decided to eat before seeking out Giles. Finding the room suitably appointed with rich leather armchairs and the odd side table, he dragged one of the latter to one of the former and sat down by the fire. It was an odd place for a meal. Blood-red walls and minimal light lent the room a mildly foreboding air, while the intricate tracery of the high ceiling made Redwald feel as if he were a small animal, bleeding out beneath the roots of a giant tree. Those parts of the wall not otherwise taken up with windows or gun cases were filled with artwork and taxidermy, such that Redwald was watched as he ate by thousands of glassy, lifeless eyes peering out of earthy paintings or set in slowly mouldering sockets.

He was squinting up at a stuffed gryphon's head, a piece of venison on the end of his fork, when he heard voices outside the door. He recognised them both instantly.

"Oryn's sake, I hate this. Don't know why I come every year," Lord Martingale said, his shadow cast through the open door by the light of the chandeliers.

"Because you're fond of Lord Hawtree?" Asplund replied as his short, broad silhouette joined the Baron's. Martingale grunted a laugh in response. "You know," Asplund continued, "what he wants is your approval. Might prove useful."

"He wants a damn sight more than that. He wants the whole thing, just like Ellswych. Greasy, ambitious little sycophant."

"You don't have to give it to him."

"I won't."

"*I* know that, but *he* needn't. Men like Hawtree can be played when you know what they want. Just like you played Captain Streich at Deyssante Point." Martingale's shadow leant heavily on the balustrade.

"He was vulnerable. Didn't understand the importance of loyalty, not like you." Asplund leant alongside his erstwhile commander and together they enjoyed a moment of comfortable silence. After a while, Asplund turned to Martingale and began to speak to him, softly.

"You know, I was very . . . very proud of you that day, Archie," Asplund said, before sliding his hand along the banister and tenderly placing it on the Baron's own. Redwald felt a flush of guilt; this seemed far more private a moment than he was comfortable overhearing. His fear was allayed by the Baron's reaction, however. Lord Martingale looked down at Asplund's hand for a moment, before taking it in his own and shaking it warmly.

"You're a good friend Gerritt, always have been," he said, patting Asplund on the back. "Couldn't ask for better; that's why I'd trust no one else with those keys." Asplund's shadow seemed to shrink a little. "Damn," Martingale said, apparently looking along the gallery behind Asplund, "the little turd has found us." Over the chatter from the entrance hall below, Redwald heard approaching footsteps and a familiar drawl.

"My Loooord!"

"Hawtree," Martingale replied before adding, in a tone Redwald had never heard from him, "Alice, dear. How . . . how are you holding up?" The shadows were now so numerous that Redwald could not distinguish any one from the rest.

"I'm well, my Lord, thank you so much for asking. And thank you both for coming! It really is lovely to see you."

114

"Our pleasure," Asplund replied, his voice a little subdued.

"Couldn't have a party without inviting the Baron and his Seneschal!" Giles cut in. "Do join us will you? I was about to show Lettie the new acquisition."

The magician started as Giles bustled unexpectedly into the Gun room, leading a woman Redwald did not recognize. Martingale and Asplund followed, muttering something non-committal, while Alice brought up the rear. None of them noticed Redwald, ensconced in the dark, and before he could announce himself Giles had already begun his lecture.

"See here, Lettie," Giles said excitedly, gesturing at an enormous painting that hung opposite the door, "remarkable isn't it?" As one of the few portraits in the Manor that did not feature Sir Julius, Redwald had to agree. Like Sir Julius in his own paintings, however, the sitter seemed oddly proportioned, with a head too small for his overlong body. Worse still, he looked positively swamped by his clothes and surroundings. On the desk beside him were overflowing piles of books, maps and navigational instruments, while the window over his shoulder showed the rippling blue expanse of Forstrand Bay and the distant Straits of Brimgard, through which every ship to and from Athonstone must pass. He himself was smothered by the royal standard, which he wore as a robe, and juggling a collection of ancient regalia. With a carved orb in one hand and a rusted sword in the other, he was forced to balance the sceptre, topped with an ivory gryphon with rubies for eyes, in the crook of his arm.

Yet this general air of clumsiness was eclipsed by the sitter's easy, roguish confidence. With one booted foot resting on a step and a playfully smug expression cast across his face, he looked for all the world like a high-class jewel thief making off with his prize. Or at least he would have, were it not for the crown which fit *perfectly* upon his brow.

"Hmmm, this piece I am liking greatly," said Lettie. Her voice was quite low and pleasantly aged. She spoke slowly and with the clarity of one making an effort in a language not their own. Redwald recognised the lilting, honeyed accent almost immediately. "This man, he is a king, no?" Giles shrugged.

"Should think so! Paid a king's ransom for it anyway. I'm told it was painted by one of your lot."

"I am thinking you are right," she said, leaning in close to examine it, "drawings are not of my . . . *expertise*, but this painter is very famous in home; Laszlo Kist. He is gone now, but coming originally from Oštrouman. We were buying many of his works fresh!" She laughed. "I am wondering, though, who is king?" Each member of the group shrugged in turn.

"It's Krysillion VII," Redwald said. He should have spoken sooner, he knew, but couldn't deny the guilty pleasure of seeing Giles jump.

"Oh, Redwald, there you are!" he said, adjusting his hair, and in his mildly disordered state Redwald once again felt that pang of recognition. The Baron merely harrumphed as the magician put his empty plate to one side and rose from the armchair.

"Evening all," Redwald said as he made to join them, glass in hand.

"This is the fruit magician?" The strange woman asked, looking at Giles. Redwald frowned.

"Oh, I should explain," Giles said, his habitual grin now restored, "I was just discussing with Lettie what magicians actually do and I told her about your spell."

"My spell?"

"You know . . . animating fruit." In spite of himself, Redwald laughed.

116

"Oh yes, that one. It's an illusion spell," he said, directing the comment at Lettie, "you can create the illusion that someone *is* where they *aren't* in a number of ways. It isn't easy, but it can be made easier if you have some . . . organic matter in their place. That particular spell uses fruit, is all," he said, gulping his wine. "It's completely bloody useless, but there you go."

"How . . . how is the case going?" Alice asked. Redwald's ears burned as he recognised how insensitive he had been. Although, in his defence, she didn't seem half so waifish as she had when they first met. Dressed in a navy coatdress embroidered with white roses and tied up with a cord, she looked immensely glamorous and in control, a serene smile offsetting a turban-tied shawl to disguise her thinning locks. Despite this overt display of confidence, however, Redwald noted that she was subtly wringing her hands. He swallowed.

"I believe it's going well. In fact," he said, "Guardsman Norris has provided me with a very helpful lead. I had wanted to discuss it with Mr . . . Giles, actually." Giles leant in to listen. Redwald paused. "Perhaps you and I could step outside for a moment?" Redwald suggested, acutely aware that he was about to discuss the weapon that might one day bore a hole in Alice's eye socket.

"I'd like to come too," Alice said, matter-of-factly. "Better I know than not, I suppose." Courage was a lot like clouds, Redwald thought. Though taking many different forms and easily dispersed, it was always recognisable.

"We'll leave you to it," Martingale said as he and Asplund made for the door. Lettie started to follow suit.

"No, my Lord, of course you're welcome to stay!" Hawtree said. "Please do indulge me, this won't take long and I was hoping to introduce you to Sir Alphyn Iudex." The Baron looked as though he were about to argue, but Asplund placed a calming hand on his

117

sleeve. They turned to wait for Giles, who grinned expectantly up at Redwald.

"It's about Sir Julius' weapons collection."

"Well, there it is!" Giles said sarcastically, as he gestured to the room at large.

"This is the *entirety* of Sir Julius' collection?"

"It's all kept here." Redwald paused for a moment, aware of the need for delicacy.

"Guardsman Norris has suggested that the . . . the fatal wound, was or *will be* caused by an antique weapon of a certain age and matching certain technical specifications. I believe, given the . . . the apparently vindictive nature of the crime, that the mur. . . the perpetrator, might seek to acquire a weapon from Sir Julius' collection, to maximise the psychological impact. However, although this room is *a* likely source, it may not be the only one. So far as you know, does anyone else in the immediate vicinity have an antique armoury? Anywhere else a perpetrator could acquire such a gun?" Giles shrugged and Alice, slightly crestfallen, admitted she did not know. Martingale and Asplund were both silent as the latter rubbed at his eyepatch.

"I am thinking you might purchase some in Trewcester, perhaps," the strange woman interjected, "but these places are not many. Otherwise, people are selling these things in Athonstone only."

"So what you're saying," Alice murmured, trying not to look at the antique weapons that lined every wall, "is that the murder weapon is in this room."

"Hopefully," Redwald replied, "because that gives us the strategic advantage. Firstly, because you can put a guard on the door, to ensure these weapons are not accessible to . . . anyone and

118

secondly, because of this." He held the roll of crimson ribbon out before them.

"What is *this?*" Giles asked.

"I enchanted it earlier today so that I can track its movement. Using the details provided to me by Guardsman Norris, I intend to go through this collection, identify any weapons that fit his specifications and tie a length of ribbon on each. I've specifically enchanted the ribbon to be cut-resistant and, once tied, it can only be *untied* by me. That way, if any weapons go missing, *even under your guard,*" he said heading off Giles' objection, "I can recover them and maybe even catch the perpetrator in the process." An uncomfortable silence prevailed for a moment before Alice broke it.

"You'll need the key to the cabinets then," she said, walking over to a large gilt clock on the mantelpiece, shifting it to one side and pulling a small key out from underneath. She placed it in Redwald's palm with ice-cold fingertips. Giles looked from Redwald to his wife and beamed.

"Great," Giles said, "so that's it! I'll have Morrimer put a guard up here right away and you can do . . . your stuff." He turned as if to leave.

"Just one more thing," Redwald said, opening his notebook to where he had copied out the weapon specs, "I need someone to walk me through the specifications, do any of the servants know about these weapons, or your gamekeeper perhaps? Ideally, I'd tag these tonight, but if that's not possible, perhaps you could put me in contact with an expert? I assume Sir Julius consulted someone on his purchases?" Giles suddenly and unexpectedly seemed rather pleased with himself.

"Well Redwald, my friend," he said, placing a hand on the magician's shoulder and manoeuvring him to face Lettie, "it just so happens that this *gorgeous* woman was actually Sir Julius' weapons dealer."

"Oh, that's serendipitous," Redwald said, cringing slightly at Giles' unwelcome touch.

"I'm sure you can discuss the rest between yourselves. Right," Giles said conclusively, clapping his hands together, "let's leave these two to get acquainted, shall we? Perhaps you can interview Lettie at the same time, Redwald? Come on my Lord, let's meet Sir Alphyn." Giles, before anyone could object, began to lead Lord Martingale out of the room, greasily enquiring as to the Baron's health as he did so. Martingale had the look of a patient but unhappy family dog left to play with the baby. Asplund nodded at Redwald before following wordlessly, while Alice paused for a moment, looking between Redwald and Lettie.

"Good luck Redwald," she murmured before turning to leave.

"Mrs Hawtree, I . . ."

"I told you, please call me Alice," she said, smiling at him over her shoulder.

"Alice, we can try and stop them getting the weapon, but we can also try and stop them getting to you. I would suggest . . ."

"Morrimer has placed a guard outside my door. Two of our men will be there all day and all night, every day of the week. When I'm not sleeping I'll either be with Giles, or surrounded by crowds, as I am tonight." Redwald nodded.

"I think that's very sensible."

"I have every faith you can solve this, Redwald," Alice said kindly and again, Redwald felt his ears burn. It wasn't right that *she* should be comforting *him*. "But please do solve it quickly," she added, her voice quavering a little. He nodded stiffly once more.

"I shall do my best."

"Thank you." With that, she began to follow the others out of the room, but a thought suddenly struck Redwald.

"Alice, wait." He strode over to her and cut a length of ribbon from the roll with his borrowed scissors. "May I?" She nodded and he tied the ribbon loosely around her bony wrist. He looked directly into her eyes. "So long as you keep this on, I can find you, do you understand?"

"I do, thank you." Her eyes glistened slightly as she said it, but she gave no other sign of her feelings. Nodding politely at Lettie, she turned around and headed back out into the party. Redwald wished he could have said something more concrete to comfort her, but he couldn't. He simply flicked open his notebook to the map and watched as a tiny red droplet separated from the larger drop and moved slowly away. Drawing a deep breath, he paused and turned to speak to Lettie.

Looking at her properly for the first time, he realised that Giles had been right; she really was exceptionally beautiful. Dressed in a flowing silk gown of a deep emerald green, she wore her black hair cropped short and a fur draped around her tan shoulders. It was hard to tell her age, but as she walked towards him, her olive legs slipping subtly from beneath the folds of her dress with every step, he imagined she was older than she appeared. It was not her looks that belied her age, however, but rather the expression of wicked, sardonic cleverness sculpted into her smooth features. It was the look of someone old enough to understand the quintessential silliness of life and wise enough to find it amusing.

"Apologies," Redwald said, extending a hand, "I don't believe we were properly introduced. I'm Redwald de Cordonnay."

"I am thanking you for your hand, Mr de Cordonnay," she replied, "but in my country, we kiss." *Czerganzans*, Redwald thought to himself. She leant in to peck him on both cheeks, but he parried her by gently taking her gloved hand and shaking it warmly.

"Welcome to Tempest," he replied. She returned his wry smile and shook his hand.

"It is pleasing to meet you, Redwald de Cordonnay, I am Laetizja of Oštrouman." Redwald felt his brain clunk like the ticking of a bell tower clock. Of course, *Lettie* was the visiting Countess Laetizja. She turned and walked over to one of the settees perpendicular to the fire, where the obligatory portrait of Sir Julius Hawtree loomed from over the mantelpiece. "Please be correcting me," she said as she sank gracefully on to the leather seat, "but I am thinking there was a de Cordonnay in Czerganza before the Revolution, no?"

"Perhaps, but no relation of mine," Redwald lied, hurriedly. "May I ask, do you prefer Laetizja or Lettie?"

"Mr Giles is calling me Lettie," she said.

"Laetizja it is then," Redwald responded as he made to join her. She laughed at that and patted the spot next to her on the sofa. Redwald sank instead into the adjacent armchair.

"You are wishing to interview me first, Mr de Cordonnay? Then perhaps we are discussing the weapons?"

"Yes please."

"Then it is pleasing for me to answer you. But first, I am curious, please be explaining to me how you are knowing which this king is." She gestured to the portrait of Krysillion VII. Redwald smiled.

"I just recognised the face. I saw another portrait of him once, many years ago, when I was studying." She shot him a sceptical, mocking look.

"This is all?"

"I have a very good memory. Especially for faces, as it happens," he said, extracting a pen from the pocket of his tailcoat. She scoffed.

"I am thinking this cannot be all. He is not looking *so* particular." Redwald finished noting the date and time, before looking up at the painting again.

"He has a very distinctive asymmetry to the line of his mouth; the right-hand corner is higher than the left. You'll note also that he shares a dimpled chin with his grandmother, Walda, Margravine of Farminster, as well as her black, curly hair." Laetizja raised her eyebrows and nodded, mildly impressed, but Redwald continued. "It's also not real. Not a forgery," he said, hurriedly correcting himself as Laetizja's eyes widened, "it's just that scene can't have been painted from life. You see that castle on the easternmost spit of the Brimgard Straits? That's Fort Durran. Krysillion VII planned it, but it wasn't completed until after he was deposed. This was probably painted for him in exile, as propaganda."

"Hmmm," she sighed, almost sensually, "you *are* good with the details". She leant back in her seat, her long, brown neck on tasteful display.

"Sometimes," Redwald conceded, "now, if I may?"

"Please, be asking your questions." Her hazel eyes looked him over, assessing him as keenly as he had assessed the portrait.

"So," Redwald began, "you were Sir Julius' weapons consultant?"

"I am a curator," she said, firmly, "but yes, I was advising Sir Julius on his collection, acquiring pieces for him. After a time, we are becoming friends."

"How did you come to meet him? Giles said you left Czerganza after the Revolution." She tutted.

"No, this is not so. I am leaving *before* the Revolution. In my family, you see, the girls . . . people were not thinking we could *do*. They are thinking that we should be marrying, having the children. Well, this idea is boring me, so I leave and I learn. After the Revolution, when the men are dying, family are choosing me as Countess, because I am having the money. This is amusing, no?" Redwald agreed that irony did indeed abound.

"And how did you meet Sir Julius?"

"Ah, this is also *before* the Revolution. My employer is sending me to Athonstone, to buy some pieces for his collection, but you see, Sir Julius is also wanting them . . . and . . . is paying me more."

"How direct of him."

"He was just so," she said, looking up at his portrait over the mantelpiece. Redwald looked at it too as he took a draught of wine. The question fled his lips before he could stop himself.

"What was wrong with his hand?"

"Why is it you are thinking this?" She inclined her head, smiled, and waited for him to show his workings. He paused for a moment.

"Well . . . every portrait of Sir Julius in this house, and there are many, prominently displays his hands, but they seem too big . . . too overblown. By contrast, I've only seen one *photo* of him and there his right hand looked off; stiff and unnatural, as if his fingers wouldn't close. My guess is that he's taken a leaf out of Krysillion VII's book; using art to conceal the truth. So I'm curious, what was he hiding?"

124

"Maybe you are right," Laetizja said, "but Sir Julius is trusting me with secrets. Why should I be telling you? Perhaps, you will be persuading me?" She slowly re-crossed her legs, so that the silk cascaded around her onto the sofa, before toying with the pendant that hung between her breasts. Redwald smiled.

"What if I said please?" She laughed and sat forward again. It was clearly the right answer.

"Very well, I am telling you, but only because you are being *so polite*." She smiled her wicked smile. "How am I saying this? Sir Julius, he was a strong man. People were knowing this, but he is wanting them to believe him . . . *invisible?*"

"Invincible."

"Just so. He is caring for this reputation; to be the powerful businessman, perhaps more than anything else. After all, this is how he is building his empire, doing his business; he is seeming strong both in body and in the mind."

"But, in his eyes at least, he had a weakness."

"Just so," she looked up at the portrait. "His right arm. It is being damaged, since birth. He is missing three fingers and the arm is shorter than his left."

"He wore gloves to disguise the missing fingers?" That would explain why they looked stiff in the photograph, Redwald thought.

"Just so. Such lengths he is going to, to hide this. I am telling him all the time: 'This is no weakness, this is no shame!' But he is not hearing me, I think." She sighed. "This is why he is dying so young; keeping his secrets, it is pulling on his heart. Then one day," she snapped her delicate fingers, "his heart is beating no more." She looked mournfully up at Sir Julius' portrait for a moment before quickly regaining her composure. "Enough about these things. You are having other questions for me?"

Redwald, his own curiosity sated, turned back to the business at hand. He continued by asking her the same questions he had put to the Hawtrees and testing to see if her account differed either from their statements or from the statement she had given to Norris. It did not. Redwald began to look a little crestfallen.

"I am not helping you?"

"No, no it's not that . . . you agree with everyone else's account."

"To me, this is sounding unhelpful for you." The Countess pursed her lips unhappily and turned to look at the weapons that lined the wall. "Perhaps I am being of more help with the weapons, yes?"

"Only if you wouldn't mind."

"Of course I am not minding," she said, as she floated to her feet, "how old are you saying is the future weapon?"

"Built anywhere from the 2070's to the 2130's." She nodded. Slipping around the end of the sofa, she headed towards the display cases furthest from the door.

"Sir Julius is, after my urging, storing his weapons in order of time. Neater," she explained, winking at him. "From here," she said, pointing to a battered-looking pistol, before walking the length of the wall and stopping beside an old crossbow, "to here, are weapons of the proper age." Redwald joined her and peered along the cases.

Unlike their counterparts nearer the door, which contained modern hunting rifles, these cases were stacked not for efficiency, but for display. Their occupants, each labelled with little printed notes, were pieces of art more than functioning weapons, many being too old to work or else deliberately disarmed by the removal of their orcite crystals or bowstrings. Angled on their stands so that the light reflected their decoration *just so,* silver frigates clashed in shimmering mother-of-pearl oceans on the butts of rifles, blunderbuss barrels were acid-etched with grapevines and flowers, while the marquetry on crossbow stocks wove polished wooden hunters into polished wooden forests. In one case, it seemed a gilded pistol had even been made to commemorate a wedding, while a topaz-eyed demon glared at Redwald from the handle of another.

"You are knowing also of the calibre?" Redwald flicked to the relevant page in his notebook to show the specifications to Laetizja and together they began to work through the pieces on display. Redwald gladly followed the Countess as she wafted like a summer's breeze along the cases, explaining each antique as she went. Initially, she confined her comments to whether or not they fit Redwald's criteria and, if so, whether they remained armed. In these cases, Redwald would note the weapon's name on a list entitled 'Suspects', unlock the cabinet, and tie a precisely cut length of ribbon around the trigger guard, before locking the cabinet once more. As they continued, however, Laetizja's enthusiasm got the better of her and she would explain each piece in detail, regardless of relevance. This, of course, was no detriment to Redwald and he listened enthusiastically each time she wandered off on a tangent.

She was expounding on the provenance of an ornate, wrist-mounted crossbow, when Redwald's eyes slipped momentarily away and met those of a woman he recognised. Staring at him from the handle of an old duelling pistol, her smooth cheeks and dark eyes had been set into the oak handle piece by delicate piece. Her hair, woven of hundreds of slivers of multi-coloured woods, was polished to a sheen and so finely made that it appeared to waft like gossamer in a non-existent breeze. Behind her, dozens of sovereign coins tumbled across the mahogany of an escutcheon's field, itself surmounted by a Vysearl's coronet.

Redwald quickly realised that it was not the woman that was familiar, but the coat of arms of which she was a part. He squinted, trying to remember where he had already seen the design, before looking to the pistol's slightly wonky, hand-written label. *Maidensworth Duelling Pistol (King's) – 2122*. That too was familiar, but Redwald still couldn't place the name.

"May I ask," Redwald said, turning to Laetizja as she finished her lecture on the crossbow, "what do you know about this pistol? I'm sure I know those arms and I've definitely heard that name before, but I'm not sure where." She examined the gun and its label for a moment, before her eyes suddenly widened.

"I am not knowing that Sir Julius is having one of these," she said, before swearing under her breath in Czerganzan. "I am not knowing *anyone* is having one of these." She began to look around as if for another.

"Are they rare?" Redwald asked.

"Just so! They were making only two for the duel," Laetizja said excitedly as she turned back to him, but her face fell slightly "Ah, but no matter. You are knowing of Krysillion VII already, so you are hearing also of the duel, yes? Or . . . perhaps you are not?" She asked hopefully. For a moment, in place of the elegant, worldly woman she had become, Redwald saw her as she might once have been; an excited little girl, fascinated by guns and keen to tell a friend all she had learnt.

"Not yet," he replied. Laetizja beamed, her sardonic veil slipping gently away.

"Ah, then I am telling you; it is a *good* story. Long ago, the Vysearl of Maidensworth is commissioning a pair of pistols for an especial duel he is to be fighting. Please be understanding, this is strange. The duelling pistols are often being kept for . . . emergencies, for using at short notice."

128

"Better to follow through on your challenge while still drunk, I suppose," said Redwald, sipping his wine.

"Just so. But the Vysearl is not drinking, he is planning the vengeance against his King; *Krysillion VII*. Why this is, we are not knowing for sure. Some are thinking that the King is seducing the Vysearldoress, some that he is not rewarding the Vysearl enough, others that the Vysearl is mad. What we *are* knowing is *how* the Vysearl is thinking he can do this. Knowing his King to be . . . prideful," she said, glancing at the painted Krysillion posing smugly with his crown, "the Vysearl is challenging him to a duel. But the King, being so prideful, is *often* fighting duels; he is fighting them well and against many foes. So, to ensure he is winning, the Vysearl is paying his gunsmith to be creating two beautiful duelling pistols for him. Of the design, the Vysearl is caring little, but is requiring especially two things. First, the guns must be looking identical in every way, even to people with the training, like me. Secondly, and of the most importance, one of the guns should *not* be firing. It is this gun that he is intending for the King." Redwald frowned.

"But surely, the King's own gunsmith would fire a test round before the duel, wouldn't he? Precisely to guard against this sort of thing?"

"This is what the gunsmith is telling the Vysearl. So instead, he is making the King's gun using a most impure, most brittle orcite crystal, which is then being overcharged. One shot and the crystal is cracking, disarming the gun. Now the guns are being tested, each gun is firing once and the King, his gunsmith, and everyone else is thinking both guns are working, but the Vysearl is knowing this is not so."

"So, what went wrong?" Redwald asked, finishing his wine. "Because, if I'm not mistaken, Krysillion VII died in Glavnigrad, bedridden with the pox. He wasn't killed in a duel."

"Ah yes, you are knowing this much," Laetizja said, winking again. "Badly for him, the Vysearl is forgetting his manners. Especially, he is forgetting his duelling . . . traditions; it is the party being challenged who is choosing his weapon first. Not knowing of the different guns, the King, as challenged party, is selecting the wrong weapon and so the Vysearl. . ." she dragged a finger across her throat.

"Ha! Of course he is," Redwald said, spinning the cap off his hipflask and taking a drink. "You're right, that *is* a good story."

"You are enjoying the poetical justice," Laetizja observed.

"Greatly," Redwald said, smiling. Yet something continued to bother him. He paused for a moment, before putting the inevitable question. "Could this gun be a suspect?" Laetizja looked it over.

"Indeed, I am thinking it is very possible. The age is right and so are the . . . *specificities*. I am wondering, though, whether this is the gun the King was *supposed* to be having, or the one he is *actually* having?"

"How could you tell? Presumably you'd have to test it?"

"Just so. They are being made identically." Redwald, emboldened by drink, looked from the pistol to one of the narrow windows sandwiched between the gun cases along the far wall.

"Could . . . could we test it?" Laetizja met his gaze.

"It is your investigation," she said, in a measured tone, "but I am warning you, this weapon . . . until now, I am not knowing any are surviving at all, either this one or its counterpart. And I am guessing," she continued, as Redwald leaned in to listen, "that if both Maidensworth Duelling Pistols were surviving, Sir Julius would have been buying both."

"I see . . . Is a test likely to damage it?"

"Likely? No. Possibly? Yes." Redwald looked at the one-of-a-kind antique that would, almost certainly, exceed in value all that he might earn in his lifetime and decided against impulsively firing a round out the window. "I'll just add it to the list," he said, noting its name and tying on a ribbon.

The pair continued down the gun cases as before, inspecting each remaining weapon as they went. By increments, Redwald began to feel more optimistic. They had so far identified only six potential murder weapons; the rest were either too big, too small or too broken. Redwald, for whom optimism was an unusual condition, took a celebratory swig from his hipflask. Surely, this was the right thing to do; either cutting the killer off at the source or else setting a trap for them.

Redwald's triumphalism proved both short-lived and premature, however. As he pocketed his hipflask, Laetizja cleared her throat for his attention. He looked up and his stomach dropped. "Oh *shit*." Bare of any weapons, the blood-red backing of the final cabinet was garishly bright. The angled iron stands were empty but for the printed labels and both doors were thrust open, albeit the glass pane was missing from the left-hand one. Redwald felt his optimism evaporate; tagging six suspect weapons was a poor defence if a further ten were on the loose.

"I am thinking these must be out for cleaning," Laetizja said, leaning in to read the labels.

"I mean . . .," Redwald sighed, "it *might* not matter; are any of them suspects?"

"I am finding it hard to say without them here, but . . . yes, yes I am thinking some perhaps are." She noted, with a hint of frustration, that she did not recognise all the names. Of those she did recognise, however, there were a few suspects. Redwald noted each one down as she read their names out; the Waters 2101, the Ausburger Snaplock 2120, and, finally, the Villantine Special 2132.

These he added to his list of suspects, before preparing a second list which included all the missing weapons. "I am most sorry that I cannot be telling you about the rest," she said, nervously toying with her pendant, "it is a shame, tripping at the last hurdle. I am being most unhelpful to you."

"On the contrary," Redwald said, snapping his notebook shut, "you've been exceptionally helpful; I can't thank you enough." She smiled.

"Still, I am thinking I could have done more. . ."

"No, you couldn't have, you've helped me make real progress tonight. It's just up to me to track the missing ones down, I suppose. I would ask Giles where they're being cleaned, but I doubt he'll . . ."

"I say, are you two *still* in here?" Before Redwald could finish his sentence, the door at the far end of the room creaked open unexpectedly. The light and noise of the Gala spilled into the quiet little space, flushing Giles along with them. "It's been *such* a looong time," Giles observed, slurring gently, "I hope you're not being *untoward*, de Cordonnay, you devil!" He swayed across the room towards them and put a hand on Laetizja's bare shoulder. Her sardonic grin subtly re-occupied her features.

"Is Alice with you?" Redwald asked.

"Well, *clearly* not. No, she's off to bed, *fully guarded*," he said raising his hands to Redwald, "just as you suggested. I assume you've made some progress here?" Giles said, looking expectantly up at them.

"Just so, we . . ." Laetizja began.

"*Excellent!* Then I'll reclaim the *gorgeous* Lettie from you Redwald, alright? Cardinal Nerezhney is here and I gather he's in the market

132

for a few of your pretty little crossbows, my dear." Laetizja turned to look at Redwald.

"You are wanting to join us?"

"That's very kind of you," he said, lacing it with enough sarcasm that she was forced to stifle a laugh, "but I had better see about these missing weapons."

"You are knowing who to ask?"

"I have an idea."

"Just so," she smiled. "Then, I am doing all I can for you?"

"*Just so,*" Redwald said, "it's up to me now."

"Come on Lettie, we don't want to keep the Cardinal waiting," Giles moaned, like an insistent toddler.

"I am staying until Borsday, then returning for home. If you are having any more questions before then, please be asking. If not, then I am most enjoying meeting you, Mr de Cordonnay, perhaps we shall be doing so again." She offered her hand to Redwald. He took it and, much to Laetizja's surprise, planted a kiss on her knuckles.

"*Sjevar Oryn'li djerristín,*" he said. Laetizja laughed.

"*May Oryn be willing it,*" she replied, translating the old Czerganzan phrase. She turned back to Hawtree, her sultry façade restored. "Come now, Mr Giles, we shall be seeing the Cardinal." Sweeping towards the door with the stumbling Giles in tow, she turned, nodded to Redwald one last time, and left. Giles, either forgetting or not caring that Redwald was still in the room, shut the door behind them.

133

The magician, now alone, cast about for a flat surface on which to write. Happily, tucked in the corner and perpendicular to the empty gun cabinet, there was a small bookcase. The wall above it was occupied by a large portrait and so the case itself was only as tall as Redwald's chest. Leaning on it, he ripped a blank page from his notebook and began to copy out the two lists; the suspect weapons and the missing weapons. The copied lists would go straight to Morrimer. If anyone in the Manor knew where the missing weapons had been sent, it would be him.

The occupants of the portrait loomed over Redwald as he carefully forced a degree of legibility upon his customary scrawl. A beautiful, fragile-looking woman in her early thirties was seated in front of a man Redwald took to be her husband. Older than her by about a decade, the man was unmistakably Sir Julius, though younger and less brutish than in his other portraits. There was even a degree of tenderness in the way his good left hand rested on her alabaster shoulder. Occasionally, Redwald's eyes would flick to the portrait's dedication as he wrote. The painting was as much a fiction as the others in the Manor, it seemed, though for more tragic reasons. Emmeline Hawtree had apparently died in 2306, two years before the picture's completion.

After expending much care on the task, Redwald finished copying the lists before compulsively checking each more times than was necessary. Finally satisfied, and aglow with alcohol and triumph, he snapped the notebook shut, wafting the adjacent loose page right into the narrow gap between the bookshelf and the wall.

He swore. The bottom of that gap would be full of all sorts of filth; fluff, dust, perhaps the odd bit of dead insect or old mange from a taxidermied head. He pulled a clean handkerchief from his pocket, to shield himself from dirt as he extracted the list. As it was, the list had not sunk to the very bottom of the gap, but had lodged itself halfway down, balanced between the adjacent wall and a small brass stud set into the bookcase.

134

Redwald's first attempt to extract the list failed. His hand was too thick for the narrow gap and both the list and the stud on which it rested were set too far back. He grumbled for a moment. He wasn't sure what a solitary brass stud was doing set into the side of a bookcase, but it was now an annoyance. He tried to shake the bookcase and dislodge the list that way, but the thing appeared fixed to the wall and would not budge.

Swearing under his breath, he was about to re-copy both lists when he hit upon an idea. Stooping a little to look at the books, he ran his finger down their spines. There was only one that looked thin enough to fit into the gap and tall enough to reach the page; *Twistle's Traditional Tales for Growing Children*. Bound in blue leather with a golden key on the cover, it seemed a shame to use it for this purpose, but he could wipe it clean afterwards.

Feeling like a ham-fisted lockpick as he leant against the case, he slid the book into the gap and moved it up past the stud. Then, awkwardly, he pressed the bottom of the list to the bookcase using one of the book's corners and began to slide the page towards the top. As Redwald pushed the page upwards, however, he was forced to hold the book flush to the wood, pressing the stud down into the bookcase in turn.

For a brief moment Redwald wrote this off as shoddy workmanship, but then he heard the hissing. It was no more obtrusive a sound than a breeze blowing through a window and, but for the relative quiet of the Gun Room, would have been inaudible. He briefly paused at that, but ultimately ignored it in favour of his singular quest to retrieve the page. He even ignored the quiet creaking that followed soon after. What he could not ignore, however, was the sudden movement of the bookcase away from him and into the wall. Losing his support, Redwald dropped the book, stumbled, and fell to his knees. The list fluttered out onto the floor in front of him, covered in dust.

"Shit."

Fussily dusting off the list before pocketing it, he rose to his feet to see what had happened. The section of wall beneath the portrait had swung backwards on a hinge, taking the bookcase with it and revealing a passage beyond. Looking closer, Redwald noted the characteristic haze around the edges of the doorway. Like the servant's doors out in the entrance hall, this was the subject of a concealment spell.

He stooped for the blue book, dusted it off and slid it back on to the shelf. He then retrieved his notebook from the top of the case and ducked beneath the portrait to look into the passage. To his left, in a dark alcove behind the hinged wall, he could just make out a system of weights, gears, ropes, and pulleys that had apparently opened the wall upon the depression of the stud. To his right, at the base of a narrow staircase which spiralled up and away from him, was an unlit orcite lamp hung from a bracket, and an adjacent lever connected to the weights.

He paused on the threshold and took a drink from his hipflask, debating whether or not to investigate. Trespassing on a client's property, secret property no less, seemed like a bad idea. At the very least, and more damning in Redwald's eyes, it was poor form. Why should he assume this hidden opening to be sinister? What if this were just another servant's passage? *All the same*, he thought, pocketing his hipflask, *this is an ill-fitting pattern*. If this *were* just another servant's passage, why hide the stud on the side of a bookcase? Why hide the passage behind a bookcase at all? More importantly, what good was a servant's passage with a four-foot-high entrance?

He quickly decided on his preferred course; he couldn't risk not knowing. Shuffling beneath the portrait, he entered the passage and stood up. Lifting the orcite lamp from its bracket, he turned the compressor and carried it up the staircase, climbing higher and higher and higher. Gradually and with each successive spiral, he lost all sense of direction.

After what seemed like an age, Redwald noticed the first trickles of cool moonlight spilling down the steps ahead of him. Hurrying upwards, he turned the last spiral and found himself in a long attic space, stretching away into the darkness beneath rough-hewn, cobwebbed rafters. The staircase itself rose beside a tall, barred window but was caged into its own corner by two chain-link screens, separating it from the rest of the room. Redwald climbed the last few steps, drew the bolt on the cage door and entered the room proper.

It seemed for a moment as if only his end of the room existed. The combined moon and lamplight revealed only the caged staircase, the tall window, and about fifteen feet of rafters and floorboards before the remainder of the room was lost in darkness. Redwald shivered.

Postponing his foray into the dark, he turned to look through the tall, barred window. Peering into the distance, he could see the valley below, the snaking river Trew, and even the tawdry banners of Hawtree's Folly, flapping and rustling from atop Martingale's Work. What he could not see, however, were any of the Manor's grounds or the village itself. These were obscured from view by the two rooves that extended past the window and sloped down to meet at a lead gutter, funnelling water to a stone gargoyle. A locked maintenance door to the right of the window opened out on to a small platform, allowing repair works to the roof. Redwald frowned. Given its position, set back into the Manor's structure and facing away from the Rise, Redwald suspected this window would be invisible from everywhere but Hawtree's Folly.

Bearings regained, Redwald turned back to the void behind him. He felt a tension in the pit of his stomach. Without being able to say precisely why, he expected to find something *very* nasty up here.

He held the lamp as high as the low ceiling would permit and gently increased the pressure on the orcite crystal, bracing himself for what he might see.

With each twist of the compressor, the yellow lamplight pushed back the clinging shade by another few inches. First, Redwald saw nothing more than additional rafters. Then, stepping forward, the rusted foot of a small bed came into view, followed by a mattress and an equally rusted headboard. Strewn on the floor around the bed were piles of toys and books, which cast grotesque, shrinking shadows as he approached. Finally, the lamplight revealed the far wall, where stood a dirty toilet, an equally filthy sink, a tin bath, and a run-down wardrobe. Redwald stopped beside the bed and looked around the room once more. This was apparently it.

Did someone *actually* sleep here? If so, who were they? It seemed an odd place for it, up here among the beams of the roof, the dust, and the spiders. Far from homely, there were neither wallpaper nor pictures here and even the floorboards were coarse. Instead, set into the beams at equal intervals were metal loops, screwed fast to the wood. The same went for the bed, where metal loops were spaced along the frame.

Somewhat underwhelmed, Redwald crouched to inspect the toys at his feet. They were old, roughly made and simple, but well-loved. Alphabet blocks tumbled like scree over little wooden animals, while a ragdoll with odd button eyes and missing hair watched him from the foot of the bed. The books were simple too, the kind one might use to teach a child to read. Gingerly lifting one from the floor with his handkerchief, Redwald began to flick through *Alfred and Isabella Visit the Bath-House*. It was a dull story, in which children could learn about proper bathing etiquette by seeing Isabella admonish Alfred on his numerous mistakes. Redwald was only half-reading it when he turned a page and stopped abruptly. His finger had touched something coarse and stiff, something foreign.

138

Moving his spectacles further down his nose, he leaned in close and angled the book towards the lantern. Caught in the binding and trailing out across the page was a black, bristly hair. It was not, however, a Human hair. Noticeably thicker, longer and more crooked than any Human might grow, this hair, Redwald suspected, had been shed by a Hob.

His stomach plunged. Were these . . . *Morrimer's* chambers? Carefully replacing the book exactly as he had found it, Redwald rose to his feet. Surely, *surely* these couldn't be the quarters of the *Head Butler*? But then, Redwald recalled, Hawtree's disdain for Morrimer had been evident. His heart suddenly racing, he looked about, ensuring he had touched nothing else and that no evidence remained of his having been there. Once satisfied, he took the lamp, re-bolted the door and hurried back down the stairs. Did Hawtree really dislike the Hob *that* much? If so, why? Redwald then recalled what Charteris had told him; that Hawtree himself had been a servant here. Had Morrimer been Giles' master? Might he, in the course of Giles' service, have given the man some reason to resent him? What could it have been? *Either way,* Redwald thought as he continued downwards, *far better that nobody know about this visit.* Morrimer, in particular, would be embarrassed by the books. It was odd for a butler not to be wholly literate; it might even be a secret that Morrimer kept from Hawtree himself.

Coming to the bottom of the stairs, Redwald replaced and dimmed the lamp, before ducking under the portrait. As he shuffled past the bookcase, he pressed the sunken stud a little further into the wood so that it sprang back out with a click. Standing up, he heard a slight hiss and the creak of weight-laden ropes behind him as the case slid back into position. The concealment charm took effect and the seam between bookcase and wall was invisible once more.

Redwald, sobered a little by the sudden panic, took a quick draught from his hipflask, emptying it. *Lesson learnt,* he thought, *straying on a client's private property isn't a good idea after all.* Having wasted enough time poking about the poor Hob's quarters, Redwald resolved to find Morrimer; he needed those missing weapons. Retrieving his empty plate and glass, he headed back out into the party, noting as he went that the Gun Room door remained unguarded.

Redwald tried to calm himself as he picked his way down one of the grand staircases. There was absolutely no reason for Morrimer to suspect Redwald of intruding, unless the magician's own nerves betrayed him. Depositing his used tableware at the end of the buffet, Redwald skirted the entrance hall once more and made for the concealed servants' entrances. Before he could even find such a door, however, a footman emerged from one carrying a tray of Arrovênnes.

There ensued a short discussion which began with Redwald explaining that he wanted to see Morrimer wherever he might be and that there was no need to disturb the butler by bringing him out into the party. It ended with the victorious footman heading off to do precisely this. *Clearly*, Redwald surmised, *it was anathema in the Hawtree household for a guest to even glimpse the inner service rooms.* He waited a safe distance from the wall and sipped a fresh glass of Arrovênnes; a consolation prize from the obliging footman.

A few moments later, the door opened again and the footman re-appeared with the jowly Hob in tow. Redwald needn't have worried about distressing him. For all that Morrimer might ultimately be responsible for a team of hundreds, on whom the success of this evening depended, he carried the burden very lightly. To the extent he displayed any emotion at all, he seemed rather bored.

"Thank you, Toku," Morrimer said, gently dismissing the footman. Redwald echoed the thanks as the young man swept off with his tray of wine. "How may I help you Mr de Cordonnay?"

"It's in connection with the case. I was hoping to ask you about Sir Julius' weapons collection, if I may?"

140

"Of course, sir."

"Thank you, I appreciate you're busy so I'll try and be brief. Firstly, I don't believe the Gun Room guard have started their watch yet, would they be able to start tonight? I'm just concerned that if we delay . . ."

"My sincere apologies, sir," Morrimer said, frowning, "I don't follow." Redwald grimaced. *Giles.*

"Ah, I see. I spoke to Mr Hawtree earlier, he said he would ask you to put a constant guard on the Gun Room. Perhaps he hasn't mentioned it, though." Morrimer's expression shifted subtly. It was the merest flutter of a muscle, a whisper of a twitch, so minute that Redwald was hardly certain that he had seen it at all. Indeed, so tiny was the expression that Redwald took a moment to figure out exactly what it was, before tentatively concluding that it had, in fact, been utter disgust, quickly and expertly smothered. The moment passed in a heartbeat and Morrimer resumed his stately, if downtrodden, bearing.

"I will send two men up as soon as we finish speaking."

"Thank you," Redwald said. "Essentially, we're trying to limit access to potential murder weapons and Sir Julius' collection seems an obvious source, better to have it guarded."

"I agree, sir."

"On that theme," Redwald said, pulling the page of copied lists from his pocket and handing it to Morrimer, "I have tagged all the weapons listed under '*Suspects*' with red ribbons so that I can track them. All the same, could I ask that the guard check in on them from time to time, just to see that they're still on their stands? I'll be checking myself," he said, brandishing the notebook, "but it would be good to have a spare pair of eyes on that."

141

"Of course, sir. I will see to that too. However, may I enquire as to the purpose of the '*Missing*' list?"

"Their stands in the Gun Room are empty and I was rather hoping you might know where they are. It's important that all potential weapons are accounted for." Morrimer scanned the list, nodding.

"I shall check our records, but I believe these are out for cleaning. Only a few items are allowed off the premises at any one time, to protect the integrity of the collection should anything happen to them."

"Is that likely? Could they be stolen in transit, for example?" Morrimer paused in thought.

"I would not call it *likely*. Sir Julius established the practice of sending them with an armed guard for added security, a practice the estate continues. However," Morrimer said, reluctantly, "nothing is impossible and I'm not myself aware of the restorer's own security arrangements."

"I see, and if a weapon were to be lost in transit . . . ?"

"In theory, the restorers would compare the inventory list we sent them with those weapons that actually arrived and alert us as soon as they discovered a discrepancy. However, that has never happened, so I'm not sure if . . ."

"They actually check."

"I'm afraid so, sir." Redwald chewed on that for a moment before pulling out his notebook. He flicked it open and looked down at the names of the missing suspect weapons. *Ausburger. Waters. Villantine.* They stood out so clearly they may as well have been written in gold leaf.

"May I ask who is restoring the guns?"

"Taylor & Booth, of Miniver Row, sir." Redwald tutted. Miniver Row was back in Athonstone, further than he had expected to go.

"Fine, I know Miniver Row. I think it might be wise for me to pay Messrs. Taylor and Booth a visit, if only to tag the remaining suspects." *Or find one missing.* He downed his Arrovênnes.

"Very good sir. May I organise a train ticket for you? I believe Dr Asplund carries an emergency supply for his duties as Seneschal."

"That would be very kind, thank you. You wouldn't also happen to know when the trains run would you?"

"I believe the first train stops at a quarter past six in the morning, sir. After that you may expect one every three hours."

"Very well," Redwald said heavily. "In that case, I had better take my leave for tonight."

"Very good sir. I shall send the train tickets and restorer's details to the Double Standard for you. I would also be happy to inform Mr Hawtree of your intentions."

"Thank you, Morrimer. I really appreciate your help."

"My pleasure, sir. Anything else I can do before you go?" Redwald paused, keenly aware of the empty hipflask in his pocket. He weighed it up for a moment before getting hold of himself.

"No that's fine, but please give my regards to Alice when you have a moment."

CHAPTER 8

A Tight Spot and a Big Case

"Athonstone – 16 Elensis 2310. His Majesty the High King today approved the attainder of Athelwulf Mullen, formerly The Rt. Chiv. Earl of Barrowmill on grounds of gross corruption, abuse of feudal privilege, and murder with malice aforethought. The sentence, handed down by Sir Alphyn Iudex, Chief Justice of the Court of Feudatories, deprives the House of Mullen of the Earldom, as well as the Baronies of Greesly and Netherford and sentences Mullen to death. The attainder follows the three-month long trial of Mullen, following the murder of his seneschal, the Reverend Leofric Lane, after the latter's discovery of irregularities in the feudal accounts."

The Crown Chronicle – Front Page – 16 Elensis 2310.

"SO RUDE!" Redwald's eyes jerked open. Groaning as he awoke, he pulled his gown close about him. "REALLY, I mean, really, what a ghastly way to carry on!" Outside the window, patchwork fields and solitary oaks glistened gold beneath the frost and rising sun. Inside, Redwald grasped the handle of his umbrella for comfort and stifled his nausea. Were he not hungover, the gentle rise and fall of the thundering train might have been relaxing.

"Mother, please just . . ."

"No! It's a disgrace, the way people behave these days. We'll have to find another one now!" It seemed to Redwald that the two-person commotion was drawing closer and, given the racket, dragging heavy cases with them. He readied himself.

Soon enough and as predicted, two faces appeared in the compartment window. *Shit.* He remembered those faces; they had joined him on the initial journey from Athonstone. The source of his discomfort, however, was not so much the presence of these people as his inability to remember their names. To his frequent embarrassment, Redwald's memory was as selective as it was potent and while he *never* forgot a face, he *rarely* remembered the associated name. *Not that it really matters,* he thought as he heaved himself upright, *calling a dog's turd delicious doesn't make it breakfast.* In any event, he doubted they would remember his name either. The younger of the two beamed at him as she slid the compartment door open.

"Mr de Cordonnay!" *Shit.* "How have you been?"

"Well, thank you." He had been about to say 'asleep' but thought better of it. "Yourselves?"

"Awful," the mother responded.

"Jolly good," Redwald said, his eyes bleary and his voice gravelly, "here, let me help with those." Stifling his self-inflicted pain, he stood and lifted their cases one by one on to the rack.

"I really should go back and say something!" The elder woman said to the younger, ignoring Redwald.

"Mother, leave it be. He had every right, it *was* a reserved compartment. Thank you so much Mr de Cordonnay, that's very kind of you," the daughter said as Redwald settled back into his corner. She looked positively mortified by her mother's behaviour.

"No problem," Redwald growled, resting his beleaguered head against the window frame.

"I mean really, would it have killed him to just let us sit there? Selfish, scruffy little man," the elder woman continued shrilly as she harrumphed into a seat. Redwald rubbed his fingers into his temples. Some people were too loud. "Untidy little devil he was too, built like a farmer and as poorly shaved. Didn't even take his hat off indoors. I've *never* been so insulted!" Given the wealth of material Redwald found that claim surprising.

"It's nice to see you again," the younger woman said hurriedly, sitting next to her mother as the latter stared sulkily out of the window. "Are you heading home? Oooh, did you solve your case?!"

"Don't be silly Elisa, he clearly can't tell you anything, it will all be confidential," the mother snapped. Redwald breathed a sigh of relief. *Elisa, that was it. Elisa . . . Brenchley, Bisley, no . . . Bewley.*

"I'm afraid the details *are* confidential," Redwald said to a deflated-looking Elisa, "but no, I haven't solved it, yet." Elisa's eyes widened.

"Ah!" She said conspiratorially, "so you're chasing a lead?!"

"Something like that."

"Is it a murder? Any suspects?" She asked, as her mother rolled her eyes. "Could it be *the butler?* Is there a butler?" Redwald laughed.

"Ha! I'm not so sur . . . . suuhuuuurr," he finished, covering his mouth as he yawned. Elisa's cheeks flushed.

"Oh I'm so sorry, I've been so rude, I hope we didn't wake you up. I know it's early, we were napping ourselves when . . ." she glanced at her mother before stopping short.

"No, no, don't worry," Redwald said, "I never sleep in public." Generally true, but then he generally never got up this early either. Something had to give. "Anyway, how have you been? You were in Stenmoor to see your uncle, I believe?" Elisa's blush quickly faded and before long she was chatting happily away about her uncle, her trip to Stenmoor, and her plans to meet her sister later that day. Aside from the apparently urgent and unnecessary reminder that said sister was a Clerk at the Court of Feudatories (*don't you know*),

146

Mrs Bewley said nothing, preferring to purse her lips at the passing countryside instead.

Having spent another reasonably pleasant journey in conversation with Elisa, Redwald bid farewell to the Bewleys at Kingsmarch station some time later, before walking across town to Miniver Row. He vainly hoped the walk might help his hangover, but it left him only sweatier, marginally more awake and, to his surprise, paranoid. During his walk, he could have sworn on multiple occasions that someone was following him, but every time he turned to look he saw nothing but the usual crowds of Athonites who, by metropolitan custom, were looking anywhere but at each other and certainly not at him. So strong was this feeling, that Redwald even wondered if it might be *him* trying a new form of torment, but that didn't make any sense. *He* didn't go in for subtlety. As it was, Redwald chalked the feeling up to the prior night's excesses, cursed himself for his stupidity and ploughed onwards. He had a job to do.

Stretching between Duke Lane to the north and Silk Road to the south, Miniver Row was more a covered shopping arcade than an actual street. Book-ended by two pairs of wrought-iron, gilded gates, it boasted some of the most prestigious and expensive emporia in the capital; the sorts of places which did not display price tags, as their customers had no need of them. Weaving between carriages and pedestrians as he crossed Duke Lane, Redwald slipped into the arcade just as the heavens opened.

Outside, pedestrians shrieked and giggled as they hurried to find shelter from the rain, but the noise was oddly muffled in the arcade itself. Redwald, striding purposefully towards Taylor & Booth, felt as though he were trespassing in a cathedral. Wealthy customers wafted between shops like worshippers between altars, the stained-glass canopy of the arcade making a persistent echo of their murmured chatter and well-heeled footfall, while patrolling doormen in green and gold livery looked askance at Redwald as he passed, his hurried demeanour disrupting the Row's almost spiritual ambience.

Redwald ignored them all, he was too distracted. Flicking his notebook open as he walked, he looked down at the enchanted map. One red droplet remained firmly in place within the Hawtree Manor outline, while another was moving slowly along one wall. A third droplet, the largest, was pressed so close against the edge of the page that it was almost flat. It might have been naïve to assume Sir Julius' collection was entirely within Martingale-on-Trew, but it mattered little. So long as Alice remained in the village, she was safe. All Redwald need do now was tag the remaining suspect weapons and any would-be assassin could be tracked.

Redwald wiped the sweat from his brow as he swept past windowfuls of gold watches, austere hats, and silk scarves. The thought of a lost weapon unnerved him. What unnerved him more, however, was the creeping feeling that he might *prefer* that eventuality. Identical orcite chandeliers, repeating along the arcade as though reflected eternally between two mirrors, whipped overhead as he strode determinedly onward. What was better; to continue the waiting game and guarantee Alice's safety or start the chase and *maybe* win the resolution he so craved?

Eventually he arrived outside a window that bore the neatly painted legend *Taylor & Booth, Antique Armourers and Restorers Est. 2186*, yet it was the frenzied mass of metal behind the glass that caught Redwald's eye. Racks of swords with etched blades and jewel-encrusted handles fanned out like peacock tails between two Giant helms, while at the centre four transparent, wire-veined ailicin shards emanated from behind a winged cuirass and glittered like dragonfly wings.

Redwald paused to examine the cuirass for a moment, before tearing his eyes away and pushing through the front door. A small bell tinkled as he entered, causing the other customers to briefly look up at him before continuing to browse. Briefcase in one hand and umbrella in the other, he headed for the leather-topped counter at the back of the shop, carefully picking his way between stands of pistols and racks of sabres.

"Good morning sir," said a voice like singing glass, delicate, tuneful, but somehow sharp. "How may I help you?" His manners forsaking him, Redwald arrived at the counter without properly looking up at the voice's owner. Setting his briefcase on the floor, he rummaged in his jacket pocket and produced a letter of introduction from Morrimer, sealed with the Hawtree arms.

"Thank you," he growled, looking up at the woman for the first time. "I have a . . . .," he paused, surprised, before quickly continuing," . . . a letter from the Hawtree Estate. I understand some of their weapons are here for cleaning?" He handed her the letter, placed the enchanted ribbon on the counter, and explained the reason for his visit, hoping she had failed to notice his initial surprise.

The woman behind the counter was an Avenar. Although Avenar looked far more like Humans than either Hobs or Giants, they could be distinguished from the former by their 'hair' or, in places, lack of it. Hers was short, black, and patterned with regular white spots like the feathers of a starling, for that is exactly what they were; soft, downy feathers. As she and Redwald talked, she ducked down behind the large mechanical till and extracted a ledger, to verify that the Hawtree weapons had, in fact, arrived. Moving a slender finger down the columns, Redwald noticed the loosely connected scales on the backs of her fingers and forearms where a Human woman might have soft hair. Her eyes, moving slowly down the page, were livid yellow and fringed with minute scales instead of eyelashes.

To begin with, an Avenar working as a restorer was odd. Generally in that trade and others like it, such as watchmaking or engraving,

Hobs predominated because of their visual acuity at close range. By contrast, Avenar eyes, famously powerful over long distances, could become strained when performing close-up work, necessitating the kind of reading glasses currently balanced on this woman's pointed nose. What had really surprised Redwald, however, was that she was female. The frequency of female births among the Avenar varied by latitude, but in all cases was very low relative to that of males. As a consequence, northern or 'civilised' Avenar women formed the nobility of their respective states and led lives both defined and constrained by their power. Finding a tan, northern Avenar woman behind a shop counter was therefore comparable to finding Emphoras IX shining shoes at Kingsmarch Station.

"It says here that a consignment from the Hawtree estate arrived on Khorsday the 36th, sir. Are these the weapons you're referring to?"

"Yes, I believe so."

"Very well sir," she said reaching for the ribbon, "I can take this upstairs and ask someone to . . ."

"Actually," Redwald said, retrieving the ribbon before she could take it, "I would prefer to inspect the weapons myself, if you don't mind." She fixed him with a piercing stare.

"I assure you our staff are more than capable."

"I'm sure they are," Redwald said, "but this ribbon's enchantment requires that I tie the knot myself. Otherwise, I can't guarantee the security of the weapon. I'd also like to see for myself that all the weapons have arrived safely. For my own sanity, if nothing else." She looked down at the letter.

"Ordinarily we do not permit non-personnel to visit the workshop," she said coolly, folding and pocketing the letter, "however, Mr Thesk has been a good friend to this firm since its foundation, so I suppose we can make an exception. Please, follow me." She ushered him through the counter hatch to a door marked PRIVATE, set into the rear wall. Unlocking the door, she then led him up a set of wooden stairs which climbed half a storey before doubling back on themselves.

"Mr Thesk?" Redwald asked as he followed her up the stairs.

"Yes sir, Morrimer Thesk."

"Ah yes, he never told me his surname. I'm afraid I didn't catch your name either."

"My name is Lophorina, sir." *Just* Lophorina. She would once have been Lophorina *of* somewhere; a privilege of nobility doubtless sacrificed in her departure from the Continent.

Lophorina crested the stairs and beckoned Redwald through into the workshop. The room was the same size as the floor below and just as busy, but instead of polished weapons on immaculate display, it was full of industry and craft. The walls were hung with tools of more varieties and sizes than Redwald could count. Pipe cleaners, pliers, paintbrushes, and planes jostled for space alongside hammers and awls, boxes of nails and tins of paint. Angled towards the minimal light from the arcade-facing window, the workbenches were spotted with restorations in progress, generally held in place by padded vices or else carefully dismantled and laid out piece by piece. One dress sword, however, was having its filigree touched in by an old Hob, who held the piece delicately in his lower pair of hands while working with his upper. *It must be nice to actually see progress in one's work,* Redwald thought, stifling a hangover-induced burp.

"Wiatrak," Lophorina said, approaching a Giant polishing a suit of armour, "I believe you took delivery of the Hawtree inventory, did you not?"

"The lot that came with a guard?" Wiatrak said, turning around to look down at her. "Yeah I took 'em. Made a start on 'em a few days ago, but I ain't finished yet. Gotta finish this first." *This* was a suit of plate armour that had once belonged to a Guard of the Blood. At almost nine feet tall, it towered even over Wiatrak who, being neither male nor female but a semale of *hes* species, was a little over seven.

"I see. Do you have them to hand? Mr de Cordonnay here would like to inspect the weapons *in person*." Wiatrak's rust-coloured forehead furrowed beneath a pair of ridged black horns.

"Ah you needn't worry about their security sir, I takes good care of 'em . . ."

"I'm sure you do," Redwald said, somewhat impatiently, "but I just need to check, for my own sake, that they've all arrived safely and are still here. I also need to tag a few of them with this ribbon."

"Ah no bother, I can do that meself," Wiatrak said, holding a hand out for the ribbon.

"No," Redwald snapped as his head pounded, "I appreciate the offer, but I and *I alone* need to do that; it's a condition of the enchantment. Now, if you wouldn't mind, please could you show me to these weapons?" Redwald flicked his notebook open to the list and presented it to Wiatrak.

"Alright sir," se said, a little huffily, "let's put yer mind to rest." A few minutes later, Wiatrak returned from the storeroom, placed a heavy-duty crate on the workbench and removed the lid. "How's about you read me yer list and I'll pull 'em out and show 'em to you. Then you can be nice an' certain." Brushing the Giant's condescension aside, Redwald did exactly that.

"Bowstrong 998?" Wiatrak lifted it from the protective straw in the crate and laid it on the bench. Redwald ticked it off his list.

"Klosterburg repeating, mother of pearl handle?" Se lay that one out too. "Quendle Type XIIA?" This process continued and in due course both the Villantine and the Waters made their appearance. Ashamed though he was to say it, Redwald was almost a little disappointed. By the time he arrived at the bottom of his list, he had resigned himself to the waiting game.

"Right," Redwald said, wearily, "last one; Ausburger Snaplock – c. 2120 – misshapen trigger." Wiatrak rummaged through the straw for a few moments before stopping, confusion spreading across hes face. Redwald and Lophorina waited. Se rummaged again more vigorously, to no avail, before running a hand wearily over hes long caprine face.

"'Ang on, it'll be 'ere somewhere." Redwald felt his stomach lurch, though he couldn't say whether it was excitement or fear. The Giant moved past Redwald and Lophorina, the floorboards creaking with every step of hes huge frame as se checked the length of hes workbench for the Ausburger. Redwald himself scanned. Apart from the nine guns they had just ticked off, he could see no others. Wiatrak cast hes eyes across the other benches from the back of the room. "Will, Jamie!" Two Hobs further down the room turned slowly around.

"Lookin' fer an Ausburger Snaplock, 22nd century, bent trigger. Seen it?" They muttered amongst themselves for a moment before agreeing they hadn't. "Ask Rufus will you?" In response, one of them grabbed a sheathed swordstick that lay next to him, leant forward and prodded an elderly Hob who was sat at the front workbench.

"RUFUS!" he bellowed at the apparently deaf old Hob. "HAVE YOU SEEN A 22nd CENTURY AUSBURGER SNAPLOCK WITH A BENT TRIGGER?" Redwald could not hear the response, but it appeared to be something along the lines of *yes, course I have, they're not very well made and they bend all the time.* "NO

RUFUS, RECENTLY." To this the elderly Hob merely shook his head. "Sorry, mate!" the swordsticker shouted back to the Giant. "Nothing doing at our end!" Wiatrak frowned.

"Could've sworn I'd seen it. Was working on a Snaplock, I'm sure." The horizontal pupils bisecting Wiatrak's enormous brown eyes flicked back and forth across the room, as if the weapon might suddenly appear before them. Redwald, however, was circling the name *Ausburger. The chase has begun.*

"Wiatrak," Lophorina said, her voice razor-sharp now, "did you check the consignment when it arrived?" The Giant rummaged in the straw again, pulled out a sheet of paper, and handed it to Lophorina. It was the inventory.

"Yeah, I checked 'em off when they arrived, jus' like yer s'posed to. Was all here on delivery."

"Then where . . ." she began, but Redwald cut her off.

"Apologies for interrupting, but if one of the weapons is missing . . ."

"We will sweep our premises fully, I assure you."

"Thank you, but I actually need information."

"What sort of information?" Lophorina asked.

"Anything, everything you can tell me about the Ausburger Snaplock. Where it was made, what it's made *of,* how many of them were produced, any distinguishing features of *that particular weapon* apart from the bent trigger; I need to understand both the extent to which it's unique and the features that make it so. If I don't actually have the thing to hand, I need to be able to describe it with sufficient precision for any tracking spell or protection charm to work." So dictated the Third Law of Magic - *The efficacy of a spell is*

154

directly proportional to the precision of said spell. Lophorina looked over at her colleague.

"Wiatrak? Do you think we could do that?"

"Yeah, I s'pose we could," se said, looking away along with workbench. "Shouldn't be too much trouble, I jus' . . ." The Giant froze.

"What is it?" Lophorina asked. Wiatrak's eyes had settled on a pile of rags at the far end of the bench where it met the wall. Without another word, se walked over to the pile, picked it up, and turned around with a smile on hes face. Redwald's stomach dropped. Sure enough, when the Giant unfolded the rags, there lay a neat little Snaplock pistol with a bent trigger.

"Told yer I'd worked on it," the Giant said, "all safe an' sound."

"*Excellent,*" Redwald said curtly, scowling at the corpse of his only lead as Wiatrak set it down on the workbench.

Simultaneously disappointed and ashamed for being so, Redwald dispensed with his remaining business as quickly as possible. Lophorina and Wiatrak examined the weapon specifications and confirmed what Laetizja had said; the Ausburger and the Villantine were likely suspects. The Waters, however, had been disarmed along with the other '*Missing*' weapons and, consequently, was no more dangerous than a cudgel. Redwald tagged the Villantine and the Ausburger, thanked the restorers irritably, and left.

Forsaking the shelter of Miniver Row, Redwald snapped his umbrella open and began the walk back to Kingsmarch Station. The weather was worse now. Rain, wind, and thunder rolled over Athonstone, cloaking its ancient streets and imperious monuments in a sodden darkness relieved only by the sharp crackle of lightning. Stilted or Giant lamplighters strode through a sea of black umbrellas and dashing carriages, twisting the orcite compressors of lamp after lamp, while officers of the Mayoral Guard, in their plumed shakos and dark capes, directed traffic across the city's heaving junctions. Redwald, briefcase and umbrella in hand, barrelled impatiently through the lot of them.

Although he had achieved exactly what he came for, he felt as though he had wasted his time. Tagging those weapons was a necessary precaution, for sure, but would it *actually* prevent the murder? How could he know if it did? By definition, the more successful he was in preventing the potential murder, the less he could understand about how it originally happened. Having to choose between success in his task and resolution of the problem was a decision he'd never faced before. He didn't like it. Swearing to himself, he reached for his hipflask and swore again when he remembered it was empty.

Having traversed Traitors' Bridge and the swollen River Cross beneath it, Redwald decided to take a shortcut through the Sett. This maze of irregular alleyways and tiny pedestrian streets was more direct than the main roads and, overshadowed as it was by ancient timber buildings with geriatric stoops and jettied floors, a little more sheltered. Yet so severe was the storm that by the time he reached the usually busy Brock Stock, an old pillory set at a six-way junction, the place was more or less deserted. Those who had homes to go to had done just that, while the rest either languished outside in the driest places available or peered out at the rain through the steamed windowpanes of pubs. Redwald thought on the ale that awaited him at the Double Standard and hurried onward.

His shoes slapping on the wet cobbles, he had turned the corner into an empty alley and was halfway along when someone shouted at him.

"Don't move!" the voice barked over the hissing rain. Redwald, unthinkingly disobeying that instruction, turned around. Cloaked in shadow at the alley's jettied entrance, about twelve feet away, stood what appeared to be a short, broad man pointing an old service revolver at Redwald's chest. The magician felt sick.

"I have . . . I have money," he said, trying to sound calm, "I don't want any trouble." His mind raced. The alley turned left up ahead, but the corner was too far and the gunman too close for him to make a run for it. He needed another way out.

"Tough shit," the figure said, growling to disguise his identity. Something began to itch in the very back of Redwald's mind. Growl or no, he had heard that voice before. "Don't want your money, either."

"Then what . . . what do you want?" Redwald stuttered.

"It's not what I want . . . it's never what *I* want," he said, and Redwald noticed his voice cracking as if from emotion, "I need you dead. I need to . . . to protect him . . . all of us. You're getting too close to . . ." the assailant was interrupted as a violent gust of wind tore through the alley, ripping the umbrella from Redwald's shaking hand.

"The FUCK ARE YOU DOING?!"

"I just dropped it!" Redwald shouted, raising his hands to chest height, one empty and the other taut around the briefcase handle. His mind was splintering with panic when, somewhere above them, a bird cawed from its roost. *The gloves.* They were still in the end pocket of his briefcase. He needed time.

"Idiot . . . fucking IDIOT . . . he won't thank me for this," the gunman muttered, "but if he won't listen I'll . . . I'll have to . . ." He cocked the gun.

"Wait!" Redwald shouted above the thunder and, to his surprise, the gunman paused. Redwald latched on to the first thing he could

157

think of. "So you're . . . you're not alone? You're doing this for somebody else?" Ever so slowly, taking advantage of the dark and the driving rain, he began to angle the briefcase so that the end-pocket was next to his free hand.

"*Alone*," the gunman growled, lowering the gun a little, "I'm always alone . . . and I'm doing this for *me* . . . alone . . . it's not about *loyalty*, it's not about *love*, it's just self-fucking-preservation; I'm no better than the GODS-DAMNED RATS!" His voice cracked again, and he raised the gun, ready to fire.

"No! We . . . we can solve this . . . some other way," Redwald said, rain pouring down his face. "If you kill me, someone will find out." He thought of *her* then and what she would do.

"What would you know?" the gunman asked, his voice even more strangled than before. "You can hide *anything* for . . . for *years*. Just as long as people are too . . . too scared or too lazy to look." Redwald gently lifted the end-pocket flap and latched on to the gloves. "Sorry de Cordonnay, and goodbye."

A massive sheet of lightning crackled across the sky, lighting up the alley and startling both men into action. Redwald ducked, lifted the briefcase to shield himself, and tore the gloves from their pocket; the attacker pulled the trigger. The bullet burst from the gun in a tongue of flame, whirling through the air and shredding raindrops as it went. Deadly accurate, it buried itself in the broad side of the briefcase; Redwald's heart was still in the firing line. As he lifted it, Redwald spun the case and threw it towards his assailant so that the bullet, delayed by the magically expanded interior, burst out the other side at an angle and tore past Redwald's right arm. As thunder shook the alley like an earthquake, Redwald tried to sprint past his assailant and out into the street.

The silhouetted gunman, however, deflected the briefcase and side-stepped into Redwald's path. Panicked, the magician flailed in the dark and landed a blow on what felt like his attacker's eye socket, before colliding and falling into the gutter with him. The man screamed with pain and discharged a wild shot into the jetty above. Redwald, blinded by water and fear, kicked his attacker away from him with a splash before scrambling to his feet and sprinting away into the darkness.

"FUCK!" the attacker shouted and Redwald ducked as a shot hissed past his ear. He darted left, then right, then right again, forcing his shaking hand into one of the gloves as he ran. He could hear footsteps. The assailant must be mere seconds behind him. Slamming his hand against a tenement wall, Redwald pushed himself down another alley before realising it was a dead-end crowded with rubbish bins. *Shit.* He made to pull the other glove onto his right hand but stopped, horrified. His fingers dripped blood-red. Stumbling against the wall as dizziness suddenly overtook him, he hesitated. It was dangerous to transform while injured. The approaching breaths and splashing footfall of his pursuer, however, forced his bloodied hand. He wrenched the glove on.

The familiar sinking, tightening feeling was instantaneous as the walls of the alley shot into the sky above him and the rubbish bins inflated to his left and right. Yet as the cobbles beneath him grew closer and the ground stretched out in all directions, he could feel the wound in his arm split and twist. His agonised groan quickly turned to a rasping caw, his nose lengthening and hardening into a beak, his mud-caked brogues stretching into scaly claws, and his gloved fingers elongating and splitting into hundreds of shiny, black feather barbs.

The pain in what was now his wing was searing, else he would have risked flying away. Instead, he hopped into the dark, narrow spaces between the crowded bins and watched as his attacker slammed into the wall and immediately pointed his gun down the alley.

"What the FUCK?!" he bellowed upon seeing it empty. He clamped his head in his hands and paced. "WHERE ARE YOU?!" he shouted into the night. Despite the pain, Redwald kept his beak shut and crouched in the damp. "WHERE THE FUCK DID YOU GO?!" Furious, the man kicked one of the bins over, sending the lid clattering across the cobbles. Redwald scrabbled further back into the darkness. "FUCK!" Another one, fetid meat and rotten vegetables mixing with the rainwater and Redwald's blood. "WHERE ARE YOU?! BASTARD!!" This time, the kicked bin skidded back across the cobbles and crashed into the group that sheltered Redwald. The attacker cocked his pistol in frustration and began shooting clean into Redwald's sanctuary, tearing holes in the metal and spraying filth everywhere. Redwald panicked.

Launching himself off the cobbles, he raked his claws against the brick wall, swept his wings beneath him, and pushed off into the air. The attacker flinched and swore as the raven flapped out of the darkness and past his head. Banking hard at the corner, Redwald forced himself up and away from the gunman, his great black wings scooping air beneath him as his right burned with every stroke.

The downdrafts from the rain made flying difficult and though the water slipped cleanly off his oily feathers, his sticky blood did not. Heaving himself between the houses and above the slick slate rooves of the Sett, he scanned desperately for home. He needed *her* help. Though little more than a blur through the rain, the old church tower off Charnel Square caught his eye as lightning crackled through the clouds. Banking violently, he made a beeline for it.

The wind buffeted him like a rowboat on the high seas and every wingbeat cost him in energy and blood. Yet each one also dragged the tower a little closer. Urging himself onward, he thought of *her*, thought of Alice, thought of all that was at stake if he failed and somehow found the strength to keep drawing breath after freezing breath. Eventually he was upon it. Pushing himself over the parapet with the last wingbeat he could muster, he crashed into the crown spire before being slammed onto the copper roof by a downdraft.

CHAPTER 9

The Devil Himself

". . . The rich man and the baby girl rode a long way over hills and through forests towards the rich man's home. As they rode, the rich man thought about a name to give the baby girl, but he could not call one to mind. Eventually they arrived at the rich man's home; a great and mighty castle. In the castle there lived a Duke. He was an old and bitter man who lived in a small tower at the very top of the castle, where he spent all day looking at pressed flowers in the dark, behind thick shutters. Though he was very wealthy indeed, he kept a small household, had few pleasures in life and worked his servants hard. He ate cold porridge and onions and he hated fun and extravagance of any sort. Indeed, though his chambers were full of dry pressed blossoms, his once magnificent gardens were brown and bare. The rich man was his seneschal and the only person in the whole world who loved the Duke and the only person that the Duke loved.

When the Duke heard what the rich man had done, he scolded him in front of the servants and demanded that the child be taken away, but the rich man refused. Instead he allowed the little girl to live at the castle with the servants who all loved her very dearly. Time passed and the baby grew into a little girl with flame red hair. The servants taught her and played with her, but the Duke insisted that she work and made her clean all the steps up to his dark tower once a day, for he did not like her. And still the little girl was nameless . . ."

The Tale of Alynore – Traditional Tales for Growing Children, collated by Dr C.F. Twistle (Allpress) 1992

It was the voices that reached him first, then the smell of lavender. He lay there and, just for that moment, everything felt right, everything fit. Wherever he was, it was clean and warm and soft.

The voices continued in the room below, distorted slightly as they reverberated up the stone staircase.

His first mistake was to move.

"Ah! Shit," he growled, as pain shot through his arm. Peeling his eyes open, Redwald found himself at home in bed. Horrified at the thought of sleeping between his lovely clean sheets while covered in gutter-filth, he made to pull off the covers and found his arm in a sling. He also discovered, pulling back the covers with his free arm, that he was clean, and that the lavender smell was his.

There was laughter from downstairs. Grimacing, he heaved himself into a sitting position. His entire body ached, as if he'd spent the night hanging by his fingertips from a sheer rockface. Swinging his legs out of bed and putting his feet into his slippers, he rocked forward and stood with a groan.

Outside, the storm appeared to have passed with the night, though raindrops still pattered against the tall, pointed windows and the old church tower whistled ghoulishly in the breeze off the bay. Tottering across to his dressing gown, Redwald pulled it on over his damaged arm, tied it with one hand, and started to ease himself down the spiral staircase.

". . . so I . . . I had to tell her," a man said between chuckles, "that . . . that she'd been *drinking* her ear drops . . . for the past *two weeks!*" Sat beside the fire in what was usually Adriel's chair, was a lean man with a wide smile and trimmed black beard, peppered liberally with white. "Oh there you are," he said as Redwald appeared in the doorway, "bellend." Adriel herself was in Redwald's usual seat, her back to the staircase. She leapt to her feet, rounded the chair and embraced him.

"Ah!" Redwald said as she bumped into his arm.

"Sorry," she moved around to his good side and squeezed him tightly, nestling her head against his chest, "what the *hell* were you doing last night?!"

"Being shot at."

"Well I know *that!*" Adriel snapped. "You gave me *such* a scare, slamming into the roof like that. You were bloody lucky I was even in." She stepped back and looked him over. "How are you feeling?"

"Stiff."

"Wahey," the man interjected. Adriel and Redwald raised their eyebrows in unison. "Oh *you're welcome!*" He said, grinning as he sipped his tea.

"To be fair, you do have Sakha to thank for the sling and the stitches; bullet grazes aren't my thing. I'll get some cocoa for you and then I want to know *exactly* what happened." She turned to head downstairs, but before she could do so he took her arm, pulled her close and kissed her.

"Thank you."

"Thank Sakha," she said, looking up at him with a mixture of affection and concern, "and be more *careful*, won't you?" With that, she turned and headed down to the kitchen. Redwald, lowering himself gingerly into his chair, leant his head against the red leather wing and groaned.

"Don't be such a baby, it's only a graze," Sakha said.

"Thanks for patching me up, I really do appreciate it. I hope I haven't . . ."

"Honestly, it's nothing," Sakha said, "Adge did most of the prep, but she was worried about you, *obviously*, and wanted a real doctor to check you over. Clearly it had to be me . . ."

164

". . . because you'll overlook my flagrant disregard for the Abuse of Magic Act?"

"I was going to say because I'm the *best*, but whatever . . . Anyway, all I did was add a few stitches and some dermaseal paste last night, gave you something to help you sleep. Thought I'd pop back in this morning to check on you."

"Thanks, I owe you one."

"Yes mate, you do," he said with a grin, before leaning forward in his seat and adopting a more serious expression. "While we're on the subject, though, you could start by being more careful with *those* things," he said, gesturing to the gloves, which rested on the low table between them, "it would have been easier to patch you up if you hadn't made the existing wound worse."

"Duly noted," Redwald replied, "but I *did* have a good reason. They were my only way out." Sakha inclined his head; his kindly face marked with concern.

"Mate, what actually happened? Were you mugged or something?" Adriel returned from the kitchen with a steaming cup of cocoa, handed it to Redwald, and promptly took the seat on the sofa, facing the fire. She too looked concerned.

"No, it wasn't a mugging, he . . . he said he wanted to kill me." He paused then, images of blood, filth, and rain swimming before his eyes.

"You spoke to him?!" Adriel said.

"I was trying to distract him so I could get the gloves out. He said I was getting too close, that he needed to protect . . . someone." The man's voice echoed in Redwald's head. He was certain he had heard it before. What's more, he was certain he knew *where* he had heard it.

"Who do you think he's trying to protect?" Sakha asked.

"*Must* be someone connected with the case," Redwald said. He then explained to them the Hawtree case, the lead he had unsuccessfully followed to Athonstone, and the peculiar challenge of preventing an incipient murder. "So, logically, he must be protecting the would-be murderer, or *murderers*. I thought it would be pre-meditated, but this . . . this is insane."

"Who are your suspects?" Adriel asked.

"I don't know," Redwald said, "bloody village is a tapestry of motive. They *all* seem to hate Giles Hawtree, but then, even he might benefit financially."

"In my experience," Adriel said, "these things are rarely about the money, but why attack the wife you like and not the husband you hate?"

"I . . . I don't know . . . yet."

"Anyway, did you get a good look at him? We'll need to go to the Mayoral Guard about this."

"No," Redwald said, "It's not worth the risk, if they find out about those gloves . . ."

"Redwald, the man tried to *kill* you!" Adriel said.

"He wouldn't be the first . . ." Adriel scowled at him.

"That's not fair."

"I didn't mean it *that way*. All I'm saying is that I can look after myself, within reason. Anyway, no I didn't see his face. Although . . ." Redwald said as he thought back on it, "there was a scuffle. I'm fairly sure I punched him in the eye and I definitely kicked him."

166

"Well, whoever it was will have a big black bruise right about now," Sakha said, "might turn yellow in a few days, but until then he should be easy to spot." He looked down at his watch. "Anyway, I'm afraid I'd better be going, my shift starts fairly soon. Thanks for the tea, Adge."

"My pleasure, thanks so much for coming," Adriel said, as Sakha got to his feet.

"Yes, thank you. I can't . . ."

"Mate, first-born child will do!" He pointed to the sling. "Dermaseal paste will help, but you'll still need to give that arm a rest for a few days and no more flying, ok?"

"Ok." Sakha patted him on his good arm.

"And be *careful* with these lunatics out there; I can't keep giving you freebies," he chuckled. "Seriously, look after yourself."

"Sooner I solve the case, safer I'll be." Redwald replied. Sakha shot him a look which succinctly expressed the concept of *bellend,* before following Adriel down the stairs to the front door. Redwald waved from the arched window as his friend headed down the street towards Charnel Square. He turned to find Adriel in the doorway. "I'm so sorry to have frightened you, sweetheart." She nodded.

"That's alright. I'm just glad you're safe," she said, crossing the room to hug him again, "and I really can't complain about *your* job being dangerous."

"I wasn't going to mention that . . ."

"*I wasn't going to mention that,*" she said, dropping her voice by a few octaves and heading for her tea, "*he wouldn't be the first person to try and kill me . . .*"

167

"Oh shut up," he said, grinning. She briefly returned his smile, before soberly looking into her tea.

"How have you been? You haven't had a . . . ?"

"Not yet," he snapped, cutting her off. She raised an eyebrow at him. "Sorry, it's just . . . he'll come when he comes. Nothing I can do about it, so I prefer not to dwell."

"I understand sweetie. Will . . . will you stay here with me a bit longer?"

"I'm sorry, darling, I really need to get back to the village. The longer I leave it, the greater the risk to Alice." Adriel nodded again. "I'll try and stay safe." She smiled.

"Better had, or I'll kill you myself."

By the time he kissed her goodbye at Kingsmarch Station, she had fed him, refilled his hipflask, and helped him retrieve his briefcase and umbrella. He had not expected to find either, but, at her suggestion, they had ventured into the Sett together to try their luck. Happily, neither item had been stolen. Less happily, they had instead been consigned to a rubbish-heap in the alley's corner, presumably by the same person who had tried and failed to prise one open with the other, further damaging them both. Having first calmed Redwald down, Adriel had helped him carry them back to Charnel Square, where he picked the shards of glass from between the pages of his books, patched the holes in his briefcase, and set to cleaning both items with soap and sponge.

Taking his preferred end compartment, Redwald stowed the now-spotless briefcase and umbrella in their usual places and waved to Adriel as the train pulled away. Gradually, inexorably, she slipped out of sight. Redwald paused for a moment, sighing, before compulsively plucking his notebook from a jacket pocket and checking the map. He saw one tiny dot moving about the Manor near a larger stationary blob and, on the very edge of the page, a larger ink spot just starting to separate from a slightly smaller one: nothing unexpected.

He shoved the notebook irritably back into his pocket, brushing the soft leather of the gloves as he did so. Sakha's warning notwithstanding, he would not be caught without them again. He sat for a moment, quietly contemplating the view as the city melted first into suburbs and then into rolling green countryside. Yet it was only a temporary respite; Adriel's question quickly resurfaced. *Why attack the wife you like and not the husband you hate?* Determined to distract himself from the case, and from her absence, Redwald leant forward with a groan, rummaged with his good arm inside the briefcase and retrieved his book. The sling initially made it hard to get comfortable, but soon his own troubles were forgotten in favour of the Third Siege of Jenever and Parothia VIII's imminent, grisly fate. For the moment at least, all was quiet.

Then he felt the gust.

Ice-cold, it whistled violently through the sealed compartment, ending as abruptly as it began. Redwald froze and shut his eyes, waiting for the inevitable. When it came, there was no mistaking it; a ragged, desperate gasp tearing the silence, as if someone on the cusp of drowning had just resurfaced. He *had* been due.

"**What are you reading, Redwald?**" A voice asked from the corner of the empty compartment. Gilded with a drawling accent so patrician that Redwald sounded like a street urchin by comparison, the voice was oddly pock-marked and grating, as if damaged by centuries of screaming. It was a strained voice, a harsh voice, such that speech itself sounded painful. "**Reeeedwaaald . . . not talking to me?**" Something in the compartment moved and Redwald heard uneven, stumbling footsteps before the adjacent seat cushion warped with a body's weight. "**Cooome ooon, boy, let's have a look.**" He flinched as a freezing hand rested on his leg

169

and someone leaned in close, their breath crackling in his ear like crushed paper. "**Ooooh yes, Jenever. Did you know, Parothia herself once asked for my help?**"

"I don't care."

"**Oooh you should; you're in exalted company. Would you believe I actually granted her wish? Could do the same for you if you'd just . . .**"

"Piss off," Redwald said, rage bleeding into his fear and self-loathing, "please just . . . just leave me alone." The hand's cold clamminess began to seep through his trouser leg like a melting ice cube.

"**Now Redwald, dear boy, is that any way to speak to such an *old* friend? Come now, how long has it been for you since last I visited?**" Redwald didn't respond. If he didn't engage, he might escape this quicker. "**Teeeell meeee,**" the voice whined as the cold, wet grip on Redwald's leg tightened. "**For my part, I last saw you in 2329; you *really* won't like that one. Your turn, *tell me*.**" Redwald shook his head, eyes still clamped shut. A pause. Slowly, the foreign hand released his leg before Redwald felt the weight shift from the seat. Staggered footsteps and a creak were followed by blissful silence, broken only by the rumbling of the train.

Redwald let out a slow, shuddering breath and opened his eyes in relief.

"**TELL ME!**" The demon roared, his scarred, lesioned face inches from Redwald's own, and with such force that the window seemed to ripple in its frame.

"5 MONTHS, 5 MONTHS!" Redwald screamed, scrabbling back into the corner and yowling as he knocked his arm against the wall.

"Oh my dear boy, you must have been missing me," the demon said, hobbling back into the opposite seat. Redwald, still panting from the shock, jumped as a flushed conductor wrenched the door open.

"What the 'ell is goin' on in 'ere?!" he shouted, oblivious to the monster in the corner.

"Go on, kill *him*. It would be easy . . ."

"Sorry, it . . . it's nothing," Redwald stammered, trying desperately to ignore his companion's blood-red gaze and jagged grin. "It's just . . . I have a . . . its Halv . . ." he stopped himself.

"It's wha'?"

"Go on, say it, say my name," the demon cooed. His raw skin split and squelched as he leaned forward, tiny cracks flickering across his naked body like moist, crimson lightning. **"Saaaay iiiiit!"**

"It . . . it was a bad dream!" Redwald said, clutching at straws. "Yes. Woke up from a bad dream . . . I've been in hospital, see?" he said, indicating his arm, "drugs must have messed with me a bit. Sorry about that." The conductor looked him up and down.

"Ah right, sorry mate. Still, can't be too careful. Gis' a shout if yer need help disembarkin'."

"Th-thanks," Redwald said and the conductor slid the door shut behind him.

"Coward. Weakling. You could have killed him right then and there," the demon snarled, the seat cushion darkening as ice melted from his skin and his sores wept. **"Pathetic."** Redwald, heart thundering in his ears, stared out of the window and fixated on anything he could, anything but *him*. If pain had a face, it would be that one. Stretched over the creature's skeletal body was skin so

171

weak that it split with each laboured breath and so riddled with ulcers, abscesses, maceration and necroses that it was impossible to tell where one affliction began and another ended. From his scalp, red raw and cracked like sun-baked mud, to his feet, pale, wet and sloughing slimy dead skin, the monster was clothed in nothing but agony. Yet, despite all this, it was his eyes, immaculately formed, perfectly functioning, with irises the colour of fresh blood and whites as clean as untouched snow, that Redwald could not bear to meet. **"You wouldn't even do me the courtesy of using my name. I *told* you to say it."**

"I don't . . . I don't know your name. Who you were . . . before . . ."

"Don't play coy. Before *this*," he said, sweeping his hands across his body like a tarred bird opening its greasy wings, **"I was nothing. I need but a single name now, and *that* one you know. You used it when first you called me."** *As blood is to summon, so corpse is to seal, cast off conceit, and strike thou a deal.* **"Do you not remember?"** As long as he lived, Redwald would *never* forget both the appeal and the cost of black magic, but if far wiser magicians before him had fallen for the same temptation, what chance did a child have? **"Come now, say the name with me boy!"** Redwald gagged as something unseen gripped his throat. **"Say it!"**

"Huh, urrrrgh," he wheezed, as his diaphragm was wrenched sickeningly downwards, dragging air through his clenched windpipe.

"Thaaat's it!"

"I . . . urrgrgh . . . I know iiiiiit . . .," he rasped, but was interrupted by what felt like a blow to the stomach, forcing a long, strained breath past his vocal cords. "Halv . . . Haaaalva'uuusss," he gasped, eyes watering.

172

"Yeeesss!" Halva'us said, leaning back into the stained seat. The magician spluttered and coughed as the demon released his organs. **"See, just do as I tell you and your suffering will end; there's a lesson to be learnt there."** Redwald wiped the tears from his eyes with his good hand, before scrabbling for a drink. **"A debt sealed in blood is no small thing. You may have let the conductor go, but I still want . . ."**

"I'm never going to do it," Redwald said, taking a mammoth swig of whisky from his hipflask and coughing.

"You *will*, one day. Because you know as much as I do that the drinking, the handwashing, your desperate quests for professional *catharsis*, these are just crutches, helping you support the mere *illusion* of control. But with me, you could have *real* power; the entire world in chains at your feet, your word as unquestioned law, and a crown to surpass all others." Redwald's fingers shook on the leather of the hipflask.

"I just want . . ."

"To save the Hawtree woman?" Redwald's eyes widened. **"Oh *yes*, I've already seen you later. As for the woman, I can save you the worry, if not the trouble; you fail. She was dead before you started."**

"No . . . I can . . . I have trackers . . . the experiment . . ." Halva'us burst out laughing, his ulcered tongue, riddled with bloody holes and stinging white matter, lolling about behind pitted lips and needled teeth.

"Take it from one who knows, boy," he said, the seat fabric clinging to his blistered back as he leaned forward, **"from one who sees all ages in an instant and to whom future, past, and present are meaningless; *she was dead before you started*. You cannot control this."** Redwald, trembling, raised the hipflask

173

to his lips again. "**Back on** *that* **crutch I see. It won't help.** *Nothing* **will help apart from . . ."**

"Never," Redwald said, swallowing a mouthful of whisky before it could burn his tongue, "I told you, I will *never* do that."

"**We'll see,**" Halva'us said, rocking himself to his feet and standing on legs so thin they should not have been able to support him. Redwald looked away, disgusted. "**But I'm willing to bet that, one day, you'll be sick of your failures, of your wasted potential, of your** *crutches.* **You'll remember kneeling at my feet, naked, bloodied, with that bitch in your lap and you'll wonder,** *what if? What if I had had the guts?* **Rest assured, Redwald,** *when* **that day comes, I will be waiting to show you.**"

Uneven footfall pattered towards the door, the compartment rattled with freezing wind once again, and then there was nothing. Nothing, besides Redwald's shaky breaths and the sound of the train.

After five quiet minutes, of which Redwald counted every second, he looked back and breathed a sigh that was almost a sob. The demon, and his stains, were finally gone. Taking a deep, shuddering breath, Redwald smothered the urge to weep like a child and instead dashed straight for the lavatory at the end of the carriage. By the time he was finished there, his eyes were as red with stifled tears as were his hands with cracked, dry skin. He had scrubbed them bloody.

CHAPTER 10

Reflections of the Past

"Looking up at the statue of Elizabeth Furneaux, enthroned beneath the leafy, crimson canopy of a Tempestian Rodor and ensconced in the quadrangle of the Inn of Sorcery that bears her name, one might be forgiven for thinking that she was a scholarly, subdued sort; a distant cousin of the begowned, greying academics that roll like tumbleweed around the colleges of Penbridge or Trewcester. Scholarly she certainly was, her contributions to the magical corpus are nigh unmatched, but subdued she certainly was not. On the contrary, she was a spy, adventurer, and accomplished swordsman, who quietly but consistently cut her own path through the tangled and bloody politics of her age.

Indeed, it was this indomitable streak and capacity for action, rather than her scholarly works, that led both to the founding of Furneaux's Inn itself and to its long-standing rivalry with the Inn founded by her one-time husband and noted profligate, the Margrave of Vanehurst."

Elizabeth Furneaux; the Lady under Red, by Redwald de Cordonnay MThaum. (Gryphon Publishing) 2332

Lifting himself higher on a languid wingbeat, Redwald surveyed the scene before him as he soared through the cool night air. Sweeping gently from the Rise to Martingale's Work, the valley below was broad and flat, thick with blue trees, quilted fields and silvered crops swaying in the wind. Twisting through the valley like a calligraphic pen stroke, the mercury Trew slipped towards the gleaming domes and spires of Trewcester, while Bethin's moonlight coaxed tall shadows from their hiding places.

Watched by thousands of stars, Redwald tucked his wings in and banked, curving cleanly through the air as he sank towards the village. Excited at the prospect, he made to dive and swoop between the bridges' piers, but stopped suddenly, unnerved. The shadows here were not the tall, elegant ones that stretched across the valley, but crooked and foreboding, and though the village's stone walls and rustling thatch gleamed a cold silver, no warmth shone from out its heartless, empty windows. The Double Standard was similarly abandoned, slumped over like an unconscious derelict, while the church's Flame Eternal had been extinguished, its open doors as empty as a corpse's dull eyes.

Unsettled, Redwald thought better of play and pulled himself back into the sky. As he climbed higher, Martingale Castle rose from behind the trees to his left, pale and crumbling like a nipped sugarloaf, while Hawtree Manor loomed ahead of him like a prison, its solitary barred window glinting in the moonlight. Yet it glinted only briefly. For no sooner had the flash crossed Redwald's beady, black eyes than it was smothered by a shadow, sweeping down the Rise as if from a broken dam.

Looking instinctively to the Rise's peak, Redwald saw something that sent a chill shivering down his spine. Hauling itself over the Rise like a crocodile dragging its bulk up a riverbank was a billowing monster so vast that it eclipsed a quarter of the night's stars. Smeared across the sky like paint, the thing's body appeared to be without form, until flashes from deep within it cast momentary shadows across its churning clouds. The storm leered down at Redwald, slanted streaks of lightning for eyes and thunder for a growl. It pulled itself closer, planting a foothold on the near side of the Rise, thunderbolts tearing chunks from the ground like claws and torrents of rain gushing across bare rock. It was coming for him.

Panicked, Redwald cast around for refuge. Yet the village below was dead and empty, the Manor and Castle were swamped in nothingness and the valley was cold and bare. As the wind whipped at his feathered head, he could see the storm dragging its huge, thunderous mass closer, crackling with anticipation. He would be delicious.

176

Then, on the cusp of abandoning all hope, Redwald saw it; a distant flame across the valley from him, flickering away at the very top of Hawtree's Folly. Against the greying countryside and empty shadows, it was warm and inviting and safe, his only chance of escape. He turned and furiously beat a retreat towards the Folly, his wings flapping harder and faster than ever they had before.

Behind him, as if sensing his decision, the storm gave chase. Dragging its vast water-filled belly over the Rise, it slipped down the near side like a boar in mud and crashed into the village. Sheets of rain turned roads to rivers and fields to floods, lightning blasted trees to smoking craters, and the wind tore chimney stacks and rooves from houses, dashing them like discarded toys upon the ground. Redwald ploughed frantically onwards, certain of death if he lingered a second too long.

Yet, above the throbbing noises of thunder and heartbeat, Redwald heard another that drew his attention irresistibly back to the village, even as he fled it. In the ward of Martingale Castle stood a man with snow-white hair, bellowing up at the storm through the rain and cursing its destruction. Temporarily distracted from the hunt, the beast turned and looked down at him, its mile-high face twisting with pleasure. It paused for a moment. Then, without warning, it leant forward and flicked the grandest tower. A thunderbolt arced from the creature's murky depths and struck the stone where its formless finger made contact. The tower teetered but remained standing. The man's shouting continued and, quick as a flash, the storm's spiteful grin became a scowl. Redwald looked hurriedly away as he flew onward. He knew what came next.

Within moments the entire valley was lit by a flash so bright that the outline of Martingale's Work lingered on Redwald's retina. A thunderous rumble followed soon after, loud enough that he could feel the air ripple beneath his wings, but not so loud as to smother the noise of cracking, crumbling stone, or of a man's roar as it warped into an anguished scream. Though he couldn't say why, Redwald felt a lump rise in his throat as the Folly inched closer.

Now done with the tower, the storm turned back to its prey. Launching itself off the Rise, the creature hurtled towards him, dragging its pall across the valley floor. Redwald looked down and saw his own shadow subsumed in the suffocating darkness of his pursuer's, plunging him into despair as the creature closed the gap.

Even as the slope of Martingale's Work was rising to meet him, so too were the clouds catching up and closing in on all sides. Soon enough, he could see only the candlelit room atop the Folly. The cold air stung his throat and his wings were on the verge of failure as icy water began to hammer down upon them, dragging him slowly into the shrouded abyss below. The encircling clouds flashed as the beast crackled. It almost had him.

Redwald, flailing in the night, made a final, desperate push as the clouds finally shut around him, trapping him in darkness. Heaving himself upwards on one final downstroke, he clamped his wings to his side, put his beak down and hurtled for where he believed the Folly to be.

The wind buffeted him and the rain scratched at his eyes, but as his dive flattened, the Folly reappeared through the mist like a lighthouse in the night. He shot like an arrow over the balustrade and in through an open door, the Folly embracing him in safe arms of solid brick. Exhausted, it was all Redwald could do to arrest his dive and slump to the floor in a heap.

The storm smashed into the Folly, screaming with rage around the corners of the edifice and rattling the windows in frustration. The solitary candle was immediately extinguished as the wind tore through the open door and dragged Redwald across the floorboards. Despite his exhaustion, he scrabbled to his feet, bowed his black head, and plucked the primary flight feather of

178

each wing with his beak. Tugged clean of his skin, the quills fell limp and became gloves once more.

Staggering to his now-human feet with the gloves between his teeth, Redwald rushed to the open door and slammed it shut. Finally, he was safe. Leaning heavily against the closed door, he took a moment to catch his breath and pocketed the gloves with shaking hands. Though his heart still thundered in his chest, the room itself was quieter than a field under snow. In fact, as he pressed his head against the cold glass, the only noises he could hear were the eerie whistle of the wind around the ramparts, the patter of rain against the encircling windows, and the muffled breaths of the woman behind him.

Once recovered, Redwald pushed himself upright and turned to look at her. She knelt on the floor at the dead centre of the room, hands behind her back and head bowed, her thinning, matted hair hanging around her face like the fronds of a willow. Lightning flashed outside, casting her stooped shadow across the floor and drawing Redwald's attention to the little table behind her. There stood the candle, trailing a wisp of silver smoke like a floating cobweb.

Redwald walked over to it, his long, slow steps echoing in the mostly empty room. She whimpered as he passed but remained still. Relighting the candle, he flooded the room with the warm glow that had first attracted him, before lifting the candlestick into the air and turning around to examine her, leaning nonchalantly on the table as he did so. Perhaps *this* would help.

The first thing he noticed was the blood. Dark and sticky, her hands and bare feet were covered in it, presumably from the wounds at her wrists and ankles where she had struggled against her rough, fibrous bonds. Her silken shift was hemmed with mud and looked sweaty and soiled, clinging greasily to her bony frame as she shivered on the floor like a lamb. She seemed weak; her energy spent. Although, Redwald noticed almost in passing, she wasn't *yet* dead.

As this thought crossed his mind, his spare hand brushed against something on the table. He turned abruptly to squint at it. He could tell it was a gun but found examining the details as difficult as looking at an eye floater. Focusing on one component simply blurred the others, so while he *could* make out a fluted barrel, a pristine trigger, a hammer, and a smooth wooden handle, he could never see them all at once.

Growling with frustration, he made to pick it up. To his surprise, the handle slipped almost magnetically up into his palm, while his finger settled likewise upon the trigger. He paused for a moment, unnerved, before carefully moving his finger and tilting the mahogany handle towards the light. Yet he was quickly disappointed. For even as the rest of the gun faded into frost and the handle sharpened into focus, he saw nothing distinctive about it, no sign of the weapon's identity. He frowned. There *had* been something there before, he was certain of it. He made to inspect the barrel, but before he could do so something caught his eye. Pushing itself through the mahogany's grain like a snake through the grass, a little sliver of pale boxwood wriggled around from the other side of the handle. It was soon followed by another and then another, until hundreds of variously coloured strips were slithering together in a tight weave over the polished handle. Upon reaching critical mass, they started to slow and settle in their turn, so that a face gradually congealed out of the confusion. *Alice.*

Redwald turned and walked over to her, carrying the gun and candle with him. Without realising it, his finger had slipped back on to the trigger.

"Alice?" She didn't respond. Placing the candle on the floor between them, he knelt and reached gingerly through her greasy hair, lifting her face to meet his. Her wispy tresses parted over her

180

features as she looked up at him, a resigned expression in her large, brown eyes. A dirty rag had been tied between her teeth. He frowned and pulled it loose. "My apologies."

"It's not your fault, Redwald."

"I'm afraid it will be," he said as he got to his feet, gun in hand.

"It won't be. You can't stop what's already done." He paused then, looking down at the pistol. *Inevitable.* If that were the case, he may as well find out *how.*

"Are you ready for it?" He asked, raising the gun to her head. He *had* to know. By way of answer, she leant towards him and placed her forehead on the barrel. "No," he murmured, "it has to be the eye."

"The eye? Why is that?" An *excellent* question.

"I'm afraid I don't know. Please tilt your head backwards, the angle has to be right. Look at the ceiling." She did so, reading the initials painted on the plaster.

"I know you can't stop it, but you'll catch him afterwards, won't you?"

"We'll see." Redwald heard the creak of stairs and the pounding of feet behind the door to his right. The sole internal door, he assumed it led to the Folly's stairwell. Ignoring the noise, he looked back down at her.

"MR DE CORD'NAY!" a voice called from behind the door. Neither of them responded. This had to be done.

"Goodbye, Mrs Hawtree. I am sorry for it."

"Please, call me-" Redwald lifted the gun and shot her through the left eye. Blood sprayed out of the back of her head and pattered like rain onto the floorboards, the windowpane behind her shattering. After swaying for a moment, the corpse slumped forward at his feet, crunching as her face struck the wood. Redwald could smell the iron tang of blood and the burning of her eyebrows.

Someone hammered on the door.

"MR DE CORD'NAY! MR DE CORD'NAY! SHE'S GONE, SIR!"

"I know that," he replied. What he didn't know was *how*. Yet as he stood there, the tiniest wisp of an idea flittered into his mind. He reached out carefully for it, as if catching a butterfly. A few more moments of patient thought and he felt sure he would have it; the *solution* would finally be his.

"YER NEEDED SIR, QUICK!" The door was now rattling on its hinges with the force of the blows.

"In a moment," Redwald growled, clamping his hands to his ears, "I need time to think." He was *almost* there.

"SIR, WAKE UP! WAKE UP NOW!" He had to leave, he knew it, but the *idea*, the *solution* was so close. Watching the door as it began to splinter and warp, he tried desperately to force the inspiration, but couldn't. At least not in time. Before the idea had fully formed, the door buckled under pressure, burst off its hinges, and smashed straight into him.

Redwald awoke with a jolt, cold sweat trickling from his brow and down his back. He was in bed, in his room at the Double Standard and had left the woman and the Folly far behind. The shouting, however, had followed him out of the dream.

"SIR! YER NEEDED!" He swung his legs out of bed, his arm throbbing with a dull pain, and stumbled across to the rattling

182

door. The landlord was waiting for him outside, illuminating the crooked corridor with an old-fashioned candle-lamp.

"Oh, thank Oryn," he said as Redwald emerged, "It's Alice, Mr de Cordonnay. Yer needed right now!"

"Why . . ." Redwald asked, his stomach tight with trepidation, "what's happened?"

"She's missing sir, taken most like." Forewarning did nothing to lessen the blow. Unable to meet the Landlord's eye, Redwald looked away into the darkness, images from the dream lingering like the sour aftertaste of bad wine. As the gunshot replayed itself over and again in his head, the taut feeling of having the answer at his fingertips ebbed away like sand through an hourglass, replaced by something far worse. Redwald wrenched himself back to the present, sick with guilt, *excitement* flaring in his chest.

"I'll get dressed and be down immediately," he said, shutting the door. The first thing he did, however, was twist the orcite lamp in his room and make straight for his jacket. Scrabbling in the pocket for his notebook, he flicked it open and held the map to the light. The Athonstone and Manor weapons' spots were both intact and stationary. His own spot, that of the master ribbon, was in the pub as expected and Alice's . . . was also stationary, *within the walls of the Manor*. He snapped the book shut. He could save her.

He dressed and hurried downstairs to the bar, briefcase in his sling-free hand. There in the dark, he found a dishevelled Guardsman Norris and the Landlord waiting for him, their leering shadows cast on to the walls by the lantern between them. Remembering Sakha's advice, Redwald scrutinised their faces, but neither had a bruise. Upon seeing Redwald, Norris stood to attention.

"Alice is gone, sir. Lord Hawtree needs us at the Manor."

"Good," Redwald said, "because that's where she is."

"What?!" Norris asked, as Redwald thanked the Landlord and swept out into the night. Waiting for them in the dark was a Hawtree coachman, perched atop a monogrammed carriage loaded with cases. Seeing Redwald's arm in a sling, Norris rushed awkwardly past him and opened the door.

"I don't understand," Norris said, following Redwald into the cabin, "how d'you know she's in the Manor?" In response, Redwald pulled out the notebook, opened it to the map and explained its workings to Norris. Meanwhile, the carriage had lurched off into the night, clattering towards the Manor.

"So," Redwald concluded, "it seems both that she's *still* in the Manor and that none of my tagged weapons has moved. So, either they've found *another* antique weapon elsewhere . . ."

"Or they can't kill her yet."

"Precisely; *yet*." He flicked open his watch. It was a quarter past four in the morning. "We need to know how much time she's got left."

"How are we supposed to . . ." Norris began, but Redwald, whose mind was racing, cut him off.

"I have an experiment running in the icehouse," he said, leaning forward with a grimace and reaching into his briefcase. He rummaged for a moment as the cabin rocked from side to side, before surfacing with Alice's birth certificate. "When we arrive, I suggest you go into the Manor with this," he said, handing Norris the notebook and the map, "tell Mr Hawtree that Alice is in the house somewhere, to put guards on every exit, and to ensure that *no one* leaves. If he can lead you to wherever in the Manor the smallest ink spot could be, then so much the better. If *any* of the larger ink spots move or separate, you *must* follow the moving part of it, do you understand?"

184

"Because . . . because they could be picking up the weapon?"

"Exactly."

"W-what about you?" Norris said nervously. "Would be good to have your help."

"You'll have it," Redwald said, looking out at the Manor as the carriage raced up the driveway, "but first I need to visit Alice-to-be."

The carriage crested the drive and crunched to a halt on the gravel. Norris pushed the door open for Redwald and the magician disembarked, thanking him. Outside, squads of Hawtree guards stalked the Manor's grounds, shining lanterns between the bordering trees and picking their way down the lawn towards the road. The guard at the front door rushed over to Redwald as Norris handed him his briefcase.

"Guardsman Norris, Mr de Cordonnay?" He said, in a distinctly Athonite accent.

"Yes," Redwald said.

"Mr Hawtree wants to see you right away." Redwald turned to Norris.

"I'll be there in a moment; this won't take long." Norris nodded and, clutching the notebook as if it were glass, accompanied the guard back into the Manor, explaining that Redwald would join them shortly. The magician himself half-marched, half-jogged up the Rise, guided to the icehouse by the lantern that hung over its door, his breath billowing in the unseasonably cold air as the birth certificate flapped from his be-slinged hand. As he hurried around the back of the Manor, he turned to see a light on in the study and was suddenly struck by the fear that he might see Alice laying there, taking her last breath before slipping magically from that moment

185

and into one already passed. No such spectre appeared, however. It was only a Hawtree guard, standing with his back to the window. Nevertheless, Redwald quickened his pace.

Contrary to Giles' promise, the icehouse was unguarded. Although, Redwald surmised as he shouldered painfully past the unlocked door, any guards that might have been there were probably out looking for Alice. His suspicion was quickly confirmed when he stumbled over the guards' chairs, stacked neatly but stupidly just beyond the threshold. The magician swore but stopped suddenly at the sound of his own voice, echoing off the icehouse's slick, slanted walls.

He looked up, through the first chamber which stretched eerily away from him and towards the second, where the dead Alice lay naked on her slab, waiting. He straightened up and approached her slowly, footfall slapping on the wet floor and stomach knotting tighter with every step, though whether with apprehension or anticipation, he dared not say. As predicted, the spell was finished and Alice's heart had fallen still forever, clamped in the apparatus beside the corpse, her life measured out in increments of bloodied water. Redwald placed his briefcase on the floor and turned to the birth certificate.

An officious, pro-forma document made of stiff, high-quality paper, the details of the birth had been crammed awkwardly into the boxes provided:

Name: Alice Penelope Hawtree

Father: Sir Julius Bretwalda Hawtree

Mother: Emmeline Heather, Lady Hawtree (born Westford-Mays)

Weight at birth: 6lbs 3oz

Notes: Mr Morrimer Thesk also in attendance, Family butler.

186

Time of Birth: 4:53 a.m. 34ᵗʰ Sussureme 2306.

Attending Physician: Dr G. Asplund (Med Reg #487546)

Closing his eyes and frowning with the effort of the mental arithmetic, he counted off the days and months. By his reckoning, a 34ᵗʰ Sussureme birth date would make the living Alice, wherever she was, 19 years 9 months and 8 days old. Armed with this information, Redwald walked around the slab and stooped to look at the vial beneath the heart, his chest tightening.

He quickly counted the years and months by reference to the lines and numbers painted on the glass. 19 years. *Not long.* 9 months. *Even less time.* The next part could be fiddly; he had to count the miniscule lines that remained between the uppermost month marker and the surface of the liquid, determining Alice's ultimate lifespan to a day's accuracy. The more lines there were, the more complex the task. He leant in, squinted, and balked.

That can't be right. Frantically, he double-checked the years and months before returning to the day markers. His heart quickened. The result was the same. Hot panic swept up his spine. Again, he counted, and again the number of days was identical, the conclusion inescapable; the experiment was useless.

He stood, doing his best to suppress his rising anger. Yet as he looked down at Alice, pale, cold and barely out of girlhood, he snapped. Swearing and cursing his own stupidity, he slammed a fist on the marble counter with such force that the stand leapt from the surface with a clatter.

Why it hadn't worked, he couldn't say. Perhaps he had opened the valve too early, perhaps his spell had been imprecise, perhaps his intentions had been insufficiently clear when casting. In any event, it had been wasted time, because the reading on the vial was *very* clear and *very* wrong. It must have been, because the future Mrs Hawtree lying before him, having apparently enjoyed 19 years, 9 months and 1 day of life, had died a little under a week in advance of her current self. He stuffed the birth certificate furiously back into his briefcase and stormed out of the icehouse, heading back to the Manor.

Barrelling past the guards on the front door and into the entrance hall, he found a prim, harassed-looking woman in middle-age, wearing an austere brown dress with a brooch at her throat. She appeared to be waiting for him.

"Where are they?" Redwald snapped.

"Upstairs sir, in Mrs Hawtree's room. Mr Hawtree is very. . ." she winced as a shout echoed down from the gallery, " . . . very distressed. Please follow me." She turned immediately and hurried up the stairs, Redwald in tow.   As they ascended, the shouts became clearer, as did the sound of someone pacing.

"Where the hell is he?! He should be here by now!"

"Lord . . . Mr Hawtree, sir. Are you sure this is the right room? See, I have the map here . . ."

"Yes, Norris, it couldn't be anywhere else. I *told* you. Now, WHERE IS HE?!" Reaching the top of the stairs, Redwald followed the woman along the landing to Mrs Hawtree's bedroom. Two ashen-faced guards were waiting outside it and, though notionally on duty, it was clear their minds were otherwise occupied.

"What is it Ofcross?!" Giles barked as the austere woman crossed the threshold. "Oh Redwald!" he added, his tone pirouetting on a sixpence, "thank heavens you're here!"

Norris and Hawtree were stood slightly apart from one another, just beyond the foot of the bed. Hawtree himself was unkempt and distressed, his green eyes wet with tears, his hair bedraggled, and his shirt was untucked and open at the neck, having been thrown on in a hurry. Redwald again felt sure he knew Giles from somewhere else, perhaps in similar circumstances, but ignored the instinct. Norris, meanwhile, had backed into a corner of the oriel window, presumably giving Hawtree room to pace, and was holding the notebook open in his hands.

"Redwald, dear fellow, where were you?!" Hawtree said as he hurried over to the magician, the woman called Ofcross slipping discreetly out of his way and closing the door behind her. "Norris told me that you were checking the experiment?!" Redwald cursed his own blood as he felt it burn in his cheeks.

"Yes, I . . ."

"*Well*, what did it say?!" Hawtree asked, a crazed look in his eyes, "I mean . . . how long do we . . . ?"

"The results were inconclusive, I'm afraid." Giles' look of desperation quickly subsided in favour of a confused frown.

"I don't . . . I don't understand, shouldn't it say . . ."

"Yes it *should*," Redwald replied, irritably, "but on this occasion the experiment rendered an impossible result."

"Well . . . uh . . . I don't know how, how that . . ."

"I'm sure it's my fault; I must have mis-cast the spell or opened the valve too early."

"Then what are we supposed to do?!" Giles shrieked, his frown breaking like a dam and unleashing another deluge of tearful panic. Redwald met his client's glistening eyes.

"Find Alice, and fast." He looked up at Norris, who flinched. "How many rooms have you got left to check?"

189

"Erm, none sir."

"*None?!*"

"We . . . we followed the map sir, checked everywhere, upstairs, downstairs, but we still can't . . ." Redwald swept across the room, dropped his briefcase by the tall mirror, and snatched the notebook from the Guardsman's hands. Looking down his nose at the map, he saw that Alice's ink spot was unmoved, but that his own was now so close to it that the two were almost merging.

"No, no this can't be right." Redwald said, looking around the Alice-free room.

"Redwald . . . Redwald please . . ." Hawtree said, following the magician with his hands clasped as if in prayer, "we need to find her." Redwald's eyes flicked from the notebook to the room and back, trying to calm himself, to process what he was seeing.

The bedroom looked much as it had on his first visit, albeit the lamps were now twisted to their full, searing brightness. Soft rose wallpaper clad the walls above a waist-high dado rail, anaemic pine panelling beneath, while the titanic four-poster faced the oriel window, looking out towards the village. Redwald frowned. Aside from the bedsheets, half-dragged on to the floor, the room showed no signs of a struggle. Everything else, from the tall mirror beside him, to Mrs Hawtree's dressing table and even the slightly wonky chair in the oriel's far corner, looked largely undisturbed. Ignoring the impulse to straighten the chair against the wall, Redwald began to pace.

"She was sleeping in here, right?" Redwald asked, watching the map as he moved, attempting to orientate his own ink spot relative to Alice's.

"Yes," Hawtree said tearfully, "but she was under guard the whole time, as *you* suggested." Hawtree, who looked on the verge of tearing his hair out, turned away for a moment, muttering to himself. "Where is he?!"

"How did you find out she was missing?" Redwald said as he skirted Alice's dressing table.

"The guards . . . they, they check in on her when they change shifts . . ."

"And the last change; when was it?"

"At four, but . . ." Hawtree said, pre-empting Redwald's next question, "that door is always, *always*, guarded; they only leave once the next shift arrives."

"So, no one could have come in through the door," Redwald murmured. Now at the headboard, he turned and looked back towards the window, even as he continued to pace. No panes were broken, and none of them had been opened, which, in any event, could only have been done from the inside. Whoever had taken Alice, they had not come in through the window either. *So, where's the other door?*

As this thought crossed his mind, Redwald looked down at the notebook once again. His blob had connected with Alice's; she could not be more than a few feet away. He halted mid-step, as if by moving he might accidentally lose his place. Looking up, he found himself in the corner furthest from the door, directly opposite the tall mirror and behind the wonky chair.

At first glance, it looked as though the chair had been angled deliberately for a better view through the window, leaving a wedge of empty space between its back and the wall. Redwald, standing in this wedge and having adjusted the map, turned to where Alice's ink spot appeared to be. He was greeted with the view of an Athonstone town house, in watercolours, hanging on the decidedly solid wall.

"No, no, no . . . shit!" Furious, he made to look down at the map again, but suddenly froze. Behind him, Norris stood shocked into silence, while Hawtree shifted uncomfortably on the spot.

"What . . . what is it?" Hawtree asked, sidling over to peer around Redwald's arm. "Isn't *that* Alice's blob, there?!" Hawtree reached out to point at the map, but the magician pocketed it before he could do so; he was not looking at the map. He was looking at the dado rail.

"She's behind the wall," Redwald whispered to himself.

"What do you mean, *behind it?!*" Hawtree snapped, before following Redwald's gaze. There in the dado rail, no more obtrusive than a brushstroke in a painting, was a shallow groove, just deep enough for a man's fingertips.

"It's a servant's door," Redwald murmured. That Giles might forget either that his servants existed or that they, like other corporeal beings, required means to get from one place to another, did not surprise him in the least. Quickly snapping to, the magician ushered his indignant client out of the corner whilst beckoning Norris into it. The Guardsman, though tired, was sufficiently alert to pick up on Redwald's expression. He unholstered his revolver.

"What is it?" Norris asked quietly.

"The wall is a door," Redwald whispered, slipping the tips of his fingers into the groove, "and she's behind it." Norris swallowed and nodded his understanding. Redwald did his best to give the guardsman an encouraging smile, before turning back to the wall. "I'll be right behind you, but be careful, if she's there, so too may be her kidnapper. I'll open it on three, if you're ready?" Norris cocked his gun in response and so Redwald fastened his grip on the rail. "On my mark; three, two, one . . ."

192

Redwald tugged. The wall swung open with ease as the concealment charm stretched and then failed. Norris pointed his shaking gun hand through the gap and charged into the passage. Redwald allowed the wall to swing back against the chair and quickly followed, his head down, his heart thundering.

Drab and grey, the servant's passage stretched ten feet from the open wall before turning right. Finding nothing in the first ten feet, Norris rushed to the corner and pointed his gun down the rest of the passage. Watching his reaction with bated breath, Redwald's stomach dropped as Norris first relaxed and then turned to shake his head. They had found nothing. Redwald, on the verge of vomiting, slumped against a wall, his heart beating so fiercely that he could feel it pulsing in his injured arm. How, how could he have made that mistake? Why wasn't she there? Why did the map say . . . ? The thought petered out as the splash of colour caught his eye. There on the floor, midway between him and the bedroom, was a red ribbon.

Hawtree suddenly appeared in the doorway, framed by the brilliant light of the orcite lamps behind him. He looked down at the ribbon, looked up at Redwald, and burst into fits of screeching tears. Rushing into the passageway, he dropped to his knees and picked up the ribbon, before looking pleadingly up at Redwald.

"I thought . . . I thought it . . . it couldn't . . . be removed . . ." Hawtree said between sobs. Redwald closed his eyes, white-hot rage coursing through him.

"It can't be *untied,* except by me." That, he now realised, was the precise wording of the spell. He had assumed that provision, along with the durability measure to prevent the ribbons being cut, would secure them completely. He had been wrong. Mrs Hawtree's kidnapper had, quite simply, rolled it off her wrist. Redwald opened his eyes again and saw the intact knot staring defiantly back at him.

"W-what about the . . . the weapons?!" Hawtree shouted as he stumbled to his feet, "what have you done?! If he can . . . if he can do this, why doesn't the kidnapper just . . ."

"You can't roll the ribbons off the weapons in that way," Redwald snapped as he heaved himself upright, "they all have closed trigger guards." He stormed past Hawtree and back out into the bedroom, as images of his lunchtime pint and of the many coupes of Arrovênnes floated before his mind's eye. Could he have foreseen this? *Should* he have foreseen this? Had he been sober, might he have tied the knot *just* a little tighter around Alice's wrist?

"What are you doing?!" Hawtree asked as he and Norris followed Redwald back out of the passage. "We need to find her *now* you idiot!" Redwald, wincing with the pain in his arm, stooped at his briefcase and retrieved his chalkboard.

"Are you gonna cast a spell to find her?" Norris asked.

"He's already done that!" Hawtree shouted, "and it hasn't bloody worked!" Redwald, ignoring them both, shunted clear some space for his chalkboard atop a chest of drawers.

"But he was trackin' the ribbon weren't he," Norris continued, as he edged towards Mrs Hawtree's pillow, "what if he tracked Missus Hawtree herself?"

"That *obviously* won't work!" Hawtree barked, wringing the ribbon in his hands even as his tears subsided, "any idiot knows you'd need a *part* of her to put in the spell, and seeing as she's gone . . ."

"There's hairs on her pillow, Mr Cordneigh . . ." Norris said, peering down at the loose strands that clung to the bedding, "Would that work?" Norris and Hawtree both looked to the magician for an answer, only to be greeted by the sight of his back.

His now-empty sling hanging limply over his shoulder, Redwald was already mid-way through plotting a spell on his chalkboard. Grasping his watch in his left hand and drawing with his right, he quickly plotted the web, circles, and lines with unfaltering precision, despite the trembling of his fingers and the pain in his arm.

"It's an idea," Redwald grimaced, as he scrawled the incantation painfully across the blue lines, obsessively re-reviewing the wording, "but you need a certain kind of magic to track her that way, and we don't have the time for it. Besides," he growled, bending over with a groan to retrieve the tributes from his briefcase, "it probably wouldn't work in a case like this . . ."

"So what . . . what *are* you doing?!" Hawtree asked.

"They discovered she was missing at 4," Redwald said, ignoring the question, "how often do the shifts change?"

"What are you . . . ? Every two hours, I think, but I don't see . . ."

"You will," Redwald said curtly, leaning over and drawing a line in yellow chalk across the top of the tall mirror's frame. Swivelling on his heel and ignoring his client's scowl, Redwald hurriedly scanned the room for a few seconds before his eyes finally alighted on Mrs Hawtree's dressing table. He strode over to it, scraped the same yellow line across the upper frame of its in-built mirror, and returned to place the last of the tributes in their respective circles. He stopped and looked down at the chalkboard, painstakingly examining every inch of it. Neither he nor Alice could afford any more mistakes. Once satisfied there were none, Redwald closed his eyes, ready for casting.

He sought that practiced state of mental silence that was, by its nature, almost anathema to him. He tried to visualise the habitually churning waters of his mind lapping gently to a mirror-calm standstill, ready for his intent to surface. Yet even as he tried, he found it almost impossible, wracked as he was with guilt and self-loathing, his nerves stretched tighter than harp-strings by the night's events. Worse, the searing light of the orcite lamps burned through his eyelids like sun through the bedroom's crimson curtains, projecting unwelcome images of Alice begging for her life. He opened his eyes.

"Would you turn the light off, please?" Redwald said, directing the comment at Norris.

"Oh, we turned it up bright so's you could see . . ." Norris began, but he quickly curtailed his explanation upon seeing Redwald's arched eyebrow. Soon the lights were off, and the room was silent once more, the darkness split by the moonlight that fell between the curtains and onto the bed. Redwald turned back to the spell and closed his eyes.

The intrusive images quickly resurfaced, but Redwald found it far easier, in the calming darkness, to either allow them to pass like nausea or else to bury them. Where the dry rasp of Halva'us' voice burned in his brain, he allowed the dense silence of the dark room to flood in and smother it, where panic or doubt threatened, he summoned Adriel's smooth, soft tones to reassure him, and where blood and viscera caked and contaminated his thoughts, he could call upon memories of clean, cool rain to wash it all away. Eventually and with some effort, he felt the requisite stillness settle upon him. He cast.

Opening his eyes, he found that the tributes had sagged to weyste. Giles, who had not calmed himself for casting, muttered angrily to himself and looked down at his watch. He quickly stowed it when he saw Redwald's open eyes.

"What have you done?! We need to find her now!!" Giles snapped. "Have you done something with this . . . I don't . . ." Norris, rooted to the spot beside the light switch, watched as Giles stomped impatiently over to the tall mirror. Increasingly agitated and on the verge of tears once more, his voice cracked as he stared

196

blankly at the room's dark reflection. "Redwald, *please*, just . . . just tell me what you've . . ." the magician nodded discreetly at Norris, who duly turned the lights back on. It was at this moment that Giles' words finally failed him. He stood in silence for a moment, transfixed. "I'm . . . I'm not . . . there."

"No," said Redwald, "you *weren't*." Norris, his work at the light switch complete, quickly appeared behind Giles and looked over his shoulder. He too was struck dumb. Norris had never seen magic before, but he had imagined it; foreign incantations and peculiar gestures, sparking flames and strange winds, colours that had noise and the abstract made flesh. Yet his first sight of *real* magic was far more subtle and far more unsettling; a mirror, in a well-lit room with three people, reflecting a dark room with none.

"What . . . what've you . . ." Norris began, but was interrupted by the sound of hurried footfall on the stairs outside. Redwald, Hawtree, and Norris all turned from the mirror to look towards the noise.

"Oh . . ." Hawtree said, surfacing from his reverie, "Oh! OH! That'll be him, *finally*." The footsteps grew louder and louder until Ofcross opened the door with a click and ushered an exhausted-looking Dr Asplund into the room. "Where the hell have you been?!" Giles snapped.

"Making sure I had everything," Asplund growled and lifted a large carpet bag into view, "better to come prepared."

"Oh," Norris said vacantly, still focused on the mirror, "I thought you was drinking with Archie till the small hours . . . the anniversary isn't it?" It was a sound observation, Redwald thought. In the course of scanning the doctor for Sakha's tell-tale bruises, of which he could see none, Redwald noted the unhealthy pallor that had faded Asplund's ruddy skin and the unsteadiness of his dragging steps. All parties present were underslept of course, but Asplund looked to be fighting a nascent hangover as well.

197

"So where is she; have you found her?" Asplund asked. Hawtree sobbed and shook his head. "Oh," Asplund replied, running a gloved hand back across his wiry hair, "Ofcross said the magician . . ."

"We're getting there," Redwald said brusquely, before turning back to the mirror and re-applying his sling.

"What happened to you, anyway?" Asplund asked, watching as the magician winced in pain. "Need a hand?"

"I had an accident," Redwald lied, "and no thanks. Now, if you don't mind, I was in the middle of something." With his good hand, he reached up to the top of the mirror and began to slowly drag his finger along the chalk line.

"What're you . . ." Asplund began, but Norris unthinkingly shushed him, much to the doctor's disgust.

"Seeing who we need to be chasing . . ." Redwald whispered, "come on, you bastard . . ." he said, his eyes fixed on the mirror-image of the wall behind the watercolour.

"Oh," Hawtree said, another sob rising in his throat, "that's my Alice." True enough, as Redwald's finger moved along the chalk line, it became clear that the reflected bed, unlike its material counterpart, was occupied. As Bethin moved across the mirrored sky, so the beam of moonlight slipped noticeably across the bedsheets, themselves shifting like hurried seafoam, displaced by the tossing and turning of spindly limbs.

"What . . . what is this?" Asplund asked as he placed his carpet bag on the bed and joined the others.

"I have enchanted the mirrors so that they re-reflect everything they witnessed between 2 and 4 this morning," Redwald said, continuing to drag his finger as he scrutinised the darkness, "we just need to find out when our suspect turns up."

"So . . . we'll . . . we'll be able to see who took her?" Giles asked, tremulously.

"With any luck. Though I must warn you," Redwald said, not taking his eyes off the mirror, "this could be unpleasant for you to watch. It may turn out . . . or rather I suspect, that the kidnapper is someone from your household staff. At the very least it's someone familiar with the Manor, in order to know about the passages . . . Aha!"

Through darkness thick as treacle, Redwald had seen movement. Specifically, he had seen the chair, then parallel to the wall, jerk forward. He immediately lifted his finger from the chalk and the scene slowed to a normal pace.

"Watch it, watch the chair . . ." Redwald said, so focused on spotting the villain that the discomfort of his companions escaped his notice entirely. The chair, stationary for a moment, began to move again in fits and starts. Though hard to tell through the darkness, it seemed the kidnapper had begun to open the wall, found an obstacle in its path and was now trying, inelegantly, to shuffle the chair noiselessly along the carpet. This they did piecemeal, until a white shape blossomed against the black, the seat of the chair edging into the moonlight. Then it stopped.

Behind the chair, the darkness was stirring. All four men held their breath as something pushed through the gap in the wall. Yet, for all that they could see its movement, they could see little else; the creeping mass that inched towards Alice was both shapeless and faceless.

Redwald whirled around and hurried across to the dressing table as, in the past, the shadow crossed the same space. Kneeling with a wince and gripping his injured arm, he positioned himself at an

199

angle to the mirror and opposite the window. With any luck, he might catch the villain's silhouette against the uncurtained windowpanes. Blood throbbed in his ears with every hurried heartbeat as he waited, hungrily, *excitedly*, for his opponent to reveal themselves. Asplund, Norris, and Hawtree all watched him in silence.

Although expecting it, Redwald started when the silhouette appeared in the mirror, shuddering as if Halva'us had run frozen fingers through his hair. Temporally distant, but physically close, Redwald almost felt as if he could reach out and touch the kidnapper, perhaps even drag them to the floor and save Alice there and then.

Instead, the shadow shuffled awkwardly, and inexorably, towards its victim, affording Redwald only the briefest glimpse of its shape as it passed across the light. Short, broad, and hooded, the kidnapper soon lurched out of frame, prompting Redwald to scuffle across to the other side of the mirror. Yet all he could see from this angle was the kidnapper's back and Alice's skeletal hand on the moonlit bedsheets. The chill returned. He would have to watch this unfold, he realised, powerless to stop it.

Heaving himself to his feet, Redwald hurried back to the tall mirror. Whatever was about to happen to Alice, loath though he was to consider it, could involve the kidnapper leaning forward into the moonlight. If they did that, Redwald thought, he might catch a glimpse of their face. But as the magician arrived and peered over Hawtree's head at the mirror, he felt disappointment sink heavily into his stomach. The kidnapper was stood directly adjacent to Alice's pillow, but the moonlight that fell on the bed stopped short of her midriff, leaving both her face, and the kidnapper's, obscured. The shadow loomed over its victim for a moment, pausing.

"Mr Hawtree," Redwald whispered, "you might not want to watch this." Giles ignored him, staring intently into the mirror with Norris, even as Asplund turned away, a thousand-yard stare in his one good eye. The shadow shifted again and there was a sudden glint as something caught the moonlight. Redwald's excitement at the prospect of a potential clue was quickly smothered by horror, however, as he realised exactly what he was seeing.

"Mr Hawtree, I . . .", it was too late. Before Redwald could finish, a glittering mist emanated from the razor-sharp point of the metallic syringe and the shadow descended upon Alice, the needle slipping silently out of the moonlight and into her throat. Beneath the sheets, her feet twitched and jerked for a moment before falling limp once more. The whole business had passed in no more than a few seconds, probably before Alice even knew what was happening.

Hawtree watched, wide-eyed, as the shadow leaned in, lifted his unconscious wife delicately from her bed and turned around, dragging the bedsheets on to the floor in the process. The top-heavy shape of one body carrying another then headed back towards the servant's door, moving in stops and starts. Redwald squinted through the darkness, grinding his teeth in frustration as he watched his last chance at a clue stumble away from him. Before the shadow could slip out of the room and into oblivion, however, it paused at the narrow opening into the passage.

After a moment's hesitation, it turned and stepped backwards through the moonlight, which glinted on its hooded, oilskin cloak. No matter how much Redwald wished it, the kidnapper never once turned their face to the light, never once revealed their identity, never once slipped up.

Instead, they knelt unsteadily, but carefully, and lay Alice on the pale carpet. Balding now in clumps, white as her sheets, and significantly gaunter than the last time Redwald had seen her, she looked ever more like her future self. The kidnapper gently placed one of her hands beneath her head and positioned her knee to support her, before standing and stepping over her towards the door. There was a brief shuffling in the darkness behind Alice, as her narrow ribcage rose and fell beneath her ivory shift.

Redwald, temporarily distracted from his task, found himself fixated on her flickering eyelids and the pallor of her bare scalp. She looked so frail that too deep a breath might crack her porcelain skin and shatter her where she lay. Then, before Redwald knew it, the shadow was back, scooping Alice into its arms and lifting her away into the night.

Redwald, fists clenched so tight that his callused, chapped knuckles had cracked and bled anew, could do nothing more than watch his efforts inch closer to failure, step by uneven step. Then he saw the key.

"WAIT!" He barked, startling the others and tapping the mirror's surface with such force that it swung backward on its hinges. He quickly readjusted it and turned to Giles, pointing with a quivering finger. "That key, it's one of yours, no?" With Redwald's tap to the surface, the entire scene had frozen, such that Alice lay stationary in her abductor's arms, the latter mid-step over the threshold into darkness. At the kidnapper's hip, however, hung a key, visible where the oilskin cloak had ridden up slightly and gleaming in the light. It was a cumbersome hulk of twisted iron, a JH within the shape of a tower, initialled in the bow of the key.

"Uhm . . . yes, yes I think so . . ." Hawtree stammered, "but I don't know what it . . . Ofcross!" The harassed-looking woman quickly re-appeared in the doorway. Redwald ushered her over and directed her attention to the mirror.

"This key," he said, pointing, "do you know what it's for, who would have access to it?"

"I'm not sure, sir," she said, wringing her hands, "but it's probably one of the other estate buildings, otherwise I'd know about it. Morrimer looks after those, I'll . . . I'll fetch him," she said, making for the door before she had even finished her sentence.

"Yes please," Redwald replied. Then the realisation hit him like a bucket of cold water. "Wait! Why isn't he here already?" She stopped, her eyes wide and flickering as she grasped for an explanation.

"I uh . . . I don't know sir. I hadn't thought about it, truth be told. First thing I knew, the alarm was raised and we were all out searching for Alice, I just assumed he was too." Redwald looked between the empty bed, the open servant's passage, and the crimson ribbon in Giles' hand.

"I haven't seen him either," Giles whispered. *No*, Redwald thought, *it doesn't make sense*. Dignified, ancient Morrimer, could it really be him? Then there was the question, Adriel's question, that still needed an answer: *Why attack the wife you like and not the husband you hate?*

"Is it possible he didn't hear the alarm? His room . . ." Redwald said, hesitant to admit his knowledge of it, " . . . it's quite . . . high up in the house, isn't it? Sound of the alarm being raised might be muffled?" Ofcross shook her head.

"Morrimer's quarters are in the basement, sir, he'd hear everything from there."

"Then what was . . ." Redwald began, but suddenly all he could see was Morrimer, standing over Alice, tied to a bedframe in that dingy little room atop the hidden staircase, Morrimer, with sole access to all of Mr Hawtree's weapons and a comprehensive list, provided by Redwald, of those under surveillance, Morrimer, who knew the Manor like the back of his gnarled old hand, who would have known both of the hidden room and of the passage that led to

203

Alice, and Morrimer, who knew exactly what the red ribbon on her wrist signified and the consequences of failing to remove it. "We need to go to the Gun Room," Redwald barked, "now!"

Hawtree, Ofcross, Asplund, and Norris all followed Redwald as he hurtled through the tight residential passages and out into the cavernous darkness of the deserted reception hall. As their footfall echoed beneath the monstrous shadows of the once-glittering swan chandeliers, the magician breathlessly described his discovery; accidentally pushing the brass stud, the staircase upwards, and the apparently secret room, littered with traces of Morrimer's presence.

Giles muttered in denial as the group swept up the staircase and past Sir Julius' enormous golden statue. He could no more believe that Morrimer would betray him, despite his "firm hand", than that there was a whole room in his house of which he knew nothing. The others, however, remained silent.

Storming into the Gun Room and across to the bookcase, Redwald frantically wrenched *Twistle's Traditional Tales for Growing Children* from the shelf and jabbed at the brass stud. The wall swung open with a familiar hiss. Giles stopped muttering. Before Norris could go ahead of him with weapon drawn, however, Redwald had ducked beneath Lady Hawtree's portrait, tripped on the bottom step in his haste, and hurtled up the staircase.

Yet even as he leapt multiple steps at a time, certain he was right, certain this was the place, he feared the very worst. Halva'us growled in his ear with a voice like scraping rocks, **"She was dead before you started,"** and another intrusive image thrust itself into his mind; an anonymous hand rolling a body over to reveal Alice's empty eye socket, wet, fleshy, and ragged like a pitted peach.

He soon saw the latticed moonlight spilling through the wire cage and on to the uppermost steps. Vaulting these, he thrust the cage door open with a clatter and looked around the room.

"No . . ." he whispered, "NO!" It was the second time in his life he had seen this wretched room, a sight far more terrible on this occasion, precisely because it was the same as the first. The room was empty.

The others joined him piecemeal, panting from their dash up the stairs. Norris arrived first, gun drawn, but Redwald gestured for him to lower it.

"No," Redwald explained as he rubbed his temples, "I . . . I was wrong . . . They're not here." Asplund and a panting Giles arrived next, followed eventually by Ofcross who, holding her skirts with one hand and leaning into the spiral with the other, completed the quintet. They looked together upon Redwald's disgrace.

He had been so sure, almost as if he could foresee it; Morrimer and Alice, here, in this room, together. Why were they not? Where were they instead?

"I'm so sorry . . ." Redwald said quietly, as Hawtree sobbed into the empty darkness, "I could have sworn . . . I mean, it just suddenly made sense. He could keep her up here and no one would know, it opens right onto the Gun Room . . . it just . . . just made sense . . ."

"What do we do now?" Norris asked Redwald. The magician sighed. He was nearing the limits of his usefulness.

"That spell you mentioned earlier, using Alice's hair. I *can* do that, but it may not help, the problem with this situation . . ."

"Just get her back, please . . . I'll do anything, anything . . ." Hawtree said, turning to Redwald and looking up at him through swollen red eyes.

"Then we need external help, publicity notwithstanding" Redwald said, bluntly, "I'm doing, and will continue to do, all I can, but this case now requires more constabulary support than we have here, so . . ." Hawtree nodded reluctantly.

"Yes, send for them. Please." Redwald turned to Norris.

"You need Lord Martingale's permission to involve the liege-lord's constabulary, don't you?" Norris confirmed both that he did and that such permission would be reluctantly given, if at all.

"He'll be out on his ride," Asplund chipped in, "he likes to ride the night away at . . . this time of year."

"I'll do my best to find him," Norris said as he hurried out of the room. Redwald sighed and turned to look out of the window, mentally checking off the elements he would need for the spell.

The cold blue of the night sky had been smeared with the bloody red of encroaching dawn and scarred with gristly pink clouds that stretched over Martingale's Work. The sun, though still behind the hill, was gilding the lower sky and silhouetting the long, low ridge as it slipped down to the valley floor. Redwald's eyes lazily traced it from right to left, but, before sloping steeply at the very end of the ridge, the clean, black line was interrupted. There, a twisted shadow loomed proudly over the waking village; Hawtree's Folly. Redwald's breath caught in his throat. *It's probably one of the other estate buildings, else I'd know about it. Morrimer looks after those.*

CHAPTER 11

Bitter Medicine

". . . For many years the Duke was mean to the girl, even as she grew into a young maiden. He said nasty things to her, teasing her for the redness of her hair and saying that she was a poor servant. One day she asked the rich man why the Duke was so horrid. At first he would not tell her, but as the years went by and the maiden took care of the Duke in the darkness of his tower, cleaning his cases full of pressed flowers, cooking his meals and helping him to bed, the rich man began to relent. So he told her. He told her that the Duke had been a kind man once, who had particularly loved his garden. This he had cared for himself and kept it vibrant and lush. Then a terrible thing had happened and the Duke's mother had died. Aggrieved by her death, he had retreated to the tower and had allowed his garden to fail. Now, the Duke was too old to revive it and had only the pressed flowers in his room as a reminder of what he had lost. The maiden listened and still she was nameless.

One day, on the maiden's 18th birthday, the King died. Throughout the land the bells rang and the search began for a new King or Queen. The old King's children tried first, as was proper, but the Crown would not accept them, for they were not worthy. Then it was commanded that the Crown should be taken to the grandest lords of the land to see if they were worthy. Two weeks later, the Crown was brought to the Duke's castle, for he was next in line. . ."

The Tale of Alynore – Traditional Tales for Growing Children, collated by Dr C.F. Twistle (Allpress) 1992

Heaving himself ever upward with wingbeat after frantic wingbeat, Redwald turned his feathered head towards the Folly. Beneath him, the patchwork fields and spotted trees glistened gold in Oryn's light, the lingering mist sparkling into nothingness before the coming day. Yet Redwald, furiously chasing the shrinking shadows to the base of the hill, was blind to the morning's beauty. His eyes, black and inscrutable, were fixed solely on his target.

The second the revelation had hit him, Redwald had voiced it to Asplund, Hawtree, and Ofcross. From that moment on, the Manor had crackled as if run through with a fuse, arrangements made as hurriedly and inexpertly as revolutionary barricades. Though most of the guards were already out searching for Alice, Hawtree had decided that any remaining in the Manor (except those guarding the weapons) would be dispatched to the Folly. He and Asplund would follow by carriage.

"But sir," Ofcross had quickly objected, "the Countess' things . . . they'll be . . . and besides, the coach will be too heavy to get up the Work and . . . McKee's out searching!" Hawtree had simply rolled his eyes and pushed past her down the staircase.

"Damn it Ofcross, I'll drive and we'll just take a few cases off. Just have them bring it out! NOW!" Ofcross had quickly followed her master down the stairs, wringing her hands like dishcloths. Asplund, however, had lingered, watching Redwald uncertainly.

"Not coming with us, are you?"

"I'll save you the weight and meet you up there," Redwald had said, gazing up at the Folly, before pre-empting Asplund's inevitable question. "The sooner you get there the better. She may be hurt, or worse . . ." Asplund, still clearly uncertain, had lingered a few moments longer before finally breaking his monocular gaze and following the others downstairs.

Once alone, Redwald had wasted no time in wrenching the window open and removing his sling with a grimace, the morning breeze tousling his salted black hair. Stretching his injured arm as he extracted the gloves, he had briefly remembered Sakha's admonition not to fly, but his friend's words had soon been drowned by Alice's imagined screams. *Hang the risk.* His wound, twisting and warping with the transformation, had burned but not broken as the room inflated around him, his bones bent beneath his skin, his hairs splintered into quills, and his long nose stretched and blackened.

Hopping gingerly up onto the windowsill, he had pushed his breastbone down, twisted between the bars and leapt off into the air, sweeping his broad, black wings beneath him as he began the race for Alice's life. Like a rushing shadow he had swept low over the gutter, wings close to his body, before the roof dropped away beneath him to reveal the Manor's lawn careening down to the woods below.

Pointing his beak at the Folly, he began to oar himself higher and higher into the sky, defying the burning pain stoked by each wingbeat. Turning briefly to check for blood, he saw Hawtree and Asplund far beneath him, bickering furiously at the gravel turnaround. Asplund, crouched low on the carriage roof, was securing Laetizja's luggage lest it fall during the climb, while Hawtree waited impatiently in the coachman's seat. They would, Redwald concluded, be late. Whatever was to be faced at the Folly, he would face it alone.

Trees and fields and brooks swept unnoticed beneath his wingtips as he hurtled across the valley, every breath and muscle straining towards Alice. Haunted by his dream and the fear that Morrimer might soon enact it, he was chased up the Work by the smell of blood, the crunching of bone on wood, and the shattering of glass. Yet it was his guilt that gave him greatest pause. Try as he might to deny it, he was lured as much by his lust for resolution as he was by his concern for Alice.

His thoughts were wrenched back to the present, however, when the sky went dark. Close enough to see the mortar between the bricks and the twinkle of windows at the observation deck, Redwald had flown into the Folly's shadow and was mere feet below his goal. Taking advantage of the updrafts that resulted from the crash of wind and hill, Redwald swept his wings down one last time, cawing in pain, and vaulted the Folly's parapet, before swooping along the encircling balcony and skidding to a halt. Wearily staggering to his feet, he pulled the primary flight feathers from each wing.

"Fuck's sake!" Hot, sticky blood was seeping through his gown and running down his arm. Stuffing the gloves awkwardly into his pocket, Redwald pulled the useless limb to his side and peered through the Folly's windows. The uppermost room was a good deal smaller than he had dreamt it and more luxuriously appointed. It also appeared to be empty. Redwald wheeled about and staggered along the balcony as the wind buffeted the tower and tore at his gown. Upon finding the window that doubled as an external door, he burst into the observation room and cast about desperately for any sign of Alice's presence. He very quickly realised there would be none. The room was immaculate and untouched; if anyone *had* been there, they had left no trace.

"Alice?!" The wind whistled in mocking reply, but the room itself was silent as the grave. Paranoid, Redwald began to kick up carpets, shift cabinets, and upend sofas, convinced that there must be some nook, some cubby hole or secret passage where Alice could be hidden from him. Once again, nothing. The only way left to go was down.

Wrenching open the only interior doorway, he found an iron staircase that spiralled down around the Folly's empty core, criss-crossed by dusty orange light. "ALICE!!!" He bellowed, the noise echoing off the bare, brick walls. Silence. Gripping the railing and allowing his injured arm to jolt painfully with every step, Redwald raced down the stairs two at a time until he reached a landing. "ALICE!!!" He listened again. This time, he heard the faintest of sounds in response, a panicked voice and a wooden rattling.

Hurrying further down, Redwald called again and waited for the echo to recede.

"Mr de Cordonnay?!" A chill ran down Redwald's spine. Coming from the ground level, it was a voice Redwald recognised, but it was not Alice's. As he leapt down the last few stairs and onto a mosaic depicting the Hawtree arms, Redwald realised that the rattling sound had been coming from the Folly's tall double doors, upon which somebody was hammering. "Mr . . . Mr de Cordonnay, what . . . how did you get in there?" Morrimer's voice, reedy, ancient and muffled by the doors, was stained with terror. The fact of Morrimer's fear alone was enough to discomfort Redwald, but finding the doors locked plunged his thoughts into absolute disarray.

"Open the doors, Morrimer!!"

"Sir I . . . I can't . . . the key . . . it's gone . . ." Redwald, enraged, began to size up the doors.

"*Where* has it gone?!"

"I don't know . . . I don't . . ."

"Open the bloody doors, Morrimer, or I'll break them down! DO YOU UNDERSTAND?!!" The hammering stopped, there was a light scuffle, and then silence. *Very well.* Redwald gripped his injured arm, took aim, and slammed his heel on the spot between the handles. The lock shaft burst through the wood and the doors crashed open. Redwald staggered out past the swinging doors to find Morrimer leaning against the rim of a fountain in the Folly's tree-lined forecourt. Yellow eyes wide and long fingers quivering like twigs in the wind, he looked close to a heart attack.

"Morrimer," Redwald asked, his voice rich with quiet fury, "where is Alice?" The Hob paled.

"I . . . I have no idea! I thought you . . ."

"I'm here looking for the *both* of you!" Redwald barked as he advanced on the butler, "What have you done with her?!"

"No, no, you . . . you can't possibly think that I . . ."

"*You* went missing in the middle of the night at the same time as Alice and the Folly Key, *you* knew the significance of the red ribbons, *you* knew the servant's passages to access Alice's bedroom, *you* even knew about the secret room . . ." Morrimer looked up at Redwald, horrified.

"The sss . . . the room . . . what, what room?"

"You know damn well which room, the one hidden above the guns, with barred windows and bugger all else in it apart from one of your hairs . . ." before Redwald could finish, the trembling in Morrimer's limbs reached such a pitch that the Hob slumped against the fountain's rim and onto the floor. Rushing over and kneeling beside him, Redwald pulled him up into a sitting position.

"Morrimer, look at me," tears rolled down Morrimer's creased grey face as he complied, though in truth he seemed to be looking more through the magician than at him, "I know *something* is going on and at the moment you're looking like the prime suspect."

"No . . . I never meant . . ." Morrimer whimpered as he clutched his head in his hands.

"Where is Alice?"

"Don't . . . don't know . . . it's not my fault . . ."

"Then *whose* is it? Tell me!"

"I never meant . . . any harm . . . thought it was . . . for the best . . . I'm sorry," Morrimer said, each sentence punctuated by wheezing sobs that racked his small, frail body.

"Morrimer, *whose* fault is it?! Who knows where Alice is?! Why would anyone hurt her?!" Morrimer blinked tearily up at him and looked, for a moment, as if he were about to unshoulder the heaviest burden of his life. But then his eyes suddenly widened, and he scrabbled back against the fountain.

"No, no I can't . . . I'm sorry . . . can't say . . . I'm sorry . . . he's here . . . he's *here*." Following Morrimer's gaze, Redwald turned to see Hawtree, Asplund, Norris and, to Redwald's surprise, Lord Martingale, cresting the dirt road that ran between the trees, flanked by the latter's dogs. Redwald grabbed Morrimer as they galloped closer.

"Who is it?! *Who?!*" Redwald snapped, before frowning to himself. "No, you're wrong, you must be. Why would any of *them* hurt *Alice* and not . . ." the question wilted on his tongue even as the answer blossomed in his head. Just as well, for Morrimer, curling up into as near a foetal position as his aged frame would permit, said nothing more; nothing that is, besides "sorry".

Redwald turned at the sound of hooves, just as Lord Martingale reined in his enormous grey mount uncomfortably close to where the magician stood. To Redwald's relief, the panting, slathering dogs padded away to explore the tower, leaving the three of them alone. Hawtree and Asplund were still a little way off, whipping the horse team up the Work, fruitlessly assisted by Norris.

"Has he said anything?" Martingale asked. Although his eyes were clear and his back ramrod straight, the Baron nonetheless appeared exhausted. Perhaps it was that his white mane was oddly deflated, as though it had been damp and dripped dry, or that his already shabby coat was soiled with fresh mud and reeking of stale water.

213

Either way the conclusion was obvious; he had spent the night in the saddle.

"Nothing of consequence," Redwald lied. *Why attack the wife you like and not the husband you hate?* Until now Adriel's question had stumped him, but as the carriage finally ground to a halt and Hawtree leapt from the box, crying and screaming at a catatonic Morrimer, Redwald felt certain that he knew the answer. As everyone else watched Norris stoop, quietly inform Morrimer of his rights, and arrest him, Redwald's grey eyes were fixed solely on the Baron. How best to punish the upstart family that muscled into your territory and used a personal tragedy to buy up your ancestral land? Ruin them? How? Banish them? You'd need cause for that, even as Lord of the Manor. Inflict on them the pain you feel every day, more acutely on this one than any other? A pain so intense that you ride the night out alone, in the rain and the darkness, unable to sleep in spite of drink. It wasn't fair to Alice, but neither had the storm been fair to Lady Martingale and her daughter, and as Martingale himself had said: *'Giles will lose his family to a storm the same as I did. Only difference is, it will be of his making.'*

Why attack the wife you like and not the husband you hate? So the 'husband you hate' can share your pain.

Before he could think on it any longer, Redwald was suddenly and violently reminded of his own pain. As the adrenaline began to wear off, so his wound began to burn uncontrollably. He clenched his teeth, groaned, and sank onto the rim of the fountain, fumbling for his hipflask. Martingale turned at the noise and noticed Redwald's bloodied hand.

"Gerritt," he said to Asplund, "see to the magician, would you?" With military efficiency, Asplund retrieved his carpet bag from the carriage, returned to the fountain, and examined Redwald. He asked no questions as he cleaned and temporarily dressed the wound, merely explaining that this was a temporary fix to prevent

214

Redwald bleeding to death. It would, Asplund said, be enough to last until the afternoon, at which point he would be free to stitch the wound up properly. Redwald, who had dulled the pain with several large draughts of whisky, merely nodded in agreement.

The ride back to the village was agonising and slow. With the arrival of the 'advance' guard from the Manor, Hawtree had set them to searching around the Folly and declared that one amongst them should drive the carriage back. Into this carriage had squeezed Hawtree, Redwald, Norris, and Morrimer, while Asplund and Martingale rode alongside, the dogs trotting in their wake. Scrutinising the Baron from inside the cabin, Redwald groggily turned the evidence over in his sleep-deprived, whisky-fogged head. It was not enough, he knew, to show that Martingale had the motive; he also needed to prove *means* and *opportunity*. Yet, as the images swirled around his mind like figments of a fever dream, the magician could not resolve the pattern, could not see *how* Martingale might kill Alice even if he wanted to. According to his notebook, every weapon remained firmly under control.

As if fatigue were not enough, Redwald's efforts were also plagued by Norris' persistent curiosity as to how the magician had made it up to the Folly before everyone else. Eyelids drooping, wound throbbing, and head clunking against the carriage wall with each bump in the road, Redwald admitted defeat. Fabricating a plausible (and legal) story to assuage the Guardsman, he declared his intention to sleep, pulled his gown close about him, and left the others to their solemn silence.

The sun was fully up by the time the party arrived back in the village. Redwald, peeling his eyelids open as the carriage crossed the toll bridge over the Trew, started at the sight that greeted him. More or less the entire village was gathered around the common, beneath the leaning willow, on the little footbridges that forded the river, or outside the Double Standard. Martingale, seeing this,

215

ordered the coach to stop. The guard duly obliged and Hawtree was roused from his fitful sleep.

"What's going on?" Hawtree began, but he was quickly interrupted by the Baron.

"Morning all," Martingale said, riding out into the middle of the common, dogs in tow, "clearly you're all aware to some degree of the events that have taken place this morning. Now I want to be honest with all of you; Alice Hawtree is missing." There was a ripple through the crowd. "We have a suspect in custody, but Alice is still out there and, unless we hear otherwise, we will assume she is alive and will *not* give up our search. *Magical* methods, however, have failed us. I have therefore decided . . . decided to request the assistance of the Ellswych Constabulary." Another ripple, discontented. Martingale smiled. "Notwithstanding our . . . personal . . . feelings towards the Ellswych Guard, I trust I can rely on you to cooperate with their reasonable requests and make them feel welcome. Just not *too* welcome. And remember, if any of them ask anything of you that is unreasonable, illegal, or even unpleasant, you know who to talk to." The crowd murmured reluctant consent and Martingale turned towards the Double Standard. "You have rooms to lodge them, Roderick? Good, I'd rather not have the bastards in my Keep."

Laughter swept across the green for a moment before the crowd dispersed at Martingale's signal. Two of the figures, however, approached the carriage, one leaning forward with his hands in the small of his back and the other holding her skirts above the grass.

"What's happened Archie?" Charteris said as he and Mrs Ofcross approached the carriage.

"Don't have all the details, Charles, you'd best ask the magician. In any case, I'm off. Got to prepare for Ellswych's lot, they're due this afternoon."

"Same," Asplund grunted, "*and* I've got to prep for your surgery later, de Cordonnay. See you at 3." With that, the Baron and Asplund turned their horses and cantered up the road towards Martingale Castle, the dogs barking excitedly in their wake.

"Surgery?!" Charteris blurted, "My dear fellow, what's happened?!" Redwald, stiff from the ride, swung open the carriage door and climbed gingerly down on to the grass. Charteris gasped on seeing the sling.

"There's no broken bones," Redwald said, wearily, "just a gash I've managed to re-open this morning. Dr Asplund has kindly offered to sort me out later."

"Honestly, old boy, how did you . . ." Charteris began, but was interrupted by Hawtree banging on the ceiling of the carriage and barking orders at the guard.

"I went to Athonstone," Redwald replied, as the carriage trundled off to the Manor by way of the Guard Station. "Had an accident while I was there."

"Looks nasty," Ofcross said, fretting. Charteris leaned in then, as if someone might be eavesdropping, which clearly they weren't.

"Say nothing you're uncomfortable with, but can you tell us what happened?" Redwald sighed inwardly. He was exhausted, in pain, and had only a few hours to catch up on sleep before his appointment with Asplund.

"Look, I'm sorry, but . . ."

"Oooh I forgot," Ofcross interjected, "I dropped your briefcase at the Inn, Mr de Cordonnay. You left it in Alice's bedroom and I thought you might need it. Sorry for interrupting," she said, looking apologetically at Charteris who merely smiled and wafted the apology away. Redwald looked between the two of them

217

beaming up at him and felt his resolve snap. In return for the promise of a future pint, he agreed to tell them what had happened. In truth it was a sanitised version, omitting Morrimer's *little* revelation and Redwald's use of illegal magic, but was otherwise accurate. Charteris shook his head.

"I don't know chums, sounds bad."

"But then," Ofcross said, "we knew it would be when he said the Ellswych Guard were coming."

"Hmmm," Redwald said, stifling a yawn, "another group of people Lord Martingale dislikes." Ofcross and Charteris shared a look.

"It's not a group so much as one person, really," Charteris said, "I might have mentioned that Lord Martingale and his liege-lord don't see eye to eye?"

"You did," Redwald said, recalling their first conversation. "Why, exactly?"

"Well, he . . . he's concerned that Lord Ellswych would like to consolidate this fief into his own Earldom, take direct control of it, you see."

"He *does* seem to have a complex about that sort of thing," Redwald observed.

"Not without reason. He made a claim you see, Lord Ellswych, that is . . ."

"After the Great Storm," Ofcross added.

"Yes, after the Great Storm, he applied to the Court of Feudatories. Argued Lord Martingale didn't have the resource to manage the fief and then accused him of criminal negligence in the running of it."

"Oh, I see . . ." Redwald said, slowly grasping the point.

"Exactly, old boy. Completely nonsense charges, of course," Charteris scoffed, "but if the Court had agreed with either one then Archie would have been deprived of the fief, leaving Ellswych free to apply for it. Blighter would have got a portion of Archie's remaining property too if the criminal charge had stuck. Perks of being a feudal overlord, you see." Ofcross nodded. Redwald, however, made a subconscious connection and voiced it without thinking.

"I suppose that happened with Athelwulf Mullen too, didn't it?"

"Who's that old boy?"

"You know . . ." Redwald said, blearily searching for the title lost in his brain fog, "the old Earl of Barrowmill." Charteris blanched.

"Yes . . . yes I suppose it would have . . . in a *murder* case." He paused uncomfortably. "But then, I think he was a tenant-in-chief, so the King would probably have taken over those properties after . . . after he was executed. I don't know," he added hurriedly as an afterthought. Nevertheless, Redwald saw concern in his eyes.

"Well," Redwald sighed, "I suppose I can see it Lord Martingale's way, now you mention it." His sympathy, however, did little to alleviate his suspicions. In fact, as he politely extracted himself from the conversation and made a beeline for his bed, Redwald began to understand how the Baron might see himself; under siege and alone, behind the walls of his ruined castle.

His rest was sporadic and uncomfortable. Sprawled at an angle across the bed and pained by the slightest movement of his arm, he hovered unwillingly on the border of sleep and consciousness, disturbed by images of missing eyes and bloodied floors. By the time of his appointment with Asplund, he was no better rested and marginally more irritable.

219

"You're early," Asplund growled, noisily unbolting his front door. Dressed in a shabby coat and gloves, and holding an imposing set of keys, it seemed he had only just arrived home himself.

"My apologies," Redwald said, knowing full well he had knocked on the door at *precisely* 3 o'clock. Asplund merely grunted, before turning and heading down the dingy entrance hall.

Redwald stooped beneath the squat lintel, shook out his umbrella, and shut the door on Asplund's prim little front garden. Navigating by the light at the far end of the corridor, he followed the doctor into his office and found him kneeling by the fireplace, gloved hands fumbling with an orcite heating unit.

Surprisingly for so snug a house, the office was a large, well-appointed room. Carefully curated cabinets and bookcases lined most of the walls, while a commanding desk occupied the centre and faced a few matching chairs. Pushed against the wall on Redwald's right was an elevated examination bed, washed grey in the anaemic light seeping through the large bay window. Outside, Redwald could see Asplund's weed-tangled back garden and St Alia's beyond, where Charteris' beehives sheltered like sheep beneath a leaning oak.

"Thank you for offering to see me," Redwald said, as the orcite glowed and Asplund rose stiffly to his feet, "I do appreciate it."

"Archie asked," the doctor replied, pausing for a moment to examine the crossed sabre and scabbard that hung from the mantelpiece and suspending the imposing keys between them. "Now, shut the door and get undressed to your waist."

Redwald duly obliged, shutting the door with a click and hanging his clothes on the hooks above the bed. Meanwhile, Asplund turned to rummage in one of the cabinets, clinking and grumbling his way through the glass contents of a drawer. "How's the arm?" he asked, almost as an afterthought.

"Hurts like hell and . . . it's been bleeding," Redwald replied, removing his shirt and finding it stained with red.

"Hmmmm," Asplund growled, turning around with a small glass vial in his hand, his good eye twitching as he sized Redwald up. "You're about 16 stone, yes?" He raised a brow as Redwald corrected him. "Ah. Will need a bit more, then . . ."

"Should I take this off . . . the bandage, that is?" Redwald asked.

"May as well," Asplund said, clumsily pulling a further vial from the drawer and heading for his desk. Redwald peeled the saturated bandages from his arm as the doctor stooped and retrieved a leather instrument case, opening it to reveal a glinting syringe. Casting his bandage aside, the magician watched as Asplund tried to fill the syringe from one of the vials, fumbling on account of his gloves.

"What's that for?" Asplund, apparently startled, swore, and dropped the vial. The little glass cylinder bounced and rolled across the desk with a delicate chiming noise as the irate doctor barked a string of furious curses, wrenched his gloves off, and caught it just as it was about to shatter onto the floor. Silence fell. Asplund, leaning heavily on the desk, gathered himself with a few quivering breaths as Redwald sat uncomfortably on the examination bed. "I uh . . . I can come back later if you're in a hurry?"

"NO! No, it's fine," Asplund snapped, standing to and hurriedly filling the syringe with the vials' contents, "it's just for the pain. Now give us your arm; this will take a little while." Without waiting for a response, he crossed the room and took Redwald's arm in his rough, hairy hands. Having squirted a few droplets from the syringe and taken note of the time, he slid the needle into Redwald's flesh and began to slowly depress the plunger.

Avoiding the sight of the needle, Redwald peered out over Asplund's head, past the weeds, and towards the church. Skimming

221

the weathered headstones, his eyes eventually alighted on a wisping smoker propped against Charteris' beehives, its nozzle weaving a thread of silver through the churchyard grass. And yet, even as the trail of smoke dissolved gracefully into the shifting air, Redwald found himself distracted by a familiar scent.

Peaty, rich, and faintly sweet, it seized him by the nose and turned his head back towards the office. *Whisky.* Curious as to the doctor's taste, Redwald scanned the room for a bottle he might recognise. The increasing strength of the smell, however, was accompanied by the creeping realisation that it was second-hand.

Redwald glanced surreptitiously at Asplund. Although the room was cold enough to bring Redwald out in goosebumps, the doctor's furrowed brow was beaded with sweat, plastering his wiry black hair to his forehead. His single bloodshot eye, set above a veined cheek as pink as ham, was fixed intently on the half-empty syringe which shuddered in his unsteady grip, as though he were barely keeping greater tremors in check. Redwald's breath caught in his throat, however, when he saw the bruise. A black and purple blotch turning a sour, piss-coloured yellow at the edges, stretched from thumb to ring finger across the back of Asplund's right hand.

"What . . . what happened to your hand?" Redwald asked quietly, stifling his mounting dread.

"Hmm?"

"How did you get that bruise?"

"Uh . . . fell off my horse this morning, you know; on the ride up to the Folly."

"Take that out please," Redwald said, urgency creeping into his voice.

"I'm not done yet."

222

"Take it out!"

"I'll be done in a minute, just . . ." Without warning, Redwald leant forward, shoved Asplund away from him, and lunged towards the fireplace. Losing his footing, Asplund staggered backwards into his desk and turned to see Redwald wrenching the sabre from the mantelpiece with a metallic screech. "THAT'S MY OLD SERVICE SWORD! What the fuck are you doing?!"

"Lift your eyepatch!" Redwald said, awkwardly brandishing the sword at Asplund with his left hand and inching towards the door.

"Why should I?"

"Because you're lying to me about the bruise on your hand; you rode a horse down the Folly, not up."

"A slip of the tongue, you idiot!"

"And that bruise is black, turning yellow. You've had that for days, not hours."

"I know how bruises work, boy . . ."

"Exactly," Redwald said, "so you must be lying to me. I just . . ." he stumbled over his words, the floor lurching suddenly beneath him. So steady and sure just seconds prior, the office warped violently around him, forcing him to grasp the bed for support and upending his sense of direction. It almost felt as if he might fall on to the ceiling. Then, as quickly as it had come, the nausea passed. Asplund glanced surreptitiously down at the syringe in his hand as Redwald, panting, confused, and painfully aware of his partial nakedness, swung the sword back up at him. "What have you given me?!"

"I've not given it all yet," Asplund growled, "if you're feeling odd it's because you've had a partial dose, now get back on the table!"

Redwald shook his head as he stifled a retch, edging closer to the door.

"No," he said, keeping Asplund at sword-point, "lift your eye patch."

"Why . . ."

"Because I *know* it was you!" Redwald barked, reaching unsuccessfully for the door handle. "I know that under that eyepatch you've got a bruise a mile wide and I know I gave it to you. I know it was you who followed me that morning, you who stalked me through Athonstone, you who shot me, you . . . you who spoke to me." He paused then, memories of the attack glittering into prominence like raindrops beneath lightning. "And so I know you're hiding something else, protecting *someone* else. Please, tell me what's going on. Where is Alice?" Asplund did not respond, fixating silently on the sabre's tip. Finally, Redwald's fingers found cold metal. He grasped the door handle tightly, mingled relief and nausea coursing through him. "It's not too late, Asplund; we can still fix this, together. Just . . . just tell me where she is." Feeling his legs begin to shake, he mustered all his courage and made his final gambit. "He's . . . he's not worth it, Gerritt, don't . . . don't do this for him."

Asplund's blue eye met Redwald's own for a moment. "You . . . you know?"

"Yes . . ." Redwald sighed, "but he . . . I'm sorry, I'm so sorry, but he doesn't . . . he doesn't love you." Like a storm cloud sweeping over a lagoon, the doctor's eye darkened violently.

"Fuck you, boy." It all happened in under a second. Knocking the sword point to one side, Asplund stepped past Redwald's guard, forced him up against the door, and bent the sword out of his hand with a grip like iron. A swift, forceful blow to Redwald's chin dizzied him as the cold metal of the syringe was forced into his abdomen, causing him to gasp and retch. The magician fought as hard as he could, but with his right hand crushed behind his back, an ape-like grip on his throat, and a needle in his belly, there was little he could do. Flailing wildly at the doctor's head with his free hand, Redwald accidentally caught the eyepatch strap and ripped it from Asplund's face. Split by a nobbled pink and white scar, the lids of Asplund's ruined eye flapped pointlessly over veined, wet flesh, the skin around the socket having turned as deep a purple as Redwald's   gown.

"I told you," Asplund grimaced, "*love* doesn't come into it. This . . . this is just what . . . what he's reduced me to. Now stop struggling," he added, his usual growl replacing the taut quaver that had briefly seized his voice, "I need to make this look like an accident." He finally emptied the syringe into Redwald before allowing the magician to fall to the floor.

"Where . . . uhhh . . . where is she?" Redwald wheezed as he pulled himself shakily up by the bedstead. Asplund ignored him, crossing the room to a tall wardrobe. "Tell . . . uhhh . . . tell me." The doctor pulled on a white surgical smock, his fingers trembling on the buttons. "We . . . we can still . . . uhhh . . . save her." Asplund cleared his throat with a high-pitched growl, turned away from Redwald, and reached up to his face. After a few moments, his staccato breaths having stabilised, he turned back to find Redwald staring up at him.

"You must have told me the wrong weight," he said, sitting behind his desk and waiting, jaw set, "stuff should've taken effect by now. Even Julius went under faster than this. At least it's already open." Redwald, keeping his eyes fixed on Asplund, managed to lift his leaden hand up to his wound, before examining his fingers. They were stained with fresh blood.

"You . . . can . . . still . . . stop . . ." Redwald said, desperately trying to stay upright and conscious. Asplund's jaw no longer looked so set, his eye was glistening.

"I . . . I meant what I said," he began, growling away the sobs that threatened to surface, "I am . . . I am sorry for this, de Cordonnay . . . for all of it." It was then that something moved.

Over Asplund's shoulder and through the window, Redwald saw a blurry white thing shuffling unevenly towards some other blurry white things. Someone was outside the church, heading for the beehives. *Charteris.* A surge of hope swelled inside Redwald like a bubble rising from an ocean vent. He had to move, now. Casting about him for something solid, he settled immediately on the imposing keys. Dragged from their hook when he had taken the sabre, they lay a few feet from him on the carpet.

"What are you doing?" Asplund said, noticing the flicker in Redwald's eyes. He rose from his seat. Redwald drew as long and as a full a breath as he could, summoned all his strength, and pushed off from the wall. Asplund, confused, rounded the desk just as Redwald fell to his hands and knees, placing his fingers on the keyring. "The fuck are you doing?!" Then, just as Asplund moved to tackle him, Redwald gripped, launched himself across the desk and hurled the keys at the window.

Asplund, eye wide with terror, watched as the keys arced across the office and shattered the window with an ear-shredding crash. Ringing shards fell to the floor like jagged rain as Redwald used his last conscious breath to scream for Charteris.

CHAPTER 12

Celestial Navigation

"It is a well-known fact that the temperament, confidence, and imagination of a magician can affect the performance and efficacy of spellwork. What is less well-known is the tendency of magic, in limited cases, to affect the magician performing it.

In much the same way as long-term work as a coal miner may leave one with black-lung or practice of law may leave one a bitter and twisted cynic, magical practitioners who spend many years channelling the Power Divine may suffer the effects, with the gravity of these effects seemingly proportional to length of service. Though a complete understanding of this phenomenon is unattainable at present, due to the sparsity of cases, anecdotal evidence does exist. One of my acquaintance was my predecessor as Lord High Conjurer; Baroness Hart-Pride. Following 50 years of practice, she has become slightly immaterial. Though this may initially appear to be a contradiction in terms, the practical effect is that she sinks anywhere from 1 to 3 inches into anything she touches. The upshot is that shaking hands is awkward, drinking tea is painful, and swimming is nearly impossible.

Though I should counsel you not to concern yourself with this and to continue your studies in earnest. Such cases are as notable for their rarity as they are for their peculiarity."

Letter dated 42ⁿᵈ Oryntide 2315 from Sir Ismay Dammelbridge, His Majesty's Lord High Conjurer, to Miss Clara Wilmot.

Redwald lurched forward into consciousness and struggled for air. As if buried beneath a pillar and lifting a cathedral with every laboured wheeze, he felt his leaden chest slowly crushing him, while an otherworldly roar, like the frenzied buzzing of a million titanic bees, permeated his body and surroundings.

Opening his eyes to find an ill-defined darkness humming around him, he looked wildly about, hoping against hope that he might be wrong. He was not. Though cloaked in dreamlike unreality, Asplund's office was unmistakable. And something was watching him. He sought it out, looking from the creaking desk to the twinkling shards of glass, the groaning cabinets and the window eclipsed by heavy curtains, but could not find it. The malign presence remained hidden, but creeping slowly towards him, as deadly and as certain as the rising tide.

Desperate to escape, he tried to heave himself forward but failed, paralysed on the examination bed and trapped between sleeping and stirring. Consumed by terror, his wide eyes swivelled towards the thing that lurked in the shadows. He could *feel* its gaze.

Fixated on a blacker patch of waiting darkness, Redwald tried in vain to scream for help. Panic piled upon panic as he tried again, begging every limp muscle and exhausting what little breath he had, but all to no avail. *Surely* someone would hear. Then a breeze blew in through the smashed windowpanes and the curtain shifted. A sliver of light swung backwards into the blacker patch and found a pair of perfect red eyes, set into pocked, lacerated flesh.

"**Back in the waking world, I see.**" Redwald screamed silently. "**Or stuck on the threshold again? Maybe if you drank less . . .**" Halva'us stared at him, eyes shimmering in the blackness like red stars in an empty sky. Redwald, unable to break the gaze, watched in horror as the demon took his first exaggerated, jarring step out of the corner, arms swinging limply by his side. A further step followed, and then another, the demon lurching towards him like a gruesome marionette, all while fixing him with a bloodied, unblinking stare.

"**You know,**" Halva'us rasped, steadying himself on Asplund's desk with a pus-dripping hand, "**I seem to remember telling you to give up. Bet you wish you'd listened now, hmm?**" Baring his jagged teeth in what might once have been a smile, the demon finally arrived at Redwald's bedside as the latter strained helplessly against himself.

Heaving his cadaverous frame onto the bed, Halva'us lay by Redwald's side as would a lover, his bone-thick limbs creating narrow valleys in the mattress and his sticky, ragged skin brushing Redwald's own. Amongst the quivering shadows that crept and crawled around the ever-quaking room, only the demon seemed solid, fixed, and clear.

"**Not going so well for you is it?**" Halva'us said, walking his fingers up Redwald's midriff, "**Don't worry, though. It'll be over soon. He's almost here. Maybe you can try and kill *him*?**" He said, as if asking a favour. "**You may as well. You can't save *her* after all . . . so why not take *revenge* instead?**" The demon growled, looking hungrily up at Redwald and licking his tattered lips with a long, slimy tongue.

"Nrrrhh . . ." Redwald said, the slightest quaver of a voice colouring his paper-thin wheeze.

"**One more time . . .**" Halva'us said mockingly, leaning closer and putting what was left of his ear to Redwald's mouth. Redwald, fingers twitching from the strain, dragged as much air as he could into his shallow lungs and tried again. The taint of voice was stronger on this breath, though still little more than a whisper.

"Nooooo . . . " Halva'us smiled and planted a scratchy kiss on Redwald's forehead, the latter's screams echoing around his own head, inaudible through paralysed jaws.

"**Suit yourself. It's only a matter of time, though.**" The muscles around the demon's ear-hole shifted beneath his skin and he looked abruptly towards the corridor, freeing Redwald from his piercing glare. "**That, I believe, is my cue.**" Lifting himself from the mattress, he stumbled from the bed and headed for the door,

229

grasping its handle with oozing fingers. Swinging it open, he looked towards someone Redwald could not see, before turning to wink at the magician. **"Until next time, then."** The room whistled with the rush of freezing wind, Halva'us stepped across the threshold, and the door slammed shut behind him.

Redwald, still paralysed, could now hear talking in the corridor. Hurried, urgent voices drew closer, arguing between themselves. The co-conspirators come to finish him, he was sure. If he didn't move now, if he couldn't break free of himself, if he didn't escape, then he would never save Alice, never get home, never hold Adriel again. *You'd better get on with it then,* she said, matter-of-factly, from somewhere deep inside him.

He looked down at his fingers and forced each to slowly bend, one by agonising one. Once the fingers were alive, the hand soon followed, then the arm, then the chest and Redwald, as if tearing free of a concrete grave, wrenched himself upward into full consciousness.

He sat up just as the door opened, poised to fight for his life.

"Oh, my dear fellow, you're awake," Charteris said, still wearing his apiarist attire, "how are you feeling?" Redwald slumped back onto the bed, a shaking hand concealing tears of relief.

"See, I told you he'd be fine!" Giles snapped, following the Reverend into the room. Behind him came Norris, two unidentified Constabulary Guard officers, and Lord Martingale. The office being now thoroughly overcrowded, Martingale lingered on the threshold and refused to meet Redwald's eye, while Norris hurried out of the way behind the desk, crunching glass into the carpet and swearing as he did so.

"Is it really appropriate to do this now?" Charteris asked, as the taller of the two new Guardsmen approached Redwald. "He's exhausted."

"We need to know, Charles," Martingale growled from the corner, "flying accusations might hit someone they oughtn't." Redwald bristled at that.

"And Alice," Giles added, "I need . . . I need to find her." The taller Guardswoman turned to Redwald.

"Mr de Cordonnay," she said, projecting and enunciating as if Redwald were deaf, "I'm Captain Westferry of the Ellswych Guard, how do you do?" Redwald growled and wiped his eyes. He felt hungover.

"Smashing, thanks." She pursed her lips.

"And your arm, how does it feel?"

"It feels better," he said, gingerly placing a hand on his taut, clean bandages, "thank you." Westferry's junior officer, a woman as fair of face and hair as Westferry herself was otherwise, returned his smile and straightened the white armband that marked her out as a medic. "So," Redwald said, before Westferry could continue, "where is Asplund?" The tension became obvious only in the breaking; a room that had been deathly still suddenly rustling like undergrowth.

"Unaccounted for", "Probably out running errands for me," Westferry and Martingale said simultaneously.

"No, no, no," Redwald muttered, shaking his throbbing head, "we have to catch him. He took Alice, he . . . he did it . . . all of it. . ." a wave of nausea swept away his words as he tried to swing his leaden feet out of bed. The medic rushed to keep him from standing.

"So it *was* Dr Asplund who attacked you?" Westferry said, notepad in hand, pencil twitching.

"Yes . . . twice . . ." Redwald said, allowing the medic to ease him back into bed.

"Twice?" Westferry began, "but I don't . . . ". Martingale cleared his throat loudly from the corner of the room.

"Unless you want anything else from me . . ."

"No of course, my Lord, I understand. Please don't feel you have to . . ."

"I don't," Martingale said abruptly, his eyes boring into Redwald's "I just want justice done. Report to me when you're finished," he snapped, slamming the door behind him before anyone could answer.

Silence lingered in the Baron's wake. Charteris, sighing heavily, dragged a chair to Redwald's bedside and groaned into it, while Hawtree paced in Martingale's vacant corner.

"Mr de Cordonnay," Westferry continued after a pause, "if you would, and in your own time, please tell me what you know about Gerritt Asplund." Redwald gathered himself, sat up in bed, and did so. He told her how Asplund had invited him to the surgery on the pretext of treating his wounded arm, before sedating and then attacking him. He told her how he had obtained that wound in Athonstone, cornered and threatened by an unknown assailant who carried a service revolver, ranted about loyalty, and spoke in an unplaceable, yet familiar, growl. He told her about the blows he landed on that assailant and how Asplund had both displayed and lied about the resulting tell-tale bruises.

He then told her of his suspicions; that Asplund must have known what train Redwald would take to Athonstone because Morrimer had asked Asplund for the tickets; that Asplund wasn't working alone and was trying to protect someone by attacking Redwald; that, his attack in Athonstone having failed, Asplund must have

232

planned to sedate Redwald, re-open his wounds and allow him to bleed to death in the surgery; and, most importantly, that Asplund had been uniquely well-placed to kidnap Alice.

The group listened intently as Redwald, a naturally fast talker, began to trip over his own tongue in an effort to keep up with his racing mind. Asplund was a practical man, the magician explained, with a long-standing connection to the Hawtree family. Having ministered to Alice's every injury and illness since pulling her from her mother, Asplund would have known the correct dosage and method for sedating her. What's more, and given his frequent visits, he would also have known the Manor itself and been as trusted a presence in it as Giles, Morrimer, or Alice, allowing him to navigate the servant's passages with ease and access Alice and Morrimer's rooms without suspicion or detection.

"It's true," Hawtree sobbed, "I trusted him with everything, he practically raised Alice before I arrived, he managed the household accounts, all the staff, knew the house back-to-front, organised my calendar. He had free rein of the estate, his own set of keys . . ."

"Wait," Redwald said, frowning. "He had his *own* keys? Then why did he take . . ." The magician stopped dead in his tracks.

"What is it?" Westferry asked.

"He. . . he must have used it as a distraction to . . . to move her," Redwald replied shakily, unable to meet Giles' eyes.

"Used what?" Westferry pressed. Redwald paused and swallowed, before allowing the acrid sentence to billow from his lips.

"The Folly Key. He must have known we'd take the bait . . ."

". . . and leave the house unguarded," Westferry finished. "So you think . . ."

"Alice was in the house when we left." Thick silence suffocated the room. "Even if we hadn't seen it in the mirror," Redwald continued, thinking out loud, "the key would have turned up missing sooner or later. Asplund might even have discovered it *missing* himself, who can say?" Redwald's heart sank.

"Gerritt couldn've got her out, though," Norris interjected, "he came up to the Folly with Giles . . . Mr Hawtree."

"Unless his accomplice was the one who picked her up," Westferry said, Redwald nodding in agreement. The pieces, hours too late, were falling into place. Before the discussion could continue, however, Giles Hawtree snapped.

"And where is she *now*?!" he screeched, finally pacing out of his corner and towards Redwald. Westferry moved as if to defend the magician, but Giles stopped short. "We have to find her! NOW, do you hear me?! I don't care about Asplund, I don't care about . . . *any* of this. We just need to find her before . . . if she isn't already . . ." Tears welled up in his eyes.

"Provided I've understood what's going on here . . . *magically* speaking . . . I firmly believe that Mrs Hawtree is still alive," Westferry said, matter-of-factly. "If the position were otherwise, the men guarding your study would have alerted us to a disturbance. Since they have not, that means the . . . predicted event . . . can't have occurred there yet, in order for her to move backwards in time. Am I getting that right?" Redwald confirmed that she was. "And as for finding her . . ."

"We was going to ask Mr Cordneigh to do his hair spell," Norris said, suddenly perking up. Redwald rubbed his sore temples in frustration.

"I told you; it won't work for Alice . . ."

"Not Alice, sir, Gerritt. We found a few of his hairs around, see?" Norris hurried over and produced a handkerchief, opening it to show Redwald a few strands of Asplund's scraggy black mane. The magician wrinkled his long nose at the hair, but the plan itself was viable.

"I . . . I hadn't thought of that," he admitted, mildly irritated by the fact.

"Will it work?" Westferry asked.

"Yes . . . yes it should do, yes."

"Good," Westferry said, snapping her notebook shut. "We have also managed to obtain samples of the . . . present . . . Mrs Hawtree's hair. So your objections notwithstanding . . ."

"I can try both at the same time," Redwald said wearily, stifling the urge to vomit.

"Then we should perform the spell at the earliest opportunity. How long till he's fit to work Lieutenant?" The silver-blonde woman gently took Redwald by the chin and leaned in to examine his eyes, taking his pulse at the same time.

"The papaver's wearing off, but only gradually; he'll feel the effects for a while. Rest a few more hours at least," she said to Redwald, "but after that it's up to you." The magician looked across at Hawtree quivering in the corner, and instantly saw Alice quivering too, but alone and helpless in the dark.

"No, I'll do it now," he said, but in attempting to stand he sent the room into a tailspin and slumped, defeated, back onto the bed. A friendly hand gripped his shoulder.

"Rest, old boy," Charteris said. "Alice needs you in good shape." Behind him, Norris and the Lieutenant escorted a sobbing Hawtree out into the corridor while Westferry looked on.

"Fine," Redwald growled, "if you could . . ."

"We'll wake you in two hours," Westferry said, "Do you have everything you need for the spell?" Redwald thought for a moment.

"Magically . . . yes, yes I do. But I also need two compasses, directional not mathematical."

"I can arrange that, anything else?" Redwald shook his head. "Good, then we'll leave you to it." Charteris rose from the chair with a groan and followed Westferry towards the door, while Redwald eased his aching frame into a sleeping position. Before Redwald could settle, however, a thought struck him.

"What about Morrimer?" Westferry stopped. "I don't think he's . . ."

"Mr Thesk will remain in custody for the time being," Westferry said, coolly. "He's catatonic, hasn't said a word since his arrest, but I'm sure he knows more than he's letting on. I want him around when he speaks again. Besides, if you're confident that Asplund has an accomplice, then I can't rule out that it might be him. Unless, of course, you have concrete evidence to suggest otherwise?" The last sentence hung in the air for a moment.

"Only what Asplund said in Athonstone," Redwald replied, after a pause, "and the way he's been behaving. I don't think he *wanted* any part of this, he . . . he's acting under orders. And I don't think he would have taken those from Morrimer."

"I see," Westferry said, as Charteris listened carefully. "And do you have any *concrete* evidence to suggest that someone *else* might have given those orders?" The implication was clear. Formally accusing a Lord in his own Barony was no small thing. Redwald paused.

"Not yet," he admitted, wearily.

"Very well," Westferry conceded, "then we shall have to see what your spell does for us. Dr Asplund's testimony will prove vital and, ultimately, finding Mrs Hawtree must be our priority. We can discuss the accomplice later. Sleep well, get better." Nodding authoritatively, she turned and walked away down the corridor, leaving Charteris on the threshold. The Reverend looked as if he had been about to follow her, but instead he waited, long enough to hear the front door clatter shut. Once certain they were alone, he turned to Redwald, kindly concern etched into his forehead.

"Listen old boy, I feel I should warn you about . . . well, you remember our conversation about Lord Ellswych? You may find that his Guard try to . . . to . . ."

"My conclusions are and will be my own," Redwald snapped, apprehending Charteris' meaning even as fatigue dragged him into oblivion. "You needn't doubt that." Charteris paused, watching as Redwald lay his pounding head upon the pillow. Then, smiling wanly and apparently comforted, he wished the magician a speedy recovery and left, closing the door behind him. His optimism was misplaced, however. For all that Redwald might lack the evidence for a formal accusation, he knew deep down who was giving Asplund's orders. Who else, but the man who had done so for the last twenty years? And so, as Redwald drifted off to sleep, his dozing thoughts were of magic, compasses, and the walls of Martingale Castle.

Hours passed and dusk finally engulfed the village, Oryn's holy fire setting the horizon ablaze as the sky proper faded from cloudy grey to star-speckled blue. Redwald shivered as he knelt over his briefcase, removing his glasses and wiping the freezing slick from his eyes. It was not raining, but a fine mist suffused the air, seeping between cracks in cloaks and defying Norris' attempts to shield Redwald with an umbrella.

"You're absolutely sure this is safe?" Westferry said, hovering over Redwald's shoulder as Charteris and Hawtree looked on. The magician sighed.

"Nothing is completely safe, but I can certainly do it. I *could* have done it inside."

"I hadn't realised you would be summoning a star."

"It's the best way to do this and I have done it many times before, although generally, as I say, *inside.*" He had at least managed to chalk the spell on to the blackboard before Westferry gave marching orders.

"I understood this to be a complicated process. And with all due respect you're quite . . . junior, aren't you? So I thought it would be safest, just in case." Westferry, having a greater knowledge of magic than most, had unfortunately presumed that entailed a greater knowledge of magic than Redwald. So, while he did save time in that he had less to explain to her, he wasted just as much in answering her partially informed questions. It was already testing his patience.

"Yes, *much* safer out here where no one else could get hurt," Redwald said, glancing at the crowd of villagers held back by Westferry's men. Holding a mixture of orcite and flaming torches against the encroaching dark, it seemed the entire village had turned out to watch the spell. Lord Martingale, however, was notable by his absence. Growling to himself, Redwald placed the penultimate tribute item on the chalkboard and began to shuffle through his briefcase once more.

"It'll be alright, old boy," Charteris said from beneath the hood of a battered old cape, "you're a fine magician after all!" Given the icehouse fiasco, Redwald could not disagree more. Even his ribbon plan had been a bust. His notebook had been the first thing he checked upon waking; none of the ink spots had moved.

"And you said you've got a link with this star eh, Mr Cordneigh?" Norris said, between chattering teeth, "don't that make it safer?"

"It makes it a bit *easier*, yes," Redwald said, as he pulled a vial of what looked like indigo snow from his briefcase, "I've summoned it before, many times."

"Why this particular one?" Westferry asked.

"Because, relatively speaking, it's not that powerful. Which made it easier for me to summon in the first place." Westferry seemed underwhelmed by that, but Redwald ignored her. Instead, he pocketed the indigo snow before shovelling some candles out of his briefcase and on to the sodden grass.

"You're getting them wet," Hawtree warned him, unnecessarily.

"Doesn't matter, these would burn underwater if you needed them to. Help me arrange them, would you?" He said to Westferry, gesturing to his be-slinged arm, "push them into the ground around the chalkboard, if you can, every 6 inches or so should do." Resembling church tapers, the candles were tall and slender, drawn to a point where the curiously shimmering wick protruded from the iridescent black wax. Redwald set about thrusting them into the ground with some force, but Westferry hesitated, fearful of snapping them. Redwald noticed. "Don't worry, you'd need to smash these over your knee to break one in half. Even then you'd struggle."

A short time later the candles stood proudly to attention, encircling the blackboard like ancient standing stones. Redwald stood up to survey their work and carefully removed his sling, holding his injured arm close.

"I think that should do it. Do you have the compasses, the hair?" Westferry clambered to her feet and handed him two handkerchiefs, each containing fibres from Asplund and the living

Alice respectively, before offering up the compasses. One was a battered old thing, but as Redwald turned it experimentally in hand, it seemed to work. The other compass was just as old, but carefully and beautifully maintained. It was set in a clean brass case with precisely painted degree lines and decorated with an illustration of Bethin at the top. Enthroned on the moon, grasping her net in one hand and her quill pen in the other, she had been minutely detailed in black ink with a single horsehair brush. Redwald carefully wiped the congealing water droplets from its face. "Is this yours?" Westferry shook her head.

"Guardsman Norris volunteered it."

"Are you sure?!" Redwald asked, turning to him, "it won't work once enchanted and, frankly, it looks rather valuable . . . and quite beautiful."

"I'm sure, sir, and it don't matter about it working none. Ain't been used as such since Gran passed anyway. I reckon she'd like it doing some good again." He smiled.

"Thank you, that's . . . that's very kind of you," Redwald said, sighing deeply and looking back down at the heirloom in his palm, "Once this is over, I'll see what I can do to fix it."

"Thank you, sir."

"Can we find Alice now? Please?!" Hawtree snapped as he fidgeted on the spot.

"We *are* against the clock here Mr de Cordonnay," Westferry said, water dripping from the peak of her cap.

"Very well, then I suggest you take a step back," Redwald replied, "this can be a smidge . . . turbulent." Norris, taking his cue from Redwald's warning glance, furled the umbrella and joined the other Guardsmen at the perimeter, followed shortly by Hawtree and

Charteris. Westferry, on the other hand, stood by Redwald's side as he positioned himself about eight feet from the board, planting his back foot heavily in the mud.

They stood in silence for a moment as Redwald carefully checked and re-checked the board, interrupted only by the murmuring crowd and the hissing drizzle. Then, satisfied that everything was in order, the magician turned to the items in his hands. Carefully pairing each compass with a handkerchief, he stowed these pairs in separate trouser pockets, before retrieving the vial of indigo snow.

"What is that?" Westferry asked, as he emptied half of it into his palm.

"It's got a few names, Trig Powder, Stardust, Castalyst, but what it *does* is light all the candles and complete the spell simultaneously, since it's the final tribute. Provided I don't cock it up, of course."

"And if you do?"

"We'll all be blinded instantly." Preparing to cast, he stilled his mind and stared blankly into the middle distance, focusing on nothing. He could not close his eyes this time; he *had* to be able to see what happened and this *had* to be quick. The greater the gap between the candles lighting and the star appearing, the greater the danger, while a delay in the opposite direction didn't bear thinking about. But the spell was simple, and his wish was blissfully clear. He exhaled, swept the Stardust in a wide arc before him, and allowed the concept to surface in his mind.

All at once the torches were extinguished. Blurred bulbs of light hovering before his unfocused eyes, they blinked out of existence immediately and simultaneously as if a switch had been pulled. *Shit.* He realised his mistake before the screams.

"EVERYBODY STAY WHERE YOU ARE!" Redwald bellowed, as a ripple of panic swept through the surrounding crowd, "and

241

absolutely do not move; your torches are still lit!" Behind him, he knew, the setting sun would likewise have vanished. That might prove unnerving.

"I'm blind!" someone screamed, "Oryn save us!" replied another.

"STAND STILL!!" The magician roared, his voice echoing across the common as he fumbled desperately with the vial in his hand, squinting pointlessly through a darkness blacker than sleep.

"Mr de Cordonnay!" Westferry barked as Redwald emptied the rest of the powder on to his palm, "what have you . . ." He cast again, hurling the indigo snow towards the board and beseeching the stars for his audience once more. This time, the powder found its mark.

Heat, light, and air exploded from the board, almost knocking Westferry to the ground. The shockwave cracked a whip upon the Rise, echoing like cannon as the now-constant gale wrenched torches from hands, forced onlookers to their knees, and dragged Norris' umbrella into what once was darkness. Now, however, the valley was aglow. Shifting streaks of pale blue light emanated from the board, silvering every leaf, raindrop, and blade of grass and casting shuddering shadows behind each.

The candles, still arrayed around the board, burnt with a black fire as they fought to suppress the blinding light. Darkness emanated unevenly from them, rising and falling as each flicker cast a further shadow onto the floor, the obsidian flames spitting and crackling in the violent wind. All present watched in stunned silence, too shocked to even scream. All that is, besides Redwald.

Silhouetted against the blazing light, he had weathered the initial blast and now bore the brunt of the ongoing maelstrom, his gown snapping around him like a flag in a hurricane. He paused for a moment, locked eyes with the thing amongst the candles, and offered a shallow bow. For there, standing weightlessly upon the blackboard and encircled by empty flames, shone Pandrammon.

242

With tremendous gravity in every measured movement, the star turned his searing countenance towards the onlookers who squinted through the brightness and trembled at the sight. Glass baubles of congealing rain shimmered with starlight as they hovered in ever-shrinking circles around him. Drawn inescapably by the sheer weight of his presence, they rippled and sprayed in the wind before falling too close and disintegrating at his touch. Draped in a cloak of sea-spray sewn from the errant wisps that lingered thereafter, the star's skin glowed blue-white, pulsing as if lit from within by a roaring flame, and spotted with luminescent hairs that swayed and flexed as if in water. The hair upon his head moved and shone likewise, while the ageless face beneath it seemed at once impossibly old and fresh from the womb; as lined as it was taut and as a smooth as it was sunken.

Yet it was not this strangeness that disturbed the onlookers most. Like meeting a person thought dead or seeing in waking life a face from one's dreams, it was the unexpected familiarity of that face that so unnerved them. For, in the blunted widow's peak, the high bridge of the pointed nose, and even the imperious frown, they saw Redwald's features reflected perfectly in Pandrammon's own. Only the eyes were different. Cavernous oblivions without end, these were filled with pinpricks of coloured light and clouds of nebular dust that hung like opalescence in glass marbles, so that where those eyes swivelled in their sockets, galaxies swivelled with them.

Turning from the crowd, Pandrammon fixed Redwald with a cold, empty stare. The magician, poised and ready, simply held his breath and waited for his cue. For all that Redwald had the power to summon Pandrammon, the star was bound neither to stay nor even allow Redwald to live. Ancient, potent creatures for whom billions of mortal lives sputtered in and out of being for every second of their passing time, stars might recognise "old" bonds, but cooperation could *never* be assumed. Finally, and after a lingering pause, the star returned Redwald's bow.

Wasting no time, Redwald reached immediately for his pockets. Holding a compass and a hair sample in each hand, he presented them to Pandrammon before raising his voice to speak over the wind. It was a language that none of villagers knew; even Charteris understood very little of what was said. Yet none could doubt the import of those words. A grand and weighty tongue, Redwald seemed elevated merely by speaking it, his customarily even tone suffused with passion and gravitas as if he were addressing an army. When Pandrammon replied, however, the language took on physical form. So powerful was the star's voice that it beat upon the chest and reverberated through the organs of all who heard it, sending clear ripples through the grass around him, as if each syllable were a pebble tossed into a mirror-still lake.

And then, as quickly as it had started, the exchange was over and the course agreed. Pandrammon lazily raised a hand and the compasses and hair rose with it, floating out of Redwald's palm and into the air like the circling water baubles. Accelerating gradually towards the star's outstretched fingers, the items turned over and over in the rain until, finally, they made contact. The reaction was instantaneous. Pandrammon seemed at first to grow, his brightness rising to intolerable levels before, with a flash and a thunderclap, he collapsed in on himself. Shrinking to a point above the blackboard faster than a man could blink, all light, heat, and noise vanished into a singularity, leaving the green in cold silence. All that remained were the smoking candles, the torch-bearing villagers, and the drizzle.

Redwald quickly approached the board and knelt, fumbling in the darkness to find the compasses. Plucking them from where they had fallen amongst the sodden grass, he turned them towards the meagre light and examined them carefully, before wrinkling his nose and tutting. *Shit.* It was not unexpected; just annoying.

"Has it worked? Certainly made enough noise . . ." Westferry said, forcing a laugh and appearing over Redwald's shoulder. She brushed the rain from her cap with faintly quivering hands.

"Sort of," Redwald replied.

"What do you mean, *sort of?*" She asked sharply.

"Well, as I explained . . ."

"Mr Cordneigh!" Norris said, bounding over with a flaming torch, Hawtree and Charteris in tow, "that's yer connection with the star, is it? He looks just like you!"

"What?" Redwald said, distractedly. "Oh no, I see what you mean. No it doesn't look like me, that's just because *I* did the summoning."

"What's wrong with the compasses, De Cordonnay?" Westferry snapped.

"Well, Asplund's is fine," he said, showing the battered old compass to the group, its needle pointing straight and true.

"And what about Alice's?" Hawtree asked, shoving Norris aside, "time is running out and we *have* to find her!" Redwald set his jaw. They wouldn't like it, but he *had* warned them.

"That may prove difficult," he said, showing them Norris' gleaming heirloom and its entirely useless needle. Flicking and flitting like a mayfly, the metal sliver skidded around the face with as much direction and precision as a petal floating on a breeze, shooting one way and then another before ticking back on itself and spinning around to the other side.

"It's an effect of the temporal displacement, I'm afraid" Redwald continued. "This spell was premised upon one important fact; that stars identify us in a way peculiar to them. We still don't fully understand it, but we do know that it's in our blood, in our hair, in our skin, and that stars can . . . track it, among other things. So here, we asked a star to use that *signature* to recalibrate a compass to point to a person, rather than North. Now that works fine with Asplund, but in Alice's case . . ."

"There's two of her." Westferry finished.

"Precisely. The needle can't point in two directions at once and even though we've only provided hair belonging to the living Alice, the signature, the code, if you like, is obviously the same both for her and her deceased counterpart."

"So we can't find her?!" Hawtree snapped.

"Not directly," Westferry murmured, lifting the battered compass from Redwald's palm. Following the needle, she turned and looked back across the village towards the Double Standard, the last spots of light before the treeline and the sloping Rise.

"What's beyond the trees?" She asked.

"Not a lot, I'm afraid," Charteris said, "that little road just there leads up to the train station, such as it is, and thence to Elmsden, a village some distance from here." Redwald frowned. Disappointed though he might be with Alice's compass, Asplund's was pointing in precisely the direction he had expected.

"What about Martingale Castle?" The Reverend gave it some thought.

"No, I think the Castle is further up the Rise than that, old boy."

"Well, wherever he is we'll find him," Westferry said, "but we need to do that sooner rather than later. THORNE!" She shouted to a rangy lieutenant on crowd control duty, "saddle the horses, we leave immediately!"

"And Alice?!" Hawtree barked.

"If we find Dr Asplund, we find Mrs Hawtree. She'll either be with him or he can tell us where she is and he *will* tell us. I suggest you turn in for the night Mr Hawtree, this could take some time . . ."

"I just . . . I just have to find her." Hawtree sobbed. "Please, promise me you'll find her. She could be *anywhere*."

"We'll do our very best. Now please, Mr Hawtree, try and get some rest." Nodding disconsolately, Giles stood in silence for a moment before Ofcross, at Norris' direction, appeared out of the crowd to take her employer back to Hawtree Manor. Redwald watched, concerned, as his client trudged solemnly into the darkness. Once he was gone, Westferry quickly turned back to the matter at hand. "Guardsman Norris, I want you to brief all my men, both here and at the Manor, on Asplund. I understand he's a trained combatant and they need to know what to expect, whether we find him or he finds us. And Mr de Cordonnay, are you fit to ride?" Redwald swallowed, uneasy. It was not that he disliked horses on principle, and he *could* ride well enough. It was just that, as with all animals, he struggled to see past the dust in their fur, the mud on their hooves, or the ticks in their flesh. In his eyes, he might as well mount a dung-heap. Yet somewhere, out there, Alice was waiting. He gritted his teeth.

"Yes, I can ride," Redwald said, angling his elbow back into the sling. His suit would need a wash.

"Good, might be helpful to have you around. You could be in for a long ride, though; we know his direction, but not his distance. He could have got quite far."

"Perhaps," Redwald said, looking through the dark towards the Castle, "but then again, perhaps not."

"Well then, let's set to it gentlemen." With that, Westferry turned and headed towards Thorne, Asplund's compass in hand, while Hawtree and Norris broke off and went their separate ways. Charteris lingered, however, as Redwald slipped the malfunctioning compass into a breast pocket.

"Are you sure you're alright to ride, old boy?" He said, kindly.

"Should be fine, I can ride one-handed. Why do you ask?" Redwald said, catching a note in Charteris' voice of which he did not approve. "You think I'm still unwell."

"You've had a long, hard, day and I'm just concerned that you seem a bit . . . how shall I say this . . . fixated . . ."

"I see."

"And I don't think it would do Alice any good if we were to jump to . . . premature conclusions."

"No, I agree," Redwald said, "*premature* conclusions can be damaging."

"Especially," Charteris continued, "if an innocent person were to take unfair blame. And it wouldn't just be that person, you understand, but their friends and dependents also, who might suffer for the innocent's absence . . . or his replacement. Do you see what I mean, old boy?" Redwald shivered. He had heard words to that effect before, in a dark alleyway, with a gun trained on his chest. *I need to . . . to protect him . . . all of us.* Redwald looked down at the gently smiling vicar.

"Yes, I see," Redwald said, "but the facts are as they are and the compass will point where it points, whether we like it or not." Before Charteris could react to that, a Guardsman approached and presented Redwald with the reins of a bay horse.

"Then, I suppose . . ." Charteris said, changing tack, "I can only hope you find the true culprit. For all our sakes." Redwald climbed awkwardly up into the saddle, took the reins in his good hand, and allowed the Guardsman to adjust his stirrups.

"I will do my best." Spurring his horse into a walk, Redwald nodded at the vicar and rode off into the dark.

At the other end of the green the Ellswych Guard had split into two detachments, one mounted and one not. The mounted division carried torches and rifles, ready for the hunt, while their colleagues on foot were keeping the clamouring crowd at bay. Westferry swung herself nimbly up into the saddle as Redwald approached, before consulting the compass, pulling her steed about, and following the needle down the woodland road. The Ellswych Guard followed at her order, trotting between the parted crowds and illuminating the canopy from beneath with their crackling torches. Rushing to keep up, Redwald cantered past the villagers and into the rear as the last of the Guard filed into the woods.

Although the party travelled at a walk, the chatter of the crowd and light of the village both quickly faded behind them, replaced by deathly quiet and an encircling darkness. Every sound seemed muffled, if not by the moisture in the air then by the velvet blackness itself. Redwald heard neither the chitterings of creeping wildlife, nor the slow patter of water droplets between the trees, only the grinding hoofbeats of the horses and his own nervous breaths.

Flanked by two torchbearers, Westferry bore the compass ahead of her as she rode up front, carefully watching the needle shift minutely with every step. Redwald peered between the bobbing heads of the Guardsmen in front of him, trying to see where she was looking, but to no avail. Frustrated, he checked the notebook once again but, as always, the same blobs remained in the same places on his crudely drawn map. No weapons had moved, nothing was happening, resolution continued to evade him. Slumping petulantly back into his saddle, he was forced instead to wait for Westferry to prove his theory for him. Absent any better option, he tried to dull the pain in his arm with surreptitious and repeated swigs from his hipflask.

After a short, silent ride the party came upon the fork in the road. To the right, Redwald knew, the road faded up the Rise towards Martingale Castle while to the left it led to the station and, apparently, Elmsden. His heartbeat throbbed in his ears as Westferry looked down at the compass. Tilting it back and forth as her horse approached the turning, she took a reading, looked pointedly to Lieutenant Thorne, and reined her horse to the right. Like one of Martingale's own hounds, Redwald could smell blood on the breeze.

Yet it was a slow, laborious chase. With each step closer to the Castle, the road became rougher, the trees encroached further, and the torches seemed dimmer. Guardsmen were forced to steer their horses clear of fallen logs and duck beneath branches while Redwald, at the back of the column, could barely see the earth beneath his horse's hooves. It was almost as if the woods, like Charteris, were trying to protect their overlord from consequence, guarding the Castle with a multitude of knotted limbs. Redwald dodged a branch and spurred his horse onward. He would not be beaten.

Westferry seemed similarly determined. Turning to her aides on either side, she began giving clear, crisp orders, which rippled down the column like echoes in a tunnel. Further torches were lit, rifles were loaded, and the Guardsmen suddenly seemed more vigilant and alert. Redwald sat up in the saddle, his stomach taut, eagerly awaiting the parting of the trees and the appearance of Martingale Castle. They *must* be close. It was then that the column suddenly shunted to a halt.

250

Frowning, Redwald stood in his stirrups and peered ahead to see Westferry and Thorne dismounting. The road ahead was narrow, but not obstructed, and Martingale Castle was nowhere to be seen.

"What's going on?" Redwald asked of the Guardsman directly in front of him. Not having received his orders, the man simply shrugged. Wincing with the pain in his arm, Redwald slipped from the saddle and hurried around to the front of the column, dodging the flicking tails of horses and dismounting Guardsmen.

"Why are we stopping?" Redwald asked, approaching Westferry and Thorne as they conferred over the compass. "The road's clear for a while yet." They ignored him, looking instead between the compass and the darkness to the left of the road. Redwald frowned before glancing over his shoulder, towards the peak of the Rise. "He's not at the Castle?"

"Apparently not," Westferry said, eyes downcast. Following her gaze, Redwald noticed the groove of clean, compressed earth that had been worn between the tree roots at the road's edge. It was unmistakably the beginnings of a path. Westferry took Thorne's torch and knelt. As she brought the light closer to the ground, so the shadows grew. In particular, those of the gleaming and regular ridges left in the clay by a heavy boot print.

"Looks new," Thorne observed. Muttering agreement, Westferry stood again and held the torch aloft, this time casting light down the path itself. Sloping steeply at first and then more gently, it meandered down the side of what appeared to be a broad gully, before vanishing into the night. Redwald looked surreptitiously down at Westferry's spare hand. The compass pointed straight down the middle of the path.

"Ready the men," Westferry commanded. The preparations were made in short order and, leaving a junior officer to care for the horses, the group quickly began its descent into the gully. Finding the path itself too slippery, they instead walked either side of it,

251

treading carefully through the crackling undergrowth. Leading the way were a line of riflemen, each paired with a torchbearer, under orders to keep their rifles raised. Behind that line came Westferry, her compass, Thorne, and ultimately Redwald.

Per Westferry's strict orders, the group moved as quietly as possible. This, she had explained, was not so much to prevent detection of their arrival, but to aid detection of somebody else's. Although Asplund was being tracked, his accomplice was not, and if they turned up and made a noise in the dark, like the cocking of a gun, for example, a second's warning could save lives. She had carefully avoided the word 'ambush', but Redwald had borrowed a revolver all the same, grasping it awkwardly in his left hand. If he met Asplund in the dark again, he wanted it to be on more even terms.

As the path continued to descend, a noise gradually filtered through the night towards them. Thorne was the first to notice. "Water," he whispered to Westferry, "maybe he thought we'd bring dogs." Westferry tilted her head. Redwald listened too and realised that the noise was coming from in front of them, the hissing of a small, fast-flowing brook. Yet as they continued, no such brook presented itself. Instead, the noise grew louder and closer until they discovered it to be the rush of a wide, rocky stream. Westferry checked the compass and directed her men to cross. One by one, they began to pick their way carefully through the water, placing one foot after the other on slippery, sodden rocks, even as the stream roared around them.

Hearing assailants with that racket nearby would be damn-near impossible, Redwald thought. Having apparently realised the same, Westferry and Thorne had turned their attentions from the submerged path to the woods and stream on either side of them, watching like hawks for any sign of movement. Redwald, unnerved by their paranoia, began to look backwards down the path as well, fearing that he might see someone silhouetted against the light from the road. It was then that they heard a gun cock.

Loud enough to be heard above the stream, it was followed immediately by a succession of further clicks as more weapons were armed. Turning quickly to the noise, Westferry, Thorne, and Redwald discovered that their own gunmen were the source. They were staring dead ahead and had stopped in their tracks.

"Captain," one of the riflemen whispered, "over there." Following the barrel of her gun, Redwald saw it too. At the very edge of the light cast by their torches was a vague brown shape, rising out of the water to about waist height. Westferry quickly gave the signal to proceed, and as the party inched closer, the shape of a man congealed out of the darkness.

Facing downriver and away from the party, he knelt in the stream with his head bowed and face hidden by his curly black hair and greying whiskers. Apparently gazing into the water that rushed around his thighs, he did not react to the Guard's presence, merely swaying on the spot as if rocked by a breeze. Redwald imagined for a moment that he might be crying. Westferry consulted the compass one last time and pocketed it before raising her revolver and stepping out beyond the line of riflemen. She gestured for them to surround the man.

"Dr Gerritt Asplund," Westferry announced over the sound of the river, "in connection with the kidnap of Mrs Alice Hawtree and the attempted murder of Mr Redwald de Cordonnay, I hereby place you under immediate arrest and require you to surrender yourself into my custody. If you resist, I am entitled to use deadly force to ensure the safety of my officers, do you understand?" A breeze blew through the trees and Asplund's head moved on his chest. He did not, however, respond.

"I need an answer, Doctor," Westferry said, her men edging around the silent Asplund. The feeling hit Redwald all at once. Something was not right.

As the most distant officer moved around to face Asplund, her rifle raised, something shifted downriver. It was a long, thin something, undulating with the flow of the stream and entirely invisible, until disturbed and revealed by the officer's leg. It looked like a knotted, pale rope, twisting and turning in the water and leading back to the doctor himself. The rifleman's torchbearer joined her, noticed the rope as well and followed it back to Asplund, lifting the torch as he did so. The rifle was quickly lowered.

"Captain, he's dead."

CHAPTER 13

A Shot in the Dark

". . . the Crown arrived in a great iron wagon, guarded by many fierce soldiers, for it was very important. When it arrived, the rich man sent the maiden to fetch the Duke. She climbed the stairs up to the tower where the old man slept and roused him from his slumber. The Duke refused to try the Crown. The maiden tried to persuade him, but he would not budge and went back to bed. Yet, outside, the trumpets were sounding over and over, for the soldiers wished the Duke to try the Crown before they moved to the next castle. Angry, the Duke bade the maiden open the shuttered windows, so that he could shout at the soldiers and demand that they leave. The maiden did so, but when the Duke went to the window to shout, he found he could not. There, before him, his castle was rich with colour again; his beautiful gardens were revived, fresh and bright and humming with honey bees, just as they had been so many years ago. The Duke saw this and knew what the nameless maiden had done . . ."

The Tale of Alynore – Traditional Tales for Growing Children, collated by Dr C.F. Twistle (Allpress) 1992

Redwald leaned back in the creaking leather armchair, compulsively polishing the dimples of the beer mug with his fingertips. He raised the glass once more and took a draught.

Although prone to mysophobic compulsions, it would be unfair to describe Redwald as a squeamish man. In fact, his "fear" was not of dirt or gore itself, but the possibility that he might be unable to clean them off. As such, the sight of Dr Asplund, dead and frozen in place in the middle of a stream, bowels nestled in his lap like a cluster of mushrooms between the roots of an old tree, had not unduly disturbed him. If anything, it had angered him.

Lowering his glass, he scowled across the bar towards Westferry and Thorne. They had set up offices at the largest table the Double

255

Standard had to offer and were poring over a map the size of a tablecloth. Around them, a collection of bedraggled Ellswych Guardsmen, Hawtree security, and local volunteers dined at whatever space could be found for them, the Landlord and his daughter delivering food and ale despite the lateness of the hour. The atmosphere was subdued, hopeless.

Much about Asplund's death remained uncertain, but, Redwald reflected bitterly, he had not died alone. He had taken their best lead with him. Westferry had therefore resorted to more old-fashioned methods. Dividing the map up into squares, she had dispatched her motley coalition to search the village and surroundings from top to bottom including, at Hawtree's insistence, the villagers' homes.

Since then, team after team had returned from their assigned sectors with nothing to report, and square after square had been filled up with bright red crosses, each plunging Redwald deeper and deeper into furious despair. Every shake of a weary head had ratcheted the tension one notch further, and while the teams themselves were quickly passed into the care of the Landlord, Redwald himself could not relax. He had failed. All of his magic, all of his efforts, had counted for nought and somewhere, alone in the dark, an innocent woman was inching slowly and painfully towards her end. Mrs Ofcross, whose visits were the sole punctuation in this miserable routine, was the only person who deigned to speak with him, though this was largely to convey frenzied queries from Giles and deliver home-made confections to the volunteers.

As Redwald had stewed in his nook beside the stairs, so Charteris had been at Martingale Castle, delivering the news of Asplund's passing. That, Redwald thought drily, seemed rather efficient. Charteris was the most obvious candidate to reclaim the keys and succeed Asplund as Martingale's Seneschal. Then, before Redwald could stop himself, his thoughts were back in the woods, with the old Seneschal.

256

The pale rope, it had transpired, was the Doctor's small intestine, a technical point that Redwald had internalised with macabre interest as the silver-blonde medic explained it to him later. Streaming out from the pile of fetid organs, it had glistened wetly in the light as Redwald approached and as the torches gathered, it had become clear that where the water flowed around Asplund, it was stained red with his blood. A crusted red sabre, grasped in his hand and frozen in place, lay across his thighs, while the keys of his Seneschalcy hung at his belt. Cold and still, Asplund might have seemed statuesque, even dignified, were it not for the hollow in his belly and the spewing, slippery rawness that had once sustained him. Redwald took another drink, unable to shake the thought that when it first emerged, it would have steamed in the night air.

Another team opened the door with a thud and Redwald was suddenly back in the room. Looking them over as they shook the rain from their cloaks, he realised with a chill that this was the last group to report in. The rest of the room seem to have noticed that too; the bar had gone from quiet to silent. The bone-white skin of Redwald's over-washed knuckles cracked and bled as he clenched a shaking fist.

The team's leader, a Guardsman, removed her cap, tucked it under her arm and marched up to Westferry's table, leaving her companions on the threshold. The conversation was short and accompanied by shaking heads. Westferry, failing to conceal her disappointment, directed the Guardsman and her team to a clear table, before inking a bright red cross in the map's penultimate square. As the low-level chatter resumed, Mrs Ofcross, who had lingered after her last delivery, rose from where she sat amongst the volunteers and made directly for Westferry. She had apparently made the same connection as Redwald.

Draining the last of his pint, he put the glass down with such force that Westferry, Thorne, and Ofcross all looked up at the noise, just

257

in time to see the magician marching across the room towards them, cradling his injured arm.

"Mr De Cordonnay . . ."

"May I ask," he hissed, "why the Castle has not been searched?" He placed a finger on the sole un-crossed square.

"I was just asking the same thing," Ofcross added indignantly, "Mr Hawtree is insisting that the *entire* village be searched, top to bottom, including the Castle."

"Do you have any concrete evidence to suggest that Mrs Hawtree is there?" Westferry said, calmly. In spite of himself, Redwald rolled his eyes.

"Surely we can draw *some* inferences? We know Asplund isn't working alone, we know he's taking *orders* from someone . . ."

"And can you *prove* who that someone is, do you have any evidence? A witness to a conversation perhaps, a scribbled note, anything?"

"No, but there's only one person who . . ."

"Then I ask again, Mr de Cordonnay, do either of you have *concrete* evidence to suggest that Mrs Hawtree is *actually* at Martingale Castle?" Redwald seethed. He did not, in fact, have such evidence. Nor from the looks of it, did Ofcross. Redwald had only suspicions; Martingale's obvious motive, Asplund's links to both Hawtree and Martingale, Asplund's clear and unrequited love for the latter, and Martingale's consequent and undisputed control over his perennial subordinate.

"How could we possibly have that when *we haven't searched the Castle*?!"

"Precisely, now you see my problem."

"*Your* problem?!" Redwald barked, "*She*'s the one who's going to die!" Mrs Ofcross put a shocked hand to her mouth and Redwald realised his error. The bar was silent again, and Redwald could feel the eyes upon his back. Westferry looked between him and Ofcross, staring down the overly inquisitive, before returning and speaking to them in a low voice.

"You may be unfamiliar with the law, Mr de Cordonnay, but I am bound by it in the commission of this investigation. In particular, by the Feudal Privileges Act 2062. To put it simply, where a noble tenant - Lord Martingale - requests the assistance of their liege lord - Lord Ellswych - in constabulary matters, the liege's constabulary must not debase or otherwise infringe upon the rights of the tenant in the commission of their duties . . ."

"What about the Barrowmill case?!" Redwald interjected, "*His* properties were searched."

"He was subject only to the High King, the rules are different," Westferry snapped, "In *this* case, under the 2062 Act, I need either Lord Martingale's permission to search the Castle, which I do not have, or a bloody good reason to override his wishes, which I'm only going to do if I'm damn sure that I'll find something. So I ask again, *what evidence do you have?*"

"I would never accuse . . . Lord Martingale himself," Ofcross whispered, "but isn't it enough that Mrs Hawtree is clearly nowhere else?" It was a weak point.

"Nowhere else *in the village*, Mrs Ofcross, she could be *anywhere* outside of it. We don't even know how long she's got left, the kidnappers could take her miles away before bringing her back for the murder, if they even do follow through . . ."

"Is the body still in the icehouse?" Redwald asked Ofcross.

"Yes she is . . ."

"Then it's still on course to happen," Redwald growled. Another weak point. He had never knowingly changed the future before. What would happen to the deceased Alice's body if he succeeded was completely unknown to him. Nonetheless, he *had* to ensure that the living Alice was rescued and while Ofcross might doubt Martingale's guilt, he did not. "As for how long Alice has left, I may have been wrong, but not *that* wrong. We're short on time."

"How can you be sure?"

"Because I'm good at what I do!" Redwald snapped, surprising himself. Westferry, however, was unmoved.

"Even if that were true, the position is the same. I need either Lord Martingale's permission, or actionable evidence that we'll find something. Without those, and absent any further magical assistance *you* can provide, Mr de Cordonnay, there's nothing else I can do about this. I suggest you both try and make yourselves useful in some other way. I'll be widening the search radius tomorrow. More volunteers are always welcome."

"Very well," Redwald spat, scratching his initials onto the sign-up sheet volunteered by Westferry and turning on his heel. If evidence she wanted, then evidence she would get. He reached for his gloves and headed for the door, quaking with rage.

"Mr de Cordonnay!" Ofcross said, almost jogging to keep up as Redwald reached the door. "What are we going to do . . . Mr Hawtree . . ."

"Tell him I'm on it," Redwald said, pulling on the first glove as she followed him out into the drizzly night.

"But what shall I say . . ."

"Anything!" Redwald snapped, turning with thunder in his eyes as she placed an arresting hand on his good arm. Letting go immediately, she stumbled backwards under the force of his glare. For a moment, silence lingered between the two of them.

"I say, what's going on here?!" asked a voice in the darkness. Ofcross and Redwald turned in unison as a sodden Charteris ambled into view, an orcite lantern swinging from his fist. Redwald, as if coming to, suddenly realised what he had done.

"I . . .I'm sorry, I was just . . ."

"We were discussing Alice," Ofcross said, cutting across Redwald's half-formed apology.

"Have we found her?" Charteris asked hopefully. His face sagged when Ofcross confirmed they had not. "Oryn protect that girl," the vicar murmured, circling himself across the chest, "what a night it's been. I had hoped . . . but all we can do is keep looking, I suppose." Redwald, abashed by his rudeness, had been avoiding the vicar's gaze. At the latter remark, however, he suddenly looked up. *Evidence or permission.*

"How is Lord Martingale?" Ofcross asked.

"I've seen him worse," Charteris confided, "but he's . . . he's struggling. Of course, who wouldn't be?"

"And did he . . ."

"I'm afraid so, back in post," Charteris confirmed, patting with a clink the ring of keys that had moved from Asplund's hip to his own. Redwald decided to seize the opening.

"And how are you?" He asked. Charteris' smile returned, if only in part.

"I've been better as well but thank you for asking old boy. How's the arm?"

261

"Improving," Redwald lied, "more worried about Alice than anything else, I must say. Who isn't, though?" Ofcross nodded.

"Indeed old boy, these are . . . trying times for us all," Charteris said, "Now yes, that um . . . that reminds me," he looked between them towards the pub. "I have a few matters to attend to, but would either of you fancy a drink . . . maybe?" Redwald slowly removed his glove and pocketed it.

"Of course, my pleasure. Mrs Ofcross?"

"No," she said, a little disapprovingly, "I had better get back to the Manor and I thought . . ."

"Very well," Redwald said, "Reverend, will you have the usual?"

"Thank you, yes, much appreciated."

"Wonderful, in that case. I'll . . . I'll see you in there. Just need a quick chat with Mrs Ofcross, to update Mr Hawtree, you understand."

"Not to worry, old boy. I'll see you in the usual spot. Good night Tabitha," Charteris said, wearily touching what remained of his forelock before turning and heading for the pub.

"Mr de Cordonnay," Ofcross said, hands wringing afresh, "I'm not sure now is the time to be drinking."

"I understand Mrs Ofcross and you're quite right, but I won't *just* be drinking. I have an idea, but I may need an hour or two to put it into action. Could you send a boy down around midnight to collect my update?" After a slight pause, she nodded. "Thank you and . . . and I'm sorry for my earlier rudeness. I didn't mean to snap." Mrs Ofcross reached into her beige handbag and unfurled a small umbrella, the drizzle now hardening into rain.

"That's ok Mr de Cordonnay. At least you care," she said, smiling awkwardly. "I'll send a boy in an hour." With that, she turned and headed off towards the Manor, bearing just enough news to ward off Giles, for the moment at least.

When Redwald returned to the warmth of the bar, he looked around and saw Charteris in the Westferry / Thorne corner, leaning over the map. He was now Martingale's official liaison after all.

Leaving the Reverend to his business, Redwald headed for the bar and ordered a pint for each of them. It was only when he leaned against the pewter counter, waiting for the Landlord to pour, that he realised his hands were shaking. He was not entirely sure *what* he had been about to do or *how* he would have done it, but he was sure that if he had been caught doing it, he would have lost both his job and his liberty, never mind the damage to his arm. Auto-transformative magic was illegal, *full stop*. Auto-transformative magic for the purposes of breaking and entering, into a Lord's property no less, was something else entirely.

The Landlord duly poured the pints, Redwald paid, and he retreated to his favourite nook, pulling up a stool for himself and ceding the chair to Charteris. Meanwhile, the Reverend finished speaking to Westferry and, instead of joining Redwald in the nook, headed across to the bar. Pausing for a moment to ensure he could be seen, he lay a few loud thumps upon the counter-top.

"Good evening everyone!" he said, as if addressing a congregation, "may I have your attention for a moment? As I'm sure you are all aware, and in addition to the ongoing tragedy of Mrs Alice Hawtree's disappearance, Dr Gerritt Asplund, long-time Seneschal of this Barony, doctor to us all and friend to many, has passed away." The room was silent. Charteris paused for a moment, gathering himself. "Lord Martingale has asked me, partly in light of the continuing search for Alice, to perform Gerritt's funeral at the earliest opportunity. I have agreed to do so. Anyone who wishes to come and pay their respects is therefore welcome at St Alia's, 4 o' clock tomorrow, when we will render Dr Asplund's eternal spirit unto Bethin and to Boros. Captain Westferry has kindly agreed that her officers will take over the searches for the duration of the service and the subsequent wake to be held at Martingale Castle." There was a general murmur of gratitude and Westferry nodded.

"Finally," Charteris said, a weariness in his voice now, "it appears . . . it appears from the circumstances that Gerritt decided to take his own life. Now I know this will be greatly upsetting and shocking for many of you, but I want to make two things clear. Firstly, you can never know what transpires in the minds of others. That knowledge is given only to Psurania, She-Of-The-Thousand-Eyes. None of you, therefore, should hold yourselves in any way responsible for Gerritt's decision. It was his to make and his alone. Secondly, if any of you are suffering from doubts, from sadness, anxious about anything at all, or struggling in any way whatsoever, I want to make it clear that I am available to you at any time, for whatever purpose. I look forward to seeing you all tomorrow."

Leaving the bar, Charteris headed over to the nook and slumped into the vacant chair with a groan, the pub humming with conversation once more. Redwald pushed a glass towards him, before raising his own.

"The dead." Charteris repeated the toast and they drank.

"I'm sorry old boy, I appreciate that must have been difficult for you to hear as well, given that . . ."

"He tried to kill me twice . . ."

"Hmmm," Charteris took a long swig.

"I thought it *might* be," Redwald confessed, "but it wasn't really. I get the feeling . . . as I said to Westferry, I don't think he *wanted* to do it. It wasn't *personal*."

"As I said, you can never know," Charteris replied, swigging again, "but you're right. He may have been a born soldier, but he wasn't an animal."

"So . . . you agree," Redwald said carefully, "you think he was acting under orders as well." Charteris, haggard as the magician had ever seen him, looked up wearily.

"Now, listen here old boy. . ."

"I'm not . . . I'm not necessarily *accusing* anyone, but you must see the logic of it, Reverend."

"It's not the logic I'm quibbling with, it's the facts. I was just with him, if he were hiding anything I . . . I would have known . . ." The unfinished sentence hung in the air like a bad smell. Doing nothing to dissipate it, Redwald instead watched Charteris' eyes flick between the magician's sling and the vicar's own pint.

"I'm sure you're right," Redwald lied, kindly, "but not everyone has access to the facts and for them, the logic might raise questions."

"Has Westferry said anything to you?"

"No. Nothing besides that she isn't allowed to search Martingale Castle." Charteris ran his fingers through his greying, thinning hair.

"No, Archie would have to actively consent to that. But then . . . why would he?"

"I rather think the Guard might be asking the contrary," Redwald said. "As far as I'm concerned, though, that's not the issue. We should be able to say, with certainty, that we've done all we can for Alice. I need . . . I want to make sure we've checked *absolutely* everywhere for her. The Castle grounds represent the only unturned stone in the village."

"But you must understand . . ."

"Reverend," Redwald said, rubbing his temples with quivering fingers, "please. I *need* to do *everything* to find her. I can't . . . I can't just stop. I can't just leave her to it. If I miss something, if I don't try hard enough, if I don't explore *every single possibility* and . . . and she turns up dead . . ."

"Then it wouldn't be your fault . . ." Charteris said, kindly.

"Yes, it would!" Redwald snapped. The feeling had overcome him without warning and as his eyes bore into the Reverend's own and silence hung between them, he felt it crawl slowly up his back. It was a hot, creeping panic, a demonic voice inside that told him over and again that he was insufficient, that he was lazy, that he had wasted opportunities, had risked disaster by doing so, and that the only remedy was to work until the problem was fixed or he could work no more. Suddenly ashamed, Redwald looked down at the table. "I'm sorry, I really am. I just . . . I'm running out of magic here. So, I'm asking for your help. Is there any way, just to rule it out, that you could persuade Lord Martingale to allow a search of the Castle? I know that puts you in . . . a nearly impossible position, but I . . . I don't know what else to do." All but the last was true, for even as Redwald gave his earnest apology, he squeezed the gloves beneath the table. Charteris paused, thinking.

"All I can do is ask."

"Thank you, thank you so much."

"But I shall have to be delicate, and I wouldn't expect an answer first thing. We are burying his best friend tomorrow after all. Which reminds me," Charteris sighed, "I had best be off. Early morning for me." He downed the last of his pint, excused himself and rose, before placing a knobbly hand on Redwald's shoulder. "You're doing a good job, old boy. Please remember that. Now sleep well and we'll see what the Vaeltava bring us on the morrow."

Redwald lingered in the bar for a while longer, staring blankly into space, before the adrenaline slump finally hit. He was asleep in his chair when the messenger boy tentatively prodded him awake. Once the boy had been dispatched, with assurances for Giles that a search of the Castle was being sought, Redwald headed for his pillow. Despite the slump, however, he did not sleep well. Instead, as the twinkling firmament shifted above him, so a constellation of mis-matched images swirled beneath the dome of his skull; an upward shot, an old gun, a secret room, a silent butler, a murderous, spurned doctor, a jealous, impoverished lord, a blameless girl displaced in time, a village map with a blank square and multiple, stationary ink spots, blood-red ribbons, keys, and a pile of steaming, reeking organs.

The morning after was sickly pale and damp with fog, crawling over the horizon like a dying animal and bringing a smell of damp decay with it. Not wishing to simply wait for Lord Martingale's response and having been hounded by further messenger boys from the Manor, Redwald reported to Westferry and was assigned to search the woods beyond the railway line. Dragging an off-duty Hawtree footman and dim-witted Guardsman along with him, Redwald compulsively searched every ditch, dell, and copse he came across, but found nothing. Nothing that is, besides the growing feeling that he should simply fly into the Castle himself and hang Martingale's response. Returning to the Double Standard, he reported the disappointing news to Westferry before turning to the Landlord.

Busy with preparations for the wake that evening, the Landlord rather grumpily confirmed that, no, Charteris definitely hadn't left Redwald any message, or otherwise been looking for him.

Redwald's stomach becoming ever tighter with nerves, he promptly volunteered for another search and was duly dispatched, a second pair of unwilling teammates in tow, his doubts growing. By the time they returned, the funeral bells were tolling. Redwald vacillated on whether or not to attend, but the draw of a potential Martingale response was too strong.

Redwald was fortunate in that he had not attended many funerals. He was even more fortunate in that at least one of those had been for somebody he had never met. This funeral, however, was different. Keenly aware that he might not be entirely welcome, he filed into St Alia's last and sought out an empty pew.

Like logs around a campfire, these were arrayed around the Flame Eternal on six sides, the seventh and eighth sides belonging to the pulpit and the private space beyond the triangular rood screen. Those pews near the centre were packed, so far as Redwald could tell, with most of the village, with Ofcross beside Norris, the Landlord and his family across from them, and Lord Martingale at the centre. As was customary, the Lord's pew was far grander than the rest. Flecked with gold leaf and supported by two carved, snarling bulls, it would usually have been reserved for the Lord and his family, but Martingale was sharing it with his tenants.

The outer pews, by contrast, were bare. Leaving the village to their warmth and subdued chatter, Redwald settled into a spot at the very end of the most distant pew, pulling his gown close against the draught that howled beneath the door. Looking absently up at the ceiling, he found that grotesque again; a demon chewing on a raven.

His darkening thoughts were interrupted, however, by the appearance of the Reverend Charteris. Dressed in pure white robes over his black cassock and draped with a long green chasuble, he mounted the steps to the jutting pulpit and placed a heavy tome upon the lectern, the Flame Eternal lighting his features from below. A group of choristers followed him from behind the rood screen, rather like ducklings following their mother, and assembled on either side of the pulpit, waiting for him to begin. The upward lighting did Charteris few favours, casting shadows of his wrinkles and aging the already old man considerably. Much as he had the night before, he looked desperately weary.

"Welcome friends, to St Alia's and to this service of remembrance and prayer in honour of our friend, Dr Gerritt Asplund." He gestured to the space directly beneath the pulpit. There, supported on an ornate cast-iron stand and lit by the flickering Flame Eternal, was a humble clay urn, cradling what remained of Redwald's would-be killer. "Today, we shall commend his body to the soil, and his spirit to the embraces of Bethin and of Boros. We shall pray that the deeds of his life are soundly judged and that, Boros-willing, his spirit might be returned to us in a new life, drawn hence by the mortal remains of the old. But first, please rise and join with me in reciting the Adulation of Oryn." There was general shuffling as the congregation rose and began to monotone in unison:

"*Oh Heaven's King, his praises sing, in Oryn's name we pray*

Whose burning light, hath ended night, and ushered forth the day

Ascension thine through darkness shines, to guide our mortal way

Our heads now bowed, but faith uncowed, we gather here and say . . .

Protect us Lord from evil, that lurks this world without

And spare us sin and sorrow, the choking fog of doubt . . ."

The Adulation's words caught in Redwald's throat as something gasped behind him and a cold, rushing wind, too strong to have blown under the church door, tugged at his gown. "**Quite the scene, is it not?**" Redwald flinched impulsively for his hipflask,

269

but restrained himself, always conscious that Martingale might see him.

"You seem surprised. Did you really think the walls of a church would protect you from *meee*?" Doing his best to ignore the sight of Halva'us' blistered cadaver as it lurched into his field of vision, Redwald hurriedly picked up the words of the Adulation again. **"*Sacred ground*,"** Halva'us continued sarcastically, leaning over the back of an occupied pew and oozing pus into the wood. **"My dear, foolish boy, did you really think that I could be *stopped* just because some *nobody* in a cassock declares something *sacred*?"** He tutted, tousling a little girl's hair in a way that she might have mistaken for a draught, soiling her pure, silken strands with ulcerated, flaking skin. **"Besides, it was in a church that we first met, was it not? Where you made your unkept promise."** He paused for a moment. **"Perhaps you could kill *this* one?"** He said, indicating the girl, **"She's veeery small, it wouldn't be difficult."** Redwald simply clenched his jaw and said nothing, doing his best to hide the shaking in his hands. At the Adulation's conclusion and Charteris' instruction, he sat, along with the rest of the crowd.

"Thank you," Charteris said, as Halva'us turned to grimace at Redwald, "Now, if I may, I should like to invite Lord Martingale to say a few words about Gerritt, who served this Manor and its Lord for many years as Seneschal." The Baron rose, made his way around the Flame Eternal, and replaced Charteris in the pulpit. Halva'us, meanwhile, was stumbling towards Redwald like a maniacal drunk, swaying atop impossibly thin legs and fixing him with a hungry stare.

"So, you're just going to sit this one through in silence, are you?" Halva'us sneered, speaking over Martingale and shuffling into Redwald's pew to take a seat, bumping his bony, scabbed legs into the magician's own as he squeezed past. It was all Redwald could do not to scream as the creature placed a tattered arm on his be-slinged shoulder and leaned in close to whisper. "**You do that more as you get older, you know, just stand there all stoic. It's so impressive.**" They both looked up at Martingale. "**Perhaps if I told you a little secret, that might loosen you up . . .?**" Halva'us cooed, his sticky tongue and lips crackling wetly in Redwald's ear. The magician looked up at Martingale. "**You're teeeempted . . .**" Halva'us observed, as the Baron concluded his brief, but impassioned, eulogy, "**I could tell you some secrets about that one, you know,**" Charteris resumed his place at the lectern, "**Or even that one . . .**" it was then that Redwald made his decision. He shook his head.

"**Noooo?**" Halva'us oozed. "**Are you sure? This is a one-time offer. Could save you a loooot of bother.**"

"NO," Redwald hissed, under cover of the congregation rising for a hymn. One deal was enough.

"**Then it's your loss, I suppose. Or rather, *her* loss,**" Redwald fidgeted, conscious that if he didn't stand for the hymn someone would notice but terrified of aggravating Halva'us if he did. "**You can't pay your debt with negligence, you know. You have to *actually* kill someone, not just let it happen.**" The opening chords of the hymn rang out on the organ and Halva'us grinned at Redwald's obvious discomfort. "**Not going to stand, Redwald? Disrespectful. What will His Lordship think?**" Redwald frantically checked on Martingale, but the Baron's gaze was fixed on the urn. "**Although,**" Halva'us continued, putting a freezing, sodden hand on Redwald's thigh, "**I suppose it would be cruel to deprive you of your search, no? Especially since we're *such* good friends.**"

"You can't bargain with me . . ." Redwald whispered, as the first judgmental glances came his way.

"**Oh, no baaaargain,**" Halva'us drawled, "**But my next visit will be faaaar worse, you can count on that. No, I'll leave you** now, but before I do; a bit of *friendly* advice. Even if you *do* get your search and even if the Baron *does* show you every little piece of his silly little castle; it won't do any good. The girl's still dead and aaaalways will be . . ." and with that he was gone, no more than a rush of cold air once again. Redwald shot to his feet, grasping the pew in front for balance.

His legs and voice shook as he forced his way through the hymn, suppressing both nausea and tears as he kept time, if not tune, with the mourners. The organ's dying notes skewing sharp as they echoed through the nave, the hymn finally drew to a close and Redwald slumped back into the pew, clutching the bench to steady himself. Though it seemed to last a lifetime, the rest of the service passed without incident. Further hymns were sung, eulogies given, and scriptures read, and when Charteris bid them stand for the last time, Redwald found himself on firm ground once more.

Following the congregation, he stood unobtrusively to one side and let them gather around the plaque to the 20th Baron and Lady Emily. There, beneath an adjacent plaque of Lord Martingale's donation, Charteris finally laid Asplund to rest beneath the church floor. Though he tried to avoid meeting them, Redwald could see that Martingale's eyes were red.

The interment ceremony over, a solemn voluntary played on the organ and the congregation gathered around Lord Martingale, preparing to lead him out into the evening and towards Asplund's wake at the Castle. Redwald, however, hung back. Standing beside a pillar, he waited as the Baron, his tenants, and finally the organist filed past, hoping for a moment alone with Charteris.

"Mr de Cordonnay," someone hissed at his elbow. It was Ofcross.

"Yes?" Redwald whispered distractedly, watching as Charteris walked behind the rood screen to deposit his smoking censer.

"The Castle . . . erm, your plan, what shall I tell Mr Hawtree?"

"I don't know," Redwald said, as Charteris re-emerged with a decanter of mead and three glasses, "but wait a second and I might have an answer for you."

Stooped and shuffling, Charteris smiled at them as he approached, sloshing the mead in hand.

"Forgive me, but I saw you waiting and thought you might fancy a drink. I know I do. Redwald I assume you're game but Tabitha, will you join us?"

"Please," she said, holding her handbag in front of her like an apron. Placing the glasses on an adjacent altar, Charteris filled and distributed them, before slumping backwards into a pew.

"What a day," he groaned, putting his feet up on a hassock.

"Not a fan of funerals?" Redwald asked.

"Not my favourite," Charteris conceded, his brow unfurrowing slightly with the first swig of mead. "Especially not on short notice; these things take a bit of preparation at the best of times. But being an ex-naval man, I think Archie is used to a degree of . . . military efficiency which can be a bit . . . difficult, shall we say."

"Well, I thought the service was lovely, Charles. Very well done," Ofcross said, smiling.

"Thank you, Tabitha, I do appreciate that." He paused for a moment, wrestling with something. "I don't suppose we've heard anything more about Alice?"

"I'm afraid not," Redwald confirmed, leaving a painful and deliberate silence in his wake. The hope that had glimmered beneath Charteris' bushy eyebrows faded.

"Ah, I see," he said. After a little contemplation, he drew a deep breath and turned in his seat to face Redwald. "About this search, old boy. Before I say anything I just . . . I just want you to know that I am concerned about Archie. It's an exceedingly difficult time for him and I just worry, as I have before, that you two might clash."

"I understand that," Redwald said, diplomatically.

"I'm also concerned about the Ellswych Guard. Given their . . . prior behaviour, I don't want any search to be . . .misused by them. Now, I'm not sure *how* they'd do that," he said, as Redwald made to speak, "but I'm just . . . I'm on the lookout. So, what I wanted to say was . . . or rather, I would just like your assurance that . . ."

"I will be sensitive," Redwald said, "and I've no desire to implicate any innocents. I just want Alice safe." Charteris nodded grimly, though he did not seem entirely comforted. "But this is all moot if we don't actually have Lord Martingale's permission. *Has* he given us permission?" The vicar paused.

"Yes, he has." Cool relief flooded Redwald as if he had quenched a burning thirst. "But there are conditions, old boy."

"I see." Redwald's stomach immediately tensed again, clamping shut like a pulled knot. "What are they?"

"Well . . ." Charteris began, carefully, "the Guard can search the grounds of the Castle however they like, but only you and Westferry can search inside the manor house. I'll be there as well . . ."

"That sounds fine . . ."

"But, when you do your search, it's up to Archie which rooms you visit. And he can stop the search entirely, if he wants to, at any time." Redwald frowned.

"But . . . doesn't that defeat the point? I mean, how do we know he isn't just . . ."

"Redwald!" Charteris snapped, taking the magician entirely by surprise, "just think, for a second, what you're asking of him. His oldest friend has just died, it's the anniversary of his family's death and you want to drag a Captain of the Ellswych Guard through his home, whose lord, might I remind you, has already tried to take that home from him. Archie doesn't *have* to do this at all, so it's the best you're going to get! I can't . . . I can't do any more for you." Exhausted, he leant forward and cradled his head in his hands. Redwald, though unconvinced, had decency enough to feel embarrassed.

"You're right," he said, "we're lucky to have a search at all, especially under the circumstances. I owe that entirely to you, Reverend. Thank you . . . for all you've done." Charteris heaved himself upright, waving the thanks away like a wasp.

"As I said old boy, anything for Alice. Besides, I shouldn't worry too much about Archie closing places off. I expect it'll just be Georgina's old bedroom."

"The former Lady Martingale?" Redwald asked. Ofcross shook her head.

"No, Mr de Cordonnay, the future Baroness Martingale . . . or she would have been. She was Archie's daughter."

"And I believe Archie has kept her room precisely as she left it, 20 years ago," Charteris added, "hence the prohibition, you understand." Redwald nodded slowly, an eyebrow arched. "Now, does either of you have the time?" Flicking his pocket watch into his palm, Redwald confirmed that he did.

With Asplund's wake about to begin, Charteris suggested they head up as soon as possible, the better to complete the search in good time and give Archie some peace. Agreeing with the Reverend, Redwald helped him tidy up while Ofcross was dispatched to

Hawtree Manor and the Double Standard, informing Giles and Westferry of the arrangement.

It was dark by the time Redwald and Charteris left the church. The morning's fog had not lifted and so their steps up the Rise were dogged by a freezing, cloying mist, clinging at their ankles and reflecting the pale lantern light directly back at them. Combined with the unkempt grass, scattered boulders, and Charteris' newfound reticence, the opaque air made the journey both difficult and unpleasant.

To reach the Castle, therefore, was a considerable relief, not least because of the bonfire crackling merrily in the courtyard. Drawing them like moths through the ruined gatehouse, Redwald felt its warmth the moment he crossed the threshold. Hot enough to burn off the fog, it had even cleared the air around the Castle, such that the keep sat like a stone in a river of shifting mist, sparks showering up to the watching stars at the collapse of each burning log.

Around the fire were clustered groups of villagers, tankards and glasses in hand, whose collective mood seemed to have lifted with the fog. To Redwald's surprise, the sombre memorial had not followed the village into the courtyard but had instead been replaced by a joyful reminiscence, signified by the rumble of conversation and the mingled aromas of grass, fire, and meat. This transition was aided, Redwald suspected, by the barrels of ale, cider, and wine that were stacked along the right-hand wall. These were tended to by the Landlord while Guardsman Norris supervised the charcoal, slowly turning three sweet-glazed hogs on a spit while flirting inelegantly with the Landlord's daughter.

Following Charteris around the fire, Redwald looked up and saw the Keep looming above them, the Manor House at its base. Built into and out of the Castle that surrounded it, the Manor House was also the only part of the structure that remained habitable. A strange, lopsided building, it sloped from a small stone tower at the left to blackened timber and chalk-white plaster on the right, embellished (or repaired) with brickwork in between. Capped with a thatched roof that seemed to slide off one side like a bad toupee, it was the architectural equivalent of a quilt designed by committee. It might even have been attractive, Redwald thought, but he felt uneasy at the sight. Practically built of nooks and crannies, he could think of no better place to hide someone.

"How's the arm?" Westferry asked as they approached. Stood to attention by the Manor House door and surrounded by her men, her arms were crossed behind her back and shrouded in a Constabulary-issue cape.

"Tolerable," he replied, still preoccupied with the house behind her, "How are you?"

"Cold," she retorted, "and looking forward to getting on with the job. Mr Hawtree and Lord Martingale are over there, so shall we . . ."

"Giles is here?" Charteris said, turning to look. Indeed he was, gathered, like a good number of other people, around Lord Martingale. Holding court to this small crowd from atop a makeshift throne of fallen masonry, Martingale grasped a tankard in one hand, and a friend's shoulder in the other. More animated than Redwald had ever seen him, he seemed to be sharing stories of Dr Asplund which, in the spirit of the wake, his listeners found greatly amusing. Giles in particular laughed heartily at each, clearly unaware that the Baron was studiously ignoring him. Charteris cleared his throat.

"Captain, I take it you're ready to proceed?" She nodded. "Very well, I'll fetch His Lordship," he said, shuffling towards the crowd, hands clasped in the small of his back. Redwald smiled uncomfortably at Westferry, smelling incoming small talk like rain on the wind.

"I should congratulate you, Mr de Cordonnay," Westferry said after a slight pause, "I didn't think we'd get to search this place." Redwald, thoroughly pre-occupied with the image of Alice trapped within while they all dithered without, accepted the compliment with a grunt. "We've searched the grounds as well," she continued, "and the ruined towers, so far as they're accessible. Found nothing. After that I gave Norris a break." Half-way across the courtyard, the merry Guardsman finally kissed the Landlord's daughter.

"Yes, I think Guardsman Norris has done his part," Redwald growled. "Presumably you found nothing?"

"I'm afraid not. If she's not in the house, she's not in the village." Over by the little crowd, Redwald watched Martingale's face rise at Charteris' approach and sink at his first words. Westferry followed his gaze. "I hope you're not having second thoughts, Mr de Cordonnay."

"How do you mean?" He said, turning to look at her.

"Well, I don't know what . . . if you've been told, but certain of the locals might not have taken kindly to our arrival and I wonder what they might have said to you. If so, you should understand that Lord Ellswych simply wants . . ."

"I don't care what either of them wants, frankly. What my client wants - what I want - is to ensure that Alice is found," Redwald said, knuckles clenched white as he waited impatiently to search the house, "So whatever dispute there was, or is, it's all just background noise to me, provided nobody stops me doing my search. I just wish we'd hurry up with it." Apparently satisfied, Westferry nodded. Martingale stumbled to his feet.

"Good. Then one more thing; I'd keep . . ." She was interrupted by a cheer from Martingale's crowd. Clinking tankards with a number of them, he turned to the courtyard at large and thrust his drink into the air with his attendants' roaring approval.

"To the next life!!!" he bellowed, sending the oldest toast echoing up the Rise.

"*And all the lives to come*!!!" came the ancient reply, the entire courtyard responding in unison. Raising their glasses, they showered the ground with drink before draining the remnants in silence.

". . . keep your wits about you, I was going to say," Westferry concluded, looking out over the 100-strong crowd that littered the courtyard, "because if we *do* find something, *they* won't like it." It was a valid point and one that Redwald had completely ignored. Following her gaze, Redwald finally appreciated the size of the crowd, the *mob*, that stood between them and the castle exit; outnumbering the Ellswych Guard 5 to 1. As Martingale approached, towering behind Hawtree and Charteris, Redwald reached into his pocket and checked for the gloves.

"Right," the Baron snarled, reaching for the door without pleasantry or delay, "let's get this over with. I trust Charles has explained the rules."

"Yes, My Lord," Westferry said, "We understand. And thank you again for . . ."

"Magician?" Martingale pressed, fist around the iron door handle, eyes boring into the wood.

"I understand," Redwald said. Apparently satisfied, if not pleased, Martingale snapped the latch open and stooped beneath the lintel. Before Westferry could follow him, however, Hawtree had poked his head around the door.

"My Lord, I wonder if I might also . . ."

"No," Martingale said, greeting his waiting dogs and slumping into an armchair without a backward glance.

279

"Leave this to us, sir," Westferry said, "we will keep you informed, of course, but this may take some time. Perhaps you should eat?" She said, gesturing to the trestle table upon which Norris was carving the first of the hogs.

"No . . ." he whispered, ashen-faced "I . . . I don't think I could. I'll wait, but please, let me know. I just want Alice to be found."

"We'll do our best," Westferry said. Nodding dejectedly, Giles turned and headed slowly back to Mrs Ofcross, whom he had left by the fallen masonry.

"Shall we?" Redwald said, ushering Westferry and Charteris politely, but quickly, into the house. They had already wasted more time than he would have liked. Shadowing them across the threshold, Redwald snapped the door shut before turning to his surroundings.

The door had opened onto a space that seemed to serve both as entrance hall and drawing room, though neither term really suited. Dominated by a gigantic stone staircase to their right and a pock-marked wall at the far end, the room's position at the base of the keep was clearly in evidence, a fact which seemed to have divided successive occupants. Some had prioritised comfort over grandeur, littering the place with knick-knacks and naval memorabilia, footstools and armchairs, while softening the stone staircase with a patchwork of rugs laid over the steps. Others had clearly favoured a return to their august roots, hanging portraits in every available space and building a fireplace against the far wall, crested with the Martingale arms and large enough to roast a horse in.

The Baron himself occupied one of the two armchairs that framed this fireplace, the dogs sleeping peacefully at his feet. Redwald observed them warily as Charteris approached, but they did not stir.

"Thanks again, Archie," Charteris said, shuffling over to Martingale's side. The Baron toyed with the half-empty tankard in his grip.

"Just want this done, Charles. Bad enough that Gerritt was involved, worse that someone else might be out there. Just want him and Alice found." *Him*. That was an interesting slip.

"My Lord," Westferry said, lingering on the threshold, "may we . . ."

"Sooner rather than later, Captain," Martingale said, staring into the fire and swigging his beer. "My patience is already wearing thin." Westferry flashed a hurried glance at Redwald and the two began to frantically search. It was not long, however, before Redwald began to consider the exercise futile.

Absent the intervention of magic, it seemed there was nowhere in the room that Alice could be hidden. Kicking over carpets to look for trapdoors yielded no results, nor did peering behind bookcases or toying with the volumes in the hopes of discovering a passage. The room contained no chests, trunks, or cupboards and there were no adjacent small rooms; even the expected nooks and crannies were sparse. The only thing that came close was the hexagonal base of the small stone tower, and even that contained nothing more than a few chairs and a bookshelf.

After a while, Redwald turned his attention to spaces between the portraits, hoping for the tell-tale blur of a concealment charm. He even searched the umbrella stand made out of an old artillery shell and the wooden model of HMS Hartspur, just in case someone had the magical wherewithal to alter their dimensions. Though it was incredibly unlikely that Alice's would-be killers were magically-trained, Redwald *had* to check, *had* to be sure. Martingale, who was watching these latter efforts, snorted.

"Once you've checked the Hartspur's brig, the kitchen is on the other side of the stairs," he said, before sinking back into his chair with a groan. "Would've thought a *magician* might have a bit more to offer here, eh, Charles?" Charteris did not respond, simply attempting to smile at Redwald.

The latter ignored them both, heading to the base of the stairs where a door led through into the kitchen. As with the entrance hall, it was a riot of well-organised clutter. Copper pots hung beside herbs over a blackened stove, while a rustic table and chairs were drawn up on the terracotta tiles. In the far corner, a door led to the larder, which Redwald found full of everything from mustard to mutton and apples to oranges, but entirely empty of Alice. As with the drawing room, he checked everywhere and everything, clattering through the kitchen cupboards and opening the screeching oven door for the merest whispers of a clue. There were none.

Westferry having also failed to find anything, they returned to the drawing room. Redwald was beginning to think that the only way of hiding a woman in this house would be in multiple pieces, but he stifled the thought with a shudder.

"My Lord, thank you for your indulgence," Westferry said, "since we have searched this floor . . ."

"You want to see the rest," Martingale groaned, "fine." Patting the dogs as he stood, he made to join them at the base of the stairs. As he passed the empty chair, however, he reached towards the headrest, compulsively stroking a head that was no longer there. Redwald quickly stifled a pang of sympathy. Whatever the man had suffered, Alice did not deserve to pay the price.

Westferry, who appeared not to have noticed the Baron's tic, stood aside to let him pass, before following him upstairs. Redwald waited for an ambling Charteris to join, before heading up as well.

The stairs led to a stone landing and what appeared to be the bricked-up entrance to the keep, a ragged, arched outline around a smooth new wall. Either side of the stone landing, where the balustrade ended roughly and abruptly, the floor became wooden, stretching out along the front of the empty keep and forming a corridor lit by softly-glowing orcite lamps. At one end, this corridor ended in a tall square window, at the other, a heavy iron-banded door. This latter door, Redwald suspected, belonged to the manor's stone tower. It was very firmly shut.

Martingale led them towards the window first. Between them, Redwald and Westferry searched a bedroom, a bathroom, and a study, with the same degree of care and measure of success as before. Moving to the other side of the staircase, they then searched a room that Redwald initially took for a bit of storage space, before realising it was Martingale's own quarters. With neither curtains, fireplace, nor wash-basin, it consisted largely of a side-table and an army camp-bed, draped with a few thin sheets. As a place to sleep, it was about as basic as you could get without sleeping on the floor; even the adjacent dog baskets looked cosier. Though quicker than the other rooms, their search yielded the same results. Dread settled on Redwald as he stepped back into the corridor, wiping cold sweat from his brow. There were only two rooms left.

Through the half-open door into the next room, Redwald could see flowery wallpaper, a small, quilted bed, an iron stove behind a grill, and what looked to be a large travelling trunk, decorated with the Martingale bull. Yet he paused on the threshold, uneasy. Though scattered with stuffed animals, toy soldiers, and dolls, the room seemed oddly sterile, as if the toys were fixed in place and the wallpaper greyed from years in semi-darkness.

The magician had little time to dwell on this, however, before Martingale joined him. The Baron flattened the upturned corner of the closest rug with the tip of his shoe, before gently closing the thick, oaken, door.

"Not in there," he murmured, as if trying not to wake someone. Redwald paused, looking at the closed door and wishing he could see through it.

"Of course, my Lord," Westferry said, placing a hand on Redwald's good arm, "we understand." Redwald, suppressing his urge to violently rebuke them all, was left with little choice but to agree.

"Fine, then it's just the treasury left. If you insist."

"We do," Redwald replied. Martingale raised a warning eyebrow and headed to the end of the corridor.

Latticed with iron, and made of a dark, imposing wood, the door to the treasury would not have looked out of place in a dungeon. Featuring a grizzled lock the size of Redwald's fist, it also faced them at an angle, a function of the way the plaster house had been built around the stone tower. Martingale reached for his keys before realising, with a growl, that he had left them downstairs. He turned to Charteris.

"Have you got Gerritt's . . . erm . . . your set, Charles?" The Reverend fumbled obligingly at his belt and handed over the Seneschal's keys. Martingale selected a particularly ugly and large one from the ring, thick enough to concuss a rat, and opened the door with a noise like an anchor chain being dragged across a hull. "Don't touch anything," he said, as the door screeched open. Redwald's heart sank. Barely big enough for a single person to stand in, the room was a glorified broom cupboard.

Lined on all sides with cupboards and display cases, interrupted only by the doorway and one arrow-slit window, the treasury guarded the very concentrated dregs of a once significant fortune, now less plentiful than the shelves on which it sat. Among a few other trinkets there was a battered coronet, placed on a folded blue and gold robe, a Baron's chain of office, the livery collars and badges of a few orders of chivalry, some knightly spurs and a battle-notched sword. Stepping over the threshold, Redwald followed the line of shelves upwards, right to the ceiling some feet above him. There, a halo of rolled papers was stuffed like honeycomb into the uppermost ring of shelves, wax seals hanging from the ends like severed heads. Comprising land deeds, titles, and estate contracts, these papers were arguably the greatest treasure here; collectively proving Martingale's right to the Barony.

But that seemed to be it. The only things here were of sentimental value or necessary to support the Baronial dignity; there was no sign of magical concealment, no trapdoors, no passages, no Alice nor evidence of her ever having been there. Panic gripped Redwald by the throat as he frantically searched the room, Alice's face floating before his eyes.

"No, no, no," he muttered to himself, "there *has* to be something." Stooping to examine the lower shelves, he was soon distracted by images of Alice that forced themselves up from the depths of his mind. Kneeling, dishevelled, and bloodied as she had been in his dream, she looked up at him with desperate eyes and that dreadful plea on her lips, *You'll catch him afterwards, won't you?* Yet the more he searched, the less he found and with every passing second, the more her imaginary face felt increasingly tangible. And then it was.

Her gaze hit him like a train, his heart skipping a beat. Blurring into reality from inside his head, a woman's eyes stared up at him from a shelf by his ankles, her polished and familiar face surrounded by a shower of sovereign coins. Redwald swore.

Before Westferry or Martingale could stop him, he stooped and lifted the Maiden of Maidensworth from her shelf, turning the familiar duelling pistol in hand.

"What the hell are you doing?!" Martingale barked, reaching in from the corridor and wrenching it from his grip, "I told you not to . . ."

"How did you get that?!" Redwald said, as Westferry and Charteris turned to the commotion.

"Inherited it, you fool. Same as the rest!"

"No you can't have, I've already seen . . ." the words tailed off as Redwald realised what he was looking at. This duelling pistol was not marked with a red ribbon. "This is the *other* Maidensworth Duelling Pistol?"

"Where do you think the Hawtrees got theirs? Couldn't sell them both, though, no matter how much Julius begged." Westferry peered at the gun.

"Mr de Cordonnay, does this weapon. . ."

"Yes, it does," Redwald said, glaring up at Martingale. "I tagged its counterpart precisely *because* it met the specifications. I would have tagged this one as well, had I known there were others around; *why* didn't you tell me?" Redwald snapped, "you were there, at the Gala, you knew I was looking for antique weapons!"

"None of your business, that's why!" Martingale replied, turning to Charteris as if for approval. But the Reverend took a while to meet his Lord's eye and when he did, his expression was riddled with doubt. "Anyway," Martingale continued, a little less sure of himself, "I knew it was safely locked away . . ."

"With a set of keys belonging to Asplund . . ."

"That's *Doctor* Asplund to you!" Martingale snapped, "The man was a hero, *is* a hero! Anyway, I thought . . . I couldn't know . . . and besides, this is the King's gun!"

286

"The one he *actually* used or . . ."

"No!" Martingale barked. "The one he was *supposed* to use: it doesn't work, it was never a threat; that's why I never mentioned it! And, frankly, because I'd had just about enough of people rooting through my affairs," he said, glaring at Westferry, "and now I *definitely* have! Get out!" Without waiting for a response, he barged into the treasury, forcing Westferry and Redwald out of it.

"We need to tag the gun!" Redwald snapped. Westferry agreed.

"My Lord, this does not assist the investigation . . ."

"The investigation is over, Captain!" Martingale said, shoving the gun back on its shelf before returning to the corridor, "at least in *my* house. Oryn knows where the poor girl is, but she's not here. Now leave me in peace!"

"I *need* to tag that weapon!" Martingale saw red. Slamming the iron door shut with enough force to rattle the windows, he rounded on the magician.

"GET OUT OF MY HOUSE BEFORE I DRAG YOU OUT!" He bellowed, reaching for Redwald's injured arm as the dogs downstairs began to bark and howl.

"Archie!"

"WHAT, Charles?!" Standing a little way down the corridor, the Reverend Charteris had cupped a hand to his ear and was listening intently.

"Do you hear that?" The Baron paused for a moment, as Redwald and Westferry both tilted their heads. Beneath the barking, there was another noise. It started as a high-pitched but muffled wailing, like a crying child heard from underwater. Then there was a tapping, as if someone were knocking hard on a distant door, the wail replaced by mangled words.

287

"I'll see who it is," Martingale said, heading for the stairs, "come on!" He gestured for them to follow, but Redwald stayed put. The noise was closer than that. Then he felt it, a banging and scraping of the floorboards as something heavy jerked and moved in the next room; beyond the door that Martingale had shut. He did not hesitate.

Crossing the corridor before an enraged Martingale could stop him, he wrenched the door open to see the trunk jerking and shifting on the floor as someone writhed and screamed within.

For a time, all was a blur. Rushing to the trunk and finding it locked, Redwald bellowed at Martingale for the key. As the ashen-faced Baron fumbled in a chest of drawers, Westferry opened a window and called down to her men, whose arrival prompted a chorus of barks from the dogs downstairs. Charteris hung back in the corridor, seemingly scared to even enter. Grabbing the key from Martingale's palm, Redwald unlocked the trunk as the Baron slumped against a wall, throwing the lid open with a bang as the Ellswych Guard arrived, weapons drawn.

Hair thinning and bruised, her wrists and ankles bloodied, Alice lay there in her greasy, soiled nightdress. She stopped screaming as the lid was opened and burst instead into tears of relief. Immediately Charteris was at Redwald's side, comforting Alice as the magician removed his sling and carefully untied her.

"It . . . it's Asplund" she gasped, as Charteris pulled the cloth from her mouth, "I saw him . . . he said . . . said sorry . . ."

"There, there, child. You're safe now . . .", Charteris began, but his words were cut short by the eruption from behind him.

As Redwald and Charteris had been seeing to Alice, so Westferry had been seeing to Martingale. Wasting no time, and as soon as the trunk was opened, she had ordered her burliest officers to subdue and arrest the Baron, who now knelt handcuffed between them, snarling up at her.

"You can't POSSIBLY believe . . . !"

"Lord Martingale," Westferry said, calmly, "I am exercising my right under Section 3 of the Feudal Privileges Act 2062 to place you under arrest . . ."

"NO!" Martingale shouted, "It's a lie . . . I had no idea she was . . . my gun doesn't even work!" He looked around wildly like a cornered animal. "This is Ellswych's doing, isn't it? He's set me up!"

" . . . on suspicion of the kidnapping of Alice Hawtree and conspiracy to murder . . ."

"I knew him for a slimy, underhanded bastard, but never thought he'd stoop this low! And how did you get Gerritt to betray me, hmmm? What price could turn the head of the most loyal, most devoted man in the whole damn Kingdom, the whole damn CONTINENT?!"

"I think you should calm down," Westferry said, having finished her pro forma speech.

"Calm down?! HOW DARE YOU?!" he said, struggling in vain against the men that flanked him. As he flailed, he caught a glimpse of Alice being lifted carefully on to his daughter's bed. "And what about you, *Captain* Westferry, how much did that scumbag pay *you* to turn a blind eye as he did *that* to an innocent girl?!" Stretching out on the quilt, Alice moaned in pain as the silver blonde medic worked at relieving the cramp in her spindly limbs.

"Escort His Lordship to the station." Martingale roared as the two men at his side hauled him roughly to his feet and dragged him from the room. At Westferry's direction, a number of armed officers followed immediately after. She then turned to Lieutenant Thorne, speaking over the sound of Martingale's furious protests as he was led away through his empty home. "There's a weapon in the treasury, we'll need that in evidence. Mr de Cordonnay, can I rely on you to identify that for us?"

"Yes . . . yes of course," Redwald said, tearing his eyes from Alice. Though still in pain, she was now breathing evenly. "I'll . . . I'll fetch it now." Without waiting for Thorne, Redwald headed out into the corridor and, for the first few seconds since Alice had been found, had a moment alone with his thoughts. For once, it was a good moment. Alice was safe, Martingale was caught, the case was as good as solved. As he grabbed the handle of the treasury door, pulling it open with a screech, he began to feel cautiously satisfied, as if the case were finally on the verge of resolution.

Thorne appeared in the doorway behind him as Redwald stooped to retrieve the Maiden of Maidensworth from where Martingale had left her. Lifting the gun into the bonfire light that spilled through the arrow-slit window, Redwald examined her with an almost spiritual reverence. Though still smiling, she no longer seemed to taunt him. Like her Hawtree counterpart, she was a thing of great beauty; her etched barrel, precise, complicated marquetry and polished hair all gleaming in the flickering firelight. It seemed almost poetic to Redwald that this had been the key; that one maiden had saved another.

"This it?" Thorne asked.

"She's the one," Redwald said, "I'll give you the ballistics report when we get back to the station, but I also know an expert who might be willing to . . ."

"Captain!" Their heads turned to the officer who had appeared at the top of the stairs. Westferry stepped into the corridor. "They've blocked our exit. Martingale is . . . talking to them." Westferry did not hesitate.

290

"On my way." Snapping orders at Thorne, Westferry commanded all of her remaining men, save the medic, to gather in the courtyard. She had barely finished speaking, however, when Charteris appeared at her shoulder.

"What are you going to do?!" he demanded. "They have a right to know what's going on. You can't just . . ."

"Unfortunately, Reverend, I *can*," Westferry said, unholstering her own revolver, "but that doesn't mean I want to. Now, since you are their Seneschal, vicar and, as of a few minutes ago, acting Lord of this fief, I suggest you help me persuade them of the merits of my position."

"Do I need to remind you that Lord Martingale is *innocent* until proven guilty?"

"*At trial.* And I want to get him there without any more fuss. Now, let's go." Without waiting for Charteris to argue further, Westferry led her men down the corridor towards the stairs. The vicar watched her a moment, brow furrowed, before conceding the logic and following her towards the courtyard. Unsure of what to do but deciding that his presence would be more likely to inflame than to dampen any tensions, Redwald wandered fitfully into Georgina's bedroom, pistol in hand. The fleeting satisfaction was gone, his stomach tight again.

Alice's limbs were now straight, and the medic was seeing to her other wounds. She was quiet, speaking only to answer questions in a rasping, overused voice and occasionally wincing as stinging anti-septic was rubbed into her lacerations. She saw Redwald and smiled. *Thank you*, she mouthed.

"You should get some rest," he said, calmly. Silently agreeing, she put her head back and closed her eyes. Redwald looked down at her, concerned, but there was nothing left for him to do. The medic would take care of her now. Before Redwald could turn

291

away, however, his gaze was drawn by something shining at her collarbone. There, at the end of a delicate chain that hung around her neck, lay a small key. To Redwald's eye, it was the only thing to distinguish Alice from her future self besides a heartbeat. *What*, he wondered, *is that for?* His curiosity was short lived, however. The noise from outside suddenly increased, and he was drawn to the open bedroom window.

Sure enough, and just as the Guardsman had described, the merry gathering of earlier that evening had shifted mood once again. Now, it stretched four people thick in a mutinous-looking arc around Martingale and his escorting officers. Hawtree and Ofcross, Redwald noted, were trapped on the outskirts, keeping a low profile as the crowd rustled with discontent, cheering and jeering as Martingale put his case and the Guard tried to disperse them. Norris, stood between the two groups, was doing his best to mediate while Martingale's dogs yapped at his feet.

"It's all lies, ALL OF IT!!" Martingale bellowed, his desperate cries echoing around the courtyard, "Why would I try to kill her?! What do I gain?! And how was I to do it WITH A GUN THAT DOESN'T WORK?!" Westferry's appearance only resulted in further jeering.

"Ladies, Gentleman, I advise you to disperse immediately!" She shouted to the crowd, who responded with a shower of drunken remarks, "Your Lord is to be detained prior to his trial for . . ."

"ELLSWYCH HAS SET ME UP!!" Martingale roared, "Corruption!" The crowd took up the chant. "If I leave here," Martingale continued, "he'll plant evidence in my home, he's finally got his Guard back in it! He'll get me for good this time!" Westferry promptly denied it and although Charteris was trying his best to calm the crowd, largely on grounds of their own safety, he was not denying a word of Martingale's diatribe.

"THE GUN DOESN'T WORK!" He bellowed again, as Westferry tried ineffectually to explain the case against Martingale to the villagers. Despite her best efforts, however, she was soon swamped by chants of "THE GUN DOESN'T WORK! THE GUN DOESN'T WORK! THE GUN DOESN'T WORK!"

Then things turned ugly. Someone, somewhere in the crowd, hurled a tankard. Redwald spotted it mid-arc, watching as it vaulted the heads of the villagers and fell towards the face of an Ellswych Guardsman. Turning over and over as if falling in slow motion, it spelled only one outcome. He decided, in that moment, to act. Turning from the window, he did not wait to see who or what the tankard struck, or whether it was a glass, a stone, or another tankard that was thrown next. Nor did he wait to see how long it took the Ellswych Guard to raise their guns, or how long it took them to fire.

Instead, he sprinted from the window, out of the room, and down the corridor. Nearly slipping on the carpeted stairs as the chant "THE GUN DOESN'T WORK! THE GUN DOESN'T WORK!" reverberated through the house, he dashed across the entrance hall and bolted out through the open door, gun in hand. A Guardsman lay on the grass, bleeding from the nose, while a number of his comrades were marching towards the crowd, truncheons held high. Though no Ellswych guns were yet pointed at the crowd, Westferry's hand was raised, ready to drop. Redwald vacillated, looking between the crowd, the Guard and the maiden's face. She was priceless. Worse, he might be wrong.

"LISTEN!" Redwald bellowed, waving to get the attention of any who would give it. "I HAVE THE . . ." a glass smashed on the wall behind him, just as a stone struck another Guardsman and Westferry's hand began to sink. *Fuck it.*

Pulling the hammer back with a click, he took aim at the stars, and pulled the trigger.

CHAPTER 14

Limited Appeal

"The party traversed the Endless Ocean for time unknown. Great storms and maelstroms did they weather and fiercely did Ærestius curse the Vaeltava and damn them for their treachery. He wept and wept and wept and none could stem his tears, for he knew that he was now the Lord of the Last Oryneans; his people and their timeless domain had fallen with the rotting of the trees. And so it came to pass that the companions became lost and so far did they travel that the stars in the firmament changed above their heads. It was then that the Vaeltava sent unto Ærestius a sign, blessing him despite his curses and the gnashing of his teeth. Through the mist they sent a gryphon, white as falling snow and blood red of eye. Gadrassix, Companion of Ærestius saw this creature and bade his master follow. It was this beast, born of the wind and the sea and the mountains, that led Ærestius and the Oromanth to the shores of Tempest and the foundation of the Realm."

The Stenmoor Chronicle, Anon. c.1580

Redwald looked at the hole in Alice's head, dissatisfied. Somewhere behind him, though he was too absorbed to hear it, the plink of a regular, repeating drop echoed around the icehouse as cold air congealed onto colder walls and dripped into a puddle.

Alone with her for the first time since his failed experiment, Redwald had just finished cleaning his instruments and was now in the process of packing them away. Yet as he lowered each piece carefully into the briefcase, something nagged at the back of his mind. It was a sensation not dissimilar to being dirty, where Redwald could *feel* the contamination resting on his hands like a film of filth. But that was not it; his hands were clean.

As he folded the brass stand, his eyes settled on Alice's empty socket. Perhaps that was it; in successfully finishing his work, he had paradoxically ensured that the case would never be fully solved. What had caused the angle of the shot? Why had 'future' Alice's head been wrapped in bedsheets? Why, when taking her, had Asplund disguised himself, only to reveal his identity to her later? And why, now Redwald thought about it, had Morrimer not alerted them to the absent Folly key before heading up there himself? The magician grimaced. It pained him to know that these questions would now exist without answers, drops without echoes, living on indefinitely now that Alice herself had survived.

Not that he would have it any other way, of course. He had at least saved her life. Snapping his briefcase shut, his thoughts turned from the living to the dead Alice. Standing up straight, he looked down on the body and paused, working up the courage to finally say goodbye.

He had not expected, or wanted, the luxury of doing so. In fact, 'future' Alice's continued existence only gave rise to further, and less comfortable, unanswered questions. Was the living Alice still at risk? Could someone yet emerge to spell her end? Given recent events, this prospect was as unlikely as it was unpleasant. And yet, Redwald thought, the alternative hardly seemed better.

What if, having succeeded here, he had created a 'new' future? One in which present Alice survived, but 'future' Alice's body remained; a necessary prompt for Redwald's actions to change the timeline in the first place. If so, Halva'us had been right all along; there was nothing he could have done to prevent her death. Redwald had simply saved one Alice at the cost of another. A particularly large drop echoed around the icehouse.

"I . . . I'm sorry, Alice," he said, quietly, "I really tried, I . . . it was all I could do."

"Was it, Mr de Cordonnay?" With a jolt, the magician remembered where he was. As Alice and the icehouse dissolved into the past, so they were replaced by a be-gowned prosecutor, gently perspiring in a baking-hot room. Peering dispassionately into the inky depths of her notes, she had yet to meet Redwald's eye.

"I . . . I'm sorry . . ." he said distractedly, "what was the question?" It was just the latest of many. Lapping at the wooden barrier that divided them from the Court, a sea of reporters and spectators listened hungrily for his response, while a squad of Guardsmen kept careful watch. Somewhere, a summer fly buzzed into the air.

"You say that Lord Martingale described Exhibit H as non-functional. Was his assessment accurate? Was the gun broken?" She gestured again to the long table beneath the judges' elevated bench. Flanked by Alice's tall mirror on one side and the open trunk on the other, the table bore a number of labelled objects, stacked on cloth-draped shelves so the eight jurors could see them. The Maiden of Maidensworth beamed up at him from beside her label card, polished features glinting in the sun. Redwald paused for a moment, peering back at her.

"No. . . " he finally whispered to himself, oblivious to his surroundings once more. By some trick of the light, it had looked for a moment as if the Maiden's left eye were burning. His trigger finger twitched.

"With apologies Mr de Cordonnay, I'm not sure the Court heard your answer. Was Exhibit H broken or not?" Redwald looked up. The crowd watched, drawing a collective breath that was followed, like a spent wave retreating from the shore, by silence.

"No," Redwald sighed, "It was quite functional." The noise rushed back on the crest of the next wave. Pens scratched, doubters gasped, the shy whispered, and the brazen spoke, but none were quiet. Yet as the crowd bristled with macabre excitement and the judges' ire was slowly roused, Redwald's eyes remained fixed upon the weapon.

Quite functional. Shooting into the stars before he could blink, a burning charge had left the barrel in a plume of smoke, dragging crimson sparks and a crackling echo in its wake. The sudden hush that followed had been deafening, a riot quelled in the span of a gunshot. He could almost feel the quaking of the handle in his palm, even now. The murmur of the crowd swelled into a rumble.

"Mr de Cordonnay," the prosecutor shouted over the noise, still fixated on her notes, "did Lord . . . did Lord Martingale . . ."

Octaves lower than any human's, the voice of Sir Rakthar Ottameer carried effortlessly over the hubbub. "If I cannot hear the witness' testimony," he said, "I shall be *greatly* displeased." Only the fly had the temerity to ignore him. "Continue."

"I'm grateful M'lord." The aged, Giant judge of the Feudal Division nodded, leaned back in his seat, and pulled his blue-lined robes close about him. "Mr de Cordonnay", the prosecutor continued, "did Lord Martingale disclose to you, at any point, that he had this weapon in his possession?"

"No," Redwald said as he met the Baron's eye, "he did not." Sat across the room and hemmed in by the iron fencing of the dock, Martingale was thinner than he had been in the spring and his face more lined. His hatred, however, was undimmed, and in fixing Redwald with an unblinking glare, he avoided the sight of the gaudy swan chandeliers that lit the scene of his humiliating trial.

"And was he aware that you were searching for a weapon, either generally or one that matched the specifications detailed by Guardsman Norris and the Countess of Oštrouman?" Though not glaring, Norris and Laetizja watched Redwald as well, sat on the benches behind the prosecution team and surrounded by their fellow witnesses. Giles and Alice were both absent.

"Yes, I believe so," Redwald said, rubbing his temples. "He was certainly present when I explained to Mr Hawtree that we were seeking and tagging antique guns."

"Did he say anything about the weapon to you on that occasion?"

"No, he did not."

"Did you ask him specifically?"

"No, I asked the group generally, but," Redwald said, hurriedly pre-empting her next question, "there were only six of us present; he can't have assumed I wasn't also talking to him." Lord Martingale's nostrils flared like a bull as sweat crept down his neck.

"I see," the prosecutor replied. She left a pregnant pause as Sir Rakthar quickly stifled an incipient murmur, casting the crowd a thunderous glance. Reaching down to her lectern, the prosecutor turned a page of her notes with all the attentiveness of someone diffusing a bomb. "Returning to your search of Martingale Castle, Mr de Cordonnay, can you tell us what happened after you found Exhibit H? What else did you find?" Redwald glanced around the room, but there was no need. Like Morrimer, she would not be testifying. Hundreds of eyes, all but the prosecutor's, stared back at him.

"We found Mrs Hawtree," he said, after a pause. Gasps fluttered around the audience like autumn leaves in the wind, but Redwald ignored them. Instead, his attentions shifted away from the gun and towards the next, and final, key exhibit. Small, dull, and unornamented, it lay on the table next to Alice's soiled slip, still on the chain that had secured it around her neck. *Almost there.*

"And how is it that you came to find her?" The prosecutor asked. Above, one of the two criminal judges flanking Sir Rakthar shifted in her seat. As the crimson lining of her robes caught the sun, so the sight of Alice's bloodied, sticky wrists flashed before Redwald's eyes. Yet it was a brief distraction. As sure as gravity, Redwald's thoughts turned back to the little key.

"It was during an argument with Lord Martingale. Because its specifications matched those of the would-be murder weapon, I wanted to tag Exhibit H in order to track it. He wouldn't permit that, however, and when I pressed the point he terminated the search. He was about to throw me out when the Reverend Charteris heard a noise, coming from a room down the corridor . . ."

"This is the room Lord Martingale had forbidden you to inspect?" Redwald quickly nodded before continuing apace. *Get to the key.*

"Despite Lord Martingale's objection we rushed straight in, of course, and that's when we saw that the trunk . . ."

"Exhibit I, My Lords," the prosecutor interjected.

"Yes, yes, Exhibit I", Redwald said, ploughing on, "Anyway, it was moving around jerkily on the floor, as if someone were struggling to get out of it. I demanded that Lord Martingale open it immediately, so he produced a key and sure enough when we lifted the lid it was Ali . . . Mrs Hawtree, trapped in there, screaming."

"Could you describe her appearance to the Court?"

"She looked exactly like the body in the icehouse," Redwald said, causing a satisfied rustling among the prosecution team. "She was bleeding at the wrists and ankles where the rope had cut into her skin, she was bruised, pale, spindly, and her hair was thinning. She was wearing the nightdress she had on when she was abducted - Exhibit J," he said, pre-empting the prosecutor again, "but she was also wearing a key, Exhibit K, on a chain around her neck, which . . ."

"Thank you, Mr de Cordonnay," the prosecutor said, cutting Redwald off. He leant forward to argue, features hardened, eyebrows arched, but he quickly restrained himself - the prosecutor had shot him her first and only direct look. Wiping sweat from his brow, he slumped back into his seat. "If I may, Mr de Cordonnay, I should like to refresh the Court on what you said at the beginning of your testimony. When describing how you set about solving a crime that had yet to be committed, you referred to three key elements. Please could you remind us of those?"

"Motive, means, and opportunity," Redwald said, patiently invoking the trinity. *Come on.*

"And, having completed your search of Martingale Castle, had you established any of these with confidence?"

"Yes; means," Redwald replied, frowning. "We found the gun." The prosecutor smiled into her notes.

"Not motive or opportunity?" Finally, the line of questioning clicked. Redwald leant forward again.

"Not completely," he said, picking up the trail. "I thought I had already established motive, and when we found Mrs Hawtree, I thought we had proven opportunity too, but I wasn't completely right in either case. It was more complicated than that."

"And how did you arrive at that conclusion, Mr de Cordonnay?"

"We figured out what Exhibit K was for." There was an audible creak as the crowd pressed close against the wooden railing and the jurors shifted in their seats, all trying to get a better glimpse of the tiny, boring key.

"What is the relevance of Exhibit K, Mr de Cordonnay?"

"It's the external key to Mr Hawtree's study," Redwald began, his words echoing around the reception hall. "And, therefore, the key

301

to this case. The one thing we knew from the very beginning was that Mrs Hawtree would eventually return to the study. From there, she would travel backwards in time to the same place, prompting my investigation. What we didn't know, and hadn't really considered, was *how* she got there. Exhibit K's presence around Mrs Hawtree's neck tells us that if she had returned to the study to die, it would be because Lord Martingale *planned* it." The Baron, impotent in the dock, could do nothing but clench his lantern jaw.

"Now you have complete opportunity," Redwald continued, as the prosecutor quietly closed her notebook. "Lord Martingale had Mrs Hawtree kidnapped and brought to him, with the means to deliver her to her doom hanging around her neck. The murder weapon was already in his own treasury. Which begs the question, however; why? What was the *motive*?" The crowd listened in silence.

"Initially, this was the most difficult part of the investigation. Mrs Hawtree had no enemies that I could uncover and was well-liked and respected hereabouts. With the discovery that the weapon was likely to come from the Hawtrees' own collection, even though it ultimately didn't, I began to speculate that the motive was revenge, not upon Mrs Hawtree, but upon the Hawtree Family generally. The more I learned about Lord Martingale, the more this motive seemed to fit." The Baron scoffed. At the far end of the room, Sir Julius' golden statue leered from beneath the mezzanine, watching the proceedings with blank, pupilless eyes. "Having lost his wife and daughter to the Great Storm of 2306, he had been forced to sell the better part of his lands and heirlooms to the Hawtrees in order to repair his demesne. This was a humiliating outcome for any baron, but anathema to one as proud as Lord Martingale. I was also made aware, through discussions with locals and by some of His Lordship's own remarks, that he especially disliked *Mr* Hawtree. As such, I came to believe that Lord Martingale wished to inflict on Mr Hawtree the pain he himself had felt in losing his wife and daughter." Redwald paused. "But then we found the key." Even the lone fly, buzzing wildly in a distant corner, fell silent.

302

"Now, Exhibit K doesn't negate revenge as a motive; killing Mrs Hawtree in her husband's intimate space with a Maidensworth pistol is a potent statement. The Deed by which Lord Martingale sold the Rise to Sir Julius is displayed in that study and the Maidensworth pistol is one of the few heirlooms left to Lord Martingale, his last ounce of pride. But Exhibit K does raise a crucial question; why go to all the effort to get her back to the study? Of course, it might be more cathartic, more powerful a message to kill her there, but it also greatly increases the risk of getting caught and consequent failure. In short, getting her back to the study is disproportionately difficult if all you want to do is kill her. Surely, someone as tactically competent as Lord Martingale would know that. So, what else did he want?" Silence.

"He wanted his inheritance back. As Lord Martingale would be well aware, if a tenant is convicted upon indictment, some of his property is forfeit to his overlord." The Baron began to furiously shake his head. "If Mrs Hawtree were killed, the entire estate would pass to Mr Hawtree, including the lands that once comprised Lord Martingale's demesne. If Mr Hawtree were then convicted of a crime, Lord Martingale could reclaim some of what he had lost . . . " This time, there were audible gasps.

"No!" Martingale said, quivering with rage, rattling the bars that encircled him with gigantic hands, "it's lies, all of it. I . . . I would never . . ."

"If a recently discharged weapon, identical to one in Mr Hawtree's collection, were found beside a deceased Mrs Hawtree, a case could be built against Mr Hawtree for murder. Given Mrs Hawtree's universal popularity and the fact that Mr Hawtree stood to gain total control over her fortune if she died, the conclusion would be obvious. After shooting Mrs Hawtree, all the plotters need do was return to Martingale Castle with Mr Hawtree's gun, thereby leaving an empty rack in Mr Hawtree's cabinet and a literal smoking gun by his wife. If a jury saw it the same way, then Lord Martingale could

303

rid himself of the Hawtrees, take his revenge, and restore a much-diminished fortune, all in a single stroke."

"You can't believe this!" Martingale protested to jury, judges, and his tenants dotted throughout the crowd simultaneously, "it's ludicrous, patently untrue. He's lying! He's a bloody liar, a charlatan, a. . ."

"The Defendant shall remain silent!" Sir Rakthar decreed, leaving a bewildered Martingale to glower at Redwald and the crowd, livid with the former and defiant to the latter.

"On that basis, Mr de Cordonnay," the prosecutor continued, "would you conclude that Lord Martingale had the *means, motive,* and *opportunity* that you sought?"

"I would."

"And would you therefore agree that Lord Martingale was ultimately responsible for and an accessory to the kidnapping of Alice Hawtree and actively conspired with Dr Gerritt Asplund in planning her murder?"

"Yes, I would," Redwald said, heavily.

"My Lords, no further questions." Triumphant, the prosecutor lowered herself onto the bench with a creak, her juniors and associates leaning in to whisper their congratulations. Exhausted but relieved, Redwald made to stand, meeting Martingale's burning glare for the last time before finally turning away. Why linger, after all? His work was done. Before he could leave the witness box, however, Sir Rakthar swivelled his great yellow eyes to the prosecutor's left.

"Witness is yours Mr Decker." *Shit.* He had forgotten the cross-examination. As Redwald sank back into his chair, so Lord Martingale's defender rose imperiously from his, noisily shuffling his notes on the lectern as he did so. A large, shaggy man, he reminded Redwald of an eager spaniel, one that had just dropped an unwanted dead animal at the foot of its master's bed. Leaving the lectern and his notes behind he began to pace beneath the judge's bench, a hand placed theatrically upon his chin in mock contemplation. Redwald watched him carefully.

"*Mr* Redwald Alberic de Cordonnay," he said after a pause, "you're a credible witness aren't you? Honest, reliable, informed?" A smile stretched across his disproportionately small face.

"I believe so," Redwald replied, tentatively.

"Really?" Decker said, turning to face the jury and hoicking his tent-like gown back on to his flabby shoulders, "your testimony so far has been *completely* accurate?" Redwald frowned, the prosecutor poised to intervene.

". . . to the best of my knowledge," he replied, his stomach tightening.

"Really? You say that, even though . . . you have already *lied* to the Court?!" The prosecutor was on her feet in a second as Decker wheeled about, accusatory finger in the air, "on the *very first* question, when asked to identify yourself, did you not mislead the Court, *MISTER* de Cordonnay?! Or should I say *Count* Redwald I of . . . Cursed Gavran in the ArchCounty of . . . Kezerganser?!" There were scattered gasps in the crowd and Laetizja raised a slender eyebrow.

"No," Redwald replied, relieved as he was exasperated.

"Aha, but is it not true that . . ."

"I *was* the last Count of Čvrst Gavran before the Revolution, yes," Redwald sighed, glaring down at him. "But as you clearly aren't aware, Mr Decker, Tempestian subjects need Crown permission to use foreign titles in this country, whether in pretense or not. I don't have such permission which means that I am, formally, *just* Mr de Cordonnay and *certainly* not a liar." It was a bold and fundamentally stupid move on Decker's part, a fact the room at large seemed to acknowledge. After a groaning pause, he turned on his heel and hurried back to the lectern.

"I would advise counsel to limit his questions to those of real relevance," one of the criminal judges tutted as Decker, in his haste, accidentally knocked his notes to the floor. Amid new rumblings from the crowd, Lord Martingale turned to glaring at his feet instead of Redwald, while even the latter burned with vicarious embarrassment. In an already-sweltering room this squeezed further droplets onto his brow, soothed only by the sudden, freezing wind that unexpectedly tousled his hair. For a brief, delirious moment, he sighed with relief. But the slap of saturated flesh on marble quickly reminded him of the obvious fact: cold winds do not blow in midsummer.

"**Reeeedwaaald.**" Relief crystallised into tension. "**Theeere you are. It has been too long, my friend, *far* too long.**" Unaided by any junior, Decker scrabbled to re-assemble his notes from the floor, but Redwald's attention was elsewhere. Try as he might, he could not ignore the squelching and cracking of skin that stretched and split over shifting bones, nor the demonic, macerated hand as it smeared pus on the wood of the witness box. "**Sooo, what is all this, hmmm?**" Halva'us wheezed, baring his needled teeth at the crowd. His perfect eyes flickered with recognition. "**Oh congratulaaations, Redwald, you caught him after all. *Weeell done*!**"

"Mr Decker, are you *quite* ready?" Sir Rakthar snapped. Turning back to the proceedings, Halva'us' attention settled on Lord Martingale. Licking his cratered lips, the demon growled gleefully.

"Yes, My Lord," Decker replied, parting the long hair that had fallen across his face, "sorry, My Lord." Pushing himself off the witness box, Halva'us stumble-ran like a toddler across the polished floor, slamming against the dock like a deranged animal and leaving pus-prints in his wake. Bile rose in Redwald's throat.

"Mr de Cordonnay," Decker continued, at an apparently random point in his notes and ignoring Redwald's discomfort, "I would . . . would like to return to a few aspects of your account, if I may . . . ."

"Loooooook at him, Redwald," Halva'us said, peering through the iron fencing at Martingale. "The proudest Lord in Tempest, reduced to a common criminal by your incisive genius. Whaaat a *victory*, Redwald, what a victory. How does it feel, hmmm? To have reduced and humiliated your opponent so completely, so *irreversibly*. Actually no, do *not* tell me . . ." Turning in a flash, his crimson eyes caught Redwald's like a hawk on a mouse. ". . . you must be *loooooving* this!" The monster's face split in grimace, a wetly crackling laugh echoing around an ignorant room.

"Would . . . would you not agree, Mr de Cordonnay, that you are relatively junior to be instructed on a case of this nature?"

"I . . . yes, a little," Redwald said, wincing as Halva'us' laugh grated on his eardrums like mashed glass.

"How could you not? The control, the *catharsis* . . ." the demon said, grasping through the bars towards Martingale ". . . you *won*, because you were *right*. It is *everything* you crave, *everything* that drives you."

"So why should we trust your testimony?"

"I'm a highly qualified magical professional," Redwald shuddered, unsure of where he was going as Halva'us' bone-sharp fingers gripped an oblivious Martingale by the chin, "of . . . of some years standing . . . Perhaps I'm not as senior as some of my colleagues, but . . . but I have a wealth of experience in this and similar areas."

"Yeeees, teeeeell them. Only your *unique* mind could have done this," the demon said, smearing an ulcered hand across the Baron's face, **"and you deserve to *relish* your victory."**

"B . . . besides," Redwald continued, "I'm not strictly testifying on . . . magical matters, just an investigation in which magic helped. As such, my . . . my seniority is . . . irrelevant."

"And how better to do that, I wonder," Halva'us said, whipping his slimy hand from Martingale's cheek with a flourish, **"than to know the *consequences* of it."**

"But," Decker continued, "why instruct someone so junior . . ."

"Relevance, Mr Decker!" Sir Rakthar growled, as Halva'us, tired of abusing Lord Martingale, lurched slowly back towards the witness box.

"First, they will convict him. Of course . . ."

"Yes My Lord, sorry My Lord. In that case, Mr de Cordonnay, I refer to your report at page 25." There was a general rustling of paper from those with bundles, but Redwald's own went untouched as he fixated on the demon inching towards him.

"How could they not? Would you believe Martingale spared no expense on this one?" He flicked the excess pus from his hand across Decker's chest.

"You refer to the fact that, when Mrs Hawtree went missing, Mr Thesk set off for the Folly without informing you he was doing so. How do you account for that?" Pirouetting as he reached the witness box, Halva'us allowed himself to fall, his spine snapping backwards over the rim. The magician choked.

308

"Such a delicious *humiliation* . . . the old soldier's most important battle, and someone else has to fight it for him . . ."

"I cannot . . . I can't testify for Morr . . . Mr Thesk," Redwald stuttered, as the demon's crusted scalp crackled on the fabric of his trousers, "but Mr Hawtree had said he was occasionally prone to confusion, being of advanced age. I doubt . . . I doubt it's any more than that and . . . and his being panicked . . . perhaps." Decker flicked to the next question as Halva'us grinned up at Redwald, sharpened teeth locked together at odd angles like spurs on twisted barbed wire.

"But when his champion fails, as fail he must, they'll drag the old man away . . "

"Very well, but at page 6, you say that Mrs Hawtree future's head was wrapped? Surely this implies that she was killed elsewhere and then moved, which seriously undermines your theory about my client framing Mr Hawtree, does it not?" Decker said, turning expectantly to the jury.

" . . . *far* away, to a deep, dark, coooold place . . ."

"I don't . . . no . . . no it doesn't undermine my theory at all," Redwald began, pressing his back flat against his seat as Halva'us splayed his scabbed arms in mock arousal, "we . . . we cannot now know *exactly* how the crime would have been committed, but it's certainly . . . certainly possible that Mrs Hawtree could have been killed elsewhere and then left . . . left at the scene to achieve the same effect . . ."

". . . they'll exchange his livery collars for chains, his titles for a number, and he will be reduced to nothing but the memory of a crime . . ."

". . . this . . . this would have reduced the risk of someone overhearing the shooting and I . . . I don't see a reason the scene

309

could not have been deliberately . . . *dressed* to imply guilt . . . I think." There was a pause as Decker hurriedly re-arranged his notes, but Halva'us lost no time in filling it. With a crunch, he swung back on to his feet as if pulled from above, ribs shifting like worms beneath his tight and tattered skin.

"*Some* friends will visit, of course, those not ashamed of him, who *actually* believe his innocence . . ."

"You refer . . . you refer at page . . . 14, Mr de Cordonnay, to your tagging of the Hawtree weapons collection," the Court flicked through their bundles, "and assert that said tagging ribbons could not be removed; is that correct?"

"But the rest . . . they'll pretend he never existed . . ."

"N . . .Not quite," Redwald said, as Halva'us swivelled aimlessly towards the prosecutor, "they could not . . . not be untied or cut, except by me . . ." Leaning in as if to kiss the prosecutor's hand, the demon opened his mouth and a crusted tongue lolled out over razor teeth, licking her as far as her elbow. Redwald stifled a retch and forced himself to look away. Across the room, Martingale's silver mane was in his hands.

"And yet you accuse my client of planning to take Mr Hawtree's weapon to imply the latter's guilt? Why, never mind how, could my client do that if you were to track the weapon with a ribbon that could not be removed?"

"And after a while, it will be as if he never did . . ." Gently, he pulled the prosecutor's sleeve back down, over the glistening streak he had left there.

"As I say," Redwald said, eyes forward, jaw clenched, and knuckles bleeding where he gripped the chair, "we cannot now know what would have happened had . . . had the plot been allowed to continue . . ."

"The fief will be granted to someone else, soon indeed . . ."

". . . but the effectiveness of a spell turns heavily on its wording, a fact exploited by . . . by Dr Asplund, when he slipped Mrs Hawtree's ribbon off intact. . . so, while it would be difficult to remove the ribbons, it's not impossible. Otherwise . . ." Redwald shuddered as Halva'us slithered deliberately back into his eyeline, "you might be right, perhaps . . . perhaps the timelines diverged when I decided to tag the weapons and the . . . the crime was doomed from then on. Even if that were true, it wouldn't stop Lord Martingale making an attempt or absolve him of kidnapping and conspiracy to murder." Halva'us leaned in close, so close that Redwald felt the demon's hot, damp breath upon his skin.

". . . and then . . . then the slow process of forgetting will begin. The older tenants will die off, the younger ones will have known no other Lord, the Castle will decaaaay, crumbling into dust like the dynasty it served and, eventually, no one will know that this place was named for a family at all . . . ."

"But surely," Decker continued, obscured from Redwald's view by Halva'us' looming face, "all of this implies that my client willingly attempted to commit a crime he knew had already been discovered?"

"Or," Redwald growled, desperate to descend from the witness box as he stared into the face of his nightmares, "one in which he'd already been proven successful; he knew she had been killed . . ." Murmurs rippled around the Court.

"*Excellent* point, dear boy. You *are* good at this. And you would have to be. By your hand, the Martingales of Martingale have *finally* been disinherited, a thousand-year line brought loooow, the last of their blood condemned for a crime he *failed* to finish. . ."

311

"Erm yes, but . . . but the search, why would my client offer a search to the Ellswych Guard if he was knowingly hiding a kidnap victim in his home?" Decker said, grasping clumsily for one question after another as Halva'us stepped slowly backward.

". . . And he *knows* it . . ." his arm, like a bone picked clean of meat, swung outward, gesturing towards Martingale. The Baron's hands were now shaking. "**He *knows* what he stands to lose. Such *exquisite* agony.**"

"I cannot testify for your client," Redwald said, transfixed by Halva'us, "but I would guess it was a tactical gamble, an attempt to prove beyond doubt that he was innocent." Stumbling back over to the dock, Halva'us watched Martingale through the bars, reaching for him like a petulant child trying to stroke a caged lion.

"**But the best part, Redwald, the best of all of this . . . is what he does *not* know - that he has already lost . . .**"

"Why kidnap her at all for that matter?" Decker said, ploughing on, "why not kill Mrs Hawtree on the night of the abduction?"

"**And so he will fight. *Fight,* as he always has done, *fight,* as he was taught, for he knows nothing else . . .**"

"I don't know," Redwald replied, tentatively watching as Halva'us tried to meet Martingale's downcast eyes, "as I say, the plan might have diverged from the intended path at any moment, perhaps the delay was compensating for a mistake or adapting to circumstances. It doesn't matter either way."

"**And as his home crumbles and his family name fades, he will bleed himself and his final friends dry in appeal after appeal, pardons sought, new evidence gathered, knowing that his chances of success and the remnants of his old life diminish with every *second* wasted . . .**" Decker, who appeared

312

to have got to the last page of his notes, patted his pockets as if he might find further questions there.

"Mr . . . Mr de Cordonnay, you . . . refer . . . referred in a prior response to Dr Asplund . . . How can you be certain that Dr Asplund was not acting alone throughout this *supposed* conspiracy . . .?" The prosecutor stood before Redwald could answer.

"Witness has already explained this, My Lord, when attacked in Athonstone by Dr Asplund, the latter indicated he was not working alone. See page 21 of Witness' report." Sir Rakthar rumbled his approval.

"Asked and answered Mr Decker," one of the criminal judges said, "move it along."

"He would turn the tide to save the sand and will spend *years* trying . . .Until, finally, one day, he will realise . . ."

"But has the witness explained why it must have been *my* client that Dr Asplund was protecting, hmmm?" he said, arms outstretched, before remembering that he was cross-examining Redwald rather than the Court at large. "Mr de Cordonnay, you assert that Dr Asplund kidnapped Mrs Hawtree and would have assisted in her murder under orders from my client. Do you *really* think that *anyone* could coerce a man like Dr Asplund especially if, as you allege, he was unwilling. If so, *why* should that person be my client?"

" . . . realise that *all* his chances are spent, his only friends have abandoned him, and that there is nothing *left* for him to go back to, even if he could . . ." Martingale looked up and Halva'us, for the first time, allowed Redwald to speak without interruption or distraction. The Court was silent.

"Asplund . . . *Doctor* Asplund . . . was a born soldier. Used to taking orders from Lord Martingale, he had served with him in the Royal Navy and as Seneschal after that."

"All tenants serve their Lords . . ."

"But few are in love with them . . ." the magician murmured. The Baron's eyes shifted, rage and shame now tainted by fragile disbelief. "I believe that Dr Asplund was in love with Lord Martingale, based on his behaviour around the Baron, his words to me in Athonstone, and his reaction when I suggested the same in his surgery. I believe it was this attachment, more than any faith in Lord Martingale or predilection for obedience, that precipitated Dr Asplund's crimes. These crimes could *only* have been committed for Lord Martingale, because *only* Lord Martingale was the object of Dr Asplund's deep and unrequited affection." It was one drop too many in an ocean of regret. The disbelief buckled under pressure and excruciating guilt pooled in Martingale's eyes, washing all else away. He was silent.

"And on *that* day, Redwald," Halva'us said, pointing, **"*this* is the face he will wear. On *that* day, he will decide that enough is enough and *finally* remove himself from the world that had forsaken him *years* before. Congratulaaations, Redwald, you should have just killed him *yourself.*"**

Though it felt an eternity to Redwald, the cross-examination was soon over. Decker's spring of improvised questions had run dry and Halva'us skulked back to the frozen waste whence he came. Finally, he was alone again. Excused by the Judges, Redwald stood, bowed to the Royal Arms and fled the courtroom immediately, eyes downcast as he swept past a shuddering Martingale.

Outside, the sun was half-way down the sky and gloriously bright, illuminating and beautifying everything below. Bees hummed through the Hawtrees' pristine flower beds and over the chequered lawn, notch-tailed kites soared on the rising thermals, and thick, green trees rustled in the warm wind. Even Hawtree Manor was improved by the summer afternoon.

But Redwald noticed none of it. Halva'us' words and Decker's questions still echoed in his head like chants in a cathedral dome, and so he grasped his open hipflask with cracked and quivering fingers. Suddenly, almost without thinking, he stopped, turning back towards the Manor. He paused, leaning away from it, but rooted to the spot, as if attached by some invisible thread. *No,* he thought, finally wrenching himself away. *It's done, she's safe, you're right. You have to be right.* And with that, he headed back into the village; only one loose end standing between him and the next train to Athonstone.

When he reached the Double Standard, he found it more or less abandoned. This was a relief. On his arrival the night before, the stone benches had been packed with villagers, basking in a balmy twilight; nevertheless, his reception had been frosty. There was a scrape as he opened the door.

"You alright my . . . Oh," said the Landlord's daughter as she turned from her work at the bar and spotted Redwald. "S'pose you're 'ere fer yer briefcase?"

"Please," Redwald sighed, as she nudged it under the bar counter with her foot. "Thanks."

"You already paid, ain't yer?" He nodded, and she returned to her chores without another word. Crossing the room, he stooped and rummaged in the case for a second, while the Landlord's daughter made a furious show of polishing the beer pumps. He stood up and cleared his throat.

"I think these are yours," he said. Gently, he lay her scissors and ribbon on the pewter counter.

"Aye," she said, and was about to turn away when he produced something else. A clean, brass compass glittered in his palm, pointing due north. "I meant to give this to Guardsman Norris at

315

the trial," he said, tentatively, "but I . . . I didn't want to hang around. Would you mind passing it on to him?" She paused.

"Ye not stayin' fer the verdict?"

"No," Redwald said, over-bluntly, "I want to go home now. Besides, that could take . . . anyway, no reason for me to stay any longer. Would you give it to him?" She came and collected it tenderly from his palm.

"'Course I will."

"Thank you." He said, making for the door without pause. He had a train to catch.

"It's just that," *Shit*, "I know the Reverend were 'oping to speak to yer, afore ye went. If ye could find a bit 'o time fer him. I know 'ed be grateful." Redwald stopped, fingers wrapped around the door ring. He paused.

"I didn't see him at the trial."

"No, 'e's up at the Castle, with . . ."

"And he specifically asked to see *me*, did he? When did he ask you?"

"'E did ask fer ye, yeah. Asked this mornin', said 'e wanted to catch ye before the trial, but couldn't make it in time." Redwald paused again. "Should'a tell 'im ye were busy?"

"No," Redwald groaned, "I'll find him." The door swung shut at his back and he turned towards the Rise.

It had been a long time since the magician and the vicar had last spoken. In fact, now Redwald thought about it, it might even have been the night of Martingale's arrest. There were some obvious reasons for this. The first was that Redwald, his work mostly done, had returned to Athonstone shortly after, there to compile and finalise his report. The second was that Charteris had been busy.

In pulling the Maidensworth trigger, Redwald had not only silenced the mob and damned the Baron, he had placed a significant burden on Charteris' shoulders. Running a fief as Seneschal was one thing, running it as acting Lord was quite another. Worse still, Charteris also had to make arrangements for Martingale's trial. Normally, it was a privilege of lordship to be tried in one's own fief. The ruins of Martingale Castle were manifestly unfit for purpose, however, and so Charteris had instead been administratively sandwiched between the Hawtrees and the Clerk to the Court of Feudatories for months.

But there was something else, Redwald suspected, in the silence between them, something that caused his stomach to knot tighter with each step closer to the ruined keep. If Martingale were found guilty, the Barony would be taken from him and granted to another. That person would then be responsible for every single soul that Charteris cared about, for better or, possibly, for worse. It was a risk that Charteris had wanted to avoid and now, thanks to Redwald, it was a real and alarming possibility.

Eventually, the woodland path having faded into the woods and the woods into the meadow, Redwald looked up and saw the Castle, shining in the sunlight. Behind the Rise the sky was clear and blue, while the grass around the keep was embroidered with a constellation of wildflowers. Above the hiss of swaying grass, Redwald could hear the humming of butterflies, ladybirds, and demoiselles as they flitted from one petal to the next. He swallowed and made for the gatehouse.

As he approached, a warm breeze wafted a snippet of conversation his way, along with the smell of food. He rounded the gatehouse corner to find three people sitting at a small table, each holding a book. Behind them, Martingale's old mansion clung to the base of the keep, the windows boarded. Charteris spotted him first.

"Redwald, old boy! Good to see you, good to see you. Do join us!" Redwald jumped as a Hawtree footman appeared from the shadow of the gatehouse, carrying another chair over to the table.

"Tea, sir?" said another, appearing at Redwald's shoulder.

"Uh no, thank you," Redwald said, as he was borne along to the table by what seemed to be an ever-growing wave of footmen. Sat with Charteris over an assembly of dainty cakes, sandwiches, and miniature pies were Mrs Ofcross and a woman Redwald initially did not recognise. Wearing a hat to shield herself from the sun, she was holding a small book with a vibrant blue cover, *Twistle's Traditional Tales for Growing Children*.

"Do have a seat old boy, there's a good chap." It was as if he had never left.

"Well I would, but I . . . I was hoping to catch a train." He flicked open his pocket watch. He had a little time. "You wanted to speak with me?" Charteris deflated somewhat.

"Really no time for anything?" Ofcross asked, plaintively. "We have fondant fancies." She indicated the cake plate with a degree of pride.

"Thank you, but I really . . ." The woman to his right, having finished the paragraph she was reading, finally looked up.

"You look worried, Redwald, is everything ok?" She smiled a sunrise smile, worn like flowers in her hair. He frowned, and slowly recognised her.

"Mrs Hawtree?" she grinned and raised a gently chiding eyebrow, "Sorry, Alice . . . how . . . how are you doing? You look well." Indeed she did. Though still very thin, she was fuller in figure than when they first met, and her pale cheeks now bloomed with a hint of colour. At her wrists, the lingering rope scars were barely visible.

"I'm getting better," she admitted, closing her book. "What about you, though? You seem . . ."

"Agitated," Ofcross agreed, to which Alice nodded approvingly. The three stared up at him. He gripped the back of the chair, feeling it all at once, the myriad doubts, anxieties, and stresses clattering ceaselessly in his head, the looming spectre of Alice future looking over his shoulder.

"Well, I . . . I suppose . . ."

"You're worried I'm still at risk, aren't you?" Alice said, quietly. Redwald balked at that, but Ofcross and Charteris simply watched her. "I read your report, you know. Only a few weeks ago, I think Giles kept it from me deliberately. *Future* me makes things a little unpredictable, doesn't she? You think there's still a chance." Redwald paused. This was a conversation he had not expected to have.

"Alice I . . . Please understand, magic is, in some ways, as much art as science. Because of that, because the borders are not *sharp*, there's always room for some doubt, especially in areas like this which are . . . *esoteric*." She smiled again. "So, for completeness, I caveated my report. There are unanswered questions here, yes, but that doesn't mean you should worry . . ."

"I'm not worried," she said, playfully toying with the knot of her headscarf, "and while we're at it, I don't think you should be either."

"That would be nice," he said, like a parent whose child has offered to repair a hole in the roof with their building blocks.

"No, I'm serious," she said. "When you . . . when you found me, I looked like her, didn't I?" Redwald hesitated.

"Yes, I'd say so."

"So you think that . . . that I wasn't far from being killed at that time, right?" Redwald paused again, but neither Charteris nor Ofcross interjected.

"Yes, that's right," he said, carefully, "To some extent, your appearance was a barometer of when . . . when you were likely to pass away." He watched her. For some reason, she seemed to take comfort in that.

"And I only looked that way, really, because I was scared. I've always been a bit . . . frail, physically, and the shock of . . . well, you know, it really got to me."

"Yes, I'm sure . . ."

"So if I *hadn't* been scared," she said, continuing the thought, "I wouldn't have looked like her and it wouldn't have been *right* for me to die at that time. Yes?" Redwald considered it.

"I . . . I suppose so." Alice beamed.

"See, that's what I thought," she said, looking between Charteris and Ofcross excitedly, "and that's why we're . . . *here.*" She shuddered a little then as she took in her surroundings. "Your report, whether you meant it to or not, taught me that fear . . . fear is a self-fulfilling prophecy. So I thought that the best thing to do would be to overcome my fears; to *stop* being scared. Starting with this place."

"The cake helps," Mrs Ofcross added.

"Yes, the cake helps," Alice grinned. "We've been coming here regularly, for our little book club." Redwald looked around the courtyard, remembering.

"To be fair, I think you undersell yourself," he said, finally managing a smile, "I wouldn't have been half as brave as you were."

"You *have* to be scared to be brave," Alice retorted, "And I was terrified. Besides, I may not have been crying all the time, but that doesn't necessarily make me courageous. I just . . . stopped. I was so scared of what might happen that I was almost paralysed; I dared not do anything in case I did something wrong. I left it all to you and Giles. No, things are different now. *I'm* different now. Look." She removed her hat and placed it on the grass, before pushing her headscarf down around her neck. Like fresh snow at first light, Redwald's doubts began to slowly melt away. Her hair, no longer wispy and loose, was now short, thick, and healthy. Patches remained, of course, but these were gradually darkening as new, strong hairs rose beside their withered forbears. "I'm *not* in danger anymore Redwald, I promise. And I owe that to you, and to Charles and Tabitha of course." Charteris waved the thanks away.

"Any excuse to sit in the sun and read a book," he said, before reaching across the table for a pie. Redwald pushed the plate towards him.

"Exactly," Alice said, "so for Oryn's sake, Redwald, have a sandwich or something. It's the least I can do. Especially since Tabitha made them." Mrs Ofcross giggled. After a deep and calming breath, Redwald agreed, standing his briefcase on the grass and lowering himself into the empty seat. He could always catch another train.

It was the right decision. Though not always easy, the ensuing conversation certainly felt necessary and, at any rate, offered the participants a measure of relief. Leaning back in his chair as he

321

nibbled on a succession of fondant fancies, Redwald listened quietly to Alice and Ofcross discussing the intervening months. It was, he sensed, an overdue venting.

They rehearsed the night of Martingale's arrest, the immediate aftermath, and the reaction of the village at large. Alice, skirting around her own ordeal, focused largely on the crisis of faith suffered by Lord Martingale's tenants, and how the loss of both the Baron and Asplund in one fell swoop was only complicated by the cause of it. Charteris, slowly chewing his miniature pie, looked balefully into the middle distance.

Ofcross, by contrast, seemed more concerned with Alice. She had suffered night terrors and aches in the weeks after her rescue, Ofcross explained, before lavishing praise on the young woman for her strength in recovery. Alice elegantly deflected this, saying she owed her health to Mrs Ofcross and to a returned Morrimer.

The Hob had now been released, they said, but still would not speak. Despite having four hands, his inability to sign with any degree of fluency left him incapable of running the house and so he had been offered a generous pension and comfortable retirement, both of which he had refused. In fact, Mrs Ofcross clarified, he had refused quite forcefully. Instead, he had returned to his old quarters and now spent his time either assisting Alice in her recovery or seeing to his own among the flower beds.

Redwald took another cake, hoping it might fill the guilty pit in his stomach. How was Giles taking this, he wondered? He doubted the industrialist would enjoy supporting a butler who could no longer buttle. Much to Redwald's surprise, Alice observed that Giles was pleased to have Morrimer back. It was he, in fact, who had suggested the Hob return to his old rooms. No, if anything, Giles was more worried about the trial and had taken to regular shoots to relieve the stress.

"I don't think he likes *riff-raff* in the reception hall." She said, rolling her eyes. Mrs Ofcross giggled again, with unexpected venom.

"And how do the rest of you feel about it, the trial?" Redwald said, looking pointedly across at Charteris. "It must be . . . tense." Uncharacteristically quiet, Charteris had been staring blankly at the gatehouse. Unlike Ofcross and Alice, the conversation appeared not to have relieved him and the silence he kept was taut and uncomfortable. Redwald could not shake the feeling that he was hiding something.

"Yes, I . . . I suppose it is," Ofcross said, "It's hard to know what to feel until we . . . until we know . . ." There was a pause.

"Until we know what the verdict is." Alice finished.

"Exactly," Ofcross nodded, "Then we can start to worry about who comes next. If he's found guilty, of course," she added, hurriedly.

"Do you know yet who it might be?" Redwald asked, trying again to meet the vicar's glazed eyes. Ofcross and Alice looked at each other and then to Charteris.

"Charles?" Alice prompted, gently patting his hand. He started.

"Hmmm, what? Sorry all, I was miles away there," he said, with a wan smile. "Discussing replacements are we?" She nodded. "Well the two most likely choices are the Earl of Ellswych, I'm sure he will have applied, and our own Giles Hawtree. Of course, anyone *can* apply, but the Court of Feudatories will only recommend the serious candidates to the High King. You generally need a blood connection to the prior Lord, well there aren't any of those, local connections, that's Giles, or enough money to be able to take care of the fief, which could be either of them." He laughed, somewhat bitterly, "So it's all to play for, as they say!"

"When do they decide?" Redwald asked.

"In effect they've already decided," Charteris sighed, "written submissions were due months ago, but they'll announce it at the end of the trial. Once a Lord is found guilty, they don't like to linger over replacing them, you see." He reached for another pie.

"And how do *you* feel about that?" Redwald asked, trying to coax Charteris all the way out of his shell.

"I'm rather keen to get it over with myself!" He chuckled.

"I meant about the candidates." Redwald said, increasingly frustrated.

"Oh I'm not worried, old boy. I think either would probably be fine. Ellswych might be busy with his other fiefs, but that could give us a measure of autonomy, and Giles has a . . . local touch." Alice cleared her throat.

"Actually I think the effect might be the same. Outside of . . . recent events, Giles generally spends quite a lot of time in Athonstone. In fact, he might even re-appoint you as Seneschal, Charles." The vicar nodded appreciatively.

"See, old boy? Same difference." Charteris said, taking a bite of his pie.

"So you're not worried *at all*," Redwald asked, incredulous, "about your fief not being properly looked after, about having an absent Lord?" Charteris swallowed.

"Not a jot. We'll manage, just as we always have done."

"Then perhaps you're worried about Lord Martingale?" Redwald asked, leaning forward. "Because I can tell you're worried about *something*."

"Well, perhaps I . . ." He left a slight pause, but Redwald impatiently filled it.

"It's just that after months of us not talking, I assumed you had called me here for a reason." Ofcross and Alice exchanged glances as Charteris appeared to work up the courage to speak, but Redwald again, could not wait. "I'm aware, you know, of how my work has impacted both yourself and the village, really I am, especially what happened with Martingale, and I know how angry it must have made you, but it simply isn't . . ." Charteris' eyes widened.

"Angry?" Charteris blurted, "My dear boy, whatever do you mean?"

"That's why we haven't spoken, right? Because of *my* part in all this," he said, looking towards the boarded-up castle, "because of me, one of your best friends is facing a life sentence and your home is about to be handed to a stranger, and although I understand . . ."

"I'm not angry with you, not at all!" Redwald stopped. "How could I be? If you hadn't done what you did . . . well it doesn't bear thinking about." He grasped Alice's hand.

"Then why . . ."

"To be honest, old boy, I thought *you* were angry with *me*." There was a flutter as the wind turned the pages of Ofcross' book. "And that's why I wanted to talk, actually. I wanted to apologise." Redwald raised an eyebrow.

"What for?"

"For doubting you." Redwald began to shake his head, but Charteris continued. "No, I need to say it. At every turn I doubted you, doubted that Archie could be behind it, doubted in fact, that *anyone* I knew could be responsible. I was wrong on two counts

325

and, because of that, we almost lost Alice." She shushed him gently, but he clenched her hand like a drowning man. "I will not make the mistake of doubting you again, Redwald. I'm sorry." Stunned into silence, Redwald looked between Ofcross and Alice, who both smiled encouragingly.

"You have nothing to apologise for," Redwald said, after a pause, "and I certainly wasn't angry either. In fact, I could not have done this without you. From my first day here, you were nothing but helpful, you persuaded Lord Martingale to let us search the Castle, you were the one who heard . . . heard Alice. Without you, we might never have succeeded. And besides, who *wouldn't* question what I was saying? Everyone else did, even I did at times. Lord Martingale, he . . . he controlled the narrative, I suppose. He knew that Giles wasn't . . ." Redwald looked askance at Alice.

"Wasn't popular in the village," she said, finishing the sentence for him.

"Well, quite," Redwald agreed, apologetically, "Martingale knew the conclusions people would jump to when Alice went missing and used hostility to the Ellswych Guard to deflect suspicion from him. It's very difficult, when someone has that kind of power, to see through the deception. Others have been misled by less. I certainly can't blame you for doubting me over him." Charteris nodded slowly, satisfied if not relaxed. He had got something, if not everything, off his chest.

"Well that . . . that's kind of you, old boy. And may I say how glad I am that we're back on the right foot?"

"Likewise," Redwald said, pausing for a moment, before a pleasant idea struck him. "A toast to celebrate perhaps?" As if by magic, he produced his hipflask from within the folds of his gown and Charteris beamed.

Only Alice did not enjoy the toast, though when it was her turn with the hipflask, she gamely tried some of its contents. Rather too gamely, in fact. She was wheezing from an over-large glug of whisky when they heard a voice from the Gatehouse.

"Rev?!" It was Norris. Charteris, whose face had been creased with laughter moments before, immediately paled.

"Y-yes Osbert?"

"They've been deliberatin' for a while now, sir, and I don't reckon it'll be long. You best come down."

Redwald had not intended to return for the verdict. Arriving in the village solely for his testimony, he had made all arrangements that morning to facilitate as quick a getaway as possible. Yet as Charteris rose sombrely from his seat and Alice helped the footmen pack away the picnic, the magician felt a sudden twinge of regret. It now seemed a shame to come all this way, do all that work, and not see how things turned out. Especially if they were about to *turn out* soon.

The sun was low in the orange sky by the time the party returned to Hawtree Manor. Shards of blinding sunlight reflected off the million mullions of the Hawtree windows and the grotesques cast long shadows over blood-red bricks. The gardens were quiet, but for the crunch of gravel underfoot and a slight rustling in a flower bed near the front door.

Morrimer, with a basket in one hand and clumps of weeds in the other three, was slowly tidying the borders. He looked up at their approach and smiled a tired smile as Alice greeted him. Then his golden eyes, glinting in the sunset, swivelled to Redwald. The magician froze. The last time they had spoken had been the last time Morrimer had spoken to anyone. On that occasion, the once reserved major-domo had been reduced to a quivering wreck by Redwald's accusations and demands.

Yet as the group approached, Morrimer placed the weeds into the basket and the basket onto the floor and glided towards them like a gilded barge upon the Trew, stately as he ever was. Peeling his weeding gloves off as if they were made of kid, he offered a hand to Redwald. The magician, rather shaken, paused for a moment before accepting the gesture and the Hob's spindly fingers closed twice around the magician's knuckles. Soon another hand, and then another was placed on top, until Morrimer was silently shaking Redwald's hand with all four of his own. His tired little eyes glistened for a moment, he nodded, and then he released his grip, turning wordlessly towards the house.

"I believe he's thanking you," Alice observed, as the Hob returned to his flowers. After offering her own thanks to the Reverend and Mrs Ofcross for the tea and cakes, she too departed, picking up the basket of weeds and ushering the old Hob indoors. The little party watched them go in silence.

"Rev?" Norris murmured after a while, causing a sombre Charteris to start, "we should probably . . ."

"Yes, of course, you're quite right my boy. . . Lead on."

At the Manor's *Sir Julius* entrance, two Guardsmen stood either side of the titanic doors, through which Redwald could hear the rumble of an agitated courtroom. With the groaning of hinges and thudding of wood, the doors were thrust open and he was struck at once by the sticky heat, smell of sweat, and noise of unrestrained gossip. Only the latter softened as the crowd turned to see who had entered, before swelling again once they lost interest. As Redwald followed Norris, Charteris, and Ofcross over the threshold, the doors were slammed shut behind him.

Looking around, Redwald saw that the Bench and jury box were unoccupied, although Decker, the prosecution team, and their respective witnesses were still at their places in the fenced-off

Court. Martingale sat alone in the dock surrounded by Guardsmen, his back to them and his head down.

"Where am I supposed to be, Osbert?" Charteris said. He was struggling to find a place to stand, so thick was the press of bodies.

"I'll take you," Norris said, as he began jostling towards the wooden barrier, "this way." He was helped in this by villagers dotted throughout the crowd who, upon seeing Charteris, stepped aside and bid others do likewise.

"Right," the vicar said, turning to Redwald and Ofcross, "this is where I leave you. Good luck everybody." He grasped Ofcross' hand, patted Redwald on the shoulder, and shuffled off in Norris' wake without further explanation, hands clenching one another where they clasped behind his back.

"Where are they going?" Redwald asked Mrs Ofcross.

"Up to the balcony," she said, mishearing him over the noise of the crowd. "Visitors aren't allowed, we'll have more space."

"No, where are *they* . . ." But it was too late, she had already slipped away from him towards the staircase. He sighed and duly followed. Together, they squeezed their way around the walls, slipped between the heavy golden ropes that barred the grand staircase to visitors, and took up a spot on the gallery outside the Gun Room.

It was odd, looking down on the Court from above. For the first time, Redwald could see behind the Bench as well. To all spectators and staff in the fenced-off courtroom, it looked like a monolithic wooden barrier, as permanent and immutable as justice itself. Yet from this angle the temporary nature of the thing was very much in evidence. Behind the façade was a platform about three feet wide, supported by a criss-cross of creaking scaffolding. Three rickety staircases led up to each of the judges' worn, hardwood seats, polished by a hundred judicial backsides and softened by second-hand cushions and the odd horsehair wig. Their desks, just under the lip of the Bench, were barely visible beneath scrawled notes, open bundles, and piles of additional documentation, passed up to them by the squadron of clerks hidden in the tiny space between the Bench and the rear wall.

Then, Redwald saw something to make his stomach turn. Behind the Bench, one of the hidden servant's doors opened and a clerk hurried out. Striding halfway along the wall, she fumbled, found the handle, and vanished through another hidden door, re-appearing moments later with the judges in tow. Ofcross' knuckles turned white on the balustrade as she noticed too, her body tensing all at once. Norris had been right. It was done.

As the judges headed for their seats, the clerk scurried towards the Bench and slipped through a small door at its base. Appearing on the public side, she marched to the exhibits table, extracted a gavel from her gown, and lay five clear strikes upon a hard wooden disk. The noise was far louder than Redwald had expected and Charteris flinched as the stark tapping reverberated through the hall. Martingale, closer to the noise, did not react. The crowd fell silent.

"Pray be silent and upstanding," the clerk bellowed, "for my Lords, the Commissioners of His Majesty's Justice." There was a scraping as those with chairs stood up, Martingale being prodded to his feet by an impatient Guardsman and Charteris wringing his hands behind his back. Sir Rakthar, whose weight made the stairs flex beneath him, was first to arrive at his chair, followed shortly by his criminal colleagues. They bowed to the room at large, the room bowed back, and the judges sat in unison.

"Be seated," commanded Sir Rakthar, and the room obliged. "Clerks, please admit the jury". Behind him, another clerk made for the servant's door out of which his colleague had first appeared. Unlike his colleague, however, his footsteps echoed in the silence. In the Court below, Redwald watched as Charteris glanced unhappily from Martingale to the judges, to a tall man that Redwald did not recognise, and finally to Giles Hawtree, deathly pale and wearing a perfectly tailored suit. None dared speak. All were waiting.

After too long a pause, there was a creak and a rustle as the jury appeared through the door in the Bench and were herded into their box. As each juror took their seat, they looked towards Martingale, some furtively, some defiantly. The clerk closed the door to the juror's box and stood to one side.

"Which among you is appointed foreman?" Sir Rakthar asked.

"I am, My Lord." An elderly woman in the front row got to her feet.

"And have you, as a jury properly assembled, reached verdicts on which you are *all* agreed?" He looked over his spectacles and down his long camel-like nose at her.

"Yes, we have My Lord." She said, glancing at a vacant Martingale. Silence.

"Then I shall ask you to deliver those verdicts as follows," he said, looking down at his notes, "On the charge of kidnapping Mrs Alice Penelope Hawtree, what is your verdict?" Redwald's stomach knotted and Ofcross' breath caught in her throat.

"Guilty, My Lord." Charteris leant forward as if in prayer and though he was too far away to tell, Redwald thought he saw a tear on Martingale's cheek. A hissing whisper was quickly stilled by Sir Rakthar's glare.

"On the charge of aiding and abetting in the attempted murder of Mr Redwald Alberic de Cordonnay, what is your verdict?"

"Guilty, My Lord." The hissing surfaced once more, and Martingale began to shake his head.

"And finally, in the charge of conspiracy to commit murder upon the same Mrs Alice Penelope Hawtree, what is your verdict?" The foreman looked at the Baron, whose shaking head was now in his hands. There was a silent pause.

"We find him guilty, My Lord." Murmuring condensed out of the air like fog, but Martingale, Charteris and Ofcross were all silent.

"Thank you, foreman," Sir Rakthar said. "The Jury is excused." He gestured and the clerks opened the jury box, ushering the jurors out through the door in the Bench. Once they were gone, Sir Rakthar called again for quiet.

"Archibald Geoffrey Maidensworth Martingale, 21st Baron of Martingale-on-Trew, please stand." He did, slowly. "Having been found guilty on all three charges that were brought before this Court, I have leave, as a Judge of the Feudal Division, to sentence you. Do you have anything to say before I pass sentence?" There was a slight growl as Martingale said something.

"Speak up, sir." Rakthar said.

"I didn't do it . . ." Martingale replied, still barely audible, his voice cracking as he spoke. Sir Rakthar merely shrugged.

"Very well. Lord Martingale, I hereby sentence you to life imprisonment for your crimes, not to be released before thirty years from the date hereof. You will be remanded into custody immediately upon conclusion of this trial and taken from this place to begin your sentence. Further, the Court orders that you pay unto the Right Chivalrous the Earl of Ellswych the sum of six hundred and twenty eight crowns, forty-five groats, and twelve pennies, being the latter's feudal entitlement out of your estate, due upon your conviction. Finally, and by order of His Majesty High King Emphoras IX, Lord of the Last, Son of Oryn, you are hereby stripped of the Barony of Martingale-on-Trew, its Keep, and all rents, dues, appurtenances, privileges, and dignities thereunto attaching. Since you are lacking in heirs either by blood or by nomination, the Barony hereby reverts unto the Crown." Outside, the sun slipped past the horizon. "Guardsmen, you may remove Mr Martingale to begin his sentence."

Opening the dock with a metallic clank, two Guardsmen gestured for him to step down. But instead, Martingale turned and looked around the crowd, picking out his tenants from among the journalists, court-fanciers, and busybodies who crowded the hall. He seemed about to speak, but then, unable to do so, turned away and was pulled from the dock by his impatient captors. The door in the Bench slammed shut behind him. He was gone.

"The Trial of Archibald Martingale is hereby concluded," Sir Rakthar announced, as whispering started anew. "The Court now turns to the matter of the Barony of Martingale-on-Trew." Either side of him the criminal judges rose, bowed to the Court, and descended the stairs, leaving the Giant alone. Rather than silencing the ongoing murmurs, the wearied-looking Sir Rakthar simply spoke over them.

"As all present will be aware, the Barony of Martingale-on-Trew has now reverted to the Crown and I come with a commission from His Majesty the High King to grant that Barony to whomsoever is most fit. I therefore call to the Bench the following persons, who have laid good and proper claim to the fief. I call, firstly, Mr Giles Hawtree of Hawtree Manor . . ." Ignoring dissatisfied mutterings from the villagers, Giles rose from his seat and was directed to stand between the dock and the witness box by one of the clerks. "Secondly, The Right Chivalrous the Earl of Ellswych, represented here by Mr William Dunnegan of Dunnegan & Bramley Solicitors . . ." The tall man whom Redwald did not know joined Hawtree at the front. "And, finally, The Reverend Charles . . ." like a cork under pressure, cheers, gasps, and applause burst from the villagers in the crowd. "SILENCE!!" Rakthar roared, with such force that Redwald could feel his voice reverberating in the balustrade. "Finally, the Reverend Charles Charteris, Rector of St Alia's Church, Martingale-on-Trew."

Still pale, still nervous, but with a faint, hopeful smile tugging at his lips, Charteris joined Dunnegan and Hawtree before the Bench, the latter struggling to conceal his surprise. Sir Rakthar cleared his throat.

"To ensure continuity of governance in the event of Archibald Martingale's conviction, the High King invited claimants to make written submissions and provide supporting evidence some months ago. I have reviewed that evidence carefully and would thank all concerned for their eloquence," he said, tilting his head slightly and unconsciously towards Charteris. "In assessing those submissions, I have absolute discretion to consider such factors as I see fit. My chief concerns, however, were twofold; proximity to and connection with the fief itself and an ability and willingness to fulfil the personal and financial duties owed by the Lord of the Manor to the Crown." He paused then and allowed his weighty words the appropriate time to settle.

"I have now made my recommendation to the High King and the High King, in turn, has made His decision." The room waited in silence, save for the faint clicking of Mrs Ofcross' fingers as she gripped the balustrade ever tighter "I therefore decree that, by order of His Majesty the High King, the Barony of Martingale-on-Trew, its Keep, rents, and all relevant attachments, shall be bestowed upon Giles Hawtree of Hawtree Manor . . ." Mrs Ofcross made a noise somewhere between a sigh and a sob, while Giles beamed from ear to ear ". . . to be borne by him and his heirs and assigns in perpetuity, until such time as his line be extinguished or he is rightfully deprived of the fief by Order of the Crown." None spoke. Then, like the first patters of non-committal rain, the crowd began to applaud one by one – a dutiful smattering of barely-feigned enthusiasm.

Concluding the proceedings with minimal additional ceremony, Sir Rakthar announced that Giles was to be formally invested as Baron the next day, before airily dismissing the Court. He was out of his seat before the Guards had even opened the doors.

Mrs Ofcross too, was in a hurry. Sniffling gently as she turned from Redwald, she made a beeline for the stairs and, ultimately, for Charteris. Now sat on the prosecution benches, he was filtering the villagers magnetically from the rest of the crowd, the former being drawn to him while the latter fled into the evening cool. A band of grateful well-wishers soon accumulated in his presence, revelling in his attempt to save their fief and commiserating him on his ill-luck. He smiled with them, joked with them, and thanked them. Nonetheless, Redwald observed, something had sagged behind his eyes, as though a pile of weyste had subsided for want of any substance to hold it up.

The magician himself remained in the gallery, vacillating. Heavy-sitting unease pooled like tar in his stomach and as he watched the chaos below, he was unsure of what to do. His first thought was to join Charteris, to try and offer some condolence, or apology. Never mind that the vicar didn't blame him, never mind that Martingale had been guilty, there was a cost to his success.

And yet, Redwald mused, this was not his catharsis to seek. Below, Mrs Ofcross had squeezed through the queueing crowd and into the courtroom, putting her arms gently around Charteris' shoulders. Some months ago, Redwald had watched a similarly tender moment unfold between Martingale and Asplund, on the very spot he now occupied. The unease bubbled thickly.

Stooping, he lifted his briefcase and headed for the stairs. It was decided; he would not intrude again. Instead, he briefly considered finding and congratulating his newly ennobled client, but a scan of the room proved Giles absent. Doubtless, he and the judges were ensconced somewhere in the Manor, sitting down to a sumptuous private dinner. Redwald grimaced.

Checking his watch as he descended the stairs, Redwald estimated he had a good hour left before the last train back to Athonstone. Plenty of time to make a subtle exit and leave this place in peace. Shuffling into the back of the queue, Redwald cast a furtive glance to his right. Charteris was facing away from him, at the centre of a crowd so large that lawyers and clerks, frantically trying to pack away, were being forced outside the boundaries of the courtroom. Redwald smiled a wan smile, turned back towards the doors, and walked straight into somebody hurrying the other way. He swore, loudly.

"Oh my, sorry about that!" said a voice from behind a stack of papers. Quickly side-stepping Redwald, the voice's red-headed owner made to hurry past, but as she did so the magician was struck by a horribly familiar sensation. It was the same sensation he had felt on meeting Giles Hawtree for the first time, on hearing Asplund's growl in a sodden Athonstone alleyway, and on seeing Krysillion VII posing in a fictional portrait. From a mere glimpse of her unruly hair and a sliver of unobscured face, Redwald recognised her with absolute certainty.

"Elisa?" She ignored him, striding past. "Elisa Bewley?" She stopped. And then she turned, and it was at that moment, with a flash of feudal blue, that Redwald realised his mistake. "Oh no, I'm sorry you must be . . ."

"Audrey Bewley," she said, placing her stack of papers on the wooden barrier. "Elisa is my sister." She pushed her clerk's gown backwards, slipping her hands into her pockets. "Are you a friend of hers? How is she doing? Work keeps me busy, I'm afraid; I don't tend to see her much."

"Uh . . . no, no I'm sorry," Redwald said, still looking her over in semi-disbelief, "I just . . . happened to meet her on a train, twice actually, a few months ago." Though completely dissimilar to her frazzled, chaotic sister in manner, they were absolutely identical in feature. It was uncanny.

"*Twice*, a few months ago?" Audrey grinned. "If I'd known my face was that distinctive, I'd have become an actress. Quite a memory you have, Mr . . .?"

"De Cordonnay," he said, hurriedly, "And thank you, but really it's only good for . . . faces." Something terrible nudged gently at the back of his mind.

"Is that so?" Audrey said drily, picking up her papers once more, "You want to watch that, Mr de Cordonnay; bit misleading if two people share one. Anyway, I must be off, but nice to meet you all the same!"

She turned and hurried off towards the Bench, totally oblivious as to her effect on Redwald. For with her parting words she had prodded sharply the terrible thing in Redwald's mind. It was no longer nudging; it was screaming and Redwald, frozen on the spot by a cold and unforgiving clarity, knew *exactly* where he had seen both Alice and Giles before.

337

CHAPTER 15

The Invoice

✦❦✦

"...The Duke turned to the maiden. He took her hand and led her down the stairs to the garden. There, the soldiers awaited him with the Crown, but the Duke refused. Instead, he called for the rich man, his seneschal, to bring his coronet. The rich man did. The Duke ordered the maiden to kneel, which she did. He placed the coronet on her head and told all present that they would be his witnesses. He was assigning his dukedom to the maiden. As such, he said, she was next in line to try the Crown. He said he was not worthy of it, as he had ignored her goodness for many years and treated her poorly. Seeing now what kind things she had done, without thought of reward, this was the only way he could think to repay her. The soldiers tried to refuse the Duke, but he said that if he could not live in a Kingdom where a maiden so good and so generous was queen, then he would not wish to live at all and would lay down in his garden and become as one with his flowers.

The leader of the soldiers relented and asked the maiden for her name. She said she could not answer as she was nameless, but the Duke said that she did have a name. He would call her Alynore, for, like the small red flower of that name, she grew in harsh climes, but made beautiful what once was bleak. So Alynore, having now a name, knelt as the Crown was placed over her head. The Crown shrank and shrank until the enchanted gold rested neatly upon her brow. Alynore was thus found worthy. And so it was that the nameless little girl became a Queen through her kindness."

The Tale of Alynore – Traditional Tales for Growing Children, collated by Dr C.F. Twistle (Allpress) 1992

Giles knelt before the Princess, hands clasped in feudal supplication. Scattered like stars around the dais, candles cast shadows of his lean features, while statues of imagined Hawtree dynasts looked down on him from the walls of the ballroom. It was full. Stretching back into the darkness and towards the reception hall were row after row of the highest-born, wealthiest, and greatest of Tempestian Society, arranged according to their rank. Dukes, Archprelates, and Margraves fronted the assembly, ahead of Earls, Lord Mayors and Grand Burgesses, while Giles' old friends and colleagues; bankers, brokers, shipbuilders and breakers came last.

Princess Alesancyn, tall, serious, and starkly beautiful, grasped a Baron's coronet in her white-gloved hands. All else was done. Giles had received public instruction on his privileges, sworn to uphold his duties, and received a trapping of nobility for each oath so sworn. First she had dubbed him, her polished sabre glinting in the candlelight. Then, after the next oath, she had girt him with his own clattering, bejewelled sword. Another oath down, two of Giles' new friends from the front row had been called to garb him with a heavy mantle, embroidered with the Hawtree arms, which they had fastened at each shoulder with a glittering cloak brooch.

All that remained was his oath of fealty, and the coronet in return.

"Do you, Giles Laurence Hawtree," Alesancyn asked, and Giles' heart leapt, "hereby make oath and swear, before Oryn, the Vaeltava, and all the stars in Heaven, and upon your prosperity, life, and honour, to uphold your duties to your Sovereign Overlord and Prince, High King Emphoras IX, Lord of the Last, Son of Oryn?" Giles paused, as if he were genuinely considering his answer, until the attentions of the room settled on him alone.

"I do," he said. And it was done.

The coronet, not yet re-fitted for Giles' head, sat a little loose upon his brow, but it mattered not. Nothing, absolutely nothing, could sully this moment. Shimmering excitement rippled through his heart and when she bid him, 'Arise, Lord Martingale' he did so to the sound of tumultuous applause. He had reclaimed, finally, his birthright.

The banquet that followed, he thought, must be the best he had ever thrown. Arrovênnes flowed like water into cut-glass coupes, fine and exotic creatures were steamed, roasted, and poached to perfection, fascinators trembled, silk and satin slipped across pampered skin, and words that carried weight passed between exalted lips. And there he sat, Giles, Lord Martingale, in the middle of it all, at the head of a horseshoe table that filled the reception hall, with a princess at his right hand.

Course followed sumptuous course, interspersed with the most elegant and refined entertainments, and after dessert the assembled notables filed onto the pier, in the small hours, to watch a fireworks display that shook the valley like an airship battle. The last rocket, whistling up into the moonlit sky like a gunshot, exploded in a haze of Hawtree green and gold, stippling the initials GH in sparks against the dark. Giles smiled. It was a good start.

Sometime later, and long after Princess Alesancyn had departed, Giles saw a few of his guests to the door and bade them farewell. As the door shut behind him, and the footmen scuttled off, he turned to look up at the statue of Sir Julius. With distaste, he remembered how it had cast a shadow across his dinner plate.

It was then, he realised, that he was alone. Those guests were the last and the reception hall was empty, apart from the nervy-looking housekeeper, his wife, and other staff, clearing the tables away.

"That went well I think," Giles said to the room at large, "if I say so myself. Assuming they *were* the last of course," he asked Ofcross. "*Is* that it?" Ofcross hesitated a moment, looking up at his wife, before shaking her head.

"No My Lord, it's Mr . . ."

"The Count of Čvrst Gavran," Alice interjected, "We spoke for a bit, but he really wants to talk to you. He's waiting. In the Gun

Room." Somewhere, a footman engaged the hydraulics, and the swan chandeliers began to dim as their crystals were de-pressurised.

"The *Count* of Čvrst Gavran?" Giles asked, intrigued. He looked up towards the Gun Room, where orange light flickered through an open door. "Yes . . . yes I'll have a chat, don't think I've met him before."

"Very good, darling," his wife said wearily, "I'll see you later, not feeling too good."

"Of course dear, see to her Ofcross will you?" Giles said, not waiting for a response.

The gun room was dark. A crackling fire danced in the grate, silhouetting the pointed nose and heavy frame of the man sat before it and casting shadows around the cases. The jagged profile of every weapon was painted in shifting black on the blood red walls.

Eschewing the soft leather settees, the man was instead leaning on a rigid wooden chair, pulled up to a table. Like a miniature city aflame before him, the firelight burned between the mingled shapes of chess pieces in disarray.

"Ah, Your . . . *Tremendousness!*" Hawtree said, "it's a pleasure to see you again, I've been hoping to speak *all* night." Spectacles glinted as a beaked nose turned towards the door, but the man's face remained obscure. In the chair opposite him, however, something moved. It was a shape that Giles had barely noticed, but the fluttering of its grotesque ears suddenly drew his attention. "Morrimer!" The mute butler did not respond. "I'm so sorry, Your Tremendousness. Morrimer! You should know better than to sit in a guest's presence. Now away with you and bring us each a brandy." Still, he did not move. Until, that is, the Count gave him a slow nod. Slipping from his seat, the Hob turned and shuffled

341

towards the door. "And be quick about it," Giles snapped under his breath.

"Yes, *My Lord*." Morrimer whispered, closing the door behind him with a subtle click. Giles turned back to his guest.

"I'm sorry about that, Your Tremendousness," his eyes settled on the chessboard as he approached. "Do you play? Perhaps we could have a . . .a game . . ." He stopped.

"Why not?" said the magician, sitting where Giles had expected a Count. "I gather you enjoy *games*". Redwald did not stand. In fact, he seemed drunk. His movements were slow and heavy, his head unsteady on his shoulders, and though his diction remained crisp as ever, he spoke more slowly than usual. There were two empty wine bottles on the floor beside his chair.

"Ah, Redwald. I . . . I was actually looking for the Count of . . ."

"*Titular* Count," Redwald confirmed, "that's me, sorry to disappoint. Fancy a game anyway?" He reached out and began to shakily herd the pieces back into place, unresponsive fingers etched with livid red splits.

"Well, I . . . it is getting quite late." Why was the magician here at all? He hadn't been invited.

"It is rather," Redwald said darkly. Something rustled over Giles' shoulder, but when he turned, all he could see was a smirking Krysillion VII and an empty corner, shifting in the firelight. "Don't worry though," the magician continued, fumbling the last piece into place, "I have a *bedtime story* for you." On the table between him and the chessboard lay two documents. One was a sheaf of papers, tied with ribbons between two marbled boards. The other was a children's book, bound in bright blue leather with embossed golden keys. Giles recognised them both.

"Oh that's *kind*," Giles said, sweetly, "but I've read your report . . ."

"Then perhaps you'd prefer the Ladies of Wellinghouse Wood?" Redwald said, tapping the blue book and looking directly into Hawtree's eyes. "Unless, of course, you've read that one too?" Giles smiled. From his place over the crackling fire, Sir Julius watched in silence.

"What colour would you like?" Giles asked, finally. He lowered himself into the empty chair.

"Red."

"Confident?"

"Chivalrous," replied Redwald, "Your turn, *Giles*." His very lips seemed wet with venom. Though watching Redwald carefully, Giles did not hesitate in his first move. He took a Peon, carved in the shape of a crouching Hob, and moved it two spaces ahead of his Bethin. Redwald surveyed the scene, slowly considered his options, and slid a Peon in front of his Oryn, a move to which Giles responded immediately, advancing with his Peon on the far right. There was a lingering pause while Redwald assessed the position, a spray of silver catching the firelight as he toyed with his hair. Giles leant forward.

"Are you alright Redwald? You seem a little . . . stressed." He grinned.

"A consequence of craving order in a chaotic universe," Redwald sighed, sliding his Prelate through the gap in his front row. "I like things to fit, Mr Hawtree . . ."

"It's Lord . . ."

". . . and when they don't, it *irritates* me." The tendons in his neck twitched with discomfort at the mere thought. "But do you know what irritates me the most?" He said, his head wobbling slightly, though whether from rage or drink Giles could not tell. "*Liars.*" Giles nodded sagely.

"I simply could not agree more." He moved a Krak carved in the shape of an armoured Giant and grinned up at Redwald.

"So you can imagine, then, how *irritated* I must be, to not only work a case where things don't fit . . ."

"Well surely because . . ."

". . . but where I also discover, once I've presented my findings in court, that the *reason* things don't fit, is because somebody has lied to me. Can you, Mr Hawtree, imagine how really, fucking *angry* that would make me?" The magician bristled.

"Well of course I'd understand, but I don't . . . don't see what you mean. You caught him, Redwald, you caught Martingale. Trying to get his hands on my estate no less, for which I'm eternally grateful. It's your go by the way." The magician copied Giles' last move without looking at the board.

"You're sticking with that story are you?" Redwald asked. "Temporal displacement presaging a plot to frame you for murder?" Giles shrugged and grinned but did not meet Redwald's eye.

"I see no other," he said, moving one of his Peons before his Prelate.

"Really?" Redwald said. "You can't *possibly* think of another explanation?" Giles looked up at him.

"No, I . . ." the magician suddenly leant over the table, nudging the chess pieces forward with the impact.

"Well I can," Redwald growled, "I *absolutely* can." Giles fell silent. "So, if you insist on repeating your story, your *lie*, then let me tell

344

you mine. Starting with this, to set the scene." He opened his report and slipped a sheet of paper on to the table. It was Alice's birth certificate. "You asked Norris to give this to me, yes?"

"Well, yes. To help with your experiment . . ."

"No," Redwald said, "you didn't. If that were true, you'd also have prepared the body. No, this . . . this sets the scene for my story *and* for yours. This was just the first breadcrumb down the path of deception, your way of misleading me from the very beginning. Because you know, don't you, that there was no temporal displacement, no magic apart from my own, and no need to provide *this*. Unless, of course, you're distracting me from the obvious point; there should be *two* of them." Giles laughed and got to his feet. "Alice never found her own body, did she? She found her sister's. And you're a *bloody* liar."

"Redwald this . . . this is preposterous." He said, pacing slowly towards the portrait of Krysillion VII. "Alice is an only child."

"On paper," Redwald said, tapping the certificate. "But alright, if you won't admit it, let me tell you what I know. My *bedtime story*." Giles did not respond. He was listening. And thinking. "Once upon a time," Redwald began, "or 19 years ago to be exact, a beautiful woman, who is married to a powerful man, becomes pregnant. The woman is Emmeline, Lady Hawtree and her husband, Sir Julius, is delighted at the news. For although he is one of the most powerful men in the Kingdom and wealthy beyond measure, his insecurities control him, torment him. Possessed of a fragile virility, he goes to ridiculous lengths to conceal a malformed hand and is constantly afraid of seeming weak, a worry that ages him prematurely. A child, he thinks, will prove his strength and vitality beyond a doubt, for they are perfect, fresh, a clean start." Giles continued along the row of cabinets, step by silent step.

"When the time comes, he permits only the most trusted family servants to be present at the birth, for he is a private and

345

controlling man. Morrimer, always at his master's side and Asplund, who is to deliver the child, are present. But Sir Julius' dreams soon turn to ash, and he is confronted with a terrible reality. In the throes of birth, Emmeline Hawtree is lost. Worse still, something happens.

I don't know *exactly* what that something is, but I know the consequence. A baby is hurt, severely, internally, but obviously enough that Asplund notices it. He advises Sir Julius that the girl cannot be cured, will always be different, and will need constant care and attention. I also know he offered to provide that care and that Sir Julius could well afford it. But Sir Julius no longer sees an injured daughter, in need of his help. Instead, he sees *damaged goods*, a new, living embodiment of his deepest shame. He resolves, as he has always done, to hide this *shame*." Giles scoffed at that, loudly, so Redwald could hear.

"Morrimer and Asplund are pressured and sworn to secrecy, the girl is sequestered within the depths of a newly-built house, and Asplund, under duress, fails to record the girl's birth. Only that of Alice Hawtree, her *twin sister,* is ever made public. Deception by omission," Redwald said, thumping the certificate emphatically.

Giles still did not respond. Now at the last cabinet, he was looking down at one of the drawers. Beside him, in the empty space overlooked by the long-dead king, he swore he heard that rustling again, or perhaps a whirring, but the corner was still empty. It was probably the pipes. He grasped the handle of the drawer and tugged gently. *Locked.*

"So, we have a secret sister," Redwald continued, "growing up under the same roof as her unwitting twin. A princess in a tower, so to speak." Giles turned and saw the magician gesturing. Next to the open gun cabinet and beneath the portrait of Emmeline Hawtree, the angled bookcase gave way to a pitch-black staircase. "Her father is cruel to her, restrains her, mistreats her, and despite

346

Morrimer's best efforts to teach her, love her, and care for her, she grows up malnourished, scarred, and still *secret*. And so it remains, for years." He watched for a moment as Giles walked back towards the fire.

"But that can't last, can it, Giles? Someone is bound to find out sooner or later, aren't they? Surely, it's only a matter of time before a clever young servant, scrubbing floors or dusting in his master's Gun Room, comes across a switch on a bookcase, enters the passageway, and finds a mistreated little girl? And when that happens, around 2315, 2316 let's say, her life will change won't it? *Surely* that servant will expose his master's cruelty, save the princess, and be her *knight in shining armour*?" Giles arrived at the fire as Redwald seized his right-hand Knight and vaulted the Peons with it.

"Or perhaps not," the magician murmured, bitterly. "Perhaps that servant is enterprising and clever and ruthless instead. Perhaps that servant knows the value of information and the ruinous effects of scandal on a great family. Even if the Hawtrees, unlike his own, are not noble." Giles was subtly reaching for the gilt clock on the mantelpiece when he felt the magician's eyes upon his face. It was an unpleasant experience, more intense that the heat of the fire, as if Redwald were reaching out and touching every wrinkle in his skin, every hair upon his brow, every cavity in his skull.

"What are you doing?" Giles asked.

"He was your father, wasn't he? The timing works."

"Who?" Giles snapped.

"The last Earl of Barrowmill. You're related, I know that much. Your mealy mouth can lie to me but your face . . . well that's different. I thought it was *yours* I recognised when I first arrived, but in actual fact, I think it was his. If he hadn't been attainted, you would have been an Earl, wouldn't you?" Redwald waited for a response, but none came. Instead, Giles crossed to the table and moved his Prelate one space forward and to the right. Distracted for a moment, the magician turned back to the board and Giles seized his chance to check under the gilt clock. The key was gone.

After a moment of contemplation, the magician moved his own Prelate and continued. "So, at this point in our story, we have a dispossessed noble boy, forced by circumstance into domestic servitude, who stumbles across the greatest piece of leverage available on one of the richest men around." Giles scanned the room. Every firearm was locked away, with a key he didn't have. As calmly as possible, he slouched back into his chair, waiting. "I think we all know what happens next, don't we?" Redwald said, acidly. Giles grinned again.

"You're implying . . ."

"*Directly accusing* you of blackmail, yes I am. And worse."

"I see," said Giles airily. His eyes settled on the rack of cast-iron fire tools to his right. The poker had a nasty hook on one end.

"Because although I admit you're clever, Giles, the leap from junior servant to Managing Director of a major company is a big one to make, especially in the time it took you to make it."

"I'm flattered . . ."

"But it wasn't enough, was it? Even with everything you had squeezed out of Sir Julius, money, power, his daughter's hand, even the opportunity to ditch your old, tarnished name in favour of his, you still wanted to return to the exalted class from which you came. You wanted a fiefdom, just as you'd been promised since birth, and no amount of factories or directorships or share certificates will ever quite match the allure of a coronet, will it?" Giles met the magician's glare and moved his Bethin.

"So," Redwald continued, "you targeted Lord Martingale. Knowing him to be heirless, you hoped he would leave the Barony to you in his will, and so you did your level best to ingratiate yourself with him. By way of insurance, however, you also used Sir Julius' wealth to throw lavish parties and galas, increase your profile and court the royals, knowing full well that if Lord Martingale were to die intestate, the Barony would revert to the Crown, and be re-assigned. Sir Julius had already left you and Alice a strong claim to it when he bought the Rise, all you had to do was make good on that head start. Which it seems, *My Lord*, you did." The bitter smile that had begun to creep across Redwald's face suddenly vanished. "And all the while . . . you let her rot in that room. Did you *ever* know her name?" His tone was almost hopeful.

"Whose name, Redwald?" Giles cast a loaded, performatively sympathetic, glance at the bottles on the floor. "My *entirely fictional* sister-in-law?" Redwald snarled.

"No! The *very real, utterly wronged* woman whose death you exploited to win yourself a Barony, with nothing more than the . . . the *premise* of a children's story," he said, slamming his fist on the blue book, "and a gullible magician!" Silence lingered, but Giles declined to answer. Instead, he re-ordered the chess pieces, rattled off their spots by the magician's blow.

"It's your turn again," he said. In the corner of his eye, the brass-handled poker glinted in the firelight.

"Very well, *keep* wasting my time," the magician growled, thoughtlessly nudging a Peon forward. "But then I suppose that's how you felt, wasn't it? Like you were *wasting your time*. Lord Martingale was hardly on his last legs; fitter than you at over twice the age, and quite clearly hated you. I believe he smelled your ulterior motive, but it might just have been that you're an outsider to the Barony like me. Regardless, you weren't going to get the title, not if he could help it. So, what could you do?" The magician left another pause, but Giles simply grinned.

"You couldn't coerce *him* into handing it over, unlike Sir Julius; you hadn't the leverage. So you decided to coerce someone else. Because of course, when you found Alice's sister . . . *and did nothing* . . . you acquired leverage not just over Sir Julius, but over all of her captors. Which, happily for you, included Dr Asplund. With the Seneschal's keys in his possession, he was the lynchpin in your plan to *force* the Barony from Martingale's hands into yours; by framing the latter for attempted murder. But it wasn't an easy ride. As much as he could, and despite your blackmail, Asplund resisted you.

You didn't need him for the set-up, however. Because you didn't plan it. When Alice discovered her sister's body in the study, you stood to lose everything that years of deception had won for you; but you were too quick. Ever the consummate opportunist, you recognised your chance to turn a potentially massive loss into your ultimate gain. You 'concluded' that a temporal displacement must have occurred, caused by an imminent murder. Of course, since Alice was an 'only child', what else could it be? You hired a magician to come and give official confirmation of your story, but deliberately chose someone junior, despite the significance of the case. Clearly, you thought inexperience and ambition, a desire to solve the case of the century, would lead that magician to exactly the conclusion you wanted; that Martingale was responsible. And you were right," Redwald said, disgusted with himself.

"Before I arrived, you had Asplund swap your functioning pistol for Martingale's dead one, which you knew to be in the Castle because Lord Martingale had refused to sell it to Sir Julius. Yet Asplund was already uncomfortable. Wary of my involvement, he wanted me to arrive, confirm the temporal displacement, and leave. With the full investigation you required, however, Asplund was concerned that I might unravel the truth, or worse, follow your lie and have Martingale arrested. Impossibly, he wanted neither outcome and made a desperate attempt to kill me in Athonstone; the cleanest solution he could think of.

Meanwhile, all you had to do was act convincingly, lead me around like a dog, and wait for an opportunity to sequester Alice in Martingale Castle. You chose your moment well, the anniversary of the Great Storm. Asplund drank with the Baron and saw him off for his habitual night-long ride, before coming to the Manor on your orders to kidnap Alice, whom stress had rendered as ragged as her sister. He was masked, of course, because the intention all along was for her to survive, to be 'rescued'.

On your instructions, Asplund then hid the kidnapped Alice in a trunk among those of the guests from the Gala. You now needed to get her out of the Manor and into the Castle. The Castle was already clear because Martingale was out riding, and everyone in the village was asleep, but you had to deceive your own staff too and, most importantly, Morrimer. He wasn't a part of your plan to frame Martingale, but he *was* implicated in the crimes perpetrated against Alice's sister. You could therefore rely on him not to seek help from the authorities, but you had to consider the possibility he might interfere in your newer plans, in order to protect Alice. You therefore killed two birds with one stone, by taking the Folly Key.

With Alice hidden and a trail laid for the already suspicious Morrimer, you merely waited for your guards to raise the alarm. Morrimer took the bait and headed straight for the Folly, acting alone as expected, lest his role in your earlier crimes be revealed. In doing so, however, he also gave the rest of us a trail to follow, which you used as grounds to order a general search, clearing the Manor out entirely. You and a reluctant Asplund now had a chance to get Alice out of the Manor and into the Castle, *on your way up to the Folly.*" Redwald sighed.

"With Alice now in the Castle, Asplund was growing desperate. Perhaps hoping he might save his reputation *and* Martingale's life,

351

he tried to kill me again, in his office, but in failing he damned them both. Forced to betray the man he loved, and now a known criminal, he went to the Castle to sedate Alice one final time, apologised to her unmasked, and went into the woods to die. All that remained was for her to be found. With the temporal displacement narrative firmly in everyone's mind, and the study key around her neck, Martingale's conviction was a foregone conclusion." The chair creaked as Redwald leant heavily against the backrest. "And so, the poor little noble boy finally gets his *just* desserts and everyone else, to the extent not dead, imprisoned, or mentally scarred, lived *happily ever after.*" He scowled at Giles, waiting for a response.

Giles, however, did not give it. Instead he smiled and, leaning forward, lazily moved a Knight, before starting to clap. It was a slow, mocking applause.

"Excellent story, Redwald, *truly* excellent. A tale for the ages. But surely you realise the evidence doesn't back it up." Redwald snarled and began to rummage in his report. "Alice is an only child, that's *public record*, Parnell's experiment proved she and the body were the *same* woman, and even your compass spell . . ."

"My compass spell," Redwald snapped, swearing as his fingers fumbled on paper, "didn't work precisely *because* they're twins. That's why Parnell's work was misleading too. Twins share their . . . their signature, their make-up, in a way that nobody else does. Because that's how stars tell us apart, it makes twins indistinguishable in most magical tests." Giles scoffed.

"Exactly my point, you can't . . ." Redwald found what he was looking for and swivelled something out on to the table. Giles looked down at it. "Oh Redwald, you really think that idiot Guardsman . . ."

"Open it," Redwald said, "last page." Tentatively, Giles reached out and picked up the booklet, turning to the final set of fingerprints.

352

There, Guardsman Norris' precise handwriting had been amended by Redwald's jagged scrawl, changing the title from *Mrs Hawtree (Deceased)* to *Miss ~~Mrs~~ Hawtree (Deceased)*. Giles smirked.

"So what? You've just . . ."

"Twins are indistinguishable in most magical tests because of their shared biotic signature, yes," Redwald said, a slight smile creeping across his face again, "But there are other ways to tell them apart. And our dear Guardsman Norris was surprisingly prescient in providing one. Did you know, for example, and I hope you find this bit of trivia as *fascinating* as I do, that twins, for all that they share nearly everything else, do *not* share fingerprints?" Giles looked at the prints on the last page, before flicking back to those on the second, labelled just *Mrs Hawtree*. His stomach turned, and he dropped the booklet on to the table. Redwald moved his left-hand Peon and leant forward. "Her name, Giles. What was it?" Giles' eyes flicked to the poker and back.

"Honestly Redwald . . . so what? You've got a booklet of fingerprints done by an incompetent flatfoot and you're saying it proves . . . what, exactly? This is clearly a mistake, just like your experiment . . ."

"My experiment was performed perfectly," Redwald said, "The heart showed that the woman in question died on the precise day her body was found, by her sister."

"Right, obviously . . ." Giles said, forcing a chuckle as he got to his feet, "And who, in this deranged narrative, are you accusing of killing her. Hmmm? Whodunnit?!" He laughed, as he leaned in to stoke the fire.

"The only person it could be," Redwald said, watching as sparks wafted up the chimney. "The only person who could shoot her at that range and from that angle. The only person for whom all the known facts actually make sense, without caveat, without doubt.

She did it. She killed *herself*. But you already knew that, didn't you Giles?" He continued to stoke the fire in silence, slowly chipping away at the white-scaled log that glowed in the hearth. "It's the only way it all fits. Again, I don't know exactly what happened, but I can make a *very* educated guess. As inevitable as it was that she would be discovered, so it was also inevitable that she might one day escape. Did Morrimer forget to close the passage behind him? Forget to lock the door? Was he supposed to tie her to her bed; did he *ever* do that I wonder? In any event, and on the day of your hunt, something went wrong. She found her way down here." He gestured to the cabinets, the taxidermy, and the blood red walls.

"Now this place is fascinating for anybody, but for a woman confined to a single, barren room for her entire life, it's heaven. She is surrounded suddenly by shiny new toys, things she has never even dreamt of, and the nature of which she *does not understand*. So, by chance, she reaches out, finds an unlocked cabinet and takes her favourite off the shelf to play. It has a picture of a girl on it, just like the ones from her books; the Maidensworth Duelling Pistol. Her death is now as inevitable as her escape. Quite by accident, and out of curiosity, she looks down the barrel and pulls the trigger. The shot goes through her head, shattering the glass pane in the open door behind her and spraying blood onto the other weapons, the same weapons you sent to Athonstone to be cleaned.

"How fortunate, then, that you returned home early from the shoot and came here to deposit your weapon. Since the reception wing is separated from the residential, you're confident no one heard the shot, and so you now have a short window in which to remove the body. You decide to act immediately. Wrapping her head with her bedsheets to ensure her blood doesn't give you away, you set Morrimer to cleaning up the mess before Alice and Laetizija return. With the servants either in the kitchen or out with the hunting party, you have space in which to carry her body through the study and out into the woods behind the house, there to bury her. But this is where it goes wrong, isn't it?" Redwald said, looking across at Giles's back. The poker quivered in his hand.

"Why did you leave her there? Did you think you had more time? Were you checking for servants? Presumably you'd never needed a shovel before, did you have to ask a weeping Morrimer where they were kept? Either way, your slowness costs you and Alice comes back to find the body of her sister in the study, where you have left it. The rest is history. You, the consummate opportunist, presented with a catastrophe partly of your own making, somehow manage to find a way to exploit it," Redwald spat. "I ask again, did you ever, even while carrying her to her grave, learn her name?" Giles stood up. Poker in hand, he moved his Bethin.

"Who else knows?"

"Her name?"

"Your *nonsense* story, Redwald," Giles smiled, twitching slightly as the noise of whirring pipes emanated from the empty corner. "Who else have you told?"

"Why do you ask?"

"Because . . . because I can make this all go away." Giles said, suppressing his rage. "I see your game, Redwald, I do. You think you can come here, on the day of my elevation, and spin some farcical story about twins, and kidnapping, and a years-long plot to keep it all secret. What do you want? What can I give you?"

"What was her name?" Redwald asked, looking drunkenly up at Giles. "Just tell me you *bothered* to learn the poor girl's name."

"I can give you *anything*, Redwald. I can make you rich. I've already made your career, haven't I? After solving my case, I . . . I can refer you. Think of the contacts I can share with you . . ."

"The name, Giles. Did you know?"

355

"Come now, Redwald, don't be stupid. You're a smart young man, I can . . . I can see that. Let's work something out. Let's make a deal."

"You already know my terms . . ."

"Does your firm do aerial work, dimensional? Think of the cross-selling. Or is it women you want? I know *many* eligible heiresses." Redwald moved his Prelate in silence. "What . . . what the fuck do you want?!" Giles snapped.

"I've told you . . ."

"I don't know her FUCKING name, ask Morrimer!" Giles bellowed, kicking over the rack of fire-tools with a clatter. The magician waited a moment, watching as Giles' mistake slowly dawned on him.

"I already have," Redwald replied. "He was *most* helpful." With a chill, Giles finally heard the words that Morrimer, the *mute* butler, had whispered on his way out. *Yes, my Lord.* He stood quietly for a moment, wondering with increasing dread what other words the Hob had re-learned. Slowly, carefully, he turned to face Redwald, looking the magician up and down before casting an eye over their game. He thought about it for a moment. He could still win. Leaning over the board, he moved his Bethin again with shaking fingers and whispered something under his breath. "What was that?" Redwald asked, wearily removing his glasses.

"Checkmate." Giles said, drawing himself up to his full height and staring dead into the magician's eyes. Redwald smiled.

"*Ironic.*" Giles swung. The hooked poker struck Redwald in the temple so hard that it broke through his skull and into his eye socket, spraying red across the mantelpiece and into the fire. Falling sideways off his chair, the magician's head struck the hearth, and cracked on the marble like a melon, red, fleshy shards sliding across the floor.

Hawtree dropped the poker with a clatter as noise erupted behind him and the whirring suddenly grew louder. He turned to see Captain Westferry, Constable Norris, and Lieutenant Thorne bursting out of the empty corner, through a gap in a curtain hanging between two adjacent cabinets. Where they pushed past and broke the curtain's downward hang, the cloth was visible, twisting over and around them like water flowing around rock, but where it hung freely, it rendered invisible everything between it and Krysillion VII's portrait. This included a recording machine that stood on a little table, it's sensitive brass trumpet fixed above a whirring cylinder.

Giles bolted. Unable to reach the door, he made for the passageway. Sliding beneath Lady Hawtree's portrait, he slammed the inner lever down and the bookcase swung shut behind him, trapping the guardsmen in the Gun Room. Tripping and scrambling up the unlit staircase, Giles smelled the magician's sweet, sticky blood on his fingers and retched.

Finally, he reached the top. The chain-link door was open, as was the door out onto the moonlit maintenance platform. He had no other choice; he would climb down from the roof. Scrabbling across the rough-hewn floor, he staggered, panting, out on to the metal platform. But then he heard footsteps; heavy footsteps, angry footsteps. He turned just in time to see a tall, ghostly figure emerge from the darkness.

"Oh gods - " he said, as the figure grabbed him by the shirtfront with such force that it knocked the wind out of him. The figure bent him backwards over the railing and leaned in close.

"Emmeline," Redwald growled, nose furrowed like the muzzle of a snarling lion, "after her mother. *That* was her name, you conniving, repugnant, mendacious little shit!" Hawtree gasped.

"But you're . . . I . . ."

"It was a puppet, Giles." Over his shoulder, Giles could see a chair and a counterpart recording machine, the trumpet of which crackled like a fire, while the magician's spectacles, laying on the seat, reflected flames that were not there. "Made of *fruit*. All you did was ruin a watermelon. And give us just enough evidence to convict you. A full confession would have been better, but once a liar always a liar, I suppose." Behind him, Giles could hear the sound of the approaching Guard. "And thank you, *Mr Hawtree*, for instructing me on this case. You'll have my invoice by Khorsday."

CHAPTER 16

The End

"A fool speaks because he has to say something; a wise man speaks because he has something to say."

Continental proverb – attributed to His Empyreal Holiness Menethis XVI 'the Silent', Hierophant of the Primacy.

Somewhere at the base of the tower, a door shut with a thud. Redwald, started from his sleep by the noise, groggily pulled himself upright in his chair. There were footsteps on the staircase. At his left hand was a half-empty bottle of excellent whisky and a cut-glass tumbler, while the embers in the grate were glowing orange. None of the orcite lamps were lit. Outside, through the tall, narrow windows and across the water, Redwald could just about see the Athon Stone and the little yellow pinpricks that were its arrow-slit windows. Beneath them, the twinkling city reflected the stars above. He sighed.

As Redwald re-filled his glass the footsteps grew louder, until Adriel was standing behind him in the living room doorway. She tutted.

"What are you doing in the dark, darling?"

"Drinking," he replied. She twisted the compressor on the lamp nearest the door. "You're back late."

"Yes," she said solemnly, slipping her coat from her shoulders and hanging it on the wall, "something needed doing."

"I won't ask," he said, groaning to his feet.

"Couldn't tell you if you did," she said with a grin, her dark eyes glittering in the lamplight. He stooped and wrapped his arms around her. "I would love to, though, you know that."

"I know," Redwald said, straightening up. He wiggled his glass at her. "One for you?"

"Not that," she said, wrinkling her nose.

"No, *obviously* not that," he said, in mock indignation. "This is *expensive*. No, I'll get you a glass of the stuff that tastes like a farmyard."

"That's expensive too!" She said, wrenching her boots off. Meanwhile, Redwald was bustling by the wine rack.

"Bloody waste of money, then," he said, handing her a glass of brandy and landing a peck on her forehead. "There you go."

"Thank you darling," she said, settling into her own chair as he re-occupied his, the sofa between them facing the fire. She looked across at his half-empty whisky bottle. "I can't tell; are you celebrating or drowning sorrows? What was the verdict?"

"Guilty, thanks largely to Morrimer's testimony."

"Oh that's *brilliant* darling, well done." She smiled. "So . . . Martingale?"

"Restored," Redwald confirmed, "with Charteris as Seneschal, and Alice as heir presumptive, apparently."

"Well that's a good result isn't it?" She said encouragingly, sensing Redwald's mood. He looked out the window, brooding. "And how is Alice, is she doing ok?"

"She's alright," Redwald said, quietly, "or as much as she can be under the circumstances." He fell silent then and Adriel watched him carefully. She could see the pattern of his thoughts and recognised the distinctive spiral.

"You've done a good thing, you know."

"Have I?" He said, taking a sip of his whisky.

"Yes darling, you have," she said firmly. "Few other people who would fight the way you have to fix their mistake. Most people would have taken Giles' offer." Redwald shifted uncomfortably.

"Few other people would have made that mistake in the first place."

"That isn't true."

"I *needed* there to be an answer," Redwald said, letting his doubts surface one by one, "I needed resolution. So I forced the facts into place, *made* the pattern work. I was . . . blinded to the fact it didn't really fit, controlled by my . . . by my insecurities." An unpleasant thought crossed his mind. "To that extent I'm no different from Sir Julius with his arm and Giles with his titles."

"Nonsense," Adriel said, angrily, "Unlike Sir Julius, unlike Giles, you knew when to stop. You knew to recognise your mistake, and to fix it. And as for wanting to solve the case . . ."

"I *needed* to solve it, it's different. It's a compulsion."

"I know how you work," Adriel said, sternly, "but even that *need*; it's part of your job. You're supposed to solve the case, to answer the question. And when the person asking the question misleads you from the start, how are you just *supposed* to see around that? You were sympathetic enough when you thought Charteris had fallen for Martingale's lies; why are you so much harder on yourself?" Redwald chewed his lip. "As I say, at least you had the courage to fix it. . ."

"I was *lucky*," Redwald said. "Gods, if I hadn't bumped into that clerk . . . an innocent man would have gone to prison on the strength of my testimony. The only reason he didn't was blind luck, nothing to do with me."

"It had everything to do with you!" Adriel said. "Yes, Hawtree deceived you, but he deceived the whole village as well. And I guarantee you that over twenty years, they will all have had their moments, those *lucky* clues that must have indicated something was going on. You think Asplund and Morrimer could go that long, keeping a secret they could happily do without, and not let something slip? There will have been signs, Redwald, a trembling of Morrimer's lip in church, an inexplicably tired Asplund, noises in the Manor, anything. The difference is, Redwald, that the village either lacked the ability to recognise when something didn't fit or failed to *do* something about it. You *did* something." Redwald turned back to the window. Then, as the first few drops of rain gradually crescendoed to a soft pitter-patter, Redwald was back in the Sett, with Asplund. *You can hide anything for years,* he said, *Just as long as people are too scared or too lazy to look.* Redwald took a swig of whisky.

"Still . . ." Redwald said, "not pleased about cocking up."

"Perfection is a pipe dream, darling. Honesty is not." Redwald grumbled, reluctantly admitting the point. Adriel smiled, before standing and coming to sit on the end of the sofa nearest him. She reached out and tenderly took his hand in her own. He sighed, comforted.

"You know darling," she said in mocking sweet tones, "seeing as you've done *so* well today, I thought you might like a treat before bed." She grinned mischievously and Redwald raised an eyebrow. "Fancy a game of chess?"

Printed in Great Britain
by Amazon

60582244R00208